Bloodpledge

The Dantonville Series - Book 2

Tima Maria Lacoba

Published By
Tima Maria Lacoba

BloodPledge
Book Two of the Dantonville Legacy

Tima Maria Lacoba

Paradox Promotions
Covers & Formatting
http://bit.ly/paradoxcovers

ISBN-13: 978-1499735789

ISBN-10: 1499735782

BOOKS BY TIMA MARIA LACOBA

Laura's Locket: A Dantonville Chronicle

BloodGifted: Book 1 of the Dantonville Legacy

BloodPledge: Book 2 of the Dantonville Legacy

BloodVault: Book 3 of the Dantonville Legacy

BloodWish: Book 4 of the Dantonville Legacy

CONTENTS

ACKNOWLEDGMENTS

Thank you to everyone – my wonderful family and friends –who urged me to continue Alec and Laura's story. To my gorgeous and amazing mum, who was there every step of the way; who listened as I read out each new page and made me endless cups of tea when I couldn't leave my desk. She's my guardian angel.

To the lovely ladies in my Writers group – Anne, Peita and Joan – not just a thank you, but hugs all around for your invaluable critiquing skills and for the fun we have when we get together.

And, of course, to my 'bestie' Claudia who is Team Dantonville's biggest fan. Where would I be without her infectious enthusiasm, boundless energy and endless supply of chocolate and candy Dracula dentures? You're a gem.

Lastly, where would a writer be without her beta readers; those lovely people who drop everything to proofread a ninety-two thousand word manuscript in less than one week? Thank you to Claudia, Olivia, Stephanie, Susan and Taylor. You ladies rock!

Finally, huge hugs to all my friends who encouraged and supported me throughout this incredible journey – Lindsay, Karen, Renee, Lisabeth and Julianna. If I've left out any names, you know who you are. This book is for you guys.

CHAPTER 1 – KEYS

LAURA

Abandoned. That's how my apartment looked after I'd been away a week. The police had been. They had even hired a cleaner to wash my ex-boyfriend, Matt's, bloodstains from the doorframe and wooden floor after the forensics people had finished. He was still in hospital recovering.

As I sorted through the mail, my fiancé, Alec, casually checked out the framed photos I kept on the dining room buffet. Looking at him, I had to remind myself he wasn't human. Up until a week ago, the only supernatural creatures I believed in were angels.

He picked up the one of Matt and myself and looked at it for a long while. I would have loved to have known what he was thinking as his face betrayed nothing.

'Who's this?' he asked as he held up another one. It was a silver-framed photo of Jenny and me taken at the Randwick races one Melbourne Cup Day. She had won a pre-cup sweep at work and asked me along.

We had gone out and bought hats and dresses especially for the occasion. Neither of us won anything on the horses, but it had been a great day out.

'That's Jenny.'

'The one who phoned you in hospital the other day?'

'Uh huh. My best friend. She helped me pick out the dress I'm wearing in that photo.' Jenny and I had known each other for years; we taught at the same primary school and had become close friends, almost like sisters. I hated not being able to tell her about Alec – and the vampire side of the family.

I noticed the way he smiled as he looked at it. I'd worn a knee-length, figure-hugging black pinafore teamed with a jade silk scarf and matching peep-toe shoes.

His eyes lit up with a devilish glint. 'I need to think of some excuse for you to wear that dress for me.'

I laughed and shook my head as I turned and walked into my bedroom to grab some clothes. Even though the walk-in closet in my bedroom at my father's house was brim-full of the latest designer wear especially selected for me, I still needed some of my old, familiar stuff. To me, it was proof I hadn't really changed. I was still Laura Dantonville, primary school teacher, but I was also the daughter of Lucien (Luc) Lebrettan, millionaire real-estate magnate, vampire and Alec's sire.

As I threw a few things onto the bed, I noticed something odd. On my dressing table, next to another framed photo of me and Matt, lay the key to my unit. It was the spare I'd given him when our relationship had become serious. I'd posted my copy of his apartment key back to him three days ago – after we broke up.

A cold shiver rippled through me. He must've come here – to my apartment, without my permission.

Alec's voice came from the living room. 'Laura, everything all right?'

'Um … yes.' I wasn't sure whether to tell Alec about this. I glanced around. Nothing else seemed different or out of place. Yet, there it was, the unmistakable evidence of my ex-boyfriend's presence.

Pushing the memories of our four months together aside, I unclipped the back of the frame, took the photo out and laid it face down on the dressing table. Later, when I had more time, I'd place it in my album. Matt had once been part of my life, even if only for a short while.

'You're very quiet. Anything wrong?' I spun around. Alec stood directly behind me. His gaze went from my face, to my hand, then to the key, and I knew I couldn't keep it from him.

Loud knocking on my front door interrupted us. 'Miss Dantonville? Are you in there?'

I groaned. That slightly croaky but belligerent voice belonged to one of my neighbours, Mrs Henderson, head of the Body Corporate. She knew all that went on, and what she didn't know, she made sure to find out. In other words, she was the local busybody. And unless I opened the door, there was a good chance she'd walk around the side of the building and press her face up against the windows to see if I was in. Matt and I once hid from her – behind the settee – pretending we weren't home. 'Checking up to see if everything's all right,' she would say.

'It's Mrs Henderson, from upstairs. I have to let her in, or she'll come noseying around the windows.'

'You know there's a solution for that.' Alec's eyes shone in mischief.

'No. Don't you dare!'

He chuckled.

I palmed the key and hurried to the door. 'Hello, Mrs Henderson. What can I do for you?'

She was in the process of rapping her walking cane on my front door again and stopped mid-action. Her wide frame filled the doorway, blocking any escape.

'Are you all right, love?' She said breathlessly. 'Such a to-do earlier in the week, what with all the police and ambulance and reporters here asking so many questions. We heard you and your young man were hurt … taken to hospital.' Her triple chins wobbled in excitement making her look like an oversized ram. 'Dreadful business, being attacked like that in your own home. Are any of us safe—?' Her eyes landed on Alec, and she stopped abruptly.

Her jaw dropped mid-speech, and her hands smoothed down her tent-like dress. Before I had a chance to say anything, nosey Mrs Henderson barged past me into the living room and made straight for Alec.

If I didn't know what a big, badass vampire he was, I'd swear he backed up a step as she sailed toward him like a battleship on a mission.

Her cat, Salieri, on the other hand, took one look at Alec,

screeched and arched it back. Its fur stood on end like porcupine quills as it hissed and ran off.

Mrs Henderson turned to me and said, 'Strange, that he'd react like that. Did the same, the night the police were here. I hope he's not getting distemper!'

That was the night I was kidnapped and Matt had been seriously injured trying to protect me. It appeared Salieri could sense the undead.

She promptly resumed her advance on Alec. 'And who might you be?' she asked in a honey-sweet voice.

'Um … this is Dr Munro,' I said. Alec was a doctor and head of Munro Research Labs, a research hospital that specialised in treating blood diseases. I'd been taken there the night I was attacked. Maris, a former lover of Alec's, had tried to kill me by taking as much of my blood as she could, but in the process it had destroyed her. I'd been shocked to discover my blood was poisonous to all vampires, except those transformed by Lucius – Marcus Antonius's son – such as Luc and Alec.

'Well, well, a doctor. And how is your nice young policeman chap? He was here this morning, you know,' Mrs Henderson said without taking her eyes off Alec. 'Saw him from my window.' I felt the blood drain from my face. Next to me Alec stiffened. Mrs Henderson continued on her merry rant. 'Oh, but you have the same eye colour! How unusual … a brother or cousin then? I had the telly on that night, you see, and didn't hear anything,' she turned to face me, 'till all these flashing lights woke me early next morning. And then a couple of nice policemen spoke to me.' She turned back to Alec. 'Are you a GP? You know, I have this mild discomfort, right here.' She placed her hand poignantly on her ample bosom.

If I wasn't so tense I may have giggled.

'Mrs Henderson,' Alec interrupted, 'I'm sure it's only mild indigestion. May I suggest some antacid.' His eyes paled. 'But just to be sure, I think it best if you return to your flat and lie down for the rest of the day.'

'Yes, lie down,' she repeated slowly, her eyes glued to Alec's.

He placed his arm around her shoulders and led her to the door. 'That's right. A cup of tea and a lie down.'

I remembered something. 'Alec wait! I need to give her my phone number, as I'll be away for a while.'

'Good point.'

'Mrs Henderson, listen carefully.' He stared into her glazed eyes and repeated my mobile number. 'Ring Miss Dantonville only if necessary. Now go and have a lie down.'

She nodded, her eyes vacant and he closed the door behind her.

'All right, this time I agree with the mesmerisation.'

'It has its merits.' He leaned back against the door, arms folded across his chest. 'So, Sommers was here. They must have discharged him this morning.'

'And he came straight here.' I sighed, held out my hand and opened my palm. Even with amnesia, Matt couldn't stop being a detective. 'It's my spare key. Matt had it. I found it on my dresser.'

Alec's brow creased. 'I noticed his scent when we arrived. I thought it must be the remnants of his blood on the doorframe. Damn!' He looked thoughtfully at me. 'Why come here? He could've sent it. And why your bedroom instead of the kitchen table?'

I shook my head. 'Don't know, but nothing else was touched,' I said when I saw the questioning look in his eyes.

'Mmmm…' His lips drew together in a tight, disapproving line, and he glanced at the window. 'There's no time for that now. We should get back, so you can have a rest before tonight's Pledging ceremony.'

The Pledging. It was scheduled for midnight, when all the Prefects from around the world would swear their loyalty to Alec and myself. It was binding on all the Brethren in their respective countries, and the penalty for breaking the oath was death. The ceremony could take several hours, and I needed to ensure I stayed awake and alert.

I placed the spare key back on my key ring. 'If Matt's got amnesia, how come he knows where I live?'

'Detective Delaney – he probably told him.'

Detective Senior Constable Dave Delaney was in charge of the investigation into the break-in at my flat and the assault on Matt and myself. He'd interviewed Alec, and then later me, at the hospital. To Matt he was both mentor and friend. They used to be partners until Matt was promoted to Detective Inspector and posted to the city.

'Of course.'

It didn't alleviate my uncomfortable realisation that Matt had been here without my knowledge. Had he hoped to regain some of his lost memory by coming somewhere he thought would be familiar? But why did he have to do it behind my back? Yet the fact he left the key behind was proof our relationship was truly over.

After locking the door securely, Alec and I headed to his car for the drive back to my father's old-Victorian, neo-gothic mansion in Vaucluse. Mrs Henderson wasn't anywhere in sight.

She must be lying down after her cup of tea, I thought. Salieri hissed at Alec as we strode past then ran and hid in a nearby bush.

I took a long, last look at my unit as we drove away. Who knew when I'd be back. Luc and Judy were keen to have me stay with them, and as long as rogue elements among the Brethren wanted to seize me for their own purposes, it was safer to remain with them.

As we drove through the wrought-iron gates of Luc's palatial residence in Fitzgerald Street, the LEDs that lined the gravel driveway lit our way to the front entrance. The only light emanating from the house was a single porch light, twinkling bulbs on the Christmas wreath on the front door and the glow from the top storey ballroom windows.

As we stepped into the hall, nobody seemed to be around. Alec flicked a switch. Light burst into every corner, illuminating the stencilled griffins and unicorns that ran the length of the plastered walls and the stuccoed ceiling with its moulded roses picked out in bold Victorian colours of red, blue and gold.

Luc's house was a relic of a grander era, when riches found on the goldfields of Swan Hill and Bathurst were poured into the lavish houses of the nouveau riche. It was one of the few stately homes that the National Trust hadn't been able to acquire, and Luc aimed to keep it that way. Thankfully, he had modernised it where required.

Well, this is home, for now. I inwardly sighed as we strolled hand-in-hand to the kitchen at the other end of the house, feeling less and less the independent twenty-first century woman I once believed myself to be.

CHAPTER 2 – JAKE'S DILEMMA

ALEC

The sun had dipped behind the horizon by the time we got back to Luc's house. Although I didn't want to leave Laura, I had to speak to Jake and the others about important matters. So, reluctantly leaving her in the kitchen with Judith, I made my way to the gym.

When my sire bought the place, nearly a century ago, he had a Roman-style bathhouse constructed on the grounds, complete with sauna and swimming pool. For the time it was considered unusual, and even eccentric. But that didn't bother Luc. I was convinced he enjoyed shocking the neighbours, especially as he and the men swam and exercised Roman style – naked. I chuckled as I strode to the other end of the garden.

The clash of steel rang out as I pushed open the heavy wooden doors. Terens and Sam were sparring with rapiers. Last week it was cutlasses. A few times I'd joined their sparring matches, to keep my own skills honed, but these men were my friends and I used that excuse to spend time with them. Being the Ingenii's bodyguard, they never missed training; never stopped being Roman soldiers, and they included me among them. It was an honour I didn't take for granted.

As usual Terens was winning, cracking jokes and making Sam laugh until he lost concentration. Cal was pushing weights. He had readjusted the balance by adding more force to the machine to cater for the strength of our kind. A light sheen of sweat covered his upper body, highlighting the Antonine crest of a coiled serpent tattooed on his chest. We all have the same image on our bodies; a symbol of our brotherhood and our shared curse. At my transformation, it had appeared on the left side of my chest marking me as Luc's man.

I looked around for Jake. Of the four men, he was the one I regarded as my best friend. A splash, and I saw him plunge into the pool. As his head surfaced, he waved me over. 'Can guess why you're here,' he said, as he swam to the side.

'Can you?'

He smiled and flicked wet hair from his eyes. 'Gonna get those clothes off and join us?'

I sat on one of the marbled benches near the pool. 'You know I've never been comfortable with the full naked bit in public.'

'You prude.' He laughed.

'Blame the century I was raised in.'

He laughed again and shook his head. 'Give me a minute, then.'

Jake and I had become close friends while I was struggling with my new nature. He was instrumental in helping me accept my transformation – by teaching me to use my enhanced senses, thereby making me a better doctor. He'd been one himself, a long time ago.

He hauled his body out of the water, strode over to the racks, took a towel from the hook and tied it around his waist before coming back to sit next to me on the bench. Water dripped down his legs and left a puddle at his feet. 'I assume it's about the three Eastern European Prefects?'

'I meant to ask you when you got back,' I replied.

'Things kind of … you know.'

I nodded. More important matters arose.

The three Eastern European Prefects, Count Timur Széchenyi, Baroness Milena Flaks and Karel von Czernin controlled the ancient territories that spanned the Czech, Slovak and Hungarian republics. Over the centuries they had raided each other's lands, killing both Brethren and non-Brethren alike. It's kept the human population in that part of Europe dangerously aware of our existence. That's why Luc had sent Jake over, not just to sort out the problem but also to convey the Elders' warnings. All three were currently in danger of losing their exalted positions; perhaps even their lives. They missed the Ritual – the ceremony that took place every fifty years to introduce the next Ingenii into our world – each fearful of encroachment on their territories by the others.

'Luc mentioned they hadn't yet responded to the Pledging summons,' I said.

'They'll be here. I'm sure of it. Especially Milena.'

He stared at his feet, brows drawn. Something was bothering him, so I waited.

'There, um … was no evidence of recent trouble. Actually, when I summoned each of them to meet me in Vienna, von Czernin and the Count Timur were faintly surprised. Not Milena.' He paused then angled his head to look directly at me. 'I didn't tell Luc all the facts. He's been too preoccupied lately, but he needs to know. There's growing tension among the Brethren in Europe, as if they sense the Curse is coming to an end, and there are just as many who fear it – like Milena – as those who long for it.'

'I see. So… she wanted to warn you?'

'Something like that. Without arousing suspicion.'

He looked away and rubbed the back of his neck. I rarely saw Jake uncomfortable, but something must have happened. He wasn't sure how to divulge it, or perhaps whether he even ought to.

In a brisk movement, he stood and strode to the edge of the pool. 'Alec, when we were cursed, none of us foresaw an entire political system built around the Ingenii. When it ends, you and Luc will lose your superiority. It was happening already – Luc's getting more nocturnal as Judy's blood weakens. And … something else.'

Judith had been the previous Ingenii, but her time was over. The gene that provides daylight tolerance wanes after fifty years and the next in line replaces them. Laura was the current Ingenii, and her induction had only taken place less than a week ago.

I rose and went to Jake's side. 'Tell me everything.'

He nodded and glanced at his brother soldiers. 'We're Luc's

men, bound to him as long as there's an Ingenii.'

I became aware of the sudden quiet around me. The clash of steel had ceased. Terens and Sam looked in our direction.

'When the Curse is lifted, we can leave his service, that is, if we choose to remain as we are,' Jake said.

I looked around and saw Cal put down the weights as he, too, gave us his attention.

If Jake wanted this to be a private conversation, then he'd lost the opportunity. Yet, I sensed he wanted the others to hear. They were brothers, in many ways; had been together for over eighteen-hundred years. Experiences such as the ones they had shared over the centuries must have created an almost unbreakable bond. I doubted they had any secrets from each other.

He took a deep breath and let it out slowly. 'Milena's looking for a powerful consort. Someone to keep the other two off her lands. Someone they'd respect.'

'I have a nasty feeling I know where this is headed,' Terens said.

Jake didn't look at him, but focused on me. 'As long as the Curse is in effect, you and Luc are feared. That's going to end once you and Laura have a child. Problem is, we don't know whether her blood will retain its potency. If it doesn't, we can expect a war, and Milena's lands will be one of the first to be overrun by rogues.' He glanced briefly at the others before coming back to me. 'So far, only we know that Laura is the Child of Light and Darkness and that you're descended from the witch who cursed us.'

We all knew the prophecy, that the curse could only be lifted when a descendant of Marcus Antonius – the Child of Light and Darkness – willingly wed and had a child with a descendant of the Pict witch who had uttered it.

I began to understand what Jake was trying to say. 'You mean, if Laura and I delay having a child, we could avert a war?' They found out only yesterday that Laura and I intend to marry.

'I know I'm asking a lot.'

'You are. But, on the other hand, if it's as you predict and the lifting of the curse results in her blood losing its potency, it also means she'll be of no use to them. Both Laura and our child will be free. So the sooner we can end this thing, the better.'

'We need you strong, Alec,' Jake said.

'Don't worry about me. I've got plans. But that's not all that's concerning you, is it?' I prompted.

'No ...'

Another silence ensued.

'Oh, for the love of ... Spit it out, Jake!' Terens said.

'All right! Milena asked me to be her consort.'

It took a second or two for his news to hit them, and then they all spoke at once.

'You're not seriously—'

'C'mon man, we need to talk about this—'

'Why you?'

Jake said, 'Who better than one of us? In one move, she gains lover and protector. Von Czernin and Count Timur wouldn't dare raid her territory, knowing that.'

'You have a point,' Sam conceded.

'I knew it!' Terens spun on his heel and sliced the air with his sword, the whoosh of angry metal echoing around the room.

'Why are you doing this, Jake?' I asked.

'I didn't say I was going to do it. But it makes sense.'

'Let her choose someone else.' Cal put aside the weights and rose from the bench.

'Like who?' With hands on hips, Jake faced them.

'Hell, she knows a lot of men just as loyal to Luc as we are. One of them should do fine,' Terens said.

'Allegiances are changing,' Jake answered.

'Jake's right,' I said. 'The Elders are worried. That's why Zhao left straight after the Ritual. Things are brewing in China as well, not just Europe.' Zhao was one of the Elders who had presided over the Ritual.

'It's as if ... I dunno ... the Curse itself were sending out signals that it's over. It's run its course,' Jake said. 'The old order's about to end.'

'You becoming Milena's consort isn't going to stave off the inevitable, Jake. Maybe delay it for a bit,' I said. 'Besides, Laura's blood might not lose its potency – after all, she's half-vampire. If anything, it'll begin with the next generation. Any children she and I have will be free of the curse and *their* blood will be normal.'

'If you're right, that gives us at least fifty years to prepare,'

Sam remarked.

'And otherwise?' Cal asked.

The same thought had occurred to me. I knew Luc had been preparing for this day. Plans he hadn't shared with his men – as yet.

Terens bent and retrieved his sword, and ran his thumb down its length. 'Looks like I'll need to keep this sharp as I've no intention of allowing a bunch of rogues to take over.' The edge in his voice was as deadly as the blade he handled.

'The Principate has to remain in some form,' Cal said. 'It's the only way to maintain the peace and keep our existence secret.'

'It will. Luc and Marcus have already taken steps. Nothing much will change for now, but when the time comes, the Elders will choose the next princeps from among themselves. Of course, the Ritual will be replaced by something else,' I said.

'And us?' Cal asked. 'All these years we've been bodyguards to the Ingenii. Where does that leave us?'

'Free to do as we want, Cal,' Jake told him, 'since we've decided to go on living.'

Part of the lifting of the Curse meant the men would be given a choice when the time came. There were two options – death, or remain a vampire forever. Long ago they had decided on life, as I had.

'Actually, I like what I do. Gives me a purpose in life,' Sam said.

'The Eldership will still need enforcers,' I stated.

'Got no problem with that,' Terens said and expertly twirled the sword in his hand.

'Neither do I,' Cal agreed.

'Jake, if you're asking Alec and Laura to hold off, I reckon you ought to do the same with her ladyship. I don't believe she's in any immediate danger, and, besides, we can keep an eye on things while Alec here can deal with those other two – Timur and Karl,' Sam suggested. 'There's only the four of us left now, and we need to stay together, unless of course you … feel something for this woman?'

Jake's gaze roamed the faces of his three companions. All nodded.

His fists tightened. 'If I do feel something for her, it's none of your business.'

'Hell it is.' Cal strode toward him.

'Ah, shit.' Terens swore under his breath.

'Whoa, whoa!' Sam stepped into Cal's path. 'There's no point you two going at each other.'

The two men faced each other, their nostrils flaring. But Sam's words had an effect. Cal and Jake were close friends, and the fear of one or either of them leaving was enough to create a tense situation.

Sam addressed Jake. 'You said something about Milena contriving the situation to get you over there?'

Jake nodded.

'Okay. What if she exaggerated a bit and it's not really protection she wants.' Jake's face darkened. 'Now hear me out,' Sam hurried on. 'What if she simply wants *you*?'

'He could be right,' Terens agreed. 'There's some prestige in having one of the original legionaries as a lover. I ought to know.' He gave a crooked grin.

Jake considered it. 'It's probable but that doesn't mean –'

'What? That she won't make the most of your position?' Cal retorted. 'This is Milena were talking about.'

Jake released a pent up breath. 'Okay, I'm listening.'

Sam continued. 'Hold off giving her your answer. Did you talk to Luc?'

Jake shook his head. 'No time.'

'Well, maybe you should. Let him and Marcus involve themselves in political entanglements, not you. That's not our job.'

'Don't want to lose you, man,' Cal said.

Jake bowed his head and thought a while. 'I haven't decided anyway. I'll wait – see how things pan out.'

Terens came over and slapped him on the back. 'Bed her, by all means, but no need to wed her. The only entanglements you ever need get involved in, brother, are the long, curvy type which wrap sweetly around your back.'

Jake shook his head, but laughed with the others. They were almost back to the easy camaraderie they'd always enjoyed, although the tense lines along Jake's mouth didn't disappear entirely.

I had my own worries. What if Laura was already pregnant?

We'd made love a number of times. As a newly invested Ingenii, she was at her most fertile. So it wasn't just the imminent Pledging ceremony that concerned me.

Never had the stakes been so high, or more personal.

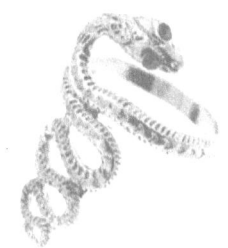

CHAPTER 3 - TOO MUCH IN ONE NIGHT

LAURA

He came in so stealthily – or so it seemed to me. I had no idea Alec was behind me until I felt his hands around my waist and his lips on my neck. He turned me to face him and drew me in for a kiss. It was a simple brush along my lips, yet it turned my knees to jelly. Pathetic really, considering I was no blushing teenager. But there it is.

Judy had left to check on progress for the Pledging ceremony in the ballroom. The delicious aroma of coffee wafted towards me as I went to pour two cups from the espresso machine.

'I thought you wanted to get some sleep before tonight?' he asked.

'Still intend to, but Judy and I got talking. You know how it is.' I shrugged.

His smile disappeared as I handed him a steaming cup. 'Laura, your blood may lose its potency once the curse is lifted. I've recently learned … there could be trouble.'

'A rebellion?'

He nodded. 'You know anything about the previous ones?'

'Yeah, Luc told me.'

If what Alec believed was right, then it was not a good time for me to fall pregnant. We'd made wonderful love several times. But what if that's all my body needed to conceive? Alec told me three days ago that now I was at my most fertile. I ran my hands over my stomach. If there were a baby, it'd be smaller than my thumbnail.

A warm glow spread through me at the thought. I wanted Alec's child, and not only because it would end the curse. I loved him. Yet what if it triggered a civil war? And if my blood reverted to human after the birth, he wouldn't have the strength to fight the rebels, and all our lives would be in danger. Everything Marcus Antonius and Luc had built up over the centuries would be jeopardised. Even from my limited experience, I knew there were those among the Brethren – cold-blooded murderers who enjoyed the thrill of the kill – who longed for a return to the days when they hunted humans as food. They weren't interested in taking a couple of polite swallows here and there. Perhaps they were like that before their transformation, but now their power and immortality only heightened those foul tendencies.

'Are you sure about my blood?'

He ran a frustrated hand through his hair. 'I checked Marcus's Chronicle, and it gives no hint, only that the curse will be lifted. I have no idea how it'll impact you.'

An idea came to me as I sipped my coffee. 'Why don't you take some of my blood and store it, you know, like the blood bank? That way you'll have a reserve supply, at least until the rebels are defeated.'

Alec looked at me. A slow smile lit his face, and then he laughed.

'What is it?'

'You are so like your father.'

What did that have to do with anything? 'In what way?'

'Laura, darling, Luc's been planning for this many centuries and he's done exactly that.'

I saw the connection and grinned. 'Problem solved, then.'

'Not entirely, but good enough for now.' He placed his cup on the table and after doing the same with mine, wrapped me in his arms and kissed me.

Suddenly he groaned and lifted his head. 'Of all the timing.'

'What is it?'

'Von Czernin's here – one of the Eastern European prefects. He's in the hallway with Luc. I have to join them.' He gave me an apologetic look.

Vampire hearing. What I wouldn't give for that. Yet, if Alec was needed, I could go and grab a couple hours of sleep. He, Luc and von-what's-his-name would probably be discussing tonight's Pledging, among other things. 'You go. I'll have a bath, then bed.'

He nodded and kissed me lightly on the brow. 'I'll introduce you to Karl von Czernin first.'

We left the kitchen and walked hand-in-hand up the stone steps to the hallway. At the other end, near the base of the marble stairs that led up to the family rooms, stood my father, Luc, with two of his men – Jake and Sam.

Sandwiched between them was a tall, brown-haired man in a long, dark green leather coat. He turned his head from Luc and looked at me. His gaze swept from me to Alec and back again. A slow smile crept across his face.

'Laura,' Alec said, 'may I introduce our Czech prefect, Count Karel von Czernin.'

'Our newest Ingenii. Just call me Karl.' He took my hand in his and kissed my fingertips. 'This is indeed a pleasure, Lady Laura.' His voice was low and designed to seduce, a trait I'd come to recognise as a characteristic feature of vampire men.

'Laura's about to get some rest before the Pledging,' Alec said and extended his arm. I disengaged my hand from Karl's, who didn't seem to want to let it go, and placed it in Alec's.

'What a pity! I would have enjoyed a closer acquaintance.' His lavender eyes sparkled, and he flashed a cheeky grin.

I was sure I heard a growl from Alec. Was it a warning, or was there something else going on? When Karl laughed and winked at him I had my answer – Alec was jealous. My female pride soared.

Jake and Sam took a step toward the stairs. Luc leaned forward and gently ran his thumb beneath my eye. 'You look tired, ma petite.'

'I am. A few hours sleep before the Pledging will help.'

'Good idea.' He kissed my brow, and with Jake, Sam and Karl following, strode up the stairs.

Alec tenderly ran the back of his fingers down one side of my face. 'Would you like me to wake you in a few hours?'

I shook my head. 'I'll set the alarm on my mobile.'

'Just let me know. I'll be with the men, in Luc's office.' He escorted me to my bedroom and kissed me before leaving.

So much had happened in the last few days, I was glad to have some time to myself.

I stepped out of my clothes, headed for the bathroom and ran the water in the ceramic tub. Several bath salts and oils sat in a nearby basket. After pouring in a few drops, I searched through the cabinets and located several candles. These I placed on the floor around the tub and lit them before flicking off the light switch.

Within minutes I was immersed in a warm, aromatic cloud. My tension eased and so did my concern about the coming Pledging ceremony.

Enclosed in my cocoon, I lay back and let the fragrant aroma wash over me, hoping it would do the same for my troubled thoughts as images of Jean-Philippe – my half-brother who had tried to rape and kill me – Alec's ex-lover Maris and her sidekick, Russell paraded through my mind. But, I reminded myself they belonged to the past.

After tonight the future, hopefully, would be safer. Alec's face appeared in my mind and I relaxed, closed my eyes and let the glow of the flickering candles create comforting patterns on the back of my eyelids.

CHAPTER 4 – BRETHREN POLITICS

ALEC

After seeing Laura to her room, I made my way down the hall to Luc's study.

Karl took out a cigarette and lit up. Of all the European prefects, I liked him the best. He actively pursued justice and honesty in all his dealings and had a dry, almost irreverent sense of humour I enjoyed, which, for some reason, seemed to grate on Jake's nerves.

Occasionally, he went too far.

'My people were right. You are in love with her.' A wide grin split his face.

'That's right, so no more hand kissing.'

He laughed and raised his hand, palm out. 'That's a promise, but it had the desired effect – I wanted to see for myself. If you weren't in love with the girl, I doubt you would have growled at me.'

Karl didn't know I was descended from the Pict witch, Eithne, who had uttered the curse against Marcus Antonius and his men eighteen-hundred years ago. So far, apart from Luc and Marcus and our trusted circle, no one else knew, nor that Laura was the prophesied Child of Light and Darkness.

That was the last thing I wanted any of my kind to guess.

'Is that what you came here to find out?' Jake asked. 'I thought it was to take the Pledge.'

'That too,' Karl answered. 'I'm just curious. No law against that.' He blew a ring of smoke into the air.

'If you don't mind, I'd rather my furniture didn't stink of cigarette smoke,' Luc said.

'Oh, so it's not concern for my health?'

Jake huffed.

Karl chuckled and stubbed out the cigarette, leaned forward in his armchair and looked straight at Luc. 'You've got trouble coming.'

'Oh?' Luc leaned back against his desk, arms folded across his chest.

I joined Jake, near one of the bookcases lining the walls.

'First of all, I don't know what Milena told you, but her territory's in no danger from me. I missed the Ritual to keep an eye on her and keep Timur's mongrels off her borders. Timur's got ambitions, and they don't just involve Milena's territories. I let her think he and I were in league to keep his trust. Stay in the circle, you know. But I think he suspects. At our last meeting he was cagey with names and details – waited till I'd gone.'

He reached into his coat pocket again, pulled out a leather glove and slid it on before extracting a small, dark object. 'Speaking of my health, recognise that?'

I certainly did. A fragment of a white-oak bullet. Lately I'd seen many of them. I'd retrieved six from Sommers's pocket the night Laura had been taken by force, and we found one in Russell's remains. He'd been shot in the back by Jean-Philippe, and within a minute, his body had disintegrated into crystalline dust. White-oak's the only substance fatal for our kind and, in the past, had been a favourite weapon of vampire hunters. But it appeared our own kind were now in possession of this deadly element, despite it being outlawed by the Eldership centuries ago when any Brethren found with it faced immediate execution. But guns were useless as the bullets travelled so slowly that any vampire could easily dodge them. One had to be taken by surprise

– shot in the back – or physically restrained while the bullet entered the body.

I pulled a handkerchief from my jeans pocket and used it to lift the bullet fragment from Karl's hand.

'We were shot at while getting into the limo at the airport tonight.' He pointed to the object in my hand. '*That* just missed me. Came straight through the window.'

I passed it to Luc, who swore under his breath and sniffed it. 'Don't recognise the scent.'

'Never thought I'd see one of those again,' Karl said.

Luc examined it closely. 'Unfortunately, I can't say the same.'

'Why's that?' Karl whipped out the gold case from inside his leather coat, took out another cigarette and lit it. As Luc frowned he added, 'I'll pay for a cleaner, if you're that particular.'

Luc dismissed the offer with a wave of his hand and briefed him about recent events and the circumstances surrounding Jean-Philippe's death. He omitted the details of their relationship, especially the fact that Laura – and current Ingenii – was his daughter. The time for that would come soon enough and, although he tried to retain an officious tone, I heard the sadness in his voice. Too late, he'd learned that Jean-Philippe had been his only son and that he'd developed an unnatural affection for his half-sister, Laura. Then had tried to rape and kill her when he realised she could never be his.

Karl shook his head. 'I'm so sorry, Luc. Hell, Jean of all people.' He looked at me. 'You had no choice, Alec. I would've done the same.'

I nodded. Jean-Philippe had been our brother, yet no one knew the madness that had been brewing and poisoning his soul. Jake later told me that Luc had brought Jean-Philippe's body back here and reverently carried it to a secluded part of the lower garden, where the morning sun reduced it to ash.

For a while no one spoke. It had hit everyone hard.

'Well,' Karl brought our thoughts back to the present situation, 'I have an idea who *that* belongs to.' He indicated the bullet casing in Luc's hand.

Luc's eyes narrowed. 'Who?'

Karl drew on his cigarette and exhaled. 'Timur and his mad sidekick, Rasputin,' he spat out, 'control most of the bad shit going on; sex trade, drugs ... you name it. They control Gregorovich, head of the Russian mafia.' He huffed. 'Rasputin doesn't hide the fact that that stinking piece of humanity's his supplier. Gets him the young ones – boys and girls. Says their blood is purer. Bastard! I'd love to kill Timur simply for turning him.'

Karl stubbed out the cigarette and placed the butt in his gold case. 'He's encroaching on our territories. Fucker's even bought up land to build another hotel in Karlovy Vary. Directly opposite mine.' He paused. 'I reckon it's a front for the blood-slave racket.'

'You sure of that?' I asked. If Karl was right, then Timur was committing a crime against Brethren Laws. It was forbidden to force humans into giving blood, especially the under-aged, since there were enough willing donors who provided their services when necessary. There was only one penalty for those caught dealing in blood-slavery – execution.

'They don't let me in on everything, but I've noticed their donsangs bringing in young humans. And they don't come out again. They were drugged – could smell it in their blood,' Karl said.

My fists clenched, and I turned to Jake. 'Go find Terens. Brief him, and then get back here with a couple of Kevlar vests.'

Jake nodded and left.

'What have you got in mind?' Luc asked me.

'What if we send a couple of the men to *escort* Timur and Rasputin here for the Pledging – surprise them.'

Karl shook his head. 'Might be too late.' He pointed to the shell casing. 'That wasn't just a warning.'

'Still, they won't be expecting one of us to show up there,' I said.

The last time any of our men had been overpowered it took nearly six of the Brethren to achieve it. I doubted Timur and Rasputin had that many around them as bodyguards. They were more likely to have human underlings who were no match for even one of our kind.

'Especially me.' Marcus Antonius strode in and closed the door behind him. He inclined his head to Luc and myself.

Karl rose from the Chesterfield and fell on one knee before him. 'My lord Marcus. This is an honour.'

Marcus indicated for him to sit. 'I heard what you said. Time I paid the European prefects a visit, while my presence still carries some clout. Find out where they're getting hold of those damned things' —he pointed to the wooden bullet in Luc's hand— 'and put a stop to his blood-slave business.'

'As long as the Principate remains, your name will be respected and your presence feared, my lord,' Karl replied.

'Let's hope.'

Luc's eyebrows shot up at Marcus's unprecedented pronouncement. Soon after being cursed by the witch, Marcus had established the Principate, then handed over his command to his son, Lucius, who now went by the Gallic version of his name, Lucien.

Not long after, Marcus went into a semi-reclusive existence, seeking redemption through penance, performing acts of goodwill. Only later he joined a monastery when the empire declared its official religion to be Christianity.

The monks knew what he was, but rather than treat him as the devil in their midst, they showed him mercy and kindness. In return, he adopted their faith. It was all recorded in his chronicle. Currently he resided in a monastery in France, still doing penance.

'If the Principate is in danger I won't stand by and see it destroyed, especially if there's something I can do. Besides, I have a vested interest.' He gave Luc a knowing look.

Luc nodded. 'My jet's on standby.'

'No,' Karl interjected. 'They're here. I flew out right after them. And they're not alone; got a whole fucking entourage!' He turned to look at Marcus. 'They've no intention of taking the Pledge, my lord. They're here to lead a rebellion. Have they presented themselves before you?' Karl's face roamed between Marcus, Luc and myself.

'No.' I answered.

'Well, there you are,' he replied.

Marcus's face darkened, and he and Luc exchanged a glance.

It was customary for visiting Brethren to present themselves before the prefect of any territory they're visiting and ask permission to enter. That was the most efficient way to maintain control of the number of Brethren in any area otherwise the human population could be placed at risk.

'Are you absolutely sure about a rebellion?' Marcus asked.

'Much as I can be, my lord. They spoke of taking "the girl", and making sure they had the numbers for a "takeover."' He shook his head. 'Timur sure wasn't on about some business deal. I'd stake my life on it.'

'We need definite evidence, Karl,' I said. 'What you've told us isn't enough.'

'Which is why I brought this.' From another pocket he produced a mobile phone, pressed a few buttons and handed it to me. 'Took it from one of his gang. All the proof you need, I'd say.'

I scrolled through a series of texts between Timur and the ex-owner of the mobile then tossed it to Luc. 'Son-of-a-bitch is planning to take Laura.' A red haze seeped into my vision, and my fists were clenched so tight, my bones began to crunch. 'Bastards want to go back to the old ways – hunt and kill. For that, they need to be rid of us, but not the power the Ingenii's blood provides.'

Luc perused the messages and passed it to Marcus. He closed his eyes for an instant and when he opened them again, they'd turned a shade lighter. 'They'll do anything to prevent the curse ending.' He turned to Karl. 'Where are you staying?'

'One of the safe houses, in Woollahra.'

'I'd rather you stay here. We've enough guest rooms. No need to risk collecting another one of these.' He held up the fragment and handed it to Marcus who turned it over in his palm.

'Yeah. See what you mean.'

'They might not just be aiming for you, but anyone who supports the Principate. Take us out one by one,' Luc said.

Karl's eyes widened. He obviously hadn't thought of that possibility. Assassinate the prefects who support the Principate faction and replace them with those from the Rebel cause. A nasty civil war could be averted as the rest of the Brethren could be cowed into submission. But that would take a lot of killing, as the majority of prefects were pro-Principate. No, I didn't want to believe that could happen, yet …

'They mustn't know you're still alive,' I said. 'I'll send out a general message to the Brethren sadly informing them of your demise. We'll tell them the car arrived with your crystalline remains in the back seat. Blame it on vampire hunters.'

The door opened. Jake, Terens and Cal walked in, each holding a Kevlar vest. Their faces split into wide grins on seeing

Marcus.

'Commander,' they said in unison and greeted him in the traditional Roman manner – hands clasping each other's forearms.

'Put those vests on,' Luc told them. 'You're going rat catching.'

'We're on a mission, boys,' Marcus said.

'Like old times.' Terens's grin widened.

'Before you head off, there's something else you need to know,' Karl said. 'This is just rumour, understand, but my informants are reliable.' He paused. 'The word is ... your little Ingenii's blood is deadly to our kind.'

Luc's hands gripped the edge of the desk, his knuckles white beneath the glare of the overhead lights. The stone surface cracked beneath his crushing fingers.

Marcus sucked in a breath.

'Questions are being asked,' Karl went on. 'Such as, since when have any of the Bloodgifted had poisonous blood? Answer? Never. So, the rumour goes, she must have vampire blood. And since she's the image of you,' he looked at Luc, 'but with Judith's colouring, well ... it doesn't take long to put two and two together, as they say.' He raised his eyebrows suggestively.

'How did this rumour begin?' I asked, hoping my voice didn't reflect the shock that went through me.

'Seems one of those involved in the recent rebellion had a mobile phone on him. Took pictures, even sent a tweet before, ah ... losing his head.'

Damn! The tension in the room rose a notch. We all exchanged glances while I figured what our next step should be.

Karl's gaze locked on Luc. 'From your silence, I assume the rumour's right.'

Luc nodded – there wasn't any point denying it.

'The infant you buried fifty years ago?' Karl asked.

'Judy's niece – she died in her sleep. The babes were swapped, and Laura was raised by her brother and his wife.'

Karl whistled long and low. 'Holy shit!' When no one spoke, he asked, 'Does she know?' Luc nodded again. 'How many others know about this?' Karl's gaze swept the room.

'You're looking at them,' Luc replied.

'Well ... hell.' He slumped back in the Chesterfield.

Laura had only learned the truth about her parentage several days ago, after the Ritual had taken place. It had come as a terrible shock to her, yet she had accepted it with grace, and Luc couldn't have been more proud. But that knowledge was best kept hidden, and from what I'd read on the stolen mobile Karl had brought, we had trouble coming all right. 'If that gets out, then what Maris planned could still happen.'

Collective curses and snarls came from the throats of every man in the room.

Karl's gaze sped from one face to the next. 'Can someone enlighten me?'

'They'd planned to mate Laura with a human – one of their minions, I expect. The idea was to use her to bear the next Ingenii for their personal use,' I said.

His eyes widened. 'Sacra!'

Luc swore as well. 'Laura's not to leave the house tonight, and during the day she's not to be left alone if she ventures out.' He nodded towards the door. Luc's teeth were gritted so hard his jaw muscles were almost protruding through the skin.

'Then the sooner we surprise those rats in their nest, the better,' Marcus said and flicked the bullet fragment into the bin next to Luc's desk.

'Bring them to me,' Luc said to him.

Marcus placed his hand on Luc's shoulder, gave him a brief nod then turned and strode from the room with Jake and Terens hard on his heels.

'Cal, scour the city; see what you can find out. Someone may have a loose tongue,' I said.

Cal nodded, and he too was gone.

I turned to Sam. 'Surveillance?'

'Up-to-date. And the area down by the water's been secured.'

'Good.'

Luc escorted Karl to one of the spare guest rooms, and I decided to drive to my apartment to collect my copy of the bloodvault key. I'd told Laura her father had been collecting Ingenii blood through the centuries; most of it was stored in the family chateau in the Rhone. Luc continued that practice when the Dantonvilles moved here in the 1850s and stored the precious vials in the cellars beneath the house.

Although the bloodvault couldn't be opened with only one key, should mine be lost or stolen, it wasn't worth the risk, so I kept it hidden in my apartment. Although I'd been there with Laura a few days ago, I hadn't deemed it necessary to bring it back, but now I realised my mistake.

'Luc, I'm going to fetch the bloodvault key. Be back soon.'

I raced down the stairs and out the front door with two things uppermost in my mind – the Pledge and Laura's safety. And then there was the delicate task of ending the curse before any move could be made against us.

Time was running out.

CHAPTER 5 – THE LAST SECRET

LAURA

I lay in the scented bath for nearly thirty minutes. The bruises Jean-Philippe inflicted had just about dissipated.

As I climbed out of the tub, my churning emotions resurfaced and threatened to overtake me, but I refused to give in. With an angry shake of my head, I crawled into bed and pulled the sheet over me. Unfortunately, my thoughts wouldn't let me rest. I tossed and turned until I could stand it no longer. What I needed was a major distraction – perhaps a nice romance novel to help my mind switch off. I had heard mention of a library on this level, and I guessed it would be near Luc's study, at the other end of the hallway.

I hopped out of bed, wrapped a short satin robe around me then opened the door and peered out. The corridor was empty.

Leaving the door ajar, I stepped out, made my way to the end of the hall and headed for the closed door adjacent to Luc's study, hoping my guess had been right. Only one way to find out. My hand gripped the handle, gave a twist, and it opened.

I stepped into the darkened room. At the far end, a solitary spotlight shone on an ancient soldier's regalia – chain mail, leg greaves, helmet and sword.

It took my breath away.

Directly beneath stood a lectern of dark wood – mahogany perhaps? – supporting a magnificent golden platform in the shape of an eagle with outstretched wings. Flanking it on either side were four tall, narrow leadlight windows. The coloured panes were dim in the darkness, yet that didn't detract from their role as silent sentinels standing guard over a sacred relic.

I inched forward for a closer view. That's when the smell of tobacco hit me. I groped the wall, located the light switch and turned it on. Stretched out on a chestnut-coloured settee, with his head facing away from me, cigarette between his fingers was the last person I expected to see – the Czech prefect, Karl von … something.

'You can come in. I'm not going to bite.' He chuckled. 'Not yet anyway.'

I didn't dare venture any further regardless of whether he was joking or not. We'd only been introduced less than an hour ago and even if my father and Alec knew him, he still might turn against them. I'd already had some experience of that. On impulse, I glanced at the serpent ring on my hand. The eyes turned black if anything was wrong, and right now, they glowed a healthy ruby-red. The Ring sensed no danger. Karl was okay.

'Impressive, isn't it?' he drawled.

'What? Oh, yes!' He was referring to the ensemble before us.

He blew smoke from between his lips. 'Belonged to Marcus Antonius.'

That aroused my interest. Luc, my father, had revealed Marcus's story to me, and the beginnings of my family legacy, but to see the tangible evidence of his former life in stark reality was something else.

I could have stood there and stared, but my curiosity overcame my reticence and I ventured into the room, my bare feet padding lightly across the deep-burgundy carpet.

It was indeed a library. Shelves filled with books – some appeared very old, if their peeling leather-bound covers were anything to go by – lined all four walls. Positioned between each bookstand were a number of padded benches. The three-seater settee on which Karl lounged was on my right and angled toward the back wall where Marcus Antonius's armour hung.

'What's on the stand?' I asked.

'His chronicle.'

'The original?' It would be the manuscript of the century if that were the case.

'Don't think so. Probably a copy.'

He finally turned his head and looked at me. My cheeks burned as he scrutinised me from head to toe. I was glad I'd slipped the robe on before leaving my room.

'I, um, came out to find a book. Didn't expect anyone to be up here,' I finished awkwardly.

He drew on the cigarette, sat up and rested his elbows on his knees. 'Yes, well. I'm supposed to be dead.'

'You mean undead?'

His chortle filled the silence. 'Depends on your interpretation.' He took a slim gold case from his hip pocket, stubbed out the cigarette and flicked the butt into a nearby wastepaper basket. 'Let's just say that someone found my existence a hindrance and tried to rectify the situation this evening. So, here I am – safe and bored.'

'You can't leave the house?'

'Unless I want to join the ranks of the dead undead.' He gave me a wide grin.

I couldn't help smiling back, feeling at ease with him. 'That's tough.'

'Yep, and it interferes with my social life. Not exactly what I'd planned for my pre-Pledge night's entertainment.' He lifted one eyebrow suggestively.

I could imagine what he had in mind. Karl was another one of those unnaturally attractive men who was irresistible to women. Collar-length, straight dark hair contrasted vividly with his lavender eyes – bedroom eyes – that were fringed by long, ebony lashes, he was every woman's fantasy.

Thankfully I already had my own awesome man, so I could appreciate Karl's charms without succumbing to them. I shuddered what would happen if he, Terens and Sam ever went out on a triple date. Heaven help the women of Sydney!

I looked away from him and focused on the armour. Up close,

I could see the chain mail had discoloured with age, as had the bronze helmet. The sword gleamed dully in the light, its edges nicked and dented. Was it the result of age or neglect? Perhaps Marcus Antonius hated the memory of the day he was cursed, or the circumstances that brought him there. I could only guess. Yet by its very presence, those three pieces acted as a constant reminder of that very thing.

'Why is it here?' I asked. 'Not locked away somewhere safe?'

He glanced up at the wall, then back at me. 'I 'spose they could do that between Elder inductions, but ....' He shrugged.

'What are they?'

'Whenever an Elder needs to be replaced, the prospective candidate is brought in here where they read aloud from Marcus's Chronicle and familiarise themselves with the terms of the Curse. Then swear to uphold the Principate.'

I didn't bother to ask how he knew that. I just assumed it was common knowledge in his world, as is the swearing in of political leaders in mine.

'Go ahead. Have a look. It isn't out of bounds.' He leaned back against the settee, hands behind his head and watched me intently as I moved to the lectern.

'Are you old enough to be an Elder?' I asked.

He laughed. 'Unfortunately. Never been tempted, though. Got plenty to keep me occupied at home.'

I walked around to the front of the lectern to see Marcus's Chronicle for myself. Resting on the golden platform, like some massive, old church Bible, was a large red leather book. The figure of a coiled golden serpent with blood-red eyes was emblazoned on the front. Encircling the whole, in vivid gold cursive lettering, ran a Latin inscription.

I had a feeling it could be the words of the curse that condemned Marcus and his men to a blood-sucking existence.

I slid my fingers along the figure of the serpent, almost expecting ... what? Some magic tingle? Since learning the truth about my birthright, I'd had to accept the reality of magic – the serpent ring on my finger was ample proof of that. However, there was no hint of anything. Marcus's Chronicle was just an ordinary book. I don't know why I felt disappointment.

'Can anyone open it?' I asked.

'Sure.'

I carefully turned back the cover, knowing full well it wouldn't be written in English. It was, after all, the chronicle of Roman Commander Marcus Antonius Pulcher, presumably in his native language – Latin.

A quick perusal of the first few pages proved me right. It was a hand written script in black ink, and along the margins, Marcus had drawn figures in Roman uniform as well as an image of a female, arms upraised, hair flowing about her like a halo.

I sucked in my breath. The female could be none other than the witch, Eithne.

'Can you read Latin?' I asked Karl.

'Of course!'

Well, of course he could, I thought. *He's probably old enough to know who-knows-how-many languages.*

'Let me know if you want me to read it for you.'

'That's okay. Luc told me the story when I saw the images on the stained-glass window on the landing.'

He nodded. 'He should know, considering he's in it.'

'What do you mean?' I glanced up from the book.

'He's Marcus Antonius's son, one of the twins. Didn't you know?'

I stared at him open mouthed. *My father,* Lucien Lebrettan, was … is Lucius? The knowledge went through me like an electric jolt. Why, that would make him nearly – I did the quick maths in my head—eighteen-hundred years old and therefore, next to Marcus, one of the oldest beings in existence. Why hadn't he told me? I thought back to his words, only now realising how cryptic and evasive his answers had been. Why had he been so reluctant to tell me? What was so terrible?

Karl unwound his arms from behind his head and sat up. 'I thought you knew.'

I shook my head.

He raised his eyebrows. 'Just don't say it came from me. If he was keeping it secret for some reason, my telling you won't endear me to him, if you know what I mean.' Just as he spoke, he straightened and swivelled his head toward the door. He groaned.

I didn't have to second-guess what was going on. Vampire hearing. He'd been overheard, and sure enough, the door opened.

Luc stood there, glaring at Karl, his fists clenched by his side.

'Leave us.'

Karl's pale face went a notch whiter. He rose from his seat. 'I assumed....'

Luc held up his hand, but said no more. Karl quietly left the room.

My father faced me, his expression changing from anger to concern. 'You should not have heard it from him.'

'It's true, then?'

He stepped into the room and closed the door. 'I planned on telling you later. You had enough to cope with, ma petite.'

Couldn't argue with that. My world had changed on learning the truth about my family heritage, and the significant part I played in it. I'd lived in blissful ignorance for many years, unaware of the existence of vampires and my family's unique bloodline. Maybe he was right about it being too much too soon.

He remained motionless by the door, hesitant, probably wondering how I was going to absorb this recent shocker.

'Does mother know?'

'Of course. I hide nothing from her.'

I raised my eyebrows. He'd kept Jean-Philippe's relationship from her. 'What about Jean-Philippe?'

'Ah. Apart from that one,' he said with an apologetic air. 'And that's because I wasn't sure. I didn't want to worry her; make her uncomfortable in his presence.'

Okay, I could accept that. 'That makes Marcus Antonius my grandfather.'

'Yes, ma petite.'

I closed my eyes and tried to come to terms with that.

'Perhaps you had better sit down,' he said, indicating the settee Karl had vacated.

'Do you want to bring out the brandy?' I asked with a half smile as I sat down.

He visibly relaxed and sat next to me. 'Am I forgiven?'

'For what?'

His face broke into an infectious grin and I had difficulty in reconciling Luc, my father, with Lord Lucien, the man who instilled fear into others of his kind. They seemed two different creatures. This Luc looked relieved I wasn't angry.

'I've lived a long time, my Laura; many lifetimes, and I've accumulated many secrets. They've kept me alive over the centuries.'

I nodded. A vampire would have to change his identity every human lifetime for fear of discovery, even his place of residence. I wondered how many houses he owned around the world.

'That must be hard.'

He shrugged. 'When there is no other way, it becomes the way.'

It occurred to me, that in all probability, the same might be awaiting me, as he and Alec believed I may have inherited a vampire's lifespan. 'Is that what I'm facing?'

His smile faded. 'Perhaps. I'm not sure how you'll be affected when the curse is lifted.'

I felt myself pale. 'You think my blood'll become normal and I'll age and die? But … Alec won't?' The sudden urge to panic swept over me. I already knew Marcus Antonius, my father, his men, and Alec would be given the choice, either to remain in vampire form or become human again. The problem with the latter is they would die within minutes as all those years of their existence caught up with them. So, where did that leave me? Would I be given a choice? Or would my blood automatically revert to normal and I would age in an instant? 'Oh, Papa!'

'No! It doesn't have to be that way, ma petite.'

'But how can you prevent it, unless you let the curse continue?'

He rose, took hold of my hands and drew me up. 'Come, there's something I want to show you.'

He led me to the wall behind the lectern, on which hung the chain mail, helmet and sword.

'Only our immediate circle know about this,' he said, and raising his right hand, he inserted his ring – also in the shape of a serpent, but with green eyes – into a cavity directly below the sword, which was invisible until you got close enough. He twisted his wrist to the left. With a click, the entire panel swung open and revealed a hidden safe.

He leaned in and withdrew a white box. As he turned back to me I saw it was made from a solid block of alabaster.

'It's beautiful.'

'Antonia liked it too. I still remember the day she bought it.' With one hand he closed Marcus's Chronicle and placed the box on top.

Antonia had died about eighteen-hundred years ago. She was Luc's twin and therefore, my aunt. The knowledge made my head swim.

Luc opened the box. I gasped. Lying in a bed of white silk was a small, oval multi-faceted, red gemstone. Its polished surface winked seductively in the overhead light. A golden serpent's head crowned the apex: attached to it was a delicate gold chain.

My father lifted the pendant and held it before me. 'This garnet vial contains several drops of blood from Antonia, Marcus and me. You have only to drink it and your lifespan will be the same as mine.'

I stared at it in fascinated silence. A faint pulse of light appeared to throb within its very heart.

'Ah, it recognises its owner,' he said. 'It originally belonged to my sister, and now it belongs to you.'

'But, why me? Surely you'd prefer mother to be with you forever?'

His eyes saddened. 'I offered it to her many years ago, ma petit. But the blood didn't respond to her as it does to you. We knew then, it wasn't meant for her.'

I didn't need to imagine the pain he must be feeling as he faced a future that would not include my mother. But Judy had mentioned she and Luc had made special arrangements for when the time was near. Maybe he had no intention of remaining without her, but that was something I didn't want to pursue. If my parents were not destined to spend millennia together in this lifetime, they were offering me the chance instead. Should my blood revert to normal once the curse is lifted, at least Alec and I will not be faced with the same heart-breaking situation.

'I believe it was always meant for you. Antonia gave it to me before she died.'

'Why didn't she take it?'

'Her second husband loved her very much, and she couldn't bear the thought of eternity without him.'

Tears stung my eyes, and I tried to blink them away. 'I don't know what to say.'

'I want you to be happy. Promise me you'll wear this always and when the time comes, you'll drink it.' Luc spread the chain and dropped it over my head so that the garnet vial rested between my breasts. 'Promise me, ma petite.'

Even though blood didn't figure high on my list of culinary delights, if it meant I could be with Alec forever, I'd drink it. 'I promise.'

He briefly closed his eyes and gave a satisfied sigh. 'Good. Your children will be free, and you and Alec will have eternity together.'

'What about Alec's position as princeps? Won't that end as well?' If my blood no longer had the power to keep him strong, he'd be in danger of losing, not just his position but also his life.

'I've had a long time to prepare. The Principate cannot end, as it's the only thing that stands between humanity and the worst of our kind.'

'How?'

Luc picked up the alabaster box and placed it back in the safe. As he swung the door closed, Marcus Antonius's armour once again dominated the wall space, the opening hidden.

He turned to me. 'My Laura, only our family is privileged with this knowledge. As my daughter, you have the right to know.'

My eyes widened. 'Perhaps you shouldn't tell me. What if I accidently blurt it out?' Like I had done to Matt when Alec first transformed in front of me. That seemed so long ago now.

He placed his hands on my shoulders. '*You* are the reason I'm doing all this. Therefore, you should know.' He dropped his hands, and from beneath his shirt, pulled out a long, golden chain from which a small key dangled. 'This unlocks a vault containing thousands of vials of blood – such as the one I've given you – gathered from Ingenii over the centuries. It's in the wine cellar beneath the house, but it's only a fraction of the amount I've stored in my chateau in France. It will give us the necessary advantage to defeat any rebellion.'

'Alec told me.'

'Did he now?' Luc raised an eyebrow.

For a moment I wondered if I shouldn't have mentioned it. My father's secrets were being revealed to me by others, depriving him of the opportunity. 'Don't be angry with him, Papa. I suggested he

36

take samples of my blood for storage in case everything goes back to normal. He only said you'd already done something similar.'

Luc shook his head. 'I'm not angry, ma petite. Alec was right to tell you. There should be no secrets between you.'

I gave a sigh of relief, not because I was afraid he'd berate Alec, but it meant there were no more surprises I'd have to deal with, except one. 'What happens when your supply runs out?'

'By then it won't matter.' He shrugged. 'The Rebels will be dead and the rest will have taken the Pledge.'

I shook my head in wonder. He'd thought of everything. Yet, a small, inner voice refused to accept it could be that simple, for even the most meticulous of plans can encounter the unexpected.

Luc patted my cheek and smiled. 'Don't look so worried. Everything will turn out well.'

'I hope so.' Another thought occurred to me. 'If there's only one key, and something were to happen to you—'

'*If,* and that's a big *if,* Marcus has a key. So do your mother and Alec. Three must be inserted simultaneously for the locking mechanism to release – in case one should go missing.'

I nodded. The famous line from *The Three Musketeers* came to mind – *All for one and one for all.* For a second I wondered if my father had known Alexander Dumas. I wouldn't have been surprised.

'Now you know all, ma petite. No secrets left.'

I leaned over and kissed my father's cheek. 'Thank you for trusting me with something so important.'

'How could I not? This doesn't affect just me.'

'You really expect trouble?'

He nodded. 'It's already begun.'

My mouth went dry at his words. I'd never been faced with a dangerous situation before, especially one involving my family. Yet, here I was, the centrepiece of a possible vampire war that could result in the death of those I loved. And there was no way the police could intervene. This was a non-human affair; a parallel world humans didn't know even existed – a war waging beneath their noses.

War. The very word frightened me. Alec could be killed. What was the use of having some magic elixir to make me immortal if the only person I wanted to spend eternity with could be taken from me? I didn't want to consider the possibility: still, I could think of no way to avoid it. If anything were to go wrong and I lost him, I'd empty Antonia's vial down the sink.

I took a deep breath and came to a decision. Every minute we spent together would be even more precious. Fingering the vial which hung from my neck, I said, 'I'd like to go to Alec.'

'He's not here right now – went to fetch the bloodvault key from his flat and keep it with him.'

Things were serious if Alec felt the key wasn't safe in his apartment. Did he really believe the Rebels capable of breaking the sanctity of the princep's domain? A shiver went through me. Going back to my room was out of the question as all tiredness had left me, and I'd probably end up pacing the carpet bare.

'I'll wait for him downstairs, in the front room.'

'Why not wait in his room?' Luc suggested. 'Come, I'll take you.' He grasped my hand. We went down the corridor, past the family rooms, across the landing to the next wing of the house and to the first door on the left. Alec had brought me up here the first time we made love. 'Since he moved out, he uses it only occasionally.'

'When did he move out?'

'Only recently. Let's see ....' He rubbed his chin. 'Oh yes, nineteen sixty.'

'That's recent?'

He chuckled. 'For our kind, it is.' Before I could ask anything further, he kissed me lightly on the forehead, turned and left.

As I went to open the door, I glanced at my ring. The eyes of the serpent changed from red to black. At the same instant Alec's face flashed into my head.

I released the handle as if electrocuted, ran down the hallway and called out for Luc.

CHAPTER 6 – THE BLOODVAULT KEY

ALEC

Laura was safe in the house. I glanced at the serpent ring every few moments to make sure of it. There was only one problem – it was difficult to discern whether it was she or I in immediate danger when the eyes of the serpents darkened. The rings always changed at the same time. I kept one eye on the road, one on the ring and my senses spread wide as I wove through the traffic to my Pitt Street apartment.

There were three hours left before the prefects were due to arrive for the Pledging – I had little time to waste. Whoever had fired those white-oak bullets at Karl was out there somewhere. Was it one assassin or more?

Vampires can normally sense, and even hear each other's conversations within a three-mile range, but my feeding from an Ingenii doubled that. If he or they were within six miles of me, I'd overhear even the faintest whisper.

The streets were filled with shoppers, as stores were open longer to cater for the Christmas rush only a week away. I felt several Brethren mingling among the shoppers. The season wasn't only a feast for humans. With so many tourists flocking into the city in the summer months, it was bumper season for vampires as well –greater choice in the hunt. They would be mesmerising humans into accompanying them into nearby Hyde Park, or into dark corners or alleyways to feed discreetly, before escorting them back.

Travelling to different cities didn't relax the rules, and with the knowledge of Maris and Russell's deaths circulating through the Brethren community, those stipulations had become further pronounced. To reinforce the No Killing rule, I whispered a reminder into the darkness, knowing my words would be heard.

'Remember: hunt but don't kill.' It was unnecessary to drain a human of all their blood, as only a few swallows were needed to satisfy a mature blood drinker.

Several, 'Yes, Princeps,' came back to me on the night air.

I eased the car into the basement parking of my apartment building and mentally scanned the immediate area before getting out. None of my kind were nearby. A car drove in and parked in a reserved spot. I knew the driver. He was human – a local businessman who lived directly below me.

We greeted each other as my private elevator arrived. Only operated by my key, it gave access to my Penthouse Suite.

Within minutes, which seemed like hours, I was home and staring at the panoramic night vista of the city. Floor-to-ceiling windows gave an unhindered view of Sydney's spectacular skyline. Like twinkling stars, the harbour reflected a million lights from the various office buildings along the foreshores.

I leant my hands against the glass, still warm from the setting sun, and looked out. 'Hear me, Karl von Czernin's assassin. I will find you.' I wanted him to think that Karl was dead.

Then I caught it. Faint laughter and, 'Not if I find you first.'

I clenched my fists. The Australian-accented voice seemed familiar, yet I couldn't place it. I ran up the steps to my bedroom in the loft. Directly above my bed hung a painting composed entirely of keys. The artist I had commissioned created a scene that could only be recognised from a distance. It was the prefect camouflage.

Separating the bloodvault key from the rest, I threaded it onto the chain that held my mother's crucifix and dropped it beneath my shirt. As I made for the elevator, the roar of motorcycles filled my ears. Several Brethren were coming.

I had only minutes.

As I got back in the lift, I picked up the presence of at least five individuals.

'C'mon, c'mon,' I willed the thing to go faster. It would have been quicker if I'd simply scaled down the outside of the building. In the dark, nobody would have seen me.

The elevator doors slid open, and I raced for the car. Five black motorcycles thundered down the ramp and surrounded me. One slid to a screeching halt inches from my legs. I knew who it was before he removed the helmet.

CHAPTER 7 – BACK UP

LAURA

Luc came hurrying back along the corridor. 'What is it?'

I held my hand up, the serpent ring facing him. 'The eyes. Look, they're black!'

Sam came down the stairs at a run. 'Laura! What's wrong?'

At the same time Karl stuck his head out from one of the rooms down the other end of the hall. 'Everything okay?'

'Alec's in danger!' There was no disguising the panic in my voice. 'I saw him, in my mind. In a room with a huge window, and … look.' I held up my hand to show them the serpent ring.

'Hell!' Sam exclaimed. 'You have a telepathic link with him?'

'Yes.'

'Try contacting him, ma petite. I'm out of range.'

I closed my eyes and concentrated on calling out to him with my mind. *Alec! Tell me what's happening. Are you okay?*

Fine, honey. Don't worry.

I breathed a sigh of relief, yet whenever he called me *honey*, it was because he was worried. The first time he did so was at the hospital after Maris had nearly killed me. I'd lost so much blood I had needed a transfusion. *I saw you.* For a moment there was silence. Then I heard his voice in my head.

I'm all right, Laura.

Then why are the serpent's eyes black? There was another protracted silence.

Alec? I waited. 'Alec!' I shouted.

Nothing.

'What is it? Tell me.' My eyes snapped open at Luc's voice.

'He said he's fine, but … something's wrong.'

Luc issued orders. 'Sam, stay here. Secure the house. Laura, ma petite,' he gripped my upper arms, 'you are not to venture out for any reason. Do you understand? Stay with your mother. Cal and I will go to Alec.' He pulled out his phone and speed dialled. 'Cal, get over to Alec's right now. There's trouble. I'll meet you there.'

'You'll need weapons,' Sam said and sped down the hall.

'Where is Alec?' Karl asked Luc.

'His apartment. He went to fetch … something.'

He'd been listening to our exchange, and his eyes darted between Luc, Sam and myself. He knew nothing of the bloodvault.

'I'm coming with you,' he said.

Luc turned to him. 'No! You can't be seen. You've been assassinated, remember? Stay here.'

'There'll be just you and Cal. What if that's not enough?'

Luc hesitated. 'Only if you cover your face. My men will be in danger if Timur and Rasputin find out you're still alive.'

He nodded, sped back to his room and re-emerged in less than a blink wearing a glittery, black Venetian Carnival mask.

'Oh, you've got to be kidding,' Sam said. He'd returned carrying several swords.

'Hey, it's the only thing I've got and if some goon hadn't taken a pot shot at me when I arrived, I'd be enjoying a very pleasant pre-Pledging party, wearing this,' he pointed to the mask, 'and nothing else.'

Sam rolled his eyes.

'It'll do.' Luc took one sword and handed another to Karl. 'I presume you know how to use this?'

Karl balanced the tip of the blade on the end of one finger then swung it proficiently around a couple of times. 'Nice weight.'

Luc nodded then turned and hurried down the corridor and out of sight. Karl followed.

I was left alone with Sam. We both glanced at the serpent ring; its black eyes stared back at us. My stomach hollowed out.

'I can't stand this.' I thought about ringing Matt, my ex-boyfriend. He was a police detective. But, then, what could he do? Not only did he have no memory of our relationship, but the existence of vampires in this city had been wiped from his mind as well. What could I tell him? Hey remember me, your ex-girlfriend? My new boyfriend is in danger from rogue vampires. Can you help? He'd probably warn me not to bother him with crank calls. I quickly ditched that idea.

'Look, Judith's up in the ballroom. Why don't you join her?' Sam suggested. 'It'll give me the chance to scan the monitors and do a quick perimeter check.'

What else could I do? 'I'll let her know what's going on.'

'No need. Luc briefed her on his way out.'

Vampire hearing, I thought. If I had a Christmas wish, that would be it.

As we made our way back down, I tried to reach Alec telepathically, but all I got was silence. Was he deliberately blocking me?

Judy met me at the bottom of the stairs, leaving Sam to do whatever it was he had to do. 'He'll be all right, dear,' she assured me. 'Alec is strong and capable.'

'I keep trying to reach him, but there's no response.'

'If he's in a tricky situation, he can't afford to be distracted.'

Like fighting for his life, maybe? I couldn't keep the thought at bay.

She ushered me into her personal sitting room, and onto one of the plush sage-green sofa chairs. The Roman blinds were half-lowered, allowing a view of the night-lit garden beyond. If I weren't so anxious, I'd be more admiring of it's fairy-tale appearance.

'Take this, dear.' Judy handed me a shot of brandy.

At this rate I'd get addicted to the stuff. Like my father, my mother believed in the curative properties of certain types of alcohol, and brandy was the family favourite. I swallowed, and the warmth of the liquid travelled through me. Pity it didn't alleviate the worry.

'Is this my future?' I asked. 'Constantly worrying about him being in danger? How did you stand it all these years with Luc?'

She gave me a sympathetic look. 'I learned to trust in Providence. *Que sera, sera,* as they say. What will happen will happen, and no amount of worry will change anything.' Judy leaned across to me and placed her hand over mine. 'I believe the Pledge tonight will help alleviate most of your concerns and guarantee your safety. After the last one, about four-hundred years ago, there was no further trouble.'

'Then here's to midnight.' I raised the glass in a salute, swallowed the last drop of brandy then placed it on the coffee table and headed for the door.

'Laura, where are you going?'

'To Alec's room, to wait for him.' The nervous tension was getting to me. If I couldn't be with him, then at least I could be in a place where I could feel his presence.

'Not a good idea, dear. Being by yourself right now isn't going to help either you or Alec.' She rose from her sofa chair, came to me and hooked her arm around mine. 'Come up to the ballroom. There's someone I'd like you to meet. She's been helping me complete preparations up there.'

'Who?'

'Wait and see.' She gave me an enigmatic smile. 'I wanted to introduce you when she arrived, but you were busy with Luc.'

I really wasn't in the mood, but maybe she was right. What would I do in Alec's room, apart from pace and worry myself sick? Perhaps a distraction was what I needed.

She placed her palm on my chest, directly over the spot where Antonia's vial sat nestled beneath my robe. 'I'm glad he told you everything. And when the time comes, at least you'll have a choice.'

He must have mentioned the vial to her on his way out.

'It's not fair … you and Luc.'

'Life's not fair, dear, but I've been loved by the best man in the world for fifty years, and that's more than most women can say.' She squeezed my arm. 'Now, no more morbid thoughts.'

Her arm still linked in mine, Judy and I made our way up the two flights of marble stairs, which led to the ballroom at the very top. I tried not to glance at the serpent ring on my other hand, for fear the eyes were still black. I sent up a quick prayer as we stepped through the open mirrored doors and gasped at the opulence that greeted me.

CHAPTER 8 – GATHERING STORM

ALEC

A black-attired cohort formed a circle around me, revving their bikes till the fumes of their engines bounced off the low ceiling. If it was meant to intimidate, it wasn't working.

Alec! Tell me what's happening. Are you okay? Laura's voice filled my mind.

For a heart-stopping second I thought she was here, despite no sense of her physical presence – her voice was only in my head. Without taking my eyes from their black-helmeted leader, I casually raised my right arm and leaned it on top of my car.

From that position I saw that the serpent's eyes had darkened. Its twin on Laura's hand would show the same. I nearly swore. Why hadn't I checked? But at least she was safe. *Fine, honey. Don't worry.*

I saw you.

She could see me? The rings were increasing the telepathic bond between us. The last thing I wanted was her worrying about me. *I'm all right, Laura.*

Then why are the eyes black?

How could I tell her I was face-to-face with a hired assassin and he wasn't alone?

Alec?

I longed to respond, but it would only serve to worry her more.

Laura's panicked voice screamed in my head again. I blocked it from my mind.

The leader removed his helmet, perched it on the handle bar of his motorbike and looked at me contemptuously from his seat. The others did the same. I did a quick scan – two women, three men. I knew them. Locals. Last time I saw them had been at the Ritual. Their leader was Roger Stockton. He'd been transformed less than thirty years ago. Unfortunately, with his sire dead, he was out of servitude and out of control.

The Elders should have appointed him a new master, but with the recent disruptions, had neglected to do so, and now it was too late. By attempting to assassinate a prefect, and being in possession of white-oak bullets, Stockton had signed his own death warrant.

'I'm here to relay a message,' he sneered.

'And for that you need company?' I indicated the hostile group that ringed me.

'You think I'd be fool enough to face you on my own? Oh no, Princeps, you should be flattered I brought so many.' He stroked his dark goatee and smiled. 'They're here to see me deliver my message.'

Some nodded. Others smiled and leaned on their handlebars. I tried to appear calm as he rose and stood before me. He was carrying white-oak. I could smell it on him, although in what form it was difficult to tell.

I leaned back against my car and masked my emotions. It takes only a fragment of the stuff to kill a vampire. I was determined that wasn't going to happen, especially now. For the first time in decades, I had something, someone to live for. 'Whose messenger boy are you?'

He stood and stared at me. The smile left his face. I guessed he didn't like being called a messenger boy. Too bad. Either that, or … 'They're that scared, huh?'

His mouth tightened. 'Rasputin's not scared of you. He's sick of you, as we all are, with your sanctimonious rules toward the humans.'

There were murmurs of agreement from his companions. I ignored them and focused on Stockton. My jibe had forced the answer out of him. Karl had been right about Rasputin, and it wouldn't have surprised me if Timur had a hand in this, too.

'He said we're gods. Immortal and superior to humans in every way,' one of the men called out. 'It's not wrong for us to kill!'

'Even so-called gods are not above our laws,' I said.

'We didn't make them. The Elders did. Rasputin's right,' one of the women said. 'He understands what we are, and the fact we need the freedom to hunt and kill. The right you've denied us.'

'The hunt wasn't denied you, only the kill.'

'What's the thrill in that? It's our nature,' she said.

'Excuse me if I misunderstood, but I thought you said you were a god, not an animal.'

Her eyes blazed, and she rose from her motorbike. I could taste the tension swirling around the group.

The woman next to her reached out and pulled her back down. 'We heard the Ingenii's blood is poison. Is that true?' she asked.

I was expecting that. Vampires were unable lie to each other. Truth has its own scent as does a lie. Were I to lie, they'd smell it immediately.

'Yes, but not to me, as you witnessed at the Ritual.'

They glanced at each other and nodded. That had me worried. Since I was the only one who could safely feed from Laura, were they to kill me, Luc would assume the mantle of princeps once again and implement his plan. The stored Ingenii blood would be given to the men, and he would instigate a massacre – civil war on a scale our kind has never witnessed before. It was a fearful scenario, and these fools were on the verge of it.

'Rasputin was right–' one of his companions said before Stockton cut him off.

'Shut it!' he called over his shoulder.

I laughed. 'That's the story, is it? Neither of *them* wants to take the Pledge, and since they're too cowardly to confront me they send a sucker like you, instead.'

He snarled, and the stench of his adrenalin drifted about him in a cloud. My body tensed. 'He's mine!' he called to the others then came at me.

His attack was rapid, but no surprise. I let him grapple me; let him think he could possibly bring me down; allow his self-confidence to be his weakness; his danger. His sneer soon turned to a grimace when he realised his attempt to overpower me was not succeeding. He was only looking foolish in front of his companions.

'Time to end this,' I said and threw him off. Crouching, I readied for his next assault.

He took to the ceiling and hung there looking down at me, twisting his head at an unnatural angle as his body moved into a better position to attack.

It gave me an idea.

I leapt over to the nearest biker, yanked him off his seat and threw him at Stockton, who sprang out of the way as the man crashed into the ceiling and fell back down at my feet. I snapped his neck before the others could react. He would be out for at least twenty minutes before his bones reknit.

The rest of Stockton's gang leapt off their bikes and scattered.

'You don't play fair, Princeps!' One of them called from behind the safety of a concrete pillar.

'I didn't agree to play fair.'

'Don't interfere!' Stockton cried, as en masse, they regrouped and moved toward me.

'Alec, we're on our way. How many are there?' Luc's voice sounded in my ears. I whipped my head around. The momentary distraction allowed Stockton to jump down, hook his arm around my throat, and kick my legs out from under me. He held me down, his fangs lowered and glistening.

'Alec!' Luc's voice sounded again, but I had no time to answer.

'I don't fight fair, either,' Stockton growled in my ear. His glove-clad right hand held a sharpened wooden stake, pointed at my heart.

I wasn't expecting that.

'Bloody hell.' One of his men said, 'he *is* going to use it!'

I tensed my neck and tucked my chin onto my chest, lessening his stranglehold. Using both hands, I grabbed hold of the arm brandishing the stake and snapped it at the elbow.

Stockton howled, releasing his grip. It gave me the chance to manoeuvre my hip and flip him onto his back. The wooden stake flew from his hand and slid beneath my car. I grabbed his neck, but was pulled back and held down on the ground by all five members of his gang members.

One of the men backhanded me as I tried to throw them off, while the smaller of the two women dived beneath my car and retrieved the sharpened stake.

'Hurry up! I can't hold him much longer,' the backhander yelled, as I strained against them.

'We can't kill him! Are you crazy?' It was the same man who swore earlier on seeing the stake in Stockton's hands.

'Shut up and do it, or you'll be joining him,' said his companion.

'No. Leave him. He's mine!' Stockton's right arm hung limply by his side as he rose and began pulling them off me.

'What are you doing?' the other woman cried. 'He was about to kill you.'

'If I wanted you dead, Stockton, it would've happened by now.' I saw my advantage and slammed together the two remaining rogues who still held my arms and threw them to the other side of the car park. They landed with a heavy thud against the concrete walls, sending clouds of dust and masonry over the few cars unfortunate enough to be parked nearby.

I became aware of Luc. He wasn't far away, and with him were Cal and Karl.

Stockton's gang sensed the same. 'Lucien's coming. I'm outta here,' one of the women exclaimed.

'I'm with you,' the other said.

They straddled their motorbikes and sped for the entrance the same instant the lights from Luc's BMW came into view. They split up and roared past him, out into the street.

Stockton and I faced each other.

'Count the days, *Princeps*,' he said, as he backed away.

I reached out to grab him, when a sharp pain exploded at the back of my head, and I fell to the ground. Voices all around me … couldn't respond.

'Alec!' Luc's voice cut through the haze.

He helped me sit up. I touched my hand to the back of my

head, and it came away with blood. It'd been a long time since I'd seen it – nineteen eighteen, in fact. The year I'd been shot. Luc saved my life that day by transforming me.

I rubbed my bloodied hand down the side of my jeans while the cut on my scalp healed, leaving neither scar nor lump as a reminder. Being a vampire had some advantages. I rose and looked around. One decapitated vampire lay at my feet, the body twitching, hands grasping for its missing head. Luc stood next to it. Blood dripped from the sword in his hand.

'This meant for you?' he asked, as he brandished the sharpened white-oak stake in his other hand. The female vampire, who'd retrieved it from beneath my car, must have dropped it when she fled. He'd covered the shaft with a handkerchief – even a splinter was fatal to our kind.

'Who else? What hit me?'

'This.' He kicked a dented bike helmet. 'I assume it belonged to him,' he said and plunged the wooden stake into the corpse. Within seconds it had turned to porcelain then disintegrated into fine crystalline dust, leaving behind only his clothes.

'You didn't get Stockton?'

He shook his head. There was no need for him to say that he could have given chase if I hadn't gone down. My fault. If I hadn't allowed myself to become so focused on Stockton, I would have sensed someone behind me. 'There were two women,' I said.

'Saw them. We'll pick them up after we've dealt with this lot,' he inclined his head toward the two remaining figures. They were on their knees, the tip of Cal's sword poised at the throat of one, while Karl held the other from behind, the edge of his blade across the man's windpipe.

They looked at Luc and myself, differing levels of fear distorting their faces. Their expressions and the strong scent that emanated from each gave them away. What they had done this night deserved no less than the death penalty. And they knew it.

Both were juveniles, transformed in the last few decades, perhaps. Their eyes gleamed with eagerness and a certain wildness that the ancient ones no longer possessed. The greater a vampire's age, the deeper their eyes reflected the experience – and often sadness – of untold lifetimes.

'They're not talking,' Cal said as I approached.

'They had plenty to say before,' I replied. The one Cal held had bravely backhanded me as his companions pinned me down – a shaven-head vampire with a "Bite Me" tattoo on the left side of his neck. 'Give me a reason to spare your life,' I said.

He looked up and glared at me. 'You're a doctor. You're not supposed to kill.'

'That applies only to humans. You don't qualify. Try again.'

'You want us to beg when you're going to kill us anyway?' his companion said.

'Not necessarily what's going to happen,' I replied. 'I don't like destroying any of my Brethren, unless I'm given no choice.'

'You tried to kill the princeps,' Luc said. 'You know the penalty for that.'

'Then do it and stop fucking with us,' the tattooed one growled.

'Speak for yourself,' the other one retorted. 'I only got sucked into this because of you.' He looked up at me. 'Stockton said we were only going to rough you up a bit, give you a message. I didn't think he was seriously going to use *that*.' With a nod of his head he indicated the bloodied wooden stake in Luc's hand.

'Too bad for you,' Luc said.

'Look, I don't know what's up between you and him but I didn't want the princeps killed, I swear.' His gaze ranged desperately between Luc and myself.

'He's telling the truth,' I said. I'd heard his voice urge the others not to kill me.

'I am. I swear it.' Sweat beaded on his upper lip.

'Would you be willing to take the Pledge?' I asked.

'You won't kill me?'

'I'm giving you a choice.'

'Hell yeah, I'll take it. Here and now if you want.' His eagerness must have disgusted his companion, for the man spat in his face.

Cal slapped the side of his sword against the man's cheek. 'Oi! Enough with the spitting.'

'Your name's Greg, isn't it?'

'Yeah.'

I'd only met him once, soon after he became one of the Brethren. Every newly created blood drinker had to be presented to the Elders. That way we could keep tabs on the vampire population in the city, and tell them when it was time to move on.

'Well, Greg, looks like you won't be dying today,' Luc said and signalled Karl to lower his sword.

The man sighed in relief, wiped the spittle from his face and sank down onto his haunches. 'Thank you, thank you.'

I looked at the other one. 'I'm offering you the same choice. Otherwise, my friend,' I indicated Cal, 'will be happy to dispatch you right here.'

Cal flashed him a grin and ran his blade from one end of the man's throat to the other without nicking the skin.

The man gritted his teeth as he glanced at the pile of black clothing that used to be his friend. His chest rose and fell rapidly as his eyes darted between the remains of his companion and me.

'I don't have all night,' I said.

'Okay, okay, I'll take the damn Pledge. But tell me, why do you care for humans so much?'

Since he was still on his knees, I crouched down till we were eye to eye. 'Without humanity we wouldn't exist. If I allowed every vampire in this city to kill in order to feed, within one generation – thirty-five years to be exact – there would be no humans left. I'm surprised your *superior intellect* hasn't worked that out.'

He had no answer.

I rose and nodded to Luc who told Cal and Karl to take them back to the house. 'Hold them in the cages in the cellar until midnight when they can take the Pledge with the others.'

As far as I was aware, the only two cages capable of holding a vampire had been destroyed in the last rebellion. They had been made of titanium.

Cal rendered the men unconscious by snapping their necks, and then Karl helped him haul their limp bodies into the boot of Luc's car. It was safer to transport them this way in case they changed their minds. They'd be out for at least fifteen to twenty minutes.

'I assume it's the same two cages Maris and Russell used?' I asked Luc as Cal slammed the boot closed.

'The same,' he replied. 'Marcus salvaged them. Said they were too good; might come in handy. He was right.'

'What about the stake on the inside?' A long wooden spike had been attached to one of the titanium bars from the inside, like some form of medieval torture device. Anyone held captive within could have been impaled easily.

'Removed it.'

'Good.' I looked around and realised I had a slight problem. There were three shiny, black motorbikes blocking the entrance to two of my neighbours' parking spots. They had to be removed. 'Help me with these will you?'

Together, Luc and I moved the bikes to a far, unused section of the car park then covered them with a tarpaulin I kept in the boot of my car.

'Karl was right. Timur and Rasputin are behind this rebellion,' I said as I strode over to collect the head and clothes of the dead vampire. 'And they know about Laura's blood. I'd say it's common knowledge now.'

He sighed and rubbed his hands over his face. 'Merde!'

'It makes the Pledging even more imperative.'

'Especially as Stockton got away. He'll warn those two rats, Timur and Rasputin.' He picked up the stake again, located the dead vampire's head and plunged the wood into the soft flesh. The skin immediately reacted with the cellulose and began to crystallise before disintegrating into dust. He dispersed it with his foot over the ground.

The car park now appeared back to normal. No one would have guessed a battle had taken place here. Satisfied, we strolled back to the car. Cal and Karl were waiting.

Karl lit up another cigarette. 'That partially makes up for my ruined evening.'

Cal chuckled and slapped him on the back. 'Tell me about this party you're going to. Just masks, huh? I like the sound of it.' They climbed into the backseat.

'Luc, I'm expecting trouble at the Pledging tonight,' I said, as we drove out. 'If the prefects know about Laura's bloodline – as I believe they do – we could face a revolt.' I swivelled and looked at him. 'What happened to me, just then, was the prelude.'

He gazed straight ahead, seemingly deep in thought. 'Perhaps ... but no one knows about your –' He stopped, glanced at me, then with a jerk of his head indicated Karl in the backseat. Luc was about to mention my bloodline.

Karl didn't know, and although I believed he could be trusted, it was too great a gamble. All the Brethren knew that Antonius, Luc and I were the only ones capable of siring children. It ensured there were Dantonville descendants for as long as the curse was in effect. I was determined Laura and I would not be a repeat of Luc and Judith, who were forced to place their child in hiding. If the Brethren suspected we were lovers, and that she was expecting our child, then so be it. As far as they knew, my blood was Antonine, and if Laura's blood was poisonous – for being half-vampire – then our child's would be the same. And by the time they realise the child was human, hopefully, it would be too late.

As soon as we arrived back at the house, I left the others, and following the sound of Laura's voice, raced up to the ballroom, eager to hold her in my arms. We had less than an hour and a half till the Pledging ceremony – enough time to imprint my scent on her. Never before had I been more determined to keep what was mine.

CHAPTER 9 – KARELIA

LAURA

The mirrored doors were wide open, revealing polished crystal chandeliers, their delicate drops catching the light and bouncing it off the mirrored walls. Magical. Even the wooden floors seemed gleamed with new vigour. I could see the intricate parquetry arrangement, which before had been hidden beneath nearly a century of dust and grime. Metal-framed chairs with plush, red velvet backs and seats had been set up in rows of ten.

'Beautiful, isn't it?' Judy exclaimed. 'The professional cleaners Luc hired scrubbed, carted rubbish away and helped set up the chairs. They've done a great job.'

'I'll say!'

I glanced around for the platform where Jean-Philippe used to have his makeshift studio. It was gone. All evidence of his presence erased – the drawings and sketches, the easel, the wall of photographs. Did Luc really have them all burned?

In its place stood a richly decorated dais, draped with purple velvet held in place with gold-coloured ribbons. Seven high-backed chairs, resembling thrones, were positioned in the centre.

Their deep-purple backs and seats matched the drapery.

I didn't need to guess that the Elders, including Luc, Alec and myself would greet the prefects there.

From behind one of the gathered drapes, a small, pale hand appeared and tied a gold ribbon around it. 'That should do it,' an unknown voice announced. A diminutive creature with short silver-blonde hair and sparkling lavender eyes emerged from her hiding place and stood, side-on, facing her handiwork, hands on hips, her eyes laughing.

She looked at me, and her pixie face lit up with enthusiasm. Pale brows arched, her face had an open, transparent look.

She looked stunning, in a Tinkerbell kind of way. I angled my head to see if she were hiding any gossamer wings, yet her eyes were a dead giveaway. This creature was, indeed, a vampire.

'Laura, dear,' my mother's voice roused me. 'I'd like you to meet Karelia.'

The pixie came toward me with hand outstretched. 'Just Kari,' she said. As she came close, I realised she wasn't much smaller than me – no more than an inch or two, but her slim, waif–like physique made her appear tiny, fae.

'Hi, I'm Laura.' I returned the warm handshake. There was something about Kari that touched me in the nicest way. I instinctively knew she could be trusted, and we would be friends.

'Kari and I have known each other a long time,' Judy said. 'She was at the Ritual, but you were too preoccupied to notice everyone there, dear.'

Understatement! Having to stand before several hundred vampires, recite some ancient Latin liturgy, then have Alec suck blood from my neck in front of them all was certainly reason enough to have overlooked a vampire or two.

'Oops, sorry.' I looked at her apologetically.

'Heck, if I had to undergo something like that, I probably would have freaked out. You were great.'

'Thanks.' I grinned.

'Judy tells me you need to choose something to wear for tonight's big do.'

'Um, yeah. I suppose. Honestly, I haven't given it a thought. Too many things have been happening.'

Judy sighed and ran her hand across her brow.

'You're tired, Mother. Come and sit down.' The moment I said it, I darted a glance at Kari. Damn! I'd slipped up and called Judy, "mother."

Kari didn't look surprised at all.

'It's all right, dear. Kari knows. I told her everything, and it's such a relief.' Judy eased herself into one of the red chairs. Kari and I pulled one each from the nearest row and sat down facing her. She grasped my hand. 'There's no point in hiding it any more, and I'm glad,' she said fiercely. 'You're my child, Laura, and I want everyone to know.'

'So do I.' I enclosed her hand in mine.

'Well, the Pledging's only an hour and a bit away,' Kari exclaimed. 'And until then, you've got yourself an unofficial bodyguard. If any rogue tries to come anywhere near you ....' Her eyes dangerously lightened, and the tips of her incisors slid down to rest on her lower lip. The pixie took on the appearance of an avenging angel – a vampiric avenging angel.

This time I wasn't going to argue. Having experienced first hand the cruelty and viciousness of creatures such as Maris, Russell, Douglas and even Jean-Philippe, I was more than happy to have someone like Karelia by my side.

'Bless you, Kari!' Judy rose from her seat and embraced her.

Just as quickly, the smiling pixie persona returned. 'Besides, I'm slightly older than one of our recently deceased Elders, so I'm stronger.'

She was referring to Maris. Judy laughed.

Hmm, how old was Kari? Terens said that Maris had been transformed by Sam but not when, although she was out of her servitude. That meant she was older than Alec, and I knew how old he was.

'Laura?' Judy was looking at me. 'You're far away, dear.'

I blinked and shook my head. 'No, only thinking.'

'She's wondering how old I am.' Kari winked at Judy and gave her a nudge.

I blushed. 'Are you a mind reader?'

'Your face says it all.' She laughed again, a light pixie tinkle. 'I was twenty-years-old in seventeen seventy-six. Work it out.'

It didn't take me long. I often gave my Sixth Graders these types of mental maths challenges. 'Two hundred and fifty-six?'

'And a half.'

'So, the older a vampire, the greater their strength.' I was learning more and more each day.

'That's it.'

'It's the major reason the Brethren fear our men,' Judy said.

Our men. Alec, Luc and Marcus – one my lover, the other my father, and the last, my grandfather, plus their men. My family. For the first time, I was comfortable with the knowledge, and it felt right.

Kari nodded. 'They could each take on a half dozen and wipe the floor with them. If Princi didn't have you though, there's no way he could fight off anyone older than himself.'

'Princi?'

'My name for him. Don't expect me to call him princeps! Too stuffy. Blah.'

She made such a face I couldn't help but smile.

'I'd rather Luc didn't "wipe the floor" with anyone.' Judy looked pointedly at her. 'Just get them to take the Pledge so we can all breathe easier.'

'Amen to that,' Kari said.

'And after, we're going to pick out the biggest tree I can find, and you're both going to help me decorate it. It'll be the Christmas I've waited such a long time for – with you, Laura, and Luc and Alec, and you, Kari. My family.' Tears glistened in her eyes as she leaned forward and grasped Kari's hand as well. 'I've been so preoccupied with everything else, I almost forgot about Christmas. I only put the wreath on the door just before you got back this evening. I intend decorating the whole house. This year will be special.'

Kari laughed and clapped her hands. 'My turn doing the mistletoe!'

'My first Christmas with my real parents,' I said. Images of past Christmas celebrations with my family scrolled through my mind. Judy was absent from each one. After her fiftieth – her coming-of-age – she had stopped coming.

'You always came to my birthday bashes. Why not Christmas?'

She sighed deeply. 'Because Luc couldn't be there. It was hard enough being at your birthday as your aunt, but he wouldn't have been able to sustain it. Look how he and John snarled at each other at the Ritual. Can you imagine what it would have been like in front of friends and family?' She shuddered. 'Christmas was a small sacrifice to make.'

I squeezed her hand. 'Not this year.'

'Okay, that's it. I'm getting teary and that hasn't happened in nearly a century,' Kari said. She stood and plucked Judy from her seat with one hand and me with the other. 'Come on, up we get. Time to dress. Let's see what you've got for tonight.'

As we strolled to the doors, Alec appeared.

'Hi, Princi sweetie.' Kari gave him a wave.

I practically ran into his open arms. He crushed me to him and his kisses seared my waiting mouth.

I heard an 'ahem,' behind me.

Alec raised his eyes heavenward, but a definite smile tugged at the corners of his mouth. 'Hello, Karelia.'

'Ooh, that sounds so formal.' She came and stood next to us. 'You need loosening up.'

I bit my lip to stop the laugh threatening to bubble up as Alec opened his mouth then closed it again. He shook his head. 'No, not even going to reply to that one.'

'Too late. You already have.' She laughed, and her eyes lit up with mischief.

'Kari, anyone ever tell you you're a pest,' Alec said.

'All the time.'

'Not surprised. But right now, Laura and I need to be alone. Excuse us.' He took my hand and led me out of the ballroom, down the stairs to his room.

CHAPTER 10 - INTERLUDE

LAURA

In Alec's room, a single tall, metal lamp gave off a weak light. There were no windows to allow in deadly sunrays, so presumably it predated the time when he became princeps. The four-poster, wrought iron bed and I were well acquainted, since we'd made love in it several times.

Alec wrapped his arm around my waist and held me close. With his other hand, he tucked my hair behind my ear. 'We have a little over an hour before the Prefects start arriving.'

'Let's not waste it.' Every minute with him was precious. Three nights ago, Jean-Philippe nearly murdered us both and, even though he was now dead, the danger was not entirely over – tonight's incident a stark reminder.

He lowered his head and kissed me with a fervency that left me breathless. I wrapped my arms around his neck and kissed him back. Our tongues meshed in a delicious tangle of desire and passion.

'What happened?' I asked between kisses.

'We had a disagreement ....'

I knew what he meant by that. 'You had a fight.'

'No avoiding it. Two of them are caged down in the cellar. Cal and Karl are keeping an eye on them till the Pledging.'

'How many were there?'

'Five – three men, two women.'

My stomach dropped. 'You could have been killed!'

'But I wasn't.'

'What if Luc hadn't arrived—'

'Shhh', he sealed his lips over mine and, as always, I melted in his arms. A while later, he murmured against my mouth, 'I probably could've handled it alone. After the Pledging tonight there should be no more *incidents*.' His lips grazed my throat.

'Promise?'

'Cross my heart.' He drew the figure of a cross over his heart. 'Luc told you about the powers of the rings. If anyone tries anything, they're ash.'

I nodded. After a previous rebellion, centuries ago, my father forced the surviving Brethren to swear an oath on the serpent rings. Those who defied it were killed when the rings flashed fire and destroyed them.

I didn't want to think about it, let alone witness something like that.

Alec could probably see the anxiety in my eyes, for he smoothed the hair from my face and said, 'The Pledge worked in the past. No reason why it shouldn't do so again.' His confidence was comforting and I released the breath I'd been holding. 'Besides,' he said, 'Pledge or no Pledge, I'll kill anyone who dares try and harm you.' A deadly edge to his voice both frightened and excited me. He lowered his head, and took complete possession of my mouth with such passion it ignited a painful throbbing in my core that only he could relieve.

His hands slid down to my waist, untied my sash. Gently he eased my robe off my shoulders. It dropped to the floor, where my camisole soon joined it. He touched the crimson vial Luc gave me, which was nestled between my breasts. It contained three drops of Marcus's, Antonia's and Luc's blood, and it would render the drinker immortal. 'Luc explained?'

I nodded.

'Would you take it?'

'Yes.' I breathed.

I couldn't tear my gaze away from his eyes. They were filled with such love, such intensity of longing I almost wished the curse wouldn't be lifted so there'd be no chance of my blood becoming normal. Yet, our children, the future....

His mouth claimed mine once again, his tongue probing deeply till I became lost to the sensations he alone aroused in me.

Slowly, he raised his head, released me and pulled his T-shirt off and dropped it on the floor. My breath hitched. No matter how many times I saw his naked torso, I was awed by his lithe, muscular body – the taut, rippling abs, the clearly defined and powerful pectorals and the strength of his arms. There wasn't an inch that wasn't hard muscle. And, he smelled divine – a strong woody scent that went straight to my head. I ran my hands along his chest, and my fingers grazed the gold crucifix he wore around his neck, the one he showed me the night we met. And right next to it, on the same gold chain, hung a small key – a similar one hung around my father's neck.

'The bloodvault key.' I looked up at him.

'Good, Luc told you. Things are moving fast.'

'Were they on motor bikes?' He would know I was referring to the vision I had earlier this evening.

'Not any more.' He cracked a smile, cupped my bottom and drew me closer. I could feel his need through the thin fabric of my pyjama shorts. He kissed me again, hooked his fingers into the top of my shorts and slowly drew them down. They dropped to my feet. I stepped out of them, and Alec picked me up and laid me in the middle of the bed.

As he straightened, I watched him unbutton his jeans. Soon, he was gloriously naked. The desire in his eyes was unmistakable, and I was sure he could hear the excited pounding of my heart as he climbed onto the bed and came toward me, parted my legs and nestled himself between them.

For a few moments we simply gazed at each other, our breathing the only sound in the room. I stroked his raven silk hair while he caressed my breast, gently rolling my nipple between his thumb and forefinger, sending pulsating waves of heat through me. Then his hand slid down the length of my body, through my feminine curls, to circle, pinch and rub the most intimate part of me. My body quivered under the sweet, sensual torture. He pressed one finger into me, then two, stretching me, preparing me for his entry as his thumb continued it's rhythmic torment.

My body arched into his touch, wanting more.

'Perfect,' he growled.

'Please, Alec!' My whole body ached for release while I rode his fingers, and my head thrashed from side to side. He grabbed the back of my head and held me still as his mouth plundered mine.

His talented fingers increased the pace until my body trembled with my climax, and as I lay panting, he withdrew them, and I whimpered. All this time, his lips hadn't left mine, and as his tongue continued to probe my mouth, he spread my thighs further and drove deeply into me.

I gasped, but there was no time for our usual teasing and playful banter. The Pledging ceremony was less than an hour away.

My body responded to his powerful thrusts, and it wasn't long until the familiar tingle of another climax began to course through me. Alec angled his hips and hit my hidden, tender spot. I writhed beneath him as he made my body sing.

'You're intoxicating, Laura,' he rasped, catching my wrists and drawing them above my head as he plunged into me, filling me completely.

I screamed, as he pushed my body into nirvana.

He bit into my neck and began to feed, taking deep draughts. His body shuddered, and a deep groan escaped his lips as his own release came. I barely felt his fangs withdraw, or the lick of his tongue and gentle kiss on the open wound. He collapsed on top of me before rolling to the side and wrapping me in his arms.

We lay like that for a few moments, breathing heavily, while my body slowly calmed.

'That's good, right?' I managed to say after a while. 'My being intoxicating?'

His chest rumbled beneath my cheek as he chuckled. 'Very good.' He brought my hand to his lips and kissed my fingertips. 'Darling, what if I ask Marcus to join us tonight?'

His question took me by surprise. Although he'd proposed three days ago, we hadn't had a chance to discuss it. I raised myself slightly and looked at him. 'You mean, marry us?'

'Yes.'

'Oh.' I sighed.

Alec frowned and ran a hand through his hair. 'But, I thought —'

'Alec, I do want to marry you, it's just that … a vampire ceremony isn't exactly what I had in mind.'

I thought of Jenny who would love to be bridesmaid. Like any other woman, I'd pictured myself walking down the aisle in a beautiful white gown – straight from the pages of *Bride* magazine – my handsome groom waiting at the altar, church bells ringing, flower girls sprinkling petals, bridesmaids, designer cake and everything that goes with a traditional wedding. At Alec's words, that lovely image dissolved and morphed into vampires dressed in black, dark, unsmiling, standing there instead of my friends, all of them looking at me as if I were the cake. I saw myself as the centre of an Addams-Family-style wedding.

He let out a breath and smiled. 'Darling, it'd be useful to have all the powerful Brethren witness you formally sealed to me in more than just a blood bond. They know the stipulations of the curse, and if they believe you're joined to me, there's little chance you'll meet someone of the witch's bloodline and bear the Child of Promise.' He smoothed the hair from my shoulder and kissed my bare skin.

'But they've got no idea whose daughter I am. Nor do they know about you, for that matter.'

He was quiet a moment. 'It's eventually going to come out – you being Luc's little girl. You know we won't be able to hide it for much longer. Someone's bound to see the resemblance between you and him, and I doubt he'll be able to blame it being an ancestral throwback.' He caressed my fingertips with his lips. 'I don't want any Brethren to know who I am, though. They need to go on believing everything's normal till our child is born, and even after – till it's too late and they're under the Pledge.'

I suppose it made sense. I couldn't fault his practical thinking. It wasn't only the Principate at stake, but our lives and even the fate of humanity – my friends, work colleagues, family. And if being married to him during the Pledging ceremony reinforced our safety – and those I loved – I was ready to sacrifice my dream wedding.

'Okay.' I nodded. 'Let Marcus do it.'

'When this is over, I promise you'll get the wedding you've always wanted. I wouldn't deprive you of that.' He gave me a dazzling smile that rendered me speechless.

I stared at him, until my brain kicked back into gear. My foster parents couldn't attend a vampire ceremony and apart from Judy and Luc and Alec's best friends, I didn't want any vampire guests – they might regard John, Eilene, and my best friend Jenny as the menu. So, a formal declaration during the Pledge solved that problem.

'A separate ceremony just for my friends and family?'

'Yes, whoever you want.'

I snuggled back into his embrace. 'You think Luc'd agree to having it in his garden? It's so lovely there, especially at sunset.'

'He'd be disappointed if we didn't. It'd be the perfect place for the wedding and reception.'

The electric clock on the bedside table caught my eye – there were only thirty minutes until midnight and I hadn't picked out a dress. I put aside wedding plans for the moment.

'I know it's time to go,' he said, as if he'd read my mind. 'Otherwise I'd make love to you all over again.'

The twinkle in his half-lidded eyes sent a tingle through me despite the fact we'd spent the last hour entwined in each other's arms. 'There's always tomorrow.' I beamed up at him.

Alec chuckled and smacked me lightly on the bottom. 'That's a promise,' he said and moved off the bed. 'I'll take you back to your room.'

'I do know the way.'

'Laura, until this Pledging takes place I'm keeping you in my sight,' he said, stepping into his jeans.

I was about to point out that I should be safe in my own father's house, but my mind replayed the incident with Jean-Philippe – it had taken place in the ballroom, where in less than thirty minutes the Pledge would take place. Goose pimples rose on my skin that had nothing to do with the house air-conditioning. I forced the memory away as I retrieved my clothes from the floor and slipped them on.

Holding hands, we exited Alec's room. The carpet seemed to magnify, rather than muffle, the pad of our bare feet. An oppressive silence filled the air, and I gripped his hand tighter.

'It'll be over soon, darling,' he said.

The weight of expectation settled on me. I glanced at the portraits of my Ingenii ancestors on the walls. Their eyes spoke of centuries of waiting … for me. I placed my hand low on my belly. *C'mon little swimmers, do your job.* My groin throbbed in response, more to do with the pleasant memory of Alec's love making than feeling his sperm making their way to my uterus.

'About time.' Kari's voice nudged me from my thoughts. 'I was beginning to think you two were never coming out.' She was sitting on the top step of the marble staircase, legs crossed, hands clasped over her knee. A broad, knowing smile lit her pixie face. 'Reckon the whole house got an ear full.'

I nearly died. She – and any vampire within hearing distance – must have heard every moan, every whimper. At one point I even screamed. Heat burned my cheeks.

'Can I add discretion to your other qualities?' Alec said dryly as we walked past her. 'Laura,' he pulled me into his arms when we reached my door, 'there's an unwritten rule among the Brethren that when any of us is being intimate, we tune our hearing elsewhere. Kari knows that. She just likes to….'

'Tease?' I finished for him.

'The word I was searching for wasn't quite that polite.'

We both laughed, and I snuggled my face into the warm strength of his chest. Alec lifted my chin and pressed his lips to mine, his tongue sliding into my mouth. I held back a moan.

Kari's voice intruded, 'Okay, enough kissy, kissy. Shoo, Princi. Laura needs to dress.'

Alec ignored her and finished the kiss. 'See you in twenty-five minutes.' He let me go and strode back the way we came.

Kari opened the door and pushed me through it.

CHAPTER 11 – PRELUDE

LAURA
My walk-in closet was full of all the clothes, shoes and accessories any girl could possibly want, hand-picked by my parents in anticipation of my homecoming. Among them were several formal gowns. Kari 'oohed' at the sight of them.

We selected three – a shimmering deep royal-purple strapless creation with a sweetheart neckline and ruched bodice, into which were sewn an assortment of crystal beads. A long, flowing A-line skirt flared out gently from below the bust.

The next was a one-shoulder, ivory, pleated Grecian-style gown with a belted waist featuring sparkling crystals and beads. Gorgeous.

There was also a stunning black number; a tight-fitting, strapless mermaid gown, which shimmered with sewn-in metallic sequins and ended in a flared, tulle tail.

It too, was lovely, but reminded me too much of Morticia Addams.

'I'm not wearing black,' I said. I liked the ivory dress. Kari preferred the lilac.

She tapped her finger against her lips, brows creased. 'Try them on.'

I slipped on the ivory dress first, enjoying the soft silkiness of the fabric as it flowed over my body. Instead of hiding it, I let the ruby vial Luc had given me dangle down over the tight bodice. It was too big – and uncomfortable – to hide beneath, and as far as I knew, it didn't have to be. To a casual observer, it was an unusual piece of antique jewellery. Who could possibly guess it's true purpose? I admired the way the precious substance within seemed to glow with a life of its own; it's vivid scarlet contrasting dramatically with the stunning simplicity of the creamy Grecian gown.

'Nice pendant,' Kari said. 'Looks amazing on that dress. Where'd you get it?'

'Um, present ... from my father.' There was no way I could tell her Luc was my father, nor what was in the vial.

She nodded in appreciation. 'If you want to wear it, you're best off leaving that purple one,' she indicated the other gown with a flick of her head, 'for another occasion.'

'I prefer the ivory colour anyway.' I did a little twirl in front of the mirror, watching the way the skirt billowed out from my legs and wondered what Alec would be wearing. He'd worn a tux for the Ritual.

'What about your hair?' Kari asked.

I hadn't given it a thought. Most of the time I tied my hair up in a ponytail – easy, no hassle and perfect for work.

'Leave it down, or,' she gesticulated with her hands, 'piled up with a long strand hanging down over one shoulder. I used to wear mine like that when I was human.'

I turned from the mirror and stared at her. It was said so nonchalantly, so ... flippantly almost, as if it was normal to drop a statement like that into a conversation. Maybe it was, in their circles, and I was now part of that. 'Did you have a choice, Kari? About becoming a vampire?'

'Of course. Jake wouldn't have done it otherwise.'

'Jake? Jake changed you?' He was one of my invisible bodyguards, part of a group of Roman soldiers under my grandfather, Marcus Antonius Pulcher's command. And, like him and the rest of the men, Jake had been transformed into vampire form by a witch's curse nearly eighteen-hundred years ago. I met him during the Ritual, yet he had known me a long time. He said he used to give me 'piggy-back rides' when I was a baby.

'Sure did,' Kari answered.

'Why?'

She laughed. 'He saved my life, Laura. I was dying. But I was lucid enough to know the choice he was giving me.'

'You were twenty, weren't you?'

'Uh huh.'

I took a breath. 'Would you tell me about it?'

'Sit down. I'll give you the quick version while doing your hair. But first,' she glanced around, 'where's your bathroom? I need a comb and hairpins.'

I pointed to the door on the other side of the room. Kari made her way there, and I pulled my mobile out of my bag. Where was I going to put it? The dress was a tight fit. *There must be something in the closet I could use.* Sure enough, nestled between an assortment of bags on one of the lower shelves, was a pearl, mesh Oroton pouch with a long shoulder strap. It was perfect. I popped my phone in, slung it over my head and let it dangle unobtrusively at my hip. Just as I sat on my dressing table seat, Kari returned, carrying a small basketful of hair accessories – pins, combs, several butterfly clips and ribbons.

'Alrighty then.' She took sections of my hair and pinned them in place. 'My parents moved from Finland to France before I was born. They named me after their homeland.'

'Why did they leave?' I watched her in the mirror. Her shoulders rose in a slight shrug.

'Work. My father was a builder. There was too much fighting in our land for that, so he and my mother moved first to Sweden, then to France. That's where he met Lord Luc. He was making improvements to his chateau in the Rhone valley. He hired Papa, and that's where I was born.'

'On Luc's estate,' I said, oddly surprised by how readily I now accepted the longevity of Brethren; thinking it nothing when discussing someone renovating their chateau several-hundred years before.

She nodded. 'The people in the village knew what he was, but because he was such a good master, they … kind of … overlooked it. Anyways, I grew up there and was engaged to be married when a fever swept through our region. Many people died. Jake tried to save as many as he could, and he did, but still....'

'Jake? Why not the local doctor?'

'He died, and besides, Jake's a physician – like Princi,' she said as she twirled and tucked several locks of my hair in place.

I'm sure my eyes widened at learning that Jake had a medical background. But then what did I know? I was only drawn into this other world a week ago, and the men hadn't been the topic of our conversation. I made a mental note to ask either Alec or Judy more about them. Who else could boast their bodyguards had once been real Roman soldiers?

Kari stood back, and with hands on her hips examined her handiwork. She nodded, moved to my other side and began to style another section of my hair. I said nothing, so as not to interrupt her flow. Her story had me fascinated.

'Mama died first while I nursed her, then Papa caught it, then me.' She grew silent, which, from my limited acquaintance with her, was probably unusual. Kari had the same sad and distant expression I'd seen on Luc whenever he spoke of the past.

'If it's painful you don't need to tell me anymore.'

She perked up and smiled. 'Nah! I don't mind. It's so long ago. Anyways, Jake couldn't save Papa—'

'He didn't ... you know, change him?'

'Papa didn't want to.'

'Why did you, Kari?' I softened my voice, hoping she wouldn't take offence at my asking.

'I didn't want to die.'

'Even if it meant living as a blood drinker?'

She flashed me a smile. 'Hey, look at the bright side – I'm forever young, and I'll never need cosmetic surgery. What's not to like?'

'I guess if you put it that way.' Yet, something in Kari's tone suggested another reason for her making such a bargain. Perhaps it was to stay with her fiancé; she said she had been engaged. Would he want to marry a vampire? 'Kari, did you marry your fiancé?'

'No.' Her expression sobered. 'He believed I died. Jake brought me into the chateau and became my mentor; taught me how to survive in my new life.'

'You two must be very close.'

'Yeah.' She lowered her eyes. The smile appeared again, less exuberant than before.

'You still live there – in the chateau?'

She shook her head. 'Got a place of my own. When I completed my juvenile stage, Jake bought me my own house and transferred several of his properties into my name. Rent from these keeps me happy. And if I ever need extra cash,' she gave me a cheeky smile, 'I go out and mesmerise some hunky billionaire into donating a few measly million into the Karelia Anakeinen fund.'

My jaw dropped. 'Jake taught you that?'

'Hell no! He'd have kittens if he knew. He thinks I manage my money well.' She moved behind me and gathered my hair in her hands. 'Well, he did provide me with a new set of skills. They'd go to waste otherwise.'

Rather than be shocked, I burst out laughing, and Karelia joined in.

'Oh, they're here,' she said, and her eyes brightened.

'The prefects?'

'No, Jake.' In a burst of speed, she finished braiding the upper part of my hair and draped a long, loose curl over my right shoulder. She raced out the door before I had a chance to slip on the matching shoes.

'Kari!' My human speed was nothing compared to hers. By the time I got to the top of the stairs, she was already at the bottom with a group of men. As I joined her, five faces turned to look at me – Marcus Antonius, Jake and Terens, and two men I didn't recognise. One stood an inch or so taller than the rest, with deep, penetrating eyes that seemed to bore into my soul. The man next to him, with his dark, curly hair and moustache, would have been handsome but for his sneer.

'Ah, our little Ingenii,' the first man drawled. 'How I was looking forward to meeting you.' If a voice could drip evil, his did. Hypnotic eyes. Strange warmth crept over me.

'Lower your eyes, snake,' Marcus Antonius snarled. I was vaguely aware of him pushing the man onto his knees.

I blinked and gripped the marble bannister as Kari stepped in front of me, blocking him from my view. 'Go back upstairs, Laura,' she whispered over her shoulder.

'Control your pet, Timur,' Alec said from behind me as he came down the stairs. His voice held a lethal tone.

Kari glanced up at him, smiled then stepped aside and went to stand next to Jake. He whispered something to her I couldn't catch; his mouth was a hard line, jaw clenched.

Alec joined me and took my hand. He was formally dressed in a lead-coloured suit with black lapels and matching shirt, and a lavender tie that set off the brilliance of his eyes. The cut of the jacket, in particular, emphasised the width of his shoulders and nearly took my breath away. It was a stunning contrast to my ivory dress and for a moment I wondered if he'd listened in on my conversation with Kari.

The moustached man spoke again. 'Why should I do that? He amuses me.'

Marcus Antonius stepped forward and backhanded him with enough force to snap his head to the side. Blood sprang from his lower lip. 'Is that how you answer your lord princeps? On your knees,' he growled.

Terens pushed him down, but Timur kept his head up and glared at Alec. 'I'll never bow to a slave!'

Kari sucked in a breath. I tensed, but Alec didn't even flinch. I'd only learnt of his servitude to my father a few days ago. It was customary among the Brethren for a newly created vampire to be trained by their sires or dammes for a century – a type of legal slavery – and Alec had only five years left before gaining his freedom. But that had been cancelled by my father, Luc, and recognised by the Elders. Alec was free – no longer at the "beck and call" of his master.

Perhaps Timur hadn't heard.

'It appears you need reminding, Count, that Lord Alec was sired by my son,' Marcus said, 'a prince whose Roman blood is far nobler than yours. By slighting him, you insult Lord Lucien and myself.'

Timur paled.

'You'll be taken before the Elders to face punishment. Escort our Hungarian prefect to the ballroom,' Alec said.

'Shall we, Count?' Terens, who had been standing behind the man, pointed the way forward with his sword.

As he was led toward the staircase, where Alec and I stood,

Timur looked at me in a way that made my skin crawl, but I dared not show it. Instead, I lifted my chin and gazed back at him. I could do bravado, too.

As he passed us, Timur closed his eyes, threw his head back and inhaled deeply. When he opened them again, he stared back at me, and I knew he could smell Alec's scent on me. His brow creased and I could see confusion in his eyes.

I gripped Alec's hand tighter.

'Don't keep the Elders waiting,' Alec reminded him.

Terens prodded Timur in the back with the sword and urged him up the imposing marble steps.

'As for you,' Alec briefly turned his attention to the other kneeling man before addressing Jake. 'Take him to the cellar and place him in the cage with the others.'

'My pleasure.' Jake tapped him on the shoulder with his sword. 'Get up and keep your eyes down.'

The man rose, his gaze locked on the ground, the knuckles of his clenched fists white as they hung by his side. It seemed the very air around him crackled with suppressed rage. I wondered if the others felt it. As Jake led him away – Kari by his side – I breathed a sigh of relief and hoped I would never have to meet the man with the penetrating eyes any time soon.

Alec's gaze followed him until they were all out of sight.

'Who are they?' I asked.

'Count Timur Széchenyi and Grigory Rasputin,' Marcus Antonius answered in his deep baritone voice. He'd remained standing in the hallway, sword sheathed.

'*The* Rasputin? The mad monk who got the Russian royal family killed?'

'The same.'

'No wonder they couldn't kill him.' From what I remembered of my high school history, he was supposedly poisoned, shot, bludgeoned and his body thrown into a frozen river by Russian aristocrats trying to protect the Czar's family. Obviously, they were unsuccessful.

Marcus Antonius's expression softened, and he came toward me. His gaze briefly lit on the ruby-crystal vial hanging down the front of my dress. 'Antonia's pendant. I see Luc told you,' he said quietly.

'Yes… Grandfather.' I wanted to know how it would feel to address him that way. He looked no older than my father.

'Long time since anyone has called me that. I like it.' He smiled. 'Keep the vial safe, child, and hidden. There's no point tempting fate, although,' he looked me up and down, 'I can see it's a challenge in that dress.'

The heat of a blush crept into my cheeks. 'I'll fix that. Don't worry.'

He turned to Alec. 'Have you told Laura our contingency plans?'

'Not yet.'

'I'll leave you to it, but don't be long. Everyone's gathered.' He cupped my face and said, 'You're in safe hands, child,' and planted a light kiss on my forehead. With that he was gone, but his words left a chill. *Contingency plans?*

Alec took my hands in his. 'Laura, in case things turn ugly tonight, we've arranged to leave through the servants' passage – the one Luc and I came through the other night—and head down to the cellar, to the bloodvault.' He must have seen the panicked look on my face, for he added. 'Darling, I'm sure things'll be fine, but just in case….' The muscle in his jaw ticked, and his gaze darted to the top of the stairs – in the direction of the ballroom.

I closed my eyes and took a deep breath. My old life – boring and predictable as it had been – seemed like a halcyon era, and for a moment I longed to turn back time and go back to being simply, Laura Anne Dantonville, primary school teacher, with no special blood in her veins. No special anything.

But then, I wouldn't have known Alec, and the thought left an empty hole deep inside me. *No, as long as he's beside me, I can face anything.*

I took another deep breath, and looked into his dark, lavender eyes. 'Let's get this over with.'

His gaze lingered on me and his fingers gently brushed my cheek. 'Did I say how stunningly beautiful you look?'

His compliment had an instant calming effect, and when he bent his head and grazed his lips over mine, I surrendered to the moment. He hoisted me into his arms, and a split second later we were outside the sliding, mirrored doors leading to the ballroom. Sprinting up two flights of stairs while kissing me was quite an achievement.

Alec lowered me to my feet. 'Ready?'

'Wait!' I remembered what Marcus had said and tucked the ruby vial into the bodice of my gown. It was a snug fit, but comfortable, and rather than the anticipated cold, it felt warm nestled between my breasts.

I felt Alec's gaze on me, and when I looked up, his eyes had darkened. We stared at each other. When the mirrored doors slid open, several hundred pale, lavender-eyed faces turned toward us.

I swallowed the tight knot in my throat.

Alec offered me his arm. We stepped in, and with a muted thud, the doors slid closed behind us.

CHAPTER 12 – ROUND ONE TO THE REBELS

LAURA

With my hand firmly on Alec's arm, I walked through the divided rows and past the standing Brethren. Never was I more aware of their otherworldliness – their absolute stillness, typical of predators, and their burning gaze, which followed us the length of the ballroom to the dais and the waiting Elders, Luc and Marcus among them.

Wasn't I one of them? Or, at least half of me? How much of those characteristics did I display? No one had ever mentioned it. I would ask Jenny next time I saw her.

The tension in the room was palpable, almost as if we'd interrupted a heated discussion. Perhaps we had. Whispers grew into murmurs. By the time we reached the makeshift stage, the two other Elders – Kwome and Zhao, whom I had first met at the Ritual – were holding up their hands for silence.

They were ignored, and the murmurs turned to vocalised questions.

'Is it true, lady, that your blood is poisonous?' someone said when Alec and I reached the dais.

My hand flew to my chest in an effort to stop the thunderous beating of my heart. *They know; they know.*

Be calm, darling. Alec's voice whispered in my mind. He squeezed my fingers when we turned to face them. 'You're out of order, Prefect O'Toole.' *Prefect from Hibernia – Ireland*, he said in my mind.

'It's an honest question, my lord Princeps. One which Lord Lucien refuses to answer,' he replied in a soft Irish accent.

This was greeted with nods and vocal assents. I gripped Alec's arm, unsure whether to answer. Luc spoke. 'All questions will be answered in due time.' His voice had a sharp edge, which silenced some who were about to speak. Their open mouths instantly shut.

Not Prefect O'Toole. 'You're not denying it then?'

Luc growled.

Timur's moustached upper lip curled into a smug smile as he stared at me from the front row. Alec must have noticed, for the arm I clutched tensed, and his fingers formed into a fist.

Oh, this is not starting well.

'Is it true, Lord Princeps?' someone else asked.

'We have a right to know,' yet another stated. 'Since none of the previous Ingenii suffered such an affliction.'

Affliction? Not as far as I was concerned. It saved my life. I was about to say so when a gentle squeeze on my arm stopped me. I glanced up to see Alec give me a barely perceptible shake of his head.

I bit my tongue, took a deep breath and scanned the pale faces before me, especially Timur's. His smile had increased. Why? Did he know who I was? How could he? It had been such a tightly guarded secret. Perhaps he didn't know. Perhaps he was stabbing in the dark, as they say, hoping to stumble on the truth and turn it against Luc and the Principate. The more I mulled it over, the more I sensed the situation would only get worse if we continued to hide the fact that I was the prophesised Child of Light and Darkness. But it was not my decision to make.

'You forget yourselves,' Alec said. 'You've all been summoned here to take The Pledge.' The power in his voice quelled any further discussion. Even Timur's smug look faded, yet the malevolence in his eyes remained.

I looked around. Jake and Terens were positioned on either

side of the room; Sam was near the door and Cal stood directly behind the last row of seats. All four cast uneasy glances at each other.

'With respect, my lord,' a lone, brave voice began, 'you ask a commitment from us, yet you're unwilling to give a reason for it. Personally, I find it an insult. My loyalty has never been in question.'

Several "Aye's" echoed around the room.

Alec, Marcus and Luc glanced at each other, and as if coming to some silent agreement, nodded. As Marcus took the other two Elders aside, Alec again addressed the crowd. 'Brethren, please be seated,' he said. 'All will be answered.'

As he and I sat down, Alec leaned over and whispered, 'Unless Luc reveals who you are, there will be no Pledge.'

The pulse in my throat hammered and I stared at him.

Alec's voice whispered in my mind again, *Breathe darling, calm.*

I closed my eyes and inhaled deeply three times, pictured my heartbeat slowing, my pulse returning to normal. A room full of vampires was not the place to show fear – it would only excite them. When I opened my eyes, many lavender gazes were still trained on my neck, but fewer then before.

Good girl.

I turned my head and smiled. 'Thanks.'

He interlaced our fingers and kissed my fingertips.

'Won't it make things worse if we tell them?'

'We have no choice. You can see their mood. Got to risk it.'

Luc crouched in front of me. 'Ma petite, it appears I can't hide you any more. There's no longer any point.' He looked at me as if waiting for my affirmation. If I didn't give it, Luc would have to create a pretty convincing lie for the unusual quality of my blood, and I had a feeling if vampires could smell emotions, they could probably sniff out a lie – and that could make matters even worse. Whatever loyalty Luc commanded could be lost. It hinged on my decision.

'If it means The Pledge can proceed, then go ahead, tell them,' I said.

He nodded, rose and stood next to my chair. From the corner of my eye I saw the other two Elders return to their seats – I would have loved to have seen their reactions when Marcus told them about me. He stood next to Luc, beckoned to our men and whispered to them in a closed huddle. They went back to their posts.

'Brethren,' Alec began, and a hush descended – out of respect, I assumed – but it may have been from a sense that something of great importance would be announced. Then again, it could have been simply out of self-preservation. Who'd want to be singled out to face the princep's wrath? Even Timur sat quietly, his gaze fixed on us. 'A few days ago, an attempt was made on the life of Lady Laura, led by one of our Elders, Lady Maris Quesnell, who is now deceased.'

This announcement was met with a general murmur. Once again, the memory of Maris's screams filled my ears as her body burnt to ash after consuming my blood.

'Was it the Ingenii's blood?' someone asked.

My hands gripped the arms of the chair. *Calm, Laura.*

I looked up to see Luc glaring at the man who spoke, but it was Alec who confronted him. 'It was and Maris paid the price for her rebellion.' His voice was dangerous.

'Ah, so there we have it,' Timur's oily voice drawled. 'But *why* is her blood so toxic?'

'The Lady Laura is part-vampire and part-Ingenii. My daughter,' Luc suddenly announced. 'And her mother is my wife – the Lady Judith.'

A second of silence greeted this pronouncement before the room erupted. I sat further back in my seat as some prefects rose and strode to the front, hurling questions at Luc and Marcus, and even Alec. Did he know about this and for how long? Why the secret? Others remained seated and spoke quietly among themselves. Jake, Cal, Sam and Terens had unsheathed their swords and blocked the exits, their gazes darting from the prefects to our besieged dais where Marcus, Luc and Alec were trying to calm the agitated crowd.

Marcus's voice boomed, 'Be seated Brethren, and all will be explained.'

'What explanation is needed for Lord Lucien fucking the Ingenii!' someone called out.

'Nothing in our laws say I can't,' Luc retorted.

'It's never been done and sets a precedent,' another added.

'For the simple reason that all the previous Ingeniis were men, and I'm not inclined that way,' Luc said.

Laughter from some of the prefects slightly defused the tense situation, and many looked at me with renewed interest. Marcus laid a hand on Luc's shoulder, but my father's fists were tightly clenched. A few of the women prefects eyed me and Alec. Were they trying to see whether he and I had a similar relationship? That wouldn't have been difficult. They could probably smell Alec's scent all over me. Besides that, the serpent rings glowed whenever our hands touched, and when we made love, the room in which we lay became bathed in a ruby aura. I glanced down at my hand. The serpent's eyes shone.

'Correct me if I'm wrong, Lord Marcus,' Prefect 'O'Toole spoke up again, 'but doesn't that mean we're in the presence of the prophesised Child of Light and Darkness? Her being the offspring of a vampire and an Ingenii? Unless, of course, my interpretation of the prophesy is wrong?' He looked from Marcus to me, and so did everyone else.

A heavy silence settled over the room.

As a teacher, I was used to being the focus of attention – by little eyes that regarded me with respect, and some awe – and I wasn't daunted by it. But what faced me now would have caused the heart of the most hardened teacher to quail, as the penetrating gaze of several hundred otherworldly eyes pinned me to my seat.

Breathe, Laura. Calm. I repeated it as a mantra, determined not to appear weak or afraid; determined to stand up for myself, especially as I had enough knowledge of the curse to answer for myself. It was time I did so.

I took a deep breath, clenched my fist, and touched Marcus's arm. 'Let me answer.' He raised an eyebrow, and a faint smile appeared. I took that for a yes and turned to Prefect O'Toole. 'Your interpretation is not wrong, and it's also the reason why my blood is lethal.' I disliked the word "poisonous".

'How long have you known, lady?' O'Toole's bright lavender eyes burned into mine. I guessed they might have been grey before his transformation, judging by his straight, ebony hair.

'Since Maris's death. Before that, I had no idea.'

'And yet the Lord Princeps drank from you at the Ritual,' he said slowly, his eyes narrowed. 'How is that possible?'

'We have the same blood,' Alec answered. 'Lord Lucien is both Laura's father and my sire, and then of course, the serpent rings chose me. You were there. You saw it.'

Prefect O'Toole inclined his head and sat down.

Alec gave a brief report of Maris's attempt to usurp the Principate and how she had been planning to use me. I shuddered at the memory. There were several gasps among the Prefects. 'Earlier this evening, I was attacked in the car park of my apartment building,' he said. 'Now you know why Lady Laura was hidden in infancy until she came-of-age, and why we insist on the Pledge. Many of you are loyal and support the Principate, but unfortunately, not all are.'

Timur kept his head down, so I couldn't see his face. Some prefects stared straight ahead, their expressions blank, while others shifted in their seats and looked at those around them. None said a word, until a tall, dark-haired woman stood and spoke.

'And what if the Principate ends, my lord? We all know the words of the prophecy: if the Destined One bears the child of one descended from the witch, that child's blood will be human – the Gift of the Ingenii will be gone. How will the Principate be sustained?' Her tightly curled ringlets danced around her waist as she spoke.

I stopped my hand from sliding onto my belly, an almost automatic response whenever anyone mentioned the words "baby", "child" or "pregnancy".

'Baroness Milena, the Principate will not end,' Alec said emphatically. 'It's the only thing which stands between us and barbarity. As long as the Elders are united in this purpose, nothing will change. We do not need to daywalk to maintain order, and as for the choice we will face on that day – if it comes – we've already made our decision. We live.'

The woman's head swivelled toward Jake. He gave her a brief nod.

'Your lands are safe, Baroness,' Alec assured her. She glanced at Jake again before resuming her seat.

Well, that's interesting, I thought and wondered if there was something between them. I made another mental note, this time to ask Alec.

'Your strength will not be as great, my lord,' Timur said. It was the first time he'd spoken since being brought here.

'Perhaps not as much, Count, but I doubt there are enough rebels to beat me and my men,' Alec replied.

'Yet two of your men were taken prisoner,' Timur retorted, his eyes narrowed, sneer in place.

I didn't need to imagine his enjoyment knowing Maris's henchmen had captured Terens and Sam and held them in cages, after she'd exposed them to the sun for several seconds.

'How would you know that?' Alec asked. 'As far as we are aware a tweet was sent, but it didn't contain that information.'

The room went quiet as everyone followed the interchange between Alec and the Hungarian prefect. Although the prefects may not have heard all the particulars of what had happened, I was sure they were putting the pieces together.

'It's common knowledge,' he asserted.

'If that's so, why did I see so many surprised faces among your fellow prefects when I mentioned it?' Alec said, almost as if he were baiting Timur or attempting to extract information, or... I finally tweaked to what was happening, and the reason why he and Rasputin were brought here under armed escort – Alec must suspect him of treachery. And, if that was true....

'That's not my problem. Only repeating what I heard,' Timur said. If he was guilty, then the confidence in his tone and demeanor were frightening. For the length of a vampire heartbeat, he faced Alec, and his eyes darted to the other Elders. Slowly his sneer faded. He rose from his seat, took a step forward and said, 'Are you accusing me of being in league with the Rebels?' After a moment of silence, he said, 'Where's your proof?'

'Right here.' Alec said, and with a nod to Sam, the entrance doors slid open.

Karl stood there, hands deep in the pocket of his trousers, a grin on his face. 'Now, who said, "The reports of my death have been greatly exaggerated"?'

Gasps and murmurs came from the crowd. Timur spun around and swore loudly. Those who had been seated on either side of him, and even behind, rose and moved away until he was isolated in the front row.

Karl strode toward the dais, his gaze fixed on Timur.

'Surprised?' He pulled from his pocket a mobile phone and held it aloft for all to see. 'It's all here – the texts you sent instructing your underlings to capture the Ingenii and overthrow the Principate. Every word condemns you.'

Timur growled and surged toward Karl, but Terens was on him in an instant, forcing him to his knees, the tip of his sword pressed to his neck. He may have been subdued, yet Timur's expression was anything but compliant. His eyes flashed defiance. Snarling, saliva dripped from his exposed fangs.

'And I quote,' Karl read the text aloud when he reached the dais, '"We kill the princeps first" —I gasped— "then the other Elders and everyone who won't join us."'

Timur struggled beneath Terens's grip on his shoulder, growling and uttering what I assumed were curses, in Hungarian.

'Interesting reading. Shall I go on?'

'Let's give the Count the benefit of the doubt,' Alec suggested. 'Perhaps his phone was stolen and someone else sent those incriminating messages.'

Karl punched numbers into the mobile. Within seconds, a ring tone came from somewhere on Timur's body. Terens leaned down, retrieved the phone and threw it to Alec, while keeping the sharp point of his sword at the kneeling prefect's neck.

'You deserve–' Alec stopped abruptly, sniffed the air and turned to Luc. 'Smoke!'

That word made my stomach drop.' Where?'

'Cellar,' Luc said. 'Sam raced down there when his security alarm went off.'

I hadn't seen him leave. It wasn't just wine stored in the cellar, but the bloodvault, and they were holding Rasputin and the two rebels there. If there was a fire… .

The prefects began to murmur among themselves, perhaps sensing something was wrong. Marcus leaned over to Alec, who whispered something back. That's when I heard the ear-piercing trill of a fire alarm coming from somewhere in the house.

'Brethren,' Marcus cried. 'We apologise for the interruption in proceedings, but we've just learnt there is a small fire in the basement. Please leave The Residence at once.'

Panic filled the room. Prefects fled in all directions – some down the staircase, others out the windows.

'My God!' Alec exclaimed, and an expression of horror crossed his face – something I'd never seen before. That alone sent a wave of dread through me.

'What's happening?'

'I need to get you out!'

The blood left my cheeks, and in spite of the warmth of the night, a sick coldness settled over me. *A fire! How?*

Alec grabbed my hand, and we ran toward the panelled wall. He flattened his palm against one side and the panel swung open to reveal a hidden passageway – presumably the same one he'd come through only days earlier. He scooped me up and ran along the dimly lit corridor and down a flight of narrow stairs. I glanced over his shoulder and Luc was running behind, followed by Jake and Cal. Directly behind them, Karl was leading the Baroness Milena by the hand.

Where was Terens? The last I saw, he was dragging a reluctant Count Timur after us.

'Alec,' Luc cried out. 'Take Laura to the jetty. Judy and Kari are already there. Get them onto my yacht.'

'What about you?' Alec said.

'Meet you there. Terens is injured.' He didn't wait for Alec's response, but turned and disappeared back up the stairs with Jake, their speed a blur to my human eyes. 'Stay with them,' I heard him say to Karl as he dashed past.

I gasped at his words. Terens!

Milena turned her head and gazed at Jake's retreating back.

'Let's go,' Alec said. I lowered my head onto his shoulder and closed my eyes as the walls and light fixtures sped by at dizzying pace. My body registered the twists and turns he took, and just as I felt we'd reached the bottom, there was a loud boom and the ground seemed to rock. Alec's step never faltered.

'Shit! There goes my Armagnac,' Cal muttered.

'How much further?' Karl asked.

'Nearly there,' Alec said. 'The side entrance.'

'Yeah, kitchen's probably gone, and Luc's best Bordeaux with it,' Cal lamented.

Seconds later, Alec stopped. I opened my eyes as he kicked open a door and stepped through it. The cool night air embraced my cheeks as we exited somewhere near the rear of the house, from a side passage lined with garbage and recycle bins, their dark contours illuminated in the glow of the inferno. A window above us exploded. Alec put on a burst of speed before sparks and glass fragments rained on us.

The entire ground floor was ablaze, and the bedroom wing on the floor above bled smoke, obscuring the stars and creating an eerie orange haze in the night sky. The wail of sirens came from the street, and the flashing red and blue lights from fire engines vied with the flames in brightness.

'This really pisses me off!' Cal exclaimed.

'Same,' Alec replied.

'Marcus's armour,' I said. 'The stained glass window, the library, all those first-edition books...' The beautiful interior, with rich and unique Gothic architecture – the lost heritage – were all burning before my eyes. What the flames didn't destroy, the water used to douse it would. I wanted to cry.

'Let's hope they put it out before it destroys the whole house,' Alec replied.

We made our way to the gate leading down to the harbour, past the expansive lawn and the wisteria-covered pavilion where the Ritual – which introduced me to the Brethren community – was held only a week ago.

Alec set me down when he stepped onto the jetty. Its entire length was lit by a string of LED lights sunk into the timber planks, their reflection dancing on the ripples that bounced off the sides of the pier. Judy stood waiting with Kari at the other end.

Beneath the dim jetty lights, Judy's face appeared ghostly pale as she ran up and enveloped us both. 'Thank God, thank God.' Then she looked past us toward the burning house and panic sprang into her eyes. 'Where's Luc? Why isn't he with you?'

'He's on his way. I can hear them,' Alec assured her. 'Terens has been hurt.'

'Oh, no!' Judy's hand flew to her mouth.

'What's *she* doing here?' Kari said, pointing to Baroness Milena.

As she and Karl approached, Baroness Milena's eyes narrowed in response. 'As a prefect, I've more right to be here than you.' She spat back and pulled her hand away from Karl's and faced Kari, fists at her side.

'Now, now, girls,' Karl said, stepping between them.

But the two continued to glare at each other until Kari turned her head and cried. 'Jake!' Her eyes were round like saucers, gazing towards the fiery darkness. 'And Luc's carrying...' Her breath caught.

Three figures made their way toward us, their silhouettes outlined against the fiery backdrop. Two were shirtless and one appeared to be carrying something large over his shoulder. Cal uttered a loud roar and sprinted toward them.

'Get him onto the boat,' Alec said when they reached us.

Sam and Cal eased Terens's semi-conscious body from Luc's shoulder and carefully carried him to the launch. Blood-soaked bandages – Luc and Jake's shirts? – bound his shoulder and chest, and where his left arm should have been. His face was ashen and taut with pain. The sickly, metallic smell of blood invaded my nostrils and I had to turn my head away to stop from gagging.

'What happened?' I asked, as we stepped into the motor launch.

'I'll kill that Hungarian bastard.' Jake said through clenched teeth.

'Timur did this?' Kari asked. She pushed Milena out of the way and slid her hand into Jake's.

'White-oak ... in ... his ring,' Terens managed to say. 'Never ... smelled it.' He groaned as the other men laid him across one of the seats in the launch and sat at either end of him.

I perched on the seat opposite and watched as Alec crouched by Terens's side, undid the bandages and examined the gaping wound. Jake sank to his haunches next to him.

'Hell!' Sam exclaimed. 'Just as well it's not his sword arm.' He glanced at Jake. 'Sure you got it all?'

Jake nodded. 'Bastard scratched him on the hand. Had to amputate his arm before the poison spread.' He touched the sword strapped to his side.

I couldn't imagine how hard that must have been for him to do.

'Fucker! I'll just add that to the list of excuses I need to rip his miserable head from his shoulders,' Karl said.

'Nice job, Jake. Bleeding's stopped. Nothing more I can do,' Alec said. 'Take him to the yacht and administer a regional.' He turned his attention to Terens. 'Jake'll give you something to kill the pain. The rest is up to you.'

My stomach hollowed out. 'What do you mean, "Jake'll do it"? Aren't you coming?'

Alec gently grasped my shoulders. 'I can't leave. As princeps, it's my responsibility to stay – make sure everything's okay.'

'Can't Luc–' I started to protest.

'He's got to check the vault and hide those cages before the firemen get down there.'

'But–'

He placed a finger over my lips. 'Darling, the Brethren are still here. I can sense them, and they need to see the Principate hasn't lost control. Now, more than ever, we need to present a picture of stability. If I run away....'

He didn't need to complete the rest for me to understand the implications – the Brethren would see it as a sign of weakness and Alec would lose all credibility, perhaps even his life. He was right. I had to let him go, although my stomach churned in revolt.

'Besides, Jake's a medic,' he continued. 'He'll give Terens a regional anaesthetic to make him comfortable. No more than I would do.'

I sighed and kissed his finger. 'So much for Marcus marrying us tonight. Be careful and ... don't be long.'

There was a pained look in his eyes as he leaned down and kissed me, long and hard, before releasing me. He turned to Jake. 'You know what to do.' With that, he, Luc, Karl and the other men disappeared into the darkness.

'He'll be okay, dear.' Judy clasped my hand and led me down the jetty, where Jake and others were already aboard the launch.

I glanced at the serpent ring and experienced a thrill of relief – the eyes glowed a healthy, and safe, red.

'We need to get Terens onto the yacht before he regains consciousness,' Jake said, as he helped Judy and myself step down into the boat.

'Will his arm regenerate?' I asked.

'During the day sleep. He was lucky.' He went past Milena to the front of the launch and steered us into the dark waters of the harbour.

I had to take a reality check, for apart from the garden-variety lizard I occasionally shooed out of my kitchen, I knew of no other species that was able to regrow an entire limb overnight. Being half-vampire, did my body have that ability? I really didn't want to find out.

Milena sat primly on the padded bench directly behind Jake, facing away from Kari and the rest of us. She'd plaited her thick, curly hair over one shoulder, presumably to prevent the wind from blowing it around.

I joined Kari who knelt by Terens's unconscious form. 'Hey, Sexy Terry,' she said, and smoothed the hair off his forehead.

'He hates it when anyone calls him that,' Jake said.

'I know,' she replied. 'If he can hear me, it'll make him mad enough to stay alive.'

Jake turned his head and smiled at her, before resuming his scrutiny of the way ahead as the boat bounced over the waves.

'He can still die, then?' I asked Kari.

'Hell yeah. Shock. Our blood flows more slowly, so there's no chance of bleeding to death, but shock is the same as with a human, and if it's bad enough, it can interfere with regeneration. But,' she added, as she scanned Terens's face, 'we're a pretty tough breed. Aren't we sexy Terry?'

'"Sexy Terry"'? I asked.

'It's short for Sextus Terentius. His real name, but no one's called him that for ages.'

A light sheen of sweat coated his brow, and in the boat's artificial light, his face appeared waxen. My heart lurched. I'd only met my father's men a week ago, yet in some respect, they'd always been in my life – unseen bodyguards, who'd made sure none of the Brethren learnt of my existence. Of the four, it was Terens I'd come to know the best. The diamond stud in his ear glinted as he'd flirted with me at the Ritual. Later, when we'd been captured by Maris – and in spite of his own painful injuries – Terens had tried to keep my spirits up and had won a special place in my heart.

I gripped his hand and said, 'Hang in there, Terens. We need you.' It could have been wishful thinking, but I'm sure I felt a gentle pressure on my fingers in response.

The launch slowed, and I peered ahead at the lights of a four-deck yacht. We pulled alongside. Jake secured it with a rope.

Stepping past Milena, he bent, whispering something in her ear. Then he hoisted Terens onto his shoulder, leapt up over the bow of the craft and landed nimbly on the main deck.

Milena rose, turned to me and said, 'Allow me to help you onto the yacht, my lady.' Presumably, we weren't going to use a ladder. I stood, and she scooped me up. With one deft leap, she cleared the bow and landed lithely on the main deck of the four-deck yacht.

Milena set me on my feet, and I waited till Kari, with Judy in her arms, joined us. Together we passed through a door that opened onto a brightly lit stateroom.

CHAPTER 13 – LINES ARE DRAWN

ALEC

'I want those two sons-of-bitches dead!' Sam growled as we ran back to the burning house.

'That makes two of us.' Karl echoed, with good reason.

'Don't ask me how,' Sam continued, 'but Rasputin managed to pick the lock, start the fire then leave the two Rebels behind to burn.'

'I heard them.' Their screams filled my ears, and I'd experienced a moment of horror as I knew it was too late to help them. 'Did you manage to—'

'Yeah.' An expression of disgust crossed his face. 'Nobody should be left to die like that. Raced up to Luc's study, grabbed the gun, went back down and shot 'em with white-oak bullets. At least they died quick.'

'And we won't have to explain any charred remains to the emergency services,' Luc finished.

That was true, although I felt responsible for their fate. I'd promised them a second chance. Leaving Rasputin unguarded had been a mistake, and they had paid the ultimate price. I was determined to see Timur and his henchman exterminated.

The acrid smell of smoke filled my nostrils as we approached. I picked out fire fighters hosing the lower storey windows from which smoke was still pouring out. Several others were inside the house, searching, calling out any survivors. One – on the street – was telling neighbours to keep their distance. I isolated Marcus's baritone from the cacophony of voices, assuring the fire chief his "brother's" guests had all been evacuated in time. Although Luc had inherited his mother's fair hair, the resemblance between him and Marcus was unmistakable. And since they appeared a similar age, passing themselves off as brothers was a necessary ruse in the human world.

It had been Marcus who'd urged us to flee, while he'd stayed behind to co-ordinate the prefects. Having resided in a French monastery for the last seventeen-hundred years hadn't dampened his ability to command.

The fire was contained to the lower and ground floors at the rear of the house, the worst damage where Rasputin had disabled the sprinklers. Sam had them installed throughout the house a few years ago. Tonight proved the worth of that decision.

'Want us to go after them?' Cal asked, as I stood transfixed by the sight of the firemen battling the flames.

Luc's eyes flared dangerously at the sight, and the anger that emanated from him was almost as scorching as the heat radiating from the house. As far as I knew, he had never been challenged on this scale. And he was torn – I could see it in his eyes – between seeking vengeance or retribution. When he turned his head and looked at me, his indecision was clear. Which side of him would win: soldier or politician?

I didn't have time to wait. 'Sam, go to the airport and locate Timur's private jet. Disable it. I don't want him leaving the country.' Without a glance at Luc, and with a nod, he sprinted away. To Cal and Karl who stood at my side, I said, 'Go hunting. Pick up Timur and Rasputin's scent. Let me know where they're holed. Don't confront them. We don't know how many of those poison white-oak rings he's got.'

They sped off.

'You okay?' I asked Luc.

'Just pissed.' The tip of his fangs glistened as he spat the words out. 'I'll go check the vault.' He sprinted around the side of the house.

I sensed two prefects stalking one of the fire fighters.

Here was another problem – too many excited humans in close proximity and the scent they exuded was like catnip to the hovering vampires. I extended my senses, knowing all the prefects would hear my voice. 'Gather at the pavilion, now. Feed later, in the city.'

I was about to turn and make my way to the pavilion when I spotted a familiar face – Matthew Sommers.

What was he doing here? The last time I saw Laura's ex-boyfriend, he'd been languishing in hospital with a head wound after an encounter with Maris's rogue group. I'd found him lying unconscious in Laura's apartment, treated him then called the ambulance, only to discover white-oak bullets in his possession. Bastard had been planning to kill us. I deprived him of his memory, though Luc would have preferred to kill him.

I moved closer to get a scent – gauge his intention – my movement a blur to the humans.

Sommers looked like he'd just gotten out of bed – hair mussed and the beginnings of a beard on his face. He stood on the other side of the road, hands deep in his jean pockets. A police car drove up and stopped a few feet in front of him. The door opened and Dave Delaney stepped out – the detective in charge of the investigation into Sommers's assault. They were colleagues.

Why were they here? Only one way to find out. I listened in.

'Matt! What the hell are you doing here at this time of night? You're still recovering.'

'Couldn't sleep. Switched on the telly and saw this.' Sommers pointed to the house. 'You mentioned my ex-girlfriend was staying here with an aunt. So....' He shrugged.

'Yeah, sorry to hear about your break-up.'

He shrugged again. 'Can't remember anything about her. Damn amnesia.'

Delaney turned his head and looked at him. 'Doctors say anything?'

Sommers shook his head. 'Don't understand it themselves.'

'You were lucky you only lost a few months. Could've been a year.' Delaney placed his hand on Sommers's shoulder. 'Take it easy, okay? Give it time.'

Sommers huffed.

Delaney titled his head toward the house. 'Did everyone get out?'

'Think so. Overheard some guy tell the fire chief that. Didn't see anyone come out, though. Check it out.' He looked up and down the street. 'They're the neighbours – in dressing gowns, right? So, where are the guests?'

He was observant.

'What did you hear?' Delaney asked.

'S'posed to be a couple hundred people in there. Neighbours said cars started coming round midnight.'

'Mmmm.'

Both stopped speaking, until Sommers said, 'First her flat's broken into, and now the house she's staying in is set alight. All in one week. What are the odds?'

They stared at the house.

'My thoughts as well,' Delaney said.

'Alec,' Cal's voice sounded in my ears. 'Everyone's assembled.'

'On my way.' I wanted to stay and hear more, but Matthew Sommers was a lesser threat then the one I currently faced.

It took me less than two seconds to reach the pavilion around which the Prefects had congregated. To any human, their pale skin, utter stillness and otherworldly beauty made them resemble garden statues – albeit clothed ones. *And I'm one of them.* It had taken a long time to reconcile myself with that fact. Now that my servitude had ended, and I was no longer regarded as a juvenile, it was time to assume the full trappings of the office of princeps.

As I alighted on the pavilion, Marcus appeared with Kwome and Zhao. They stood behind me, while Luc, who had returned from inspecting the bloodvault, stood by my side. He gave me a nod, indicating all was well. Considering the strength of its construction – a double layer of reinforced titanium that was flood, fire and nuclear bomb proof – I would have been surprised if there had been any damage.

Karl perched on the top step and lit a cigarette.

I did a quick scan to see how many of the original two-hundred-and-twenty prefects had remained. By their absence, the nine who were missing publicly declared their allegiance to the Rebel cause.

I stood and faced them. Taking the executioner's sword from Marcus's hand, I raised it in the air. 'Brethren, we are at war. Tonight was round one to the Rebels, those who would see the Principate and the Brethren law destroyed, who want to bring us back to the dark ages and the killing times, when humans knew of us and hunted us to near extinction. Is that what you want?'

There were cries of 'No!'

'Look around you.' I pointed the sword. 'See who's absent. See who took the opportunity to run rather than take the Pledge. I can guarantee you'll find them at Timur's side, decimating the human populations in their territories. Once they're done there, yours will be next.'

'He's already encroaching on mine,' Karl remarked. 'His minions are opening hotels and dealing in blood slaves. Young humans are disappearing. The decimation has begun.'

'Imagine if he had the Ingenii in his possession,' I added.

Prefect O'Toole swore, as did a few others. All of them owed their exalted positions to either Marcus or Luc, and as long as they remained loyal and kept the Brethren laws, they enjoyed autonomy in their regions. The Elders rarely interfered, and the few times they did, it had been at the behest of a prefect. Should Timur and the Rebels win, all that would end.

'Brethren.' Marcus stepped forward. Almost as one, each of the prefects fell to their knees. 'I remember the days of chaos and hiding. Should this rebellion spread, and more humans be killed, it's only a matter of time before they believe in our existence again. For the last two-hundred years we have enjoyed anonymity and unprecedented freedom to live inconspicuously among them. Their populations have grown, and we have fed well. We have forgotten what it's like to fear the vampire hunter; to fear white-oak. The Principate is the only thing which stands between our existence and disaster.'

'My lord, you will always have our support,' one said. This was followed by cries of, 'Aye.'

Marcus placed his hand on my shoulder. 'Here is your princeps. Show him your allegiance.'

'You have it,' O'Toole said, bowing his head in deference.

One by one, all the prefects did the same.

'Brethren, the lines are drawn,' I said. 'I declare in the presence of you all that Count Timur Széchenyi, Grigory Rasputin, and all who support and shelter them, are hereby proscribed. Their properties and all their possessions are default to any who deliver their heads to the Eldership, and their territory is to be transferred to the hands of the Eldership until a Principate prefect can be appointed.'

'Count Timur Széchenyi, Proscribed. Grigory Rasputin, Proscribed.' Marcus's voice resounded like a death knell. I was sure, wherever he was hiding, Timur could hear.

Luc repeated the condemnation, as did the other two Elders. This was then picked up and recited by prefect after prefect until the last voice sounded, and the garden once again fell silent. Any vampire within range would have heard. I particularly hoped Stanton and his gang, who had attacked me earlier this evening, knew the danger they were in.

War had been declared.

CHAPTER 14 – THE YACHT

LAURA

We stepped down into a sunken living area that would easily accommodate a large group of guests. Leather sofas and ottomans were scattered throughout the room, their beige tones complimenting the blonde parquetry flooring and alabaster ceiling from which shone a string of downlights. In the centre sat a glass-topped coffee table with a pile of magazines on one end and a small, bronze art deco statue of a nude dancing female on the other, while wall-to-wall windows offered an unhindered view of the ocean beyond.

The whole gave an illusion of space and light.

Several plump cushions lay scattered on the carpeted floor, presumably from the sofa on which Jake had laid Terens. Jake was in the process of removing the shirts that had been used to bind the amputation. I heard him suck in a breath as he removed the last piece. 'The regeneration should have started by now.' His voice was tinged with fear.

Milena stood behind as Kari, and I knelt on the floor next to Jake. I tried to keep my eyes averted from the raw, open wound. It made my stomach turn. I sent up a silent prayer for Alec's safety and glanced at my ring – the eyes of the serpent glowed red.

Please stay that way.

Terens's breath came in short, sharp gasps. His head tossed from side to side and his eyes flickered open once or twice.

'He needs blood,' Jake said.

'Coming up,' Judy called.

She had crossed to the centre of the room, to a built-in bar. The large mirror behind the counter reflected a range of glasses, tumblers and decanters any pub would have been proud to own. It effectively divided the spacious room in two. Her voice came from within it. I heard the ping of a microwave, and then she appeared, hurrying toward us with a bag of blood.

Jake took it from her, lifted Terens's shoulders and placed the straw end of the bag into his mouth. 'C'mon, brother, drink.'

Slowly, Terens's mouth moved and he began to suck, weakly at first, then his eyes shot open and he drank hungrily.

'Another one, Judith,' Jake said. 'And bring the medical kit.'

Judy raced back to the bar while Kari and I sat on the floor, looking helplessly on. 'Is there anything I can do?'

'Hold this,' he indicated the blood bag, 'so I can inject him with the painkiller.' As he maneuvered out from behind Terens, he motioned for Kari to hand him some cushions. 'Put 'em here.'

She placed them behind Terens's shoulders. The bloody stump that had been his arm and the blood bag I held at his mouth made my stomach heave. But there was no way I'd give in to sickness. Terens had been there for me, and now it was my turn to return the favour. Swallowing hard, I forced the bile back down and concentrated on the diamond stud in his ear, which winked at me from between the strands of his dark auburn hair.

Judy sat on an armchair next to the sofa and rested her hand on Terens's shoulder as Jake swapped the blood bags and injected Terens – with a strong painkiller, I assumed – in a couple of sites around his shoulder. Soon, Terens's breathing eased; he stopped sucking – the bag was nearly empty, anyway – his eyes closed and his body went limp.

I looked at Jake. 'Is he asleep?'

Jake nodded. 'I added a strong sedative to the anaesthetic. It'll keep him out for hours.' He took the blood bag from me and placed it into a plastic bag from his medical kit, together with the syringe, empty cartridge and the shirt-bandages, and strode over to the bar.

Kari brushed the hair from Terens's forehead. She'd risen from her kneeling position and sat on her haunches by the sofa. 'Look!' she exclaimed. Her gaze was on Terens's bloody stump. 'It's regenerating.'

Curiosity overcame my disgust, and I glanced down. It was amazing and spooky to see the blood vessels heal themselves. A light film developed and sealed the open wound, which soon changed to healthy pink skin.

'Man, he had me worried there for a bit.' The relief was clear in Jake's voice. They'd fought together for over eighteen-hundred years, and today – as far as I knew – was the first time they'd come close to losing one of their number. Very close.

'I find it interesting that an Ingenii, and a half-vampire one at that, has an aversion to blood,' Milena said.

Her voice startled me. I'd been so focused on Terens, I'd quite forgotten about her. She sat on one of the ottomans, one elegant, light-blue trousered leg crossed over the other, manicured hands clasped in her lap. Head cocked to one side, she regarded me as though I were a specimen she hadn't encountered before. Perhaps I was. After all, how many half-vampire, lethal-blooded, part-immortal women could there be?

'It's the human side of me, I suppose.'

'Mmmm.' Her delicate eyebrows rose. 'That can be a handicap.'

I couldn't tell if she'd meant that sincerely or she was being facetious, but something in her tone grated on me. 'In what way, may I ask?'

Judy's hand squeezed my shoulder. I briefly turned my head and looked up at her, but her gaze was fixed on Milena.

'You're in the company of blood drinkers,' she remarked, as if that explained everything. 'You won't find soft drinks in the refrigerator.'

Yep, she was definitely grating on my nerves. For one thing, I didn't like soft drinks – never drank the stuff. I felt like saying, No kidding, Sherlock! when Kari chipped in. 'I think she's doing brilliantly. I didn't see you holding the blood bag for Terens.'

Milena's eyes narrowed. 'I wasn't speaking to you, peasant. That's twice you've insulted me tonight. Be silent!'

In less than a blink, Kari was on her feet, bristling like a angry kitten. I was sure she would have hit Milena if Jake hadn't caught her around the waist and hauled her aside. 'Kari, calm down,' he said.

'You heard what she called me?'

'Yes, and she's about to apologise.'

'I will do no such thing.' Milena bit back.

'Yes, you will,' Jake said, enunciating each word. 'Whatever Kari's background before her transformation, it's irrelevant now. She's Brethren, and you will respect that, or it's the last you'll hear from me.'

The air crackled between the two vampire women, but at least there was no show of fangs. Well, at least not yet. Milena's gaze flicked between Jake and Kari. 'I regret my hasty words.' She eventually conceded.

'Satisfied?' Jake asked Kari before he let her go.

'Yes,' she said grudgingly, but I couldn't help noticing the way she leaned back into Jake's chest, the way I did with Alec. I wondered if Jake knew, or even guessed, that Kari was in love with him.

'Sshhh.' Jake suddenly hissed. His head turned toward the windows. 'Listen.'

I couldn't hear a thing except gentle lapping of water against the sides of the boat. 'What is it?' I whispered.

'Princi's making a special announcement,' Kari whispered back.

Alec! My heart jumped. I glanced at the serpent ring. All was well. What I would've given to have vampire hearing; to hear his deep, rich voice and enjoy the delicious tingle it always sent through me. 'Tell me.'

'He and the Elders proscribed Count Timur and Rasputin, and anyone who supports them,' Jake said. From the serious expression on his face, I guessed it must be something bad.

'Wow,' Kari's eyes were wide, 'I've never heard anyone proscribed before.'

'And I hope you never will, again,' Jake said before looking at me and Judy. 'It's rarely invoked, and only when one of our kind has committed a crime so heinous there's no other choice. It was used by the old Roman emperors, like being made an enemy of the state. The proscribed one was killed, sometimes their families, too, and their lands and all their possessions given to the one who denounced them, or to the state. Same went for anyone who helped them out.'

Milena added. 'Can't think of a better person it could happen to.' Her eyes gleamed.

I looked down at Terens. In some small measure, this was recompense for what Timur had done to him. He wouldn't need to seek revenge – Alec had done it for him. I glanced at my ring. All was well. My princeps was safe, and so was I.

The yawn came from nowhere. My planned afternoon nap had not eventuated. It was now past two in the morning, and the adrenaline, which had kept me going the last couple of hours, had worn off.

'Go to bed, dear,' Judy leaned over and said quietly. 'Alec could be a while, yet.'

I didn't want to go without seeing him, but my eyelids were getting heavier, and soon they'd close of their own accord. Yet, I wondered how could I possibly sleep after everything that had happened. I was shocked by tonight's events, and by the viciousness of those who opposed the Principate; who would stop at nothing to kill any of us, by any means.

Another yawn. My body and mind were at odds, but it seemed my body was winning.

'You're right.' I rose. Problem was, I had no idea where the bedrooms on this massive yacht were, and no change of clothes. I started heading towards a comfortable-looking sofa, when Judy took my elbow.

'This way, dear.'

She steered me out to the deck and I caught a glimpse of the star-filled night before we descended a set of stairs to a long, well lit corridor interspersed with narrow recesses filled with diminutive statues of naked females. Judy escorted me past numerous doors, each one emblazoned with gold-coloured Roman numerals.

'All the guest bedrooms are on this deck. There are twelve and two of them are the VIP rooms near the front – the "fore end," I think they call it. Here's yours.' Judy stopped at the end of the corridor, opened a door with the Roman numeral for one and flicked on the light.

My breath nearly left me. I had expected a bunk and a porthole, but I should have known that there would be nothing that simple on my father's yacht. A white-panelled cabin greeted me, furnished with a queen-sized bed draped with a striped cover in my favourite colours – light-and dark-blue. It sat resplendent on a raised carpeted platform, which extended to include an ebony-topped bedside table with lamp. Accessorising it was a similarly coloured desktop built into the wall, on the other side of the room. Overhead lights formed an arc above the bed and illuminated a set of built-in shelves with books held in place with a metal bar. A dark-curtained, rectangular window – no porthole here – at the far end of the room, and a painted scene of yachts on Sydney Harbour hanging above the bed, completed the scene.

I bent and removed my shoes, enjoying the velvety tickle of the plush carpet, its expanse of white broken up by wavy stripes of blue and pale grey.

'It's lovely!'

Judy beamed, moved further into the room and pressed her hand on part of the glossy panelling. It sprang open to reveal a built-in wardrobe. 'I had it filled two weeks ago.'

She had done the same with my room in the house. They'd had it entirely refurbished in preparation of my homecoming. There had been enough clothes and accessories to warm any woman's heart. I'd been stunned, and it made me realise what a great sacrifice they'd made to keep me safe; how much they'd missed me and longed for the day when I would, once again, be home with them – with my biological parents.

'You're spoiling me, you know that?'

Judy laughed. 'Not at all, especially now there's no telling when we'll be back in the house again. There's sure to be a lot of damage and Luc'll want it repaired straight away.'

And that could take a few weeks – maybe months. Were we expected to live on the yacht in the meantime? I had to admit, that prospect sounded okay. After all, I was on summer holidays and being on a beautiful yacht, cruising the harbour seemed not a bad idea. I'd always loved boating, but my job ate most of my free time, and my weekends were often taken up with marking assignments and preparing lesson plans.

I yawned, and looked longingly at the bed.

'Goodnight, Laura dear. There'll be enough time tomorrow to show you around – the gym and sauna on the upper deck, the jet skis.' She kissed my cheek. 'Oh, before I forget. To your left,' she pointed to the wall opposite the bed, 'is your ensuite bathroom. Sweet dreams.'

I hadn't noticed any door. 'Where's the handle? How do I open it?'

'Like the built-in,' she said on her way out. 'Push on it with the palm of your hand.'

I debated whether to take a peek or wait until morning. My curiosity won out, and I flattened my palm against the smooth panelling. The door popped open revealing immaculate white tiles with splashes of turquoise glass between them. A recessed shower behind an opaque screen stood in one corner, a toilet and bidet in another. Fluffy sea-blue towels hung from the railings. I promised myself a shower in the morning.

Curiosity satisfied, I dropped the pearl, mesh pouch with my mobile phone on the bedside table, unzipped my dress and draped it over a chair next to the desk. I checked the built-in, rummaging through each drawer for nightwear. After choosing a midnight blue, satin nightie, I slipped it on then sank into the soft comfort of the bed. Just as I was about to close my eyes, the boat came alive. A deep hum started, followed by the sound of a clunk from somewhere aft, and I felt the slightest movement. Jake must have weighed anchor and was steering the yacht out of its mooring. Moving it closer to the jetty maybe? Alec, Luc and the other men were still at the house.

He's going to pick them up, I thought, as another yawn stretched my jaw. To the soothing rhythm of the boat's engines I closed my eyes.

CHAPTER 15 – DIAMONDS AND DEALERS

ALEC

After we'd dismissed the Prefects, Marcus told me he'd be leaving with Zhao and Kwome to discuss the election of a female Elder. I agreed. Since the demise of Maris, the position had been left open and now, more than ever, the Brethren needed to see continuity in the Principate.

I glanced at the yacht, longing to join Laura; longing to have her in my arms. Unfortunately, there was something I needed to do that couldn't wait. 'Luc, I'm going to pay a visit to Dawson. Find out what he's heard. See you back at the yacht.'

I'd spared the life of Martin Dawson, Brethren, a diamond merchant and former white-oak dealer, in return for information, and even though none of his previous contacts – those we hadn't caught and executed – dared approach him, he still managed to find out who possessed the stuff and where it might be hidden.

He might also know where Timur and Rasputin are holed up, I thought, as I raced through the dark city streets. Fire engines blocked the driveway and humans milled around the entrance gates. People were filming the scene on their iPhones. It would be on Youtube – and around the world – within minutes.

I reached the George Street building and rode the elevator to the first floor, walked down the corridor to his showroom and pressed the bell. I was pleased to see the blood sign smeared on his door. Timur and Rasputin would find no shelter, no refuge among Brethren loyal to the Principate whose doors were smeared – in their own blood – with the image of the sword and twin serpents. It was then washed off, making it invisible to humans, but not to vampires.

Dawson's voice spoke through the security intercom. 'Can I help you?'

'It's Dr Munro.'

'Please, come in.'

A click, and the door swung open. As I entered, Martin Dawson bowed his head. 'Good to see you, my lord princeps.'

'You know why I'm here.' I shut the door behind me.

'Not for a social meeting, I gather. Follow me.' He led the way past the store counters to a back room I'd been in before. It doubled as a walk-in safe and private meeting room, sound proofed to prevent Brethren ears from listening in. 'Never can be too careful,' he said, indicating for me to sit.

Apart from the metal cabinets standing shoulder-to-shoulder along the walls, the only other pieces of furniture in the room was a solitary table, covered with black velvet, and two chairs. He sat in the other.

'Where's your staff?' I asked.

Dawson used his niece and nephew – twins – to man the counters rather than employ other Brethren. It made sense, as their loyalty and silence was assured, particularly as they owed their lives to him. At the age of twenty-two, both were diagnosed with terminal leukaemia.

'Sent them home to smear the blood sign after we heard your damnatio.'

Damnatio. The feared Brethren damnation – the Proscription. It was the first time I'd ever had to resort to it.

'Wise move. Now,' I leant my arms on the table, 'have you heard anything?'

'Such as?' He gave me an innocent look, but I knew better.

I rose and strolled to his side of the table. 'Don't play games with me, Dawson. I could rescind that execution order at any time. I want to know where they're hiding.'

His chair scraped across the floor as he tried to back away from me. 'No one tells me anything anymore, not since... I'd tell you if I knew. Believe me!'

I didn't enjoy intimidation, yet characters like Dawson seemed only to respond when such tactics were employed. And if that's what it took to find Timur and keep Laura safe, then so be it.

'No rumours, then?'

He scratched his head, making his wiry hair stick up. 'There was one, but I only caught the tail end. It didn't make sense.'

'What?'

'Something about, "not in a house ... couldn't be sensed". That's all I heard.'

He was telling the truth. Although it wasn't much, it was better than nothing. Yet, if he'd heard correctly what did it mean? 'When?'

'Two nights ago, at one of our regular feeding spots. They were too intent to notice me.'

'Who?' I leant on the arms of his chair and brought my face close to his.

'I don't know. Only heard their voices.'

'You sure you weren't sensed and given a false lead?'

'I'm sure.'

I straightened and strode back to my seat, turning his words over in my head. Timur was still in the city, of that I was certain, and his puppet Rasputin was probably with him. Would Stockton, and what was left of his gang, be with them also? And what about the white-oak bullets? How were the Rebels getting hold of them? It was pointless to ask. Fifty years ago I had asked, and he was lucky to still be alive. But since the introduction of the Internet, everything had changed. Traffic in those bullets, among the Brethren, was impossible to police. Still, anyone found in possession.... I looked at Dawson. He was clean; no smell of the stuff on him. That's not to say he wasn't involved in other nefarious dealings, but that was beyond my jurisdiction.

'Anything else I can help you with, Princeps?'

I could sense how badly he wanted me out of his shop. My presence was bad for business. But I wasn't finished yet. Laura and

I should have been joined tonight after the Pledging, and that had been disrupted. I'd caught the disappointment in her voice. Since Dawson was unable to provide me with all the information I wanted, I decided to prolong his agony just a little longer.

I sat back in my seat and folded my arms.

'I don't know any more!' The dismay on his face was almost comical.

'I need a diamond ring,' I said.

In an instant, his expression turned from wary to business-like, and he grinned. 'I can help you there. What are you after?'

'What can you show me?'

'For you, nothing but the best.' He jumped up – I could sense his relief – unlocked one of the metal cabinets, removed a couple of trays and placed them on the table. Then, very carefully, he emptied the contents of both. Diamonds of various shapes and sizes spilled out and glittered on the dark velvet.

I picked up a few and examined them. They were all well cut, but somehow not what I imagined she would like. Many were too large and gaudy. Laura was elegant and graceful with a softness about her that I wanted the ring to reflect.

'Nothing here you like, Princeps?'

'They're all beautiful, but I want something different.'

He stared at me a moment, 'Uh, um... okay, in that case,' he moved to another cabinet and unlocked it. 'Let me show you this.'

He took out a small, purple velvet pouch and handed it to me. I peered inside at a delicate heart-shaped stone with a pink centre like a soft heart. As I lifted it to the light, its myriad colours shifted and changed, and the rosy fire in its core turned to amethyst.

I had found Laura's ring. 'This one.'

'Knew you'd like it. One of the nicest pieces I've seen in a long time, and exquisitely cut. What about the setting? Gold or platinum?'

'Gold. Plain band so as not to detract from the stone.'

Even though I hoped she would like the heart-shaped diamond, Laura deserved to have a choice. 'I'll bring the young lady here to choose for herself, but make sure you include that.'

He was too shrewd to ask who it was for, but I knew he would guess.

'Don't worry, Princeps, if the lady doesn't like it, I'll have no trouble selling it.'

We shook hands, and I left.

The run back to the house took only a few minutes. The emergency services had left, and so had the neighbours.

Sommers's car was nowhere to be seen. *Good, I don't need him haunting my steps.*

Jake had moored the yacht at the jetty, and I could hear the men's voices on board. Sam had returned as well. As I passed the wisteria-covered pavilion near the water's edge, I stopped and inhaled. The heavy, floral perfume clouded his scent, but it was unmistakable. Sommers! He was here. Looking around, I took another breath. He was here, all right, behind one of the large fig trees. That position would give him a perfect view of the yacht – and us.

Damn! I didn't know whether to be annoyed by his persistence or admire his tenacity. Whichever, he had to be stopped. But, not right now. I was happy to let him sit there the rest of the night. His human hearing couldn't pick up our conversation from that distance, so for now, he posed no danger.

I leapt on board and made my way to Laura's room. From her gentle breathing, she was asleep. All the same, I rapped gently on her door before opening it. In the darkness, I moved to her side and knelt by the edge of the bed. Her face was toward me, lips slightly parted, tantalising and inviting, her long hair spilling over the pillow like liquid bronze. My hands itched to touch her face, to feel her silken softness, but it might wake her. Instead, I leaned down, kissed her brow and whispered, 'Pleasant dreams, my darling.'

I closed the door quietly behind me and joined the men in the wheelhouse, on the topmost deck.

Sam sat at the helm, Luc, Cal and Jake lounged on deck chairs, while Karl, Milena and Kari occupied a padded bench by the wall.

'Sommers is out there, watching the boat.' I stood next to Sam and leaned back against the console.

'Been keeping an eye on him,' Sam said. 'As long as he stays there, he's no threat.'

'I told you, you should've killed him.' Luc rose, strode to the side of the boat and glared in the direction of the trees where Sommers lurked.

'Why's he here?' Jake asked.

'On the news,' I jerked my head in the direction of the house.

Luc snorted. 'That's all we need.'

'Who's Sommers?' Milena asked.

Jake filled her in on the details. I assumed that Karl must have told her the dangerous double game he'd played to keep them both safe. And from the way her gaze shifted continuously between the two men, it appeared as if she were weighing up the merits of them both.

'Then I agree with Lord Lucien. You should've killed him,' she remarked.

'I don't regret my decision. You never know, it might prove to be a providential one.' I had a feeling and hoped I was right. 'How's Terens?'

'He's okay. The arm's regenerating.' Karl twirled an empty, red-stained glass in his hands. A positive. The sweet aroma hung in the air. 'We put him in one of the cabins.'

'Find out anything from Dawson?' Luc turned and looked at me.

'Not much. Only overheard snatches. Something about Timur not being somewhere he can be sensed. Not in a house.'

'What the hell does that mean?' Cal said.

'What, like in a plane?' Jake's brow creased. 'You can't keep flying round and round. At one point you've got to land and refuel. Unless...' he had everyone's attention. '... it's in the desert. Far enough away that you and Luc wouldn't be able to hear.'

'Not his jet,' Sam remarked. 'I've disabled it. Waited for him to show, but he didn't.' I glanced at his hands. They were streaked and smelled of grease.

I shook my head. 'A plane would be impractical. More like....' As I tried to make sense of it, a thought occurred to me.

'Go on,' Luc prompted.

'Water masks scent.' I gazed at each of them in turn. 'I'm guessing they're on a boat. That's why he didn't return to his jet. He doesn't need it.'

'If you're right, he's one clever bastard,' Sam said. 'There are thousands of boats in these waters.'

'But how many are large enough for his entourage? He and his sidekick aren't alone.'

'I agree,' Luc said. 'A rebellion on the scale he's planning needs a lot of supporters.'

'Narrows down our search somewhat.' Sam spun his seat around to face the console and began typing into the computer. 'I'll start with the larger motor yachts and see who's hired or bought one recently. Then check out any new arrivals.'

'We don't have much time. The Proscription's changed everything,' Karl said. 'Now that there's a price on Timur's head, he'll be desperate to get back to Hungary – secure his territories.'

Karl didn't need to state that his own lands would be under threat if that were allowed to happen. The Principate could lose Eastern Europe.

I had to act.

There were only a couple of hours of darkness left. If Sam could ferret out Timur's hiding place, I could follow it up in daylight hours – without Luc. As Judith's blood lost its potency, so did his daylight tolerance. For the first time in nearly eighteen-hundred years, Luc was returning to the nocturnal habits of the Brethren, although his great age still made him a formidable foe. But could I risk boarding a vessel alone? Chances were, Timur could have human minions on guard, possibly armed with white-oak. Yet I could speed past without them knowing I was there, find Timur and Rasputin, and execute them both. End of problem.

Could it be that simple?

CHAPTER 16 – THE BEST LAID PLANS

ALEC

Come sunrise, the men retired to their cabins below decks. Only Luc remained, and he was about to join Judith. Sam had managed to identify at least four boats that fitted Timur's needs; three charted in the past week, while the other was a private yacht that sailed into the harbour yesterday.

As far as I was aware, the human owner had no connection with the Brethren. Still, it was worth checking. All four yachts were moored nearby. I would take the launch and inspect them, and if Timur and Rasputin were on board one of them, I was prepared. I loaded the white-oak bullets into the gun, wrapped it in plastic – in case I needed to get in the water – placed it in the holster and strapped it around my shoulder. It was well hidden by my T-shirt.

Even this early in the morning, the harbour teemed with watercraft. It was to be expected in summer when tourists flocked here to enjoy a warm Christmas and the famous fireworks of New Year's Eve.

The first yacht I located was moored at Rose Bay, only three-

and-a-half nautical miles south. It was a tri-deck yacht, roomy enough to take a larger party, but small enough to avoid suspicion. Somehow it didn't fit the image of the Hungarian prefect, but it was best to check.

It took less than twelve minutes to cover the distance from Watson's Bay, where Luc had moored the yacht, and round the bushland peninsula of Sydney Harbour National Park. In the sheltered waters of Rose Bay, a scattering of leisure craft, fishing boats and dinghies bobbed precariously in the backwash of a passing ferry. Over there – my first target lay at anchor.

I slowed the launch and circled it, looking for human guards. There was no sign of anyone, and I couldn't get a scent. The water blocked my sense of smell. I would have to get on board.

Maneuvering the launch alongside, I crept on deck and ducked lower than the windows of the main stateroom. No voices, but several heartbeats came from the lower decks – slow, steady, human. Humans sleeping. In the corridor, I picked up scents again. There were no Brethren on board. My hunch had been right. This boat was too modest for Timur.

Back in the launch, I checked the printout Sam had given me and decided to try for the largest of the vessels, a five-deck megayacht moored in Double Bay – less than one-and-a-half nautical miles to the south-west. It was more in keeping with Timur's style – grand and ostentatious.

Five minutes later, in the wake of a commuter ferry, I was hidden from the giant yacht. As the ferry slowed and pulled into the wharf, I cut the engine and dropped anchor near the marina. The vantage point gave me a clear view. No one appeared to be moving about. Listening for voices, I picked up snippets of conversation, enough to deduce that Timur and Rasputin were on board.

I removed my shoes, slid into the water and swam the short distance to Timur's yacht. Not needing to breathe, I could remain submerged as long as necessary, and if they were expecting me, I hoped they wouldn't peer into the depths. I broke through the surface and climbed onto the main deck.

Once on board, I detected the presence of several humans, some I assumed to be part of the charter-boat crew – captain, first mate, navigator, cook and cleaner.

My presence wouldn't remain undetected for long. A puddle was forming at my feet. No matter how fast I moved I'd leave a soggy trail behind. I didn't bother to check the serpent ring, knowing its eyes would be black.

No time to waste. I pulled out the gun, removed the plastic wrapping, and after checking to make sure it was dry, took the stairs down to the lowest deck. If this yacht followed the standard pattern of design, the crew's bedrooms would be here, below the waterline. For Timur and his entourage, it would be ideal sleeping quarters – no windows, no chance of sunlight seeping through to endanger the vampires within.

I stopped, inhaled, and detected the presence of ten Brethren – Timur among them – and two humans. Yet I picked up no hint of Rasputin. Where was he? I passed through the exterior door and entered a narrow corridor.

Voices – human guards. There were at least two guarding the door to Timur's room. They were discussing football results. I rounded the corner, raced toward them and knocked them unconscious before they knew I was there. The door they guarded was locked. I broke it and walked in.

Timur was supine on the bed, deep in the coma-like vampire sleep.

I withdrew my gun and aimed for his chest, too intent on my quarry to register a change in scent, or hear approaching footsteps.

'Drop the gun.' A familiar voice came from behind.

Damn! Sommers. What is he doing here? I retained my stance and turned my head. He was pointing a gun at my back. 'What are you doing here?'

The smell of white-oak filled my nostrils. Son of a bitch! Luc had been right; I should have killed him.

'Preventing a murder. As I said, put the gun down.'

'You've no idea,' I said over my shoulder. 'This man,' I waved my gun, 'is a killer! If he's not stopped—'

'That's the law's job, not yours. You've got three seconds to drop it or I fire!'

Tension resonated through his body like a coiled spring. I didn't have time for this. The ship's engines started and the anchor rattled. One of the guards groaned and swore. Soon the other one would be awake as well – his companion would see to that.

To give the impression of surrender, I lowered my gun, spun on my heel and struck Sommers on the side of the head. My speed would have been like a blur to him. As he went down, I snatched the gun from his hand and pocketed it.

One guard was now fully conscious. He stood in the doorway, eyes wide, blocking my escape. 'Princeps,' he muttered. He kicked his still unconscious companion in an effort to rouse him. Before I could stop him, he pressed the red alarm button on the wall behind him. An ear-splitting shrill reverberated throughout the boat.

My opportunity to execute Timur had gone.

Sommers! The man was becoming the proverbial thorn in my side. For a moment I was tempted to leave him to his fate. Instead, I picked up his unconscious body and threw it over my shoulder, pushed the guard out of my way and raced down the corridor at breakneck speed. Behind me, I heard yelling and gunfire, but at this speed there was no chance of being hit.

Startled humans appeared in the doorway ahead. I barged past, ran up the stairs onto the main deck and was about to jump into the water when I spotted an aluminium dinghy. It hadn't been there before, so I assumed Sommers had used it to follow me here.

Holding him tightly to my shoulder, I leapt off and landed in the dinghy, dumped him in the passenger seat and searched his pockets for the key.

Seconds later I was speeding back to my launch near the marina. I glanced behind to see the megayacht leave its moorings and head toward open sea. Several humans ran around the main deck like disorientated ants, looking out over the railings, some with binoculars, some pointing. Something whizzed past my ear and I caught the whiff of white-oak. I swore and pushed the throttle to maximum.

Soon, I was easing the aluminium dinghy alongside my launch. I secured it to the stern, hauled Sommers – still unconscious – from the seat and climbed into my boat. The marina was quiet. Few people were about in the early morning, and thankfully those who were weren't looking my way. Just to be sure we didn't attract any unwanted attention, I lay Sommers along one of the padded benches, folded his arms over his chest, crossed one leg over the other and placed a cap over his face. He looked the picture of relaxation. Satisfied, I removed my leather gloves, slipped them in my back pocket then whipped off the wet T-shirt and dropped it on the seat. After checking that Sommers was still out, I started the engine and sped back to the yacht.

I tied him to a chair in the main salon then perched on the edge of one of the sofas directly opposite him. My wet jeans squelched on the leather. I didn't want to leave Sommers unattended in case he regained consciousness.

I sat and gazed at his bowed head, shaking my head at his tenacity. He must have waited behind that tree all night before following me. There were dark circles under his eyes and stubble on his chin. It would have been so easy to have left him with Timur's thugs. But something in my nature baulked against it. I toyed with the idea of mesmerising him again and placing him back in his car. He'd wake up believing he'd parked there and fallen asleep. Yet that didn't seem an adequate solution to the problem. Mesmerisation worked best on the weak minded, where its effects were permanent. Matthew Sommers was not of that ilk, and it would be only a matter of time before he either worked it out, or his memory returned.

'What am I going to do with you, Sommers?' I said, before sitting back and debating whether to restore his memory. I'd taken it away for good reason; otherwise Luc would've killed him. Not because he'd been courting Laura, but on account of the white-oak bullets I'd found in his pocket. The only humans in the past who'd ever used them, were vampire hunters. They were the enemy. I wasn't supposed to save my enemy.

Sommers woke. He lifted his head, blinked a few times, saw me, and his eyes widened. Realising his predicament, a string of obscenities left his mouth as he struggled against his bonds.

I knew it would take too much time to try and explain everything to him. It had been difficult the first time, yet I'd had no other choice, given the circumstances, and Matthew Sommers had become the first policeman in this country to learn of our existence. For a while I'd rectified that situation, but now....

I lifted his jaw and made him look into my eyes. 'Matthew Sommers, you are to remember what was forgotten.'

He stared at me, a host of expressions flitting across his face as the memory of the last six months flooded back to him. His hands flexed several times then finally closed around the arm of the chair in which he was imprisoned. The wood cracked under the strain. Sommers's eyes blazed with anger and hatred – and I couldn't entirely blame him.

'You bastard!' He spat and lunged forward, straining against the rope that bound him. 'It was you! You erased my memory. Why?'

'I saved your life. The others wanted to kill you after I found those white-oak bullets on you.'

He looked at me in surprise, and then his eyes narrowed and his expression hardened. 'Why didn't you?'

Interesting. He skipped the fact I'd mentioned those deadly bullets, almost as if he didn't see the need to justify their possession. 'When it was easier to erase your memory? I don't kill if I don't have to.'

I went to the bar, took out the last bag of blood, poured it into a glass and warmed it in the microwave then went back and sat down. 'As you can see, we have our own supplies.' I gulped it down.

His face paled, and he turned his head away. 'Must you do that in front of me?'

I laughed. 'Just proving a point.'

'What the hell were you doing back at that yacht? Trying to make another point?'

He was deliberately avoiding the fact I'd saved his life. Was he ignoring it so he'd feel no sense of obligation? But I had no intention of letting it go. 'Exactly what I brought you here to discuss.'

He glanced down at the ropes binding him to the chair. 'Some discussion method you use.'

'Gets a reluctant party to listen.'

He glared at me. 'I'm listening.'

'I spared your life, and now you're going to return the favour.'

His eyes narrowed. 'If you think I'm going to help you kill someone, forget it.'

'You were ready to kill me.' I pulled a couple of white-oak bullets from my pocket. 'Look familiar?' I slammed his loaded gun on the coffee table.

Sommers sucked in a breath. 'You're not human so it doesn't count.'

'How easily you justify it. But I didn't bring you here for a philosophical argument. What I want to know is why you had those particular bullets on you when I wiped your memory of all knowledge of my kind?'

His stare never wavered, but it had no affect on me. Eventually his gaze shifted to somewhere over my shoulder, and the view out of the windows behind me.

'I ordered them after checking up on your mob on the Internet; same night Lebrettan threatened me,' he said through clenched teeth. 'I wanted to wipe you all out.' His eyes connected with mine again, the challenge in them clear. I didn't respond. 'They were on my doorstep when I got out of the hospital the other day; had no idea what they were for, of course.' He sneered. 'So I googled it. Amazing what you find on there. When I heard about the house fire, something ... bugged me. I don't know why I packed it—' he jerked his head in the direction of the gun on the table '—just did. Came in handy after all.' He smiled. 'I always follow my instincts.'

More's the pity, I thought. 'This time your instincts were wrong. The man you saw me about to execute is a vampire named Count Timur Széchenyi – a criminal sentenced to death for endangering the human race; for planning to murder men, women and children in order to feed. He's the leader of a rebellion to turn humanity into farmed vampire fodder.'

I gave him time for this to sink in before I added, 'And you prevented me from stopping him.' To verify, I pulled my gun from its holster, emptied the cartridge onto the coffee table. 'Yours. The ones I pulled from your pocket, and as you know, lethal only to vampires.'

From his frown I could see the first inklings of self-doubt. Maybe we could find some common ground. I leaned toward him and delivered the final blow. 'He wants Laura.'

His eyes widened, confirming my fears, and the risk I took in returning his memory. He'd been in love with her before I wiped his mind, and now he was again. But there was nothing he could do about it. Laura had broken it off with him.

'Untie me and we'll talk,' he said.

I slipped on my leather gloves, re-loaded my gun and placed it back in my holster. The remaining bullets I pocketed before untying Sommers. 'We're at war, and it's going to spill over into your world. I can't stop it. But we know who the Rebels are, and we're after them. I thought you should know.'

He stood and faced me. 'Thanks for the advance warning. Can you protect Laura?'

'She's well guarded.'

Sommers rubbed his stubble, looked around, no doubt taking in every detail of the room – exits, what he could use as a weapon if he needed, and he probably guessed he was on Luc's yacht. 'Got anything a human can drink?' he asked.

'Coffee?'

'Yeah. I remember you drank that at the café.'

'Over there.' I indicated the bar. It had a coffee maker at one end, a convenient installation for human guests. 'After you,' I said. Although my reflexes were superior to his, I had no intention of turning my back on him.

He stood against the counter as tense and wary as a cornered animal, while I fitted the capsules into the machine. 'Black or white?'

'Black.'

'Why did you follow me?' I asked.

'Curiosity.'

'And the dinghy?'

'From the guy next door. Told him I was undercover and he let me borrow his boat. Had a feeling I might need it.'

How enterprising.

His face screwed up. 'Shit! I left it tied up.'

'Don't worry. We came back here on it.'

'Why did you restore my memory? Wouldn't it have been better if I didn't know about you lot?' he asked, when I slid him a mug of black coffee.

'It would've eventually come back, and rather than have you following me about, I need you to understand what's at stake.'

A faint smile turned up the corners of his mouth at the unintended pun as he brought the mug to his lips. 'This is good,' he said, after a few sips. He stared down at it and a shadow drifted across his face. 'What do you want from me?'

'Your co-operation. Kill me or Luc or any of our men and there'll be nothing standing between you and the real monsters.

They'll take Laura—' there was no way to avoid this. Sommers had to know '—impregnate her with one of their human underlings and raise the baby for themselves. You know what that means.'

He slammed his cup down and coffee splashed onto the counter. Laura had told him the power of the Ingenii blood. He understood the consequences. 'We can track that yacht, board it—'

I shook my head. 'Too late. The guards will have already moved Timur and Rasputin—'

'Wait! Did you say, "Rasputin"? *The* Rasputin?'

'Yes.'

He moved to the windows, dug his hands into his jeans pockets and stared out. 'Bloody hell. Please don't tell me Jack the Ripper's one of your mob, too?'

'No.' Neither of us spoke, until I said, 'Go home, Sommers. Get some sleep. You're exhausted. And you're still getting over that head injury.'

He turned his head to look at me, opened his mouth as if to speak, then closed it and went back to staring out the window. 'I don't get how you can be a doctor, and ... and ... God, I can't say it!'

'Go home, Sommers.'

'Yeah.'

He straightened his shoulders and headed toward the door, pausing momentarily at the coffee table where I'd left his loaded gun. 'You won't need it,' I said, hoping the warning in my voice was enough. 'I'm not your enemy, Sommers.'

Both his hands were balled into fists as he strode out of the room. I followed him onto the main deck and watched as he made his way through the garden and out to his car. I listened for the sound of his car's engine retreating into the distance.

'Alec? Where are you?'

Her beautiful voice wiped all trace of Sommers from my mind. *Coming, darling.*

CHAPTER 17 – MORNING TO OURSELVES

LAURA

The room was dark when I woke, but enough light came from behind the heavy curtains for me to check my watch. It was after eight, so I'd had at least six hours sleep. The other side of the bed was empty and hadn't been slept in. I wasn't surprised. After last night's disaster at the Pledging, Alec and Luc had probably used the night hours to counteract the damage caused by Timur and the creepy Rasputin. But it was morning now. I crawled to the end of the bed, pulled back the blue-striped curtains and looked out.

Sunlight danced on the turquoise waters and glinted off the windows of houses on the other side of the bay. *Another glorious day in paradise.* Some eyes never see it – Kari, Karl, Milena, and Luc's men. I wondered if they missed it. Others of their kind did and were rebelling against the Principate to attain it – to attain me.

In spite of the sun's warmth, I shivered.

'Alec, where are you?' I whispered, knowing he would hear.

In less time than it took to blink, my door opened. Barefoot and bare chested, arms braced against the doorframe, he looked down at me. He looked good.

'Right here. Why aren't you still asleep?'

I shrugged. 'Had enough.' That's when I noticed his wet jeans. 'Have you been swimming?'

He glanced down and laughed. 'Something like that.'

I couldn't resist adding, 'You ought to take them off.'

He gave me a slow smile, closed the door and began to undress. I watched, dry-mouthed, as he dropped them to his feet, kicked them aside and walked toward me in all his naked glory.

Seconds later, my nightie lay on the floor and we were making love. Afterwards I traced his tattoo with my fingertips before doing the same with my lips. He tasted salty. What had he been doing while I slept? I was about to ask when I felt him harden against me. 'Alexander Munro, aren't you satisfied?'

'I will be after this,' he said, trying to roll me beneath him.

I squealed and shot towards to the other end of the bed. Alec laughed, grabbed my ankle and dragged me back to him. He must have had a grand view of my naked backside and from the look on his face I'd say he appreciated it.

'Come here,' he purred.

I laughed and tried to kick my ankle out of his grip – to no avail. Alec lunged, wrapped his arm around my waist and pulled me back onto the pillows. He succeeded in pinning me beneath him.

'Surrender?' he asked.

'Never.'

'In that case, you leave me no choice.' A wicked glint lit his eyes. He caught my hands and held them above my head, while with the other hand he tickled me. I squealed and squirmed and laughed till tears ran down my face.

'I surrender! I surrender!'

Alec stopped and swivelled toward the door. 'Shhh! Judith's walking past.'

I bit my lip to stifle a giggle. If only she could see the position he had me in. After a while I asked, 'Is she gone?'

'Yes.' He relaxed and turned back to me. 'Now, where was I?'

'I surrender?' I said.

His grin widened, and he showed me his idea of surrender terms, after which we lay in each other's arms, contended.

Alec was quiet as his hand roamed up and down my back. I sensed he was tense. Before I could question him he said, 'Laura, there's something you need to know, to hear from me, rather than someone else.'

The tone of his voice sent a wave of apprehension through me. I sat up and pulled the cover over my breasts. 'Like what?'

He sat up and looked into my eyes. 'I saw Sommers last night. He was out on the street, talking to Delaney.'

Well, well, Matt was out of hospital. Why did Alec have such a worried look on his face? What had he heard? 'What was he doing here?'

'The fire was on the late news.'

'But it was about two in the morning. What was he doing awake?'

'Couldn't sleep, or so I heard.'

I wasn't surprised that Alec had listened in. With his superior hearing it would've been too tempting. And naturally, he would want to know why Matt was here. But I had a feeling there was more to it. So I waited.

He took a deep breath and let it out slowly. Now I was really worried.

'Sommers's amnesia wasn't the result of his injury,' he said. 'I erased his memory.'

The next few seconds ticked by as his words sank in. Alec had mesmerised Matt into forgetfulness and he hadn't told me. No wonder he'd said I might hate him after he'd rescued me from Maris and Russell. At the time his words didn't make sense – but they did now.

I clutched the bedcover tighter to my breast. 'Why would you do such a thing?'

'Remember the white-oak bullets I found on him?'

I nodded as my throat had constricted.

'In our world anyone found in possession is executed.'

'But,' I swallowed, 'he's human.'

'As were those who hunted our kind in the past. All that matters is intention. If he didn't know about us or why he had those things on him, he'd no longer be a threat.'

'You wiped his memory to save his life?'

He didn't answer, but then he didn't have to. I didn't need to second-guess what may have occurred if he hadn't done so – either Luc or one of the men would have killed him.

I didn't know whether to be angry or love him even more for protecting Matt. 'I should slap your face for letting me believe it was his injury.'

'If it'll make you feel better,' he said almost flippantly, but his voice was grim and anxiety shone from his eyes.

'Why tell me now?'

'His memory's come back.'

I clapped my hand over my mouth. I'd been so thankful Matt couldn't remember our relationship – wouldn't miss me, or feel the pain of my leaving him.

'Laura, we tracked down where Timur's hiding, and early this morning I went after him. Sommers followed me, misinterpreted the situation and tried to arrest me. I knocked him out, brought him back here and restored his memory so I could reason with him.'

'Misinterpret, how?'

Alec explained and I felt the blood drain from my face. He could have been killed. Timur and Rasputin were the real monsters and had to be stopped. I understood that, and the course of action he had to take – risking his own life to keep everyone else safe. In spite of the hurt and anger I felt at his duplicity, I threw my arms around his neck and pressed myself close to him, now more than ever, fearful of the underworld of which I was part – into which I'd been born. And now Matt was involved.

Alec held me tight and murmured into my hair. 'My darling, do you forgive me?'

'You could've been killed.' I pulled back to look at him. 'Why did you go alone? Where was Luc?'

He shook his head. 'Judith's blood's waning, and Luc's losing his day tolerance.'

He'd had no choice but to go after Timur alone. My stomach convulsed. 'Promise me something,' I said.

'Anything.'

'Never keep secrets from me again.'

'That's a promise.' Drawing me back into his arms, he chuckled. I felt his body relax.

I rested my head on his shoulder. 'Now what happens?'

'I'm working on it. In the meantime, you need to eat. I'm

going to make breakfast.'

I raised my head and gave him an incredulous look. The last time he "made" me breakfast, he'd ordered it from a café near his penthouse. 'If this is by way of an apology for keeping the truth about Matt's memory loss from me, it'd better be spectacular.'

He laughed, leaned down and kissed the curve of my breasts then leapt out of bed, picked up his wet jeans off the floor and strode from my room.

CHAPTER 18 - BRUNCH

ALEC

I went to the room they reserved for me on the yacht, took a quick shower and changed into fresh clothes. Thoughts of Laura consumed me, and our lovemaking played through my mind. I couldn't remember the last time I laughed and had fun during sex; enjoying the teasing then watching the growing climax in my lover's eyes just before her glorious release. She was my mate; my other half, and I would die for her.

It was well into mid-morning and only Luc and Judith were awake. The rest of the men were deep in their day sleep, so I wouldn't see any of them until sunset.

I went up to the main deck, through the salon and past the dining room before sensing Judith's presence in the galley.

'I didn't expect to see you up.' She was making a pot of tea and presumably would take it back to the room she shared with Luc. The tray was laden with cup, saucer, sugar and biscuits. Not that Luc would eat any of it, except via Judith's blood.

'Laura's awake,' I said, as I opened the stainless-steel refrigerator. 'Going to serve her breakfast in bed.'

'Alec, I hope you're not expecting....'

I stuck my head in the fridge. 'There's nothing in here.'

'Of course there isn't. I haven't had time to restock. Everything happened so suddenly. We just have the basics – tea, coffee, dried milk, biscuits.'

Something spectacular, Laura had warned. Now what?

'Try this,' she said and handed me a glossy pamphlet. 'It's one of my favourite restaurants, and they deliver. When your order arrives, arrange it nicely on a tray and take it up to her.'

'You're getting to be as bossy as Luc.'

'Am I?'

'Yes.' I smiled and waved the pamphlet. 'But thanks for this.'

'Good luck,' she said, picked up her tray and left.

I scanned the menu, chose something that hopefully Laura would like and gave them a call.

CHAPTER 19 - TEASE

LAURA

When Alec left, I bounced off the bed and headed straight for the shower. Thanks to him, I smelled of seawater. After standing beneath the multi-jet showerhead for nearly twenty minutes – I figured I had time, being convinced he was going to order something rather than cook it – I wrapped a fluffy towel around myself, plaited my hair and draped it over one shoulder. Now, should I dress or get back into bed, naked, and wait for him? The latter idea sounded more fun.

I straightened the bed, rearranged the pillows and climbed back in, with the summer sheet barely covering my breasts. To make them more prominent, I rubbed my nipples till they stood erect and peeked through the thin coverlet. I made myself comfortable and waited for the door to open.

I didn't need to wait long. I'd timed it perfectly.

'Your brunch, my lady.' He bowed as he entered but nearly dropped the metal tray he carried when he looked up.

I smiled and exposed one leg from beneath the cover.

Alec stood there, staring, but I could feel the burning path his gaze left as it travelled over me.

'Smells yum' I said.

'It certainly does,' he said at last. I knew he wasn't referring to my breakfast … or was it brunch?

He stalked toward me like a panther, placed the food on the table and ran his hand along the inside of my leg. As he reached my thigh I withdrew it beneath the covers, glanced at the tray and patted my lap.

His eyes narrowed and a smile lifted the corners of his mouth. Without a word, he put the tray on my lap. There were three separate dishes. My stomach growled in anticipation, completely ruining my little tease act. From the corner of my eye, I glimpsed his smile widen.

I lifted the first silver lid and viewed the array, my senses seduced by the mouth-watering aromas. The first dish contained half-a-dozen king prawns barbequed in – I sniffed – mango and lime sauce. The largest dish had a pair of quails in aspic arranged on a bed of barley with cashews, mushrooms and various greens. The last – dessert – was rich, dark and velvety chocolate mousse topped with a black cherry.

No way he cooked this. But I appreciated the effort it took to order it. A solitary red rose finished the ensemble. I inhaled its delicate scent. 'Thank you.'

Alec took my hand and kissed it. 'My pleasure.' He pulled up a chair and leaned it back against the wall. With his arms behind his head, each taut muscle accentuated, he was the image of every woman's dream centrefold. *My centrefold.*

Time to have some fun.

I picked up a prawn, tipped my head back, lowered it into my mouth then slowly withdrew it. 'Mmmm!' As he stared, I bit it off at the tail. I did the same to the next and the one after, until they were all gone.

His eyes turned a deep, dark purple.

I pushed aside the empty plate and lifted the lid from the quail. Steaming, a delicious aroma wafting up, I closed my eyes, inhaled deeply and slowly licked my lips.

'Laura.'

I looked up. Alec's eyes were burning. I smiled, bit my lip and picked up the tender meat, letting the sweet juices run down my fingers.

'This is delicious,' I said as I savoured each piece before languidly licking the sauce that had trickled down the side of my hand.

Alec swallowed.

I wanted to see what would happen if I sucked each finger clean instead of using the napkin.

Alec's eyes widened, and he inhaled sharply.

Never in my life had I played a man in such a way. I loved it.

'Laura.'

'Mmmm?'

'You keep doing that and I doubt you'll finish that meal.' His eyes had darkened further.

I feigned innocence. 'Doing what?'

He smiled wickedly, and my stomach flipped as the memory of the heights to which he could bring me.

He breathed hard. 'What a tease.'

'Oh?' This time, I picked up a small, round potato and popped it into my mouth. 'You'll taste this later.'

Alec's eyes blazed. 'How about now.'

He leaned forward, grabbed the tray off my lap and dumped it on the bedside table. 'My turn to eat,' he said, and dragged me further down the bed, threw aside the sheet and parted my legs.

Now *I* swallowed.

Keeping his eyes on me, he lowered his head between my thighs.

I bucked as his tongue tasted and savoured me and his hands stroked my already sensitive skin. I grabbed the rails of the bedhead behind me and held tight as he took me to new heights of ecstasy.

'Who's teasing now?' He chuckled and went back to his delicious torture. He drove me on and on, until I cried out in pleasure, and he bit down and fed from my inner thigh.

A sense of tranquility suffused my body, and my breathing evened out. I let go of the railing and ran my hands through his soft, raven hair. Never had I been so thoroughly sated, so utterly content, and so at one with a man – and he was drawing blood from me.

I closed my eyes and basked in the afterglow while he drank.

When he lifted his head and gazed at me, his eyes were glazed and a drop of blood stained his lower lip. I was transfixed as his tongue slid across his lip and drew it into his mouth. Alec's gaze remained riveted on me as he sucked my finger, his tongue laved the tip, exciting me once more.

He stood and removed his clothes. Moving slowly, he kissed his way up my body, interlaced his fingers with mine and surged deep into me.

A moan escaped my lips as my body surrendered to the passion, and the ecstasy of being utterly possessed.

We spent the day making love; making the most of the brief time we could come together before nightfall, and the dangers that brought with it. Somewhere in between I managed to finish my dessert, and afterwards Alec held me to him and gently stroked my face.

I must have fallen asleep. A noise woke me. My pearl mesh pouch was buzzing. Or rather, the mobile phone inside it. I glanced at Alec but he was asleep. I picked up the phone and checked the caller, but no name appeared. I pressed the answer button. 'Hello, Laura here.' My voice was croaky.

'Miss Dantonville? I thought it best to ring you—'

'I'm sorry, who is this?'

Alec stirred.

'Mrs. Henderson, love. I think you may have had an intruder in your flat last night. I wasn't sure whether to call you. It was early in the morning, well late last night actually, four a.m. Salieri woke me up. Perhaps I should have called the police.'

I was suddenly wide awake. 'No, it's okay, Mrs. Henderson. If the police need to be called, I'll do it.'

Alec sat up, alert.

'He scared the life out of me.' She went on. 'I was fast asleep, you see. To see what the fuss was about, I went to the window and had a look. There was no one out there; no car, only motorbikes. Three big black ones.'

It was like a brick had settled in my stomach – the group of rebels who had attacked Alec had been on motorbikes. I glanced his way. His mouth was set in a tight line. 'Tell her someone's on the way,' he whispered.

'Mrs. Henderson, I'm on my way.' I hung up.

'No! You can't come. It's too dangerous.' He bounded off the bed.

'It's them, isn't it? The ones who attacked you last night?'

'Stockton.' Alec looked dangerous as he grabbed his clothes off the floor and threw them on.

'He's one of them?'

'Rasputin's henchman.'

'I'm coming with you.' Not waiting for his reply I leapt out of bed and headed for the built-in wardrobe.

'No, you're not.'

'Alec, it's my flat. I'll know if anything is missing or been moved or … whatever.' I found my underwear and put them on.

Alec was silent. I turned my head to look at him.

'All right, but the moment I say, we have to leave.'

'Okay.'

'Five minutes, Laura,' he said as he headed out the door.

In less than a minute I had thrown on a belted T-shirt dress, slipped on a pair of sandals and re-plaited my hair. I grabbed my phone and dropped it into the front pocket of my dress on the way out.

Alec was pacing the floor in the corridor, talking on his mobile phone. He ended the call when I came out and dropped it into his back pocket. As he looked at me, his eyes softened. 'Pity the day couldn't end on a better note.'

'We had the best part.' I reached up and kissed him. The taste of my blood still lingered on his tongue.

He returned the kiss with equal fervour. 'Let's go.'

With his arm around my waist, we dashed off the yacht and made our way along the jetty, dread settling in my stomach at what I would find.

CHAPTER 20 – UNINVITED GUESTS

LAURA

I stared out the car window as Alec drove. It was Monday afternoon, and although it wasn't peak hour, the traffic was heavy. What should have been a fifteen-minute trip took nearly double. I couldn't keep my feet still, nor my knees from bouncing as Alec wove through the clogged streets.

What would I find in my flat? I clenched my fists.

We turned into my street, and everything seemed normal. But then, how many people knew what went on in their neighbours' places?

Alec parked the car in front of my unit block, came round the side of the car and opened the door for me. I practically ran to my front door.

Alec caught up to me and grabbed my hand. 'Careful.' He lifted his head and took a deep breath before opening the main doors to the building.

'Can you smell something?' I asked.

'Human and Brethren. They were here.'

I tightened my grip on his hand.

He raised his other hand and checked the serpent ring. Its eyes were red. No danger. I released a strangled breath and held out my key for him, but before he turned it, the door swung open – the lock was broken. He glanced at me, tucked me behind him and took a step in. Another deep breath. 'Three of them,' he said. 'At least ten-to-twelve hours ago.'

'Why would they come here?'

Alec shook his head.

My apartment looked as if a whirlwind had gone through it – furniture upturned, the stuffing from cushions torn out and strewn around the place, framed pictures lying on the floor, their glass coverings shattered. The vase in which I'd placed Alec's flowers lay broken on the floor, the water soaked into the carpet. What was left of his note lay beside it, torn to shreds.

They're not going to make me cry.

I released Alec's hand and spun around. At least the cabinets hadn't been touched. Perhaps they realised, sometime during their rampage, how much noise they were making. The kitchen appeared intact. There was no broken crockery or evidence of damage.

'I'd better check my bedroom. 'I'd better check my bedroom.' The word "sickened" didn't even come close to how I felt by this violation.

'I'll see what I can do here,' he said, and as I raced for the bedroom, I heard him righting the furniture.

I wasn't prepared for what confronted me. Bits and pieces of fabric – all that was left of my clothes – were strewn on the floor. The bedcovers had met the same fate. The spilled contents of my jewellery cases littered my dressing table. Some of my framed photos were smashed, while others lay face down on the mess.

It was too much. I let out a cry then covered my mouth with my shaking hands.

Alec reached my side in an instant. 'Laura …Of all the madness.' He looked stunned.

'They cut up my clothes; shredded them!' Amidst the rubble, I recognised the remains of one of my favourite dresses. I bent and picked it up. 'Look! I bought this for my birthday and wore it the night we met at St Andrews. Oh, Alec.'

He wrapped me in his arms. 'I'm so sorry, darling.'

I clutched the remains of my beautiful dress in one hand and the front of Alec's T-shirt in the other, unable to hold back a sob.

'I promise we'll catch them.'

'It's not the things; it's the memories. Why would they do this?' My voice choked.

'Sending a message, I suspect.'

Something caught my eye. I left the security of Alec's arms, stepped over one of the piles and picked up a framed photo I kept beside my bed. It was one of Jen and me, taken at the Melbourne Cup races. It was strange. The photo was missing, and I couldn't see it anywhere among the piles of clothing remnants. What on earth would they want with it?

I showed Alec. 'Why would they take this?'

He frowned, and then his eyes widened. 'Is there anything here that would have Jenny's scent on it?'

It took a moment for me to realise what he meant. 'Um, let me think. A book. She lent me a book. Believe it or not, about vampires.' The book wasn't on the bedside table where I'd left it, so I rummaged through the debris on my bedroom floor.

'What does it look like?' Alec asked.

'White and red cover.'

He and I searched every shelf and beneath every piece of furniture in the room without finding it.

'Definitely not here,' I said.

'Ring her. Tell her to come and stay with you on the yacht for a few days.'

'You think she could be in danger?'

'I'm convinced of it. Ask her to come before nightfall.'

'To stay on a boat full of vampires?' I looked at him incredulously and the words tumbled out of me. 'How am I going to hide the fact they only come out at night? And how on earth am I going to tell her about you? She still thinks I'm dating Matt. There's no way I can reveal what you are, or the whole Ritual bit. And what about my real parents? Do I tell her? She'll have to meet you eventually, I suppose. I was just hoping it wouldn't come so soon. Give me time to think.' I ran out of breath.

'Laura, Laura darling,' he said softy, gripping my upper arms and turning me to face him. 'It'll be fine.' He sounded confident, assuring and strong. 'Just tell her what you told the police. She doesn't need to know my eating habits.' His mouth turned up at the corners.

I took a deep breath and let it out slowly. 'Okay. She knows I was treated at your hospital and the rest ....'

'The rest is none of her business.'

'I hate lying; you know that. We've never really had secrets from each other, and now I have this overwhelming one.'

'If it's any consolation, Judith couldn't tell anyone about you,' he said gently.

Well, that one hit home. I couldn't begin to imagine the pain my mother must have suffered having to keep my existence a secret, not just from friends but her own family. My dilemma paled in comparison. 'You're right.'

'Maybe one day, just not right now, darling, although there's no harm with revealing the truth about your parentage; if you want.'

'I'm okay with that.' *Besides, Jenny's safety is more important.* It then occurred to me that Jenny may not have heard about the fire- I hope. If she had, I would've received a panicked phone call by now. We were on school summer holidays so the odds of her hearing it on the daytime news – TV or radio – were high. I pressed speed dial and waited for her to answer.

'Hey girlfriend. What's up?' She sounded relaxed.

'Hi Jen. What are you doing the next few days?' I thought it best to get straight to the point. Sunset wasn't too far away.

'Nothing in particular. Why?'

Unlike me, Jenny had no family. She'd been orphaned as a child, raised by a great aunt, and was currently single. Her ex left when he found out she couldn't have kids.

'Come and stay a few days. Have Christmas with me and the family.' An image of "my family" popped into my head – both the human and the non-human. I shook my head.

'Oh Laura hon, that'd be great! I didn't fancy spending Christmas with Aunty Dory at the nursing home. I was kind of, well, still working out what to do. Sure it's okay?'

'Of course it is, and we'll be on a yacht.'

'Wow! When can I come?' She laughed.

'I'll pick you up now.'

She laughed again. 'Whoa, hon, I need to sort a few things

first; I'm not as organised as you. Gimme a couple a hours and I'll drive there.'

I wasn't happy but I couldn't press her without explaining why. 'Okay, but come as soon as you can. Drive to the front of Aunt Judy's house, the address in Vaucluse, and text me when you get there.' It felt strange referring to my mother as "aunty", although that's how I'd known her all my life. I much preferred "mum" now that I knew the truth, yet for all our sakes I had to maintain the pretence. If only I could tell Jenny everything.

'I'll see you then.'

'Get there before dark,' I insisted.

'Will do.' She hung up.

I stared at the phone wondering how this was going to work.

As if reading my mind, Alec said, 'It's not the best solution, but for now it's all we have.'

I looked around the remains of my apartment, and a tear slid down my cheek. I swiped it away. 'How dare they! And now they're threatening my friends.'

'Not if we catch them first, darling.' His arms around me were like a warm cocoon.

'This is my place; my sanctuary.'

Alec lifted my chin. 'When this is over, I promise we'll make a new one, just for us. You can fill it with whatever you like, however you want it.'

'All our own?'

'All ours.'

I turned in his arms and surveyed the compact two-bedroom apartment I'd called home for the past eleven years. 'I loved living here,' I whispered.

As we stood there, banging sounded on the door. I jumped. 'It's Mrs. Henderson, for sure. If she gets suspicious, she'll ring the police.'

'Don't worry. I'll handle it.' Alec went to the door and opened it a fraction, enough for her to see him, but not enough for her to glimpse the lounge area.

'Hello, Mrs. Henderson,' he said.

'Oh! It's you again. I, um, saw your car and … is Miss Dantonville here?' She tried to peer around him but Alec blocked her view.

'Yes, I'm here, Mrs. Henderson,' I called as I began a hurried clean up.

'Is everything all right, love? I heard sounds coming from here last night, things crashing and banging.' Alec leaned nonchalantly against the doorway, further blocking her view.

'Fine. Fine. It must have been a cat. Nothing to be concerned about,' I said and began to hiccup! *Crap!* It happened each time I tried to lie – like an inbuilt lie preventer.

'Cat? You don't have one. Are you sure everything's okay, love?' Her voice was breathless.

'Mrs. Henderson everything's—'

'Fine, really,' I said and joined Alec. She was puffing after climbing the stairs to my apartment, while trying to bend her considerable bulk and peer through his legs. 'It must have got in through the window. There's no need to worry any further. Thank you for ringing me.'

'It's my responsibility, you know, to keep an eye on this building.' Her eyes narrowed. 'Well, if you're absolutely sure, love. But weren't your windows all closed?' She tried peering around my shoulder.

'Um, no. I forgot one.' I hiccupped again. *Crap!*

'Surely if there was a cat, my Salieri would have known. But he jumped on my bed, hissing, and refused to come out from under the cover.'

'A possum?' I sounded increasingly desperate.

'There are no possums in this area, love.'

Alec cleared his throat – I'd never heard him do that before – turned his head and looked at me with one raised eyebrow. I knew what he was asking – mesmerisation. I hated the idea of it, but Mrs. Henderson was so persistent.

I nodded.

'Look at me, Mrs. Henderson,' he said, his voice low and hypnotic. 'A large possum entered Miss Dantonville's unit. It only caused minimal damage. Nothing to worry about. Salieri needs you.'

Her eyes glazed over as she repeated what Alec had said.

'Goodbye, Mrs. Henderson.' He closed the door and turned to me. 'You don't need a guard dog with dear Mrs. Henderson around. I wonder why Luc bothered.'

I rolled my eyes. 'I'm so glad she doesn't know about my hiccupping. That would have given it all away.'

'And she never will.' He drew me into his arms.

'That's twice now you've had to mesmerise her.' Later I'd ask how many times he could do that to a person without it causing some form of damage.

'Persistent, isn't she?' he remarked.

'You have no idea.'

'I think I'm beginning to.' His mouth curled up into a smile. With my nosey neighbour dispatched, it was time to get back to the problem at hand. 'Let's lock it up for now, till you decide what you want done with it,' he suggested.

I sighed and gave a small nod. 'How long do you think we'll be on the yacht?'

'A few weeks, till repairs on Luc's house are completed.'

'What about your apartment? Couldn't we go there?' I pulled out of his embrace and looked up at him.

'I'd love you to, but I can't guarantee your safety there any more than here. It's not geared for security the way Luc's place is. I've never needed it.'

'Bugger. So your apartment's been abandoned, too.'

'I'm hardly there anyway.'

I reached up and ran my arms around his neck. 'So for now, do we sleep in your cabin or mine?'

'Which would you prefer?' He gave me a slow smile.

'You've already sampled mine. My turn to check yours out.'

His hands wandered to my backside and squeezed me closer. 'We can always toss for it.' He leaned down and kissed me. 'Much as I'd love this to continue, it'll be dark in a couple of hours. Anything here you'd like to take with you?'

I looked around and shook my head. 'Nothing. I have more than enough to wear at Luc's.'

'All right. Quick tidy up, then lock it.'

The broken and unsalvageable objects we placed in storage boxes I'd kept from when I moved here. As we left we dumped it all in the garbage bins. In the remaining time, we cleaned up the mess and I bagged the ripped clothing. After a long, last look at my home of eleven years, I closed the door and – after some fiddling – Alec managed to secure the lock.

CHAPTER 21 – BEST FRIENDS AND LOVERS

LAURA

By the time Alec and I drove back to Vaucluse, it was early evening and the sun was casting long shadows on the gravelled path leading past the house to the jetty. Luc must have organised for the repairs to begin. Warning signs had been erected on the steel barricades that now blocked access to the sides and rear sections of the mansion – the areas most damaged by the fire. Although the main driveway, the front entrance and rest of the house were unaffected, a sign had been placed on the door, directing all enquiries to the site office – Luc's yacht.

'It's our temporary floating residence,' Alec said. 'It ensures the locals know we're on the premises.'

I could understand that. Why give burglars an open invitation.

'Is that what you call it, The Residence? I heard Marcus mention it.' It reminded me of the White House or Buckingham Palace. Perhaps that was the vampire equivalent of the position my family held in their world – my world, too, I had to keep reminding myself.

'Yes. Wherever the Ingenii and princeps currently reside. For the last seventeen-or-so-hundred years Luc has held that position so it's become synonymous with him.'

'What if we want to live somewhere else?' My ancestral family "seat" was not exactly the sort of permanent home I'd envisaged for myself. Yet I could appreciate the practicality its size afforded – a place to house my father's entourage, accommodate high-ranking visiting Brethren and host those special ceremonies human eyes could never be allowed to see.

'I'd build something new, but it'd have to be large enough to function in the same way as Luc's. It's the *Princeps Oblige* – Obligation of the Princeps,' he said, as we strode past the giant fig trees and the blue wisteria-covered pavilion where Alec had kissed me for the first time, during the Ritual.

The memory would always remain with me – whenever I smelled the delicate scent of wisteria mingled with the heady perfume of fallen frangipanis on the soft summer air, I thought of our first kiss.

I leant my head against his arm and tried to imagine what our house would be like. 'No gargoyles,' I said. I wanted a home, not a museum; a place for children to run and play.

'That's a promise.' He smiled, and kissed the tips of our interlaced fingers.

The yacht windows glinted gold in the light of the setting sun, although no light came from the portholes on the lower decks. Their occupants must be still sleeping until it was dark enough to rise. I prayed Jenny would get here before then.

Luc and Judy sat on the open upper deck, each with a glass in hand. Luc's was red – red wine or A positive? Judy beckoned for us to join them. The deck gave an unhindered view of the bay and, in the distance, the magnificent sandstone cliffs – the North Heads – that acted as a natural gateway to the Pacific Ocean beyond.

Alec approached Luc, bent and whispered something in his ear. I guessed it had to do with the break-in at my flat.

'Excuse me, ma cherie,' Luc said to Judy. He got up and went indoors with Alec.

'Everything okay, dear?' Judy asked, as she watched them leave.

I sat next to her on the curved settee and looked out at the darkening water. 'Someone broke into my unit. Alec sensed it was the same group who attacked him last night.'

She sucked in a breath and placed her drink on the table. 'Did they take anything?'

'A book Jen lent me.' I turned and gazed in the direction of the garden, half of which was now in shadow. *What's keeping her?* 'He thinks they might be after her, to use her against us. I phoned … invited her to stay with us for a few days. Is that okay?' I angled my head and looked at her.

'Oh, my dear. Of course it is. We have room enough.'

'She's in danger because of me.' Unable to sit still, I went to the railing and strained my eyes to see past the trees, in case I could spot her walking down the path, although I'd asked her to text me first. She wouldn't know the way. *Maybe I should wait for her outside. And put yourself in danger?* My inner voice warned. I dug the phone from my pocket. No message. My fingers pressed into the railing.

Judy stood next to me and placed an arm around my shoulders. 'It's not your fault. These Rebels will do anything to take control.' She gazed in the same direction. 'When did you ring her?'

'Um, a couple of hours ago.'

'There's still time, dear. It's not dark yet.' Although her voice sounded calm, I felt her body tense. 'Put her in the room opposite yours. It's not being used.'

We stood for a few minutes in silence and watched as the LED lights flashed on and lit up the length of the jetty. My phone buzzed and I dove my hand into my pocket to retrieve it.

A message from Jenny. 'I'm at the front gate. Where R U???'

'Finally! She's out front,' I said to Judy, with a mix of relief and trepidation.

'Tell her to drive in and park in front of the house, near the rose bushes, and we'll meet her there.'

I'd never been afraid of the dark, but recent events and the knowledge that there were powerful, immortal beings out there who envied my family's privileged position, had changed all that. Luc's grounds were safe, I told myself – his security would immediately detect intruders, and Luc and Alec were only a whisper way. They were more powerful than any of their enemies. Yet the niggling fear remained.

Judy turned her face toward the stateroom through which Luc and Alec had disappeared. 'Luc,' she said, 'Laura and I are going to the front of the house to pick up a guest.' The phone in her dress pocket rang a second later. 'He says to go. They'll be watching.'

Ah, vampire hearing. I breathed easier.

She linked her arm through mine, and we walked briskly the few hundred metres, or so, to the front drive. My stomach clenched as I wondered how I would handle this – my best friend in the company of vampires for the next few days. Plus, there'd be no hiding the fact I'd broken up with Matt once she met Alec. *That* was unavoidable. I sighed. It would probably be so much easier to blurt everything out and hope for the best.

Jenny's white Subaru was parked exactly where she'd been directed. The boot was open and the upper half of her body was bent over as she tried to lift something from its depths. She wriggled her jeans-clad backside and dragged out a large suitcase, which she dumped on the uneven gravel surface with a crunch. She slammed the boot shut and gave me a huge grin.

'I owe you, big time,' she said.

'For what? After the incredible birthday present you gave me.' Jenny had got me front row seats to the Edinburgh Military Tattoo, performing for the first time in Sydney. She knew I loved the bagpipes. She and I were going in February. Alec, of course, was coming too. I was thrilled when he told me he had his own set.

'Anyway, how are *you*?' Her large brown eyes shone as she gave me a hug.

'Fine.'

'No after effects, like dizziness or anything?'

The bump on the head I received when abducted by rogue vampires hadn't caused any lasting damage, only a headache. 'Nope. I'm really fine.'

As I pulled out of the hug, Jenny caught my hand. 'Wow! Nice ring. Where did you get that?'

'Um, birthday present. Got it last Friday.'

'Who from?' She examined it more closely.

'My aunt Judy,' I responded mechanically, hoping that would end the interrogation. How could I possibly tell her that "Aunt Judy" was my mother?

'Hello Jenny. Nice to see you again.' Judy moved forward and offered her hand.

Jenny looked her up and down and returned the shake. 'You. Look. Amazing!' She knew Judy and I shared the same age retarding gene, and that "my aunt" was a few weeks off celebrating her centenary. But she didn't know that – unlike Judy – I had stopped ageing. Jenny was only thirty-four and she once jokingly asked if I would share my blood with her so she could look as young.

Judy laughed and good-humouredly patted her own cheek. 'Good moisturiser. Now, let's get back to the yacht.'

It was getting dark.

'What *is* this place?' Jenny absently picked up her bag. Her brown eyes widened and roamed past me to the house. 'It's a bloody castle.'

'Sorry I can't show you inside. There was an … um …' Jenny knew my lying handicap, so I didn't want to risk it.

'A minor accident. Fire in the cellar, an electrical fault,' Judy finished for me.

'Come on, Jen. The yacht's out in the bay.' Eager to get all of us safely aboard, I helped her carry her bag.

'Whose yacht is it?'

'Mine and my husband's,' Judy replied. 'It's called, *My Judy*.'

'How romantic,' Jenny said and looked at me with raised eyebrows. I'd never mentioned the existence of an "uncle" before. At the time, I didn't know there was one.

In the few minutes it took us to walk from the car back to the garden, the sun had set, and the first stars peeped between the clouds. It was a calm, warm evening. The branches of the trees were still, yet a slight breeze brushed against my skin and drifted through my hair, almost as though something – or someone – had run past at high speed. The shock that someone could be here, undetected, made the blood drain from my cheeks. I spun around but saw no one.

'What is it?' Jenny asked.

I had nearly wrenched the bag from her grip. 'Nothing. Just thought I heard something. Probably a possum.'

I glanced at the serpent ring on my hand. It glowed a rich scarlet, so there was no danger. My heart resumed its normal beat. Could it have been my imagination?

Jenny chuckled. 'Bats, more like it. With all these fig trees, I'm not surprised.'

Judy let out a sudden laugh then quickly bit her lip.

If fruit bats were the only problem I'd be thrilled. 'Let's get to the boat.' I doubled my pace.

'Is that yours?' Jenny's mouth hung open when we reached the jetty and she saw the yacht. 'It's like a mini cruise liner.'

Indeed it was. All four decks were hung with multi-coloured lanterns that illuminated its sleek length, their reflections a glittering rainbow along the water. Lights shone from every window and porthole – its occupants had woken for the night. I needed to get Jenny on board before she met any of them. That time would come soon enough.

'C'mon, let's get you settled in your cabin, and then we'll have a cuppa,' I said, as Judy led the way onto the main deck. *I'll tell her everything when the time's right. Not now.*

'I'll join you girls later.' Judy left, and we descended the stairs to the bedrooms.

Jenny looked about and shook her head in awe. 'What money can buy.'

'They've put you in the VIP room, Jen.' We strolled down the carpeted corridor to the fore, as Judy had called it.

'What's her husband do?'

'Real estate.'

She whistled. 'That explains it.'

'That's my room.' I pointed at a door with the gold Roman numeral, I, on it. 'And this is yours.' I opened the opposite door, bearing the numeral, II on it, and switched on the light.

Jenny's eyes widened. 'Oh, am I going to enjoy these next few days.'

So am I. In spite of everything, it was lovely to have her here. She was my link to the human world, a piece of life I could view as "normal." I wanted to hang onto that for as long as possible.

I stepped aside to let her through.

Her room was identical in layout to mine, with its white walls and queen size bed set at an angle, a built-in desktop with black trim and accompanying chair. But that's where the similarity ended – my room had a blue colour scheme, hers was light green. The splashes of wavy green lines on the carpet matched those on the curtains and silky bedspread, complimenting the scene of a coral reef in the framed watercolour above the bed.

'Have you eaten?' I sat on the edge of the bed as Jenny hoisted her bag onto the floating desk, flipped open the lid and began to unpack.

'Yeah, hon, don't worry. But that cuppa sounds good.'

'Press the white panelling and it'll pop open,' I said, when she searched for somewhere to hang her clothes.

'Huh! Now don't look, cos I'm hiding your Christmas present in here. Haven't had time to wrap it.'

Crap! Presents. I made a mental note to go shopping at the first opportunity. 'That's why your bag was so heavy.'

Jenny laughed. 'Not telling. You'll just have to wait.'

She removed her toiletry bag and whistled when she opened the door to the ensuite bathroom. 'Nice. How long can I stay?'

'As long as you want.' *Till we catch those who trashed my unit and took your book and photo.*

When she was ready, I took her to the bar in the main salon where I'd noticed an espresso machine. 'Take a seat,' I said.

Jenny perched on one of the stools, leant her elbows on the counter and cupped her chin in her hands. 'Now, tell me what happened.'

'Tea or coffee?'

'Coffee, thanks.'

I added the coffee capsules and while the machine bubbled away, told her what had happened last Tuesday night, minus any reference to vampires, my kidnapping and torture by the nasty female vampire who wanted me dead. But I had to admit to Alec's rescue – well the version we'd given the police – and being brought to his hospital instead of to Royal Prince Alfred.

By the time I finished, the coffee was ready. I poured out two cups and handed her one.

'Thank God you were okay. Have you seen Matt since getting out?'

I nodded. 'He's okay, but this next bit's complicated.' I took a deep breath and mentally rehearsed what I was about to say. 'The bang on the head damaged his memory. For the first few days he didn't remember me. Amnesia. Doctors said he might not get it back.'

Jenny's mouth fell open. 'You can't be serious!'

'He lost about six months.'

'Holy crap.'

I shrugged and steeled myself for the next bombshell. 'We broke up.'

'What do you mean?'

'What I said: we broke up.' I sipped my coffee and hoped the caffeine would stimulate my brain cells into providing plausible answers.

She stared at me while the news sank in. 'But ... he and you ...'

'He didn't remember me, Jen. Nothing. Zero. Zilch. And he wasn't interested in me either.' I thought it best to leave out his parting words. They were anything but flattering.

'Oh, Laura, I'm so sorry,' she said in a disbelieving tone and placed her hand over mine.

'Why are you sorry? You're not responsible.'

'Well, it's what people say, isn't it?' She left her seat and placed her arms around me in a comforting embrace, ever the mother hen. In spite of the seriousness of our conversation, I couldn't help smiling, till she said, 'What's the complicated part? You said for the first few days. Oh, you mean his memory's come back and he wants to make up?'

'Jen, it's too late. I, um....' I clenched my coffee cup. 'I'm in love with Alec Munro.'

She released me and nearly fell back onto her bar stool. 'The doctor who treated you?' I nodded. 'This is happening way too fast, Laura. Okay, he saved your life, but that's no reason to fall for the guy. You only met him a few days ago.'

'That's got nothing to do with it. We've spent a lot of time together and, I've gotten to know him. Sometimes it takes only a day to see a man's qualities.'

She looked at me for a couple of seconds. 'Well, I don't know what to say, hon.'

Jenny was being cautious, and I could understand why. She was the one who usually fell easily for a handsome face and muscular body, only to regret it later. How could I prove to her that wasn't the case with myself and Alec?

'You must meet him.'

'I need another one of these first.' She held out her empty cup. 'Got anything stronger?'

I opened one of the glass cabinets and spied several bottles – wine, brandy, whisky, liqueurs and an unopened Hunter Valley red. I found a couple of glasses and filled them. 'What'll we toast to?'

'You. That you're safe, and to your happiness.'

We clinked glasses. I drank, more out of relief than anything else. It had gone better than I anticipated. *Hurdle number one accomplished?* Perhaps. Yet I knew Jen well enough to know there'd be more questions later.

'Poor Matt,' she said.

I was about to tell her about the young emergency doctor to whom Matt had been giving all his attention, when Terens walked in, wearing nothing but a short towel slung low around his hips. His arm had regenerated completely – not even a scar remained.

Jenny nearly dropped her glass.

He went straight to the fridge, opened it and peered in. 'Hey, where's the juice?'

I blinked in disbelief. How on earth was I going to explain him? That was my first panicked thought, quickly followed by another when I saw the serpent tattoo on his chest. It was identical to my ring.

'Terens!' Alec appeared from nowhere. 'There's more in the gym fridge.'

'Just heading there,' he said, closed the door and turned to Jenny and me. He sent us both a dazzling smile. 'Hi, pet and friend.'

Terens always called me "pet".

Jenny's eyes were as wide as saucers as she looked from Terens to Alec and back again.

I had hoped to introduce Alec to Jenny tonight, but hadn't planned on her meeting any of his friends – and especially not in the shape of a half-naked Adonis!

'Then go there now. You're not exactly appropriately dressed,' Alec said, indicating with his head for him to leave.

'Hey, I've got the vitals covered,' he retorted, without taking his eyes off my best friend.

Jenny reacted as she always did when faced with an unusual

situation – she laughed. So did Terens, and as his eyes moved to her throat, his pupils dilated.

Oh crap! 'Jen this is Doctor Alec Munro, and this––,' I said, indicating Terens,

'Is my friend, Terens,' Alec finished for me. 'Who's just leaving.'

Terens ignored him, pulled up another bar stool and placed it right next to Jenny. 'Jen is it? Nice to meet you.' He raised her hand and kissed her fingertips.

Jenny's eyes glazed over. It was the first time I'd seen her lost for words.

'Beautiful name for a beautiful woman.' As he released her hand, he brushed the back of his fingers down the curve of her neck.

Jenny froze and gaped at him.

Alec gripped his shoulder. 'I'm sure the ladies would appreciate some time alone. Let's leave them to it.' There was no mistaking the warning in his voice.

Terens dropped his hand and gave a little chuckle. 'Until next time, lovely Jen.'

He rose, turned to Alec and gave him a light punch in the shoulder before striding from the room.

Jenny stared after him, looking shell-shocked.

I glanced up at Alec, who gave me an apologetic shrug.

He extended a hand to her. 'It's a pleasure to meet you. Laura's told me about you – all good,' he added with a smile when Jenny briefly turned to me with a questioning look.

'Ah, nice to meet you too.' She shook his hand.

'Now, if you'll excuse me.'

'Alec, wait, I need to ask you something.' I turned to Jen. 'Won't be a sec.' The breeze I'd felt against my cheek earlier this evening, when there had been no wind, still bothered me. We walked to the door.

'What is it?'

'In the garden, just before we came here, I felt something brush past me,' I whispered.

'Nothing to worry about. It was Karl. He and Milena thought it best to get back to secure their lands from a Rebel attack – especially from Timur. They left soon after sunset,' he whispered back.

That explained why I hadn't seen anything. 'Okay, that's all I needed to know.'

He gave my hand a gentle squeeze and left the room.

I turned back to Jenny.

'They. Are. Gorgeous. That guy Terens, is off the scale.'

I grinned. What was there to say?

'And what's he doing running around here in just a towel? Not that I don't appreciate it, mind.' She grinned.

Well, there was no hiding this. 'He's, um, part of security.'

Jenny's eyebrows shot up. 'Just how rich is your aunt Judy's man if he needs his own security?'

'Very.'

'That doctor?' She pointed with her thumb in the direction Alec and Terens had taken.

I nodded. 'That's him.'

'What's he doing here? And how come he's friends with that gorgeous minder?' She gave me her suspicious look – head lowered, lips pursed. 'What are you not telling me, Laura?'

My stomach dropped, and my mind went blank in a desperate search for a convincing story. There was no way I could tell her the truth, but I didn't want to lie. Jenny would know straight away. Like the rest of my family, she knew I'd hiccup if I had to lie. It always made her laugh, although I doubted that would be the case this time. 'Well, actually, you see—'

'Oh Laura! They're into drugs aren't they?' Her eyes widened and she sucked in a breath. 'That's why Towel Guy has that weird snake and sword tattoo on his chest. It's the same as your ring. Your aunt's bloke is some sort of drug baron, isn't he? Is that what you can't tell me?'

'What? No. He's absolutely legit. No drugs, Jen. Honestly, you really think Judy ... ah, my aunt, would have anything to do with a crook?'

'Then what? I'm not moving from here until you tell me.' She leaned forward, folded her arms her arms and waited.

I was trapped.

'Thought I'd join you ladies for coffee.'

At the sound of Alec's voice, her head swivelled around.

Relieved, I smiled at him. He'd obviously been listening to

our conversation, and on this occasion I could forgive him, for he could surely concoct a better story than I and get away with it. *He's had more practice.*

'Please do,' Jenny said. 'Perhaps you might have some answers.'

'To what?' He made his way to my side of the bar and placed another capsule in the espresso machine.

'What Laura's not telling me.' Jenny had that obstinate set to her jaw that I knew so well. Here come the questions – she could be like a bulldog when determined on a course.

'Honestly, Jen, nothing to tell.'

The coffee machine began to gurgle and he placed a mug under the nozzle. 'What would you like to know?'

I was sure Alec wasn't about to blurt out he was a vampire; so what he had in mind would to be news to me, too.

'For starters, how come you're here, and so familiar with the, ah, staff.'

I sighed and glanced briefly at Alec. His expression gave nothing away as he continued to gaze at Jenny, although the trace of a smile hovered at the corner of his lips.

'If I can assure you that nothing is amiss and Laura isn't involved in anything illegal, will that satisfy you?'

Jenny looked directly at me. 'Yes.'

'Since you know about Laura's rare blood type, I assume you also know about Judith's?'

Jenny gave a slight frown and nodded.

'I'm Judith's doctor. My hospital specialises in treating various blood diseases, and Judith's been instrumental in aiding our research. I come here a lot. Over time, I've gotten to know the family and the *staff* well.'

Jenny's face coloured, but she didn't look away. 'Okay.'

'Can we stop the interrogation now?' I asked.

'One last question.'

I raised my eyes to the ceiling.

'How come you were at Laura's flat when she and Matt were attacked?' She narrowed her eyes.

'Testing my new car navigation system. Tell me you've never done that?'

It was the same story we told the police.

'Is that why you took Laura,' she quickly glanced at me, 'to your hospital instead of the local one?'

'Exactly. They're not equipped to deal with such an unusual blood type. She could have died before the ambulance got her to Royal Prince Alfred.'

Jenny's eyes flared, and she gazed up at Alec with new respect. 'I had no idea.'

'Alec saved my life, Jen.'

'Okay, fine. But that doesn't explain why Terens has the same tattoo as your ring, Laura.'

I usually appreciated Jenny's keen eye, but not today.

'Hummppphh! Never noticed,' Alec replied. 'Must be a coincidence, nothing more.'

She looked down at his left hand. 'Then why are you wearing the same ring? What the hell's going on?'

Jenny would have to be told. I could see no way out. My heart sank.

Alec glanced at me, his eyes pale. Revealing the truth – at this stage anyway – was out of the question, and he was asking my permission to mesmerise her. I wanted to yell, No! as I hated the very thought of it, but did we have a choice? Jenny simply wasn't ready to know the truth about my connection to the "undead". Or was she?

Sadly, I gave in. 'I'm so sorry, Jen.'

'For what?'

'Look at me, Jenny,' Alec said, his voice low and hypnotic. Unable to disobey his command, she turned and her eyes locked onto his. 'The tattoo on Terens's body—'

I grabbed his arm. 'Alec, no. Please wait.' Regardless of the danger, I didn't want her mesmerised. It felt wrong, dishonest. I didn't want her, of all people, to be a casualty of my family's secret. Jenny was as close to me as a sister, and it mattered that her mind remained her own.

'Laura—'

'Matt knows the truth. Can't we trust Jen too?'

He looked at me long and hard, and slowly his eyes returned to their normal shade. 'If she can't take it—'

'I know, but I have to try.' Inwardly I prayed I was right.

Jenny blinked at me, a confused look on her face. 'What were you saying?'

I took her hands in mine. 'Jen, I need you to keep an incredible secret. Promise me you will.'

She frowned. 'Laura, you're not involved in—'

'No! Just shut up and listen. Don't say a word till I've finished. Okay?'

She pursed her lips, but after a moment said, 'Go for it.'

I took a deep breath. 'You know how my blood stops me from aging normally? Well, it's because I'm part vampire, on my father's side.' Her eyes popped. 'And it's also special. It allows his kind – vampires – to walk about during the day.' My cheeks were burning by this point. 'He feeds from me.' Her eyes darted to him, then back to me. 'And Judy's the same – her blood, that is – because she's my real mother. And her husband, Luc, is my father. I only found this out on my birthday. They hid me with John and Eilene – my aunt and uncle – to protect me from rogue vamps who want me. Or rather, they want my blood. And before I let you say anything, I'm not nuts, nor on drugs or playing a rotten trick on you.' I stopped for a moment as I ran out of breath, grabbed my phone, brought up Mum and Dad's number on the screen and showed it to Jenny. 'Look, you can check with them if you like.' I finally stopped and watched Jenny's face.

She gazed at the screen then up at me. 'You finished?'

'Yeah.'

'That's brilliant!' She held out her empty glass.

Alec and I glanced at one another – he with raised brows – as I refilled her glass. It was not the reaction I had expected. Where was the sceptical expression, the sarcastic remarks or pitying looks implying I needed therapy?

'I don't get it, Jen. You believe me? Just like that?' I snapped my fingers.

'Hon, I can tell if you're lying and you're not good at bullshit, which is why you've never been able to play April Fool's Day jokes on your students. Besides, it makes sense of something I overheard your mum say to your aunt when I was helping you move, something about your blood not being mature yet, and… the Brethren? I thought it was about your funny genes.'

'The Brethren is what they call themselves,' I said, almost in a daze. 'You believe in vampires?'

'Sure. I've been researching it for years. I never told you in case you thought I was weird. My secret.'

Alec laughed, filled the mug with coffee and handed it to me. Its delicious aroma had a reviving effect. I took a deep gulp and stared at Jen, wondering whether to strangle or hug her. 'And all this time I've been worried sick about telling you. Honestly Jen, I could just slap you.'

Jenny grinned at me before her gaze slid to Alec, and she seemed to be appraising him anew. 'You're for real?'

'As I live and breathe, but don't ask to see my fangs. Last time I did that it backfired.' He gave me a sidelong glance, followed by a grin.

How that man could turn my insides into jelly with just one look was unbelievable. On the night we met, he transformed in front of me. I screamed and everyone in the cathedral came running. My family's eighteen-hundred-year-old secret was blown in one night.

'He scared the life out of me first time he did it,' I said.

'Oh wow, I am so vindicated.' She took a couple more deep swallows of her wine.

I drank my coffee and shook my head. Who would've guessed that my best friend was a closet goth?

'What's with the tattoos and the ring?'

'My family crest – sign of the Dantonvilles. All my father's men have it on their chests, including Alec.'

'That is so cool. So,' she paused and cocked an eyebrow at me, 'that story, in your flat...?'

'All true, Jen. Matt was knocked out by a bunch of rogues who kidnapped me, and Alec risked his life to save me. But I'd lost a lot of blood. That's how I ended up in his hospital instead of with Matt at RPA. We had to modify the story for the police.'

'Does Matt know?'

'He does,' Alec said.

Jenny grimaced. 'What about those rogues?'

'We've dealt with them,' Alec replied. 'If you have any more questions, I know the perfect person to ask.'

I looked at him curiously.

'Terens,' he said, and a wicked smile played around his mouth.

I bit my lip to stop the laugh. Terens had forced us to confront Jenny with the truth. If he hadn't shown up half-naked, displaying the clan tattoo, she might still be in blissful ignorance. On the other hand, he may have done us a favour. At least now none of us would have to pretend around her, and that was liberating. And since Jenny believed in the existence of vampires, and had proved she could keep a secret, it was a win-win situation all around.

Mentally, I thanked Terens.

As expected, Jenny's eyes shone at the mention of his name.

Alec's mobile rang. He fished it from his back pocket and checked the screen before answering. 'Munro.' His expression changed and the hand holding mine tightened.

'Ow – Alec!'

He let go and I massaged my hand.

'Any fatalities?' he said. My chest constricted. His lips were taut as he listened and stared into the distance. 'Lock down. If the police come, you know what to do.' He listened again before saying, 'Excellent. Bring them to The Residence and make sure any altercations are cleaned up. And, Amanda, I don't want any humans involved... Good.' He pressed the "end call" button and slid the phone back into his jeans pocket.

'What is it?' I asked. The word "fatalities" had me worried, and who was "Amanda"?

He refocused on me. 'Rebels attacked one of the safe houses. Thankfully no one hurt. It was a drive-by shooting.'

A cold pit opened in my stomach. This was it – the war Alec had predicted. Hostilities had broken out, as they say.

'What's going on?' Jenny asked.

'Jen, I need to tell you something,' I said. 'There's a war –'

'Which safe house was it?' Terens appeared, sweat beading on his skin, and with the same towel draped around his hips. There was none of the playful teasing he'd exhibited earlier. His face was grim.

Jenny swivelled on her bar stool at the sound of his voice and nearly slipped off.

'I've received a frantic call too. Different safe house.' Luc strode in. Either he must have been in the dining room the whole time – unlikely – or there were other rooms I didn't know about on this deck. 'Rebels have launched simultaneous raids.' His eyes lightened.

Jenny gasped and left her seat to stand next to me. 'Him too?'

I nodded. 'That's my father, Luc.'

She glanced at me then back at Luc, before gulping down the rest of her wine.

Jake came in, followed by the others. The room was suddenly crowding. 'I got one, too,' he said, holding up his phone. He, Sam and Cal also had towels draped around their hips. They must have been with Terens in the gym.

'Are they all vampires?' Jenny whispered, her eyes wide as she took in each new arrival.

I nodded. 'Don't be afraid, they won't hurt you.'

'Right now, I don't care. Check out the abs,' she whispered in my ear.

I found myself caught between two conflicting emotions, not sure how to react – whether with surprise at my best friend's fearless admiration of male vampire anatomy, or apprehension at the turn of events.

'Hey, new girl.' Kari stepped out from behind Jake and sniffed. 'Human.'

'Everyone – this is my friend, Jenny,' I said, when all eyes turned to her.

'She's staying with us for a few days,' Alec added. He introduced each of them in turn. Terens gave her a curt nod. Then Alec spoke so low and fast I couldn't follow, but whatever he said, the others nodded.

I guessed he must have told them why she was here – and that she knew about us, for there were one or two raised eyebrows. Whether it was from disapproval or the fact she could be in danger, I couldn't tell. But whatever, I felt responsible for putting her in this position. She had to stay till it was resolved.

'Welcome aboard, Jenny,' Luc said. 'I hope you won't feel uncomfortable with us around.'

'Thanks, I'm fine.' Jenny had a natural confidence that I'd always admired, but right now I wasn't sure if that, or two glasses of red wine, made her appear so relaxed in the present otherworldly company.

'If you don't mind, we have important things to discuss.' Luc looked at me. 'Laura, ma petite, if you wish to join us you're welcome.'

And leave Jenny without company? That wouldn't be right. 'Thanks, but I should stay with my guest. You, or Alec, can tell me later.'

'I understand.' He turned to the men. 'Get dressed and bring the weapons. My office.' Luc turned on his heel and disappeared the way he had come.

The men sped off. Jake whispered something to Kari before he too, left. She nodded, came over to us and perched on the bar stool Jenny had vacated.

Before he joined Luc, Alec drew me aside. 'Laura, until we can end this thing, the safest place for you and Jenny will be right here, on the yacht.' He glanced at Kari. 'Kari will be here to protect you. She's well trained.'

Kari flashed me a grin.

'What about during the day?'

'Either I or Luc'll be here always. All the rules are being broken, darling. The Rebels have their own donsangs doing their bidding. It isn't safe even during the day.'

'Crap. I wanted to do Christmas shopping.'

He cracked a smile. 'Order online.'

I knew the danger we faced and I certainly didn't want to add to it, especially with Jenny in the picture. 'I'll have to warn her.'

'Do that while I talk to Luc and the men. We have to work out our next move.' He leaned down, kissed me then strode away.

I ignored the sick butterflies in my stomach as I watched his retreating back.

Kari slid off the stool and came towards us. She linked her arms through ours and said in a cheerful voice, 'So, what are we doing tonight?'

CHAPTER 22 – ROUND TWO TO THE PRINCIPATE

ALEC

'What do we do about these raids?' Cal asked.

He and the others returned, dressed and with swords strapped to their sides. Terens carried two blades slung across his back.

Several Kevlar vests lay on the floor. 'Put those on,' Luc said and added through gritted teeth, 'We're going hunting. I want to find those rats.'

'Pity these things don't come with long sleeves.' Terens picked one up. 'I don't fancy losing another arm.' He unclasped the straps that held both swords in place and lay them on Luc's desk.

'Still better than taking a hit to the heart with white-oak,' Sam said. 'No doubt the Rebels will have an ample supply.'

'Just give me Rasputin, that's all I ask.' Terens removed both swords from their scabbards. Holding them out at eye level, he sighted along their lengths. The light from the lamp on Luc's desk caught the glint of razor-sharp edges. He crossed one over the other and snapped the hilts closed, bringing both swords together in a scissor-like action.

I imagined Rasputin's head caught between those blades. *Only a matter of time.*

'How are we going to do this?' Jake asked.

Something bothered me about the drive-by shootings at the safe houses. 'Jake, what time exactly did you get that call?' I whipped my phone out.

'Uh,' he checked, '9.15.'

'Where from?'

'Rocks.'

That was the safe house closest to us. We could be there in minutes. 'Mine came 9.18 from Bondi.' I looked at Luc.

He had his phone out and was gazing at the screen. '9.20 from Parramatta.'

'Less than two minutes apart, and each one further away. Anyone see a pattern here?' I looked from man to man as I dropped the phone back into my pocket.

Luc swore. 'They're trying to draw us out – away from the yacht.'

I nodded. The Rebels were attempting to separate us from Laura. No one had to say it aloud. We all knew why.

'Now what?' Cal asked.

'Give them what they want,' I said. 'And what they won't expect.'

Luc sat back in his chair and crossed his arms over his chest. 'What do you mean?'

'When I spoke with Amanda, she said Brethren, here in the city, are retaliating by banding together to guard The Residence. She's even organised a group to hunt down all the Rebels they can find.' Amanda was Brethren, and she and her donsang ran one of the best safe houses in the country. Those without donsangs of their own found healthy, willing donors under her roof. She prided herself on the quality of blood she provided – drug, disease and cholesterol free. Not that the latter really mattered, but the blood simply tasted better.

Luc nodded. 'That's good.'

'The only place left for them to hide will be underwater,' I said and glanced at my ring. The serpent's eyes had turned black.

Luc sat up and gripped the edge of the desk.

'Hell! They're probably right under us.' Sam pulled out his

phone. 'I'm activating the underwater lights and cameras. Since we can't sense them around water, I'll catch 'em the human way. I need to see the CCTV screens.' He headed for the door.

We raced behind him as he dashed out and up another set of stairs that led from the fore to the uppermost deck to the wheelhouse.

He sat at the helm and pointed to a screen on the control console. 'There! See that? A shadow.' Sam had installed high-speed cameras to capture the rapid movement of our kind.

We looked closely. A section of the screen went blank. He swore. 'One camera's been knocked out.'

Terens stripped off his Kevlar vest, T-shirt and shoes, grabbed his sword and dived headlong into the water.

'Damn! After nearly two-thousand years and he still doesn't wait.' Jake growled, as he struggled out of his vest.

As Cal and I dived in, I heard Luc tell Sam to stay behind and keep monitoring the CCTV screen.

As I plunged into the water, my eyes adjusted to the watery murkiness. Keeping my back to the yacht's keel, I looked around. I was face to face with more than a dozen snarling Rebels. They floated just out of reach.

Terens tried to engage them, but with little success. He may be unequalled with the blade, but underwater his movements were slowed. The Rebels ducked out of his reach and his sword sliced harmlessly through water.

There they stayed, threatening, yet not moving. What were they waiting for?

When I lunged and tried to grab the Rebel nearest me, not only did he evade my grasp but he swam further from the boat and bared his fangs. Further and further out he went, turned and faced me again. And waited.

It was more than a gesture of defiance. It was almost a game. Was he trying to incite me to chase him? I glanced around to see if they were doing the same to Luc. They were. From the corner of my eye, I saw Jake dive under the keel. Presumably, Cal was there. Was he experiencing the same problem? The Rebels ringed us, and every second that passed, they moved a few feet further out.

It appeared as if they were trying to lure us away from the yacht, and there was only one reason for that – Laura. I decided to head back to the surface when Stockton appeared.

The line of Rebels parted. He swam through and bared his fangs. I reciprocated, but headed for the surface instead. He shot forward and raised his fist to me, staying just out of reach. Six others gathered around him and did the same. That's when I caught the glint of a gold ring, in the shape of a wolf's head, on each of their hands. It was Timur's personal insignia. Protruding from the wolf's forehead was a small, dull spike.

My God! White-oak! It could be nothing else. Stockton's grin was confirmation.

The men must be warned. But how? My voice wouldn't carry underwater. Luc and Terens were on the other end of the keel, Jake and Cal on the other side. If I could only get to Luc… he and I were the fastest.

Stockton, with his six companions, came at me like torpedoes, fists aimed and pointed at my chest. Just a scratch and my life would be over.

I clenched my fists, waited till they were close, and then dived, hoping their momentum would propel at least one of them into the keel. The sound would carry and alert Luc and Terens. The thud of Rebel fists connecting with fiberglass gave me what I wanted.

Luc turned his head. Several Rebels hovered near him, ready to attack. Yet they didn't. Luc had a ferocious reputation in battle, and he was old. Very old; like his men. The older a vampire, the greater their strength and speed.

The only reason I could stand with the "old ones" was by virtue of the Ingenii blood. It was the only advantage I had over the Brethren, and I was determined to use it.

I pointed to the Rebels, then my ring and mouthed "white-oak". His eyes lightened. 'Cal, Jake,' I added, and pointed with my thumb to the other side of the yacht. He nodded, dived under the keel and the Rebels went after him.

Terens. I needed to let him know. Several Rebels bore down on him.

Only one thing to do – force them to turn on themselves. *If they desire to throw off all restraint, let's see how far they're willing to go.* Would they return to the animal-like savagery of vampire-kind that existed before Marcus Antonius imposed order?

Stockton's gang regrouped and charged at me again. I surged upwards, twisted and grabbed one of them from behind, careful not to touch the ring. I squeezed his wrist till the bones gave way then ripped off his hand. The man's mouth opened in a gurgled scream. I hurled him in Stockton's direction. Even though our blood flowed slowly, sluggishly even, it was seeping steadily from both the man's severed forearm, and the hand I held. I could smell it. So could they, and like hungry sharks at a fresh kill, they turned in blood lust on their companion and tore him apart.

I had my answer. If they could do this to one of our own kind, I didn't have to imagine what they'd do to humans.

Before throwing away the severed hand, I removed the wolf's-head ring. I placed it on my own little finger then looked around for Terens. He must have taken advantage of the momentary lull – one Rebel came hurtling through the water like a missile and struck another of Stockton's group. The white-oak ring he wore struck home – within seconds, the victim's body crystallised and disintegrated, leaving behind a gossamer trail as it floated away on the current.

Several Rebels fled; those who hadn't joined the feeding frenzy. But we had another problem. Enough blood had been scattered to attract a large grey shark, soon joined by others. The Rebels scattered as the sharks homed in on the scent of blood. They gulped down the dismembered remains of the other vampire.

Only Stockton and two women I recognised remained – the same two who had attacked me in the car park. One bared her fangs before she turned and swam after the others. Her companion followed, leaving Stockton behind.

Something touched my shoulder. I spun around ready to attack.

'Rasputin?' Terens mouthed.

I'd been too preoccupied to give Rasputin a thought. A sickening realisation went through me. If he hadn't been on the other side of the boat, then the Rebels had been nothing but a diversionary tactic that may have allowed Rasputin to sneak onto the yacht. There was no knowing how many Rebels were involved in this, but if my guess was right he wouldn't have gone on board alone as Sam was too dangerous an opponent. It would take at least five of them to overpower him, leaving Rasputin free to go after

Laura. And Sam wouldn't know about the deadly wolf's-head rings. Nor would Kari, and she was guarding Laura.

I spun around again, only to see that Stockton had gone. He'd done his job.

I shot to the surface.

CHAPTER 23 – WE MEET AGAIN

LAURA

Kari's cheerfulness bolstered me. My father and Alec had everything under control, so there should be nothing to worry about – at least, that's what I told myself. But shutting off those pesky doubts was another matter. I looked at the serpent ring on my hand. It's little, red eyes twinkled up at me. That was a good sign – for now.

Jenny was peppering Kari with questions. She was insatiable for everything about vampires. Kari seemed happy to comply and Jenny's eyes got wider with each of her answers.

'You're how old?' Jenny's eyebrows had risen halfway up her forehead.

'Young compared to some,' Kari replied.

The sound of a splash followed by one, two, three others had me running to the windows. They were locked, but strong lights lit the watery depths to a few metres.

'What's happening, Kari?' Her extraordinary hearing could pick up the men's conversations.

She and Jenny were soon on either side of me.

'They think there might be Brethren down there. They're checking.'

I glanced at my ring again. This time, the eyes were black. My hands began to tremble, so I tucked them under my armpits. Not only was Alec in danger, but I'd brought Jenny here for her safety and now that appeared to be a mistake. 'How many?' I asked Kari.

She shook her head. 'Dunno. We can't sense each other around water, but Sam's got the underwater lights on. C'mon. Top deck.' She took my arm and started for the door. Then she stopped and hissed.

The sound made the hair on my nape and arms lift. I grabbed Jenny's hand and pulled her behind me. The door flew open. A tall man stood there silhouetted against the night sky, his inky hair a dark cloud over his low brow. Those unnaturally large and mesmerising eyes could belong to no one else.

Rasputin.

I'd hoped never to meet him again.

'Good evening, ladies.' He smiled, revealing gleaming white teeth – and fangs – framed by a jet-black, ducktail beard.

If I'd thought he looked evil the first time, the creature who stood before me embodied the very essence of malevolence – an almost-physical darkness, one that could squeeze hope from you. It clutched at my heart like an invisible hand, and I shivered from its icy touch.

As he stepped into the room, two other men appeared in the doorway and moved to stand by his side. Like him, they were dressed in black and water dripped from their clothes. They swam here?

Kari sniffed and hissed again. 'They've got white-oak.' She locked me behind her with one hand before crouching.

Rasputin's reptilian eyes were mocking as they scanned the room, looked past her and settled on Jenny. My blood froze. He pulled something from his pocket, and I recognized the missing photograph from my ransacked flat.

'Looks like we have both little birds, but I'll only be needing one.' He ripped the photo in two and let it drop to the ground.

'What the hell does he mean by that?' Jenny whispered in my ear.

My stomach somersaulted. She would have to be told. 'They

nicked the photo of us at the Melbourne Cup, and that book you lent me – it had your scent. I was worried they'd go after you to get to me.'

She inhaled sharply. 'That why you asked me here?'

'To keep you safe, yes.'

'And yet you're not, are you?' Rasputin grinned.

Jenny's fingers squeezed mine, and her other hand grabbed my arm.

'Come lady, you've already disrupted my plans, and unless you wish to see your friend killed, I suggest you come willingly.' He beckoned me with a wave of his fingers.

A wave of revulsion swept over me. *Where are the men? Where's Alec?* I called out to him with my mind, but there was no response. My hands shook.

Kari sucked in a breath. 'Keep away from her you big ape or I'll rip your ugly head off!'

He raised one eyebrow. 'You comparing me to a simian?'

'If the monkey suit fits,' she spat, and edged us back toward the bar. Kari was older, so I knew she'd be faster and stronger than Rasputin, and hopefully, his henchmen as well. Somehow I doubted even he would be arrogant enough to meet her head on. No wonder he resorted to using white-oak.

Rasputin moved a step closer and raised his hand, exposing the strange-looking ring he wore. It was in the shape of a wolf's head, and a tiny, spike emerged from the forehead as he pressed it. 'Useful little trinket,' he said. 'It only takes a scratch, and ash.'

It had to be white-oak.

His men laughed, fanned out and encircled us. Their black leather pants and ankle-length chunky boots squelched as they moved. One eyed Kari, the other Jenny. I glanced behind me. My best friend's usual sparkle had gone, her eyes wide with fear. 'Stay behind me, Jen.'

'Come lady,' Rasputin said. 'There's not much time. I promise you'll be treated well.' His voice was melodious and hypnotic, and his eyes – I couldn't break away from their gaze. 'One word from me and my men will kill your friends.'

It sounded so reasonable, an easy decision to make. Then all would be well. I wanted to do as he asked, yet another part of my mind screamed against it. My feet began to move. I couldn't stop myself.

'That's right, come to me, my lovely one.' He took another step toward me.

'No!' Kari's voice intruded, and she held me in place behind her. The urge to slap her rose up in me, and I struggled as much against myself as I did against her arm.

I knew what he was doing, but I was powerless to do anything about it.

'That's it, my lovely. Break free. Come to me. You know you want to. Your family and friends will all be safe.' His voice purred, and I was suffused with a sense of longing, wanting …

From somewhere in the distance, I heard Kari urging Jenny not to let go of me. She was yelling at that beautiful voice, telling it to shut up, threatening to chop off its tongue and feed it to the sharks.

No! I tried to pull away and go to him but felt myself dragged back.

'Laura, please.' Jenny pleaded.

A burning sensation on my finger, spreading to my hand. My mind was fuzzy. Still that voice, now more insistent. I had to obey.

'Come!'

My hand was burning. The pain was so intense I blinked and looked down. The eyes of the serpent were glowing; their deep scarlet filled my vision and enveloped my mind, and the fuzziness that had settled on my consciousness like a dark cloud was swept away by its blinding light. My mind belonged to me again.

'No.' I said. 'I'm not coming with you.' The burning pain in my hand receded.

'I tried to make it easy for you, lady.' Rasputin's voice no longer oozed magnetic appeal. 'I so abhor violence.' With a jerk of his head and a hiss, he indicated for his men to act.

Kari edged us back toward the bar then took up a fighting stance – slightly crouched, hands at the ready. Snarls filled the room.

Think, Laura, think! There had to be something I could do. Then it came to me. My blood was poisonous to vampires. It had killed Maris, and if the threat of just being touched by it terrified Russell, why shouldn't it have the same effect on Rasputin's henchmen?

I whispered over my shoulder to Jenny. 'Find a knife. Anything sharp.'

Behind me, Jenny rummaged through a drawer. 'No knives. A corkscrew?'

'Perfect!' It had a sharp point. I grabbed it and, keeping my eyes on the advancing henchmen, gave myself a short, sharp stab in my middle finger. *Ouch!* Blood welled up.

Holding my hand up as the blood dripped down onto my palm, I faced my would-be abductors. 'I'm sure you've heard what my blood can do to you. Come any closer and you'll feel it.' I raised the corkscrew as well. 'My blood's on this and I won't hesitate to use it.' *As good as a syringe.*

Rasputin's henchmen stopped and cast a glance at their leader.

Ha – a bleeding finger and corkscrew as deadly weapons.

Rasputin stroked his beard and smiled. 'Well done, lady. You win this round. But I assure you, the next one belongs to me.'

His gaze flicked over my shoulder, and his smile faded. The black-leathered henchmen retreated to stand next to him.

'Don't bet on it.' Sam appeared, sword poised. Blood was splattered on his grey shirt. He angled his head toward me. 'Well done, Laura. If anyone of them tries to get close, go straight for the heart.'

'I will,' I said, hiding my fear. Pricking myself in the finger was all the stabbing I ever wanted to do.

Rasputin hissed again and jerked his head toward Sam. His men hesitated, glanced at one another, shook their heads and dived out through the windows. It didn't matter that they were closed. They crashed through the glass and disappeared into the water.

Kari laughed. 'Looks like monkey boy's on his own.'

Sam and Rasputin faced each other.

'Sempronius.' Rasputin's voice took on that honey-sweet tone again, this time aimed at Sam. 'We are Brethren. There's no need to fight one other.'

Sam stood his ground. Could he resist when I couldn't?

'Poor Sempronius, always the guard at home, forever stuck behind a computer. They only ask you when there's no one else. How it must irk you.'

How was it possible that such an evil man, as Rasputin, could attune his entire demeanor to appear so sympathetic?

Sam's sword hand shook. 'Not true.'

'They don't appreciate you. I would never leave a great warrior such as you behind. Come join me.'

Sam's sword hand lowered.

'Oh, no!' Jenny cried.

'Sam!' Kari and I called out simultaneously.

'Don't listen.' I said.

'Deliver the Ingenii to me and I promise you'll have your every desire.' Rasputin pointed at me and smiled that evil smile.

Sam raised his sword and turned toward us. Helplessly we watched him fight an inner struggle, his face contorted in a grimace. His legs propelled him forward, even as we saw him try to force his sword arm down with his other hand.

Rasputin's voice took on a deeper, more persuasive tone. 'Good, Sempronius. Bring the Ingenii to me and I promise you'll never be left behind.' Sam's eyes lost focus. He gave up the fight.

Oh crap.

I still held the bloodied corkscrew. My finger had stopped bleeding, but I didn't want to use it on Sam. Anything but that.

Sam raised his weapon and grabbed for me. Kari stepped in front of him. He threw her aside as if she were made of paper. She crashed into the settee at the other end of the room overturning it.

Jenny screamed.

I backed up, the corkscrew held before me like a weapon. 'Sam, don't. Remember who you are – Luc's man. Fight it!'

He stopped. A frown crossed his face.

I heard a sharp intake of breath behind me and turned my head. Judy stood in the doorway, staring at Rasputin, her face livid. 'Don't you dare touch my daughter!'

Where she'd been all this time, I had no idea, but her presence seemed to rattle Rasputin. He growled at her then yelled at Sam, 'Bring her to me! This minute!'

When Sam took another step toward me, Judy sprang between us, a wooden pool cue held aloft. Over his shoulder, I saw Kari rise and launch herself at Rasputin. They rolled on the floor in a tangle of arms and legs.

Sam blinked, dropped his sword and sank to his knees. He clutched his head and groaned.

Kari had Rasputin on his back, one hand around his throat, the other encircling his wrist, the white-oak ring only inches from her face. Although her age was in her favour, I knew Rasputin would play dirty and negate any advantage she had. My hunch was proved right when Rasputin said, 'Join with me, Karelia my sweet. I need you.'

She wavered. Within a second, he had her pinned against the wall, the wolf's-head ring with its deadly spike a hair's breadth from her face.

'Kari!' I screamed. Throwing the corkscrew aside, I pushed past Judy and grabbed Sam's fallen sword.

'Laura, no!' Judy called out.

'That's a white-oak spike in his ring.'

'Oh God,' Judy cried, and as I raised the sword, she ran toward Rasputin and slammed the pool cue against the back of his head. Wood splintered in all directions. He barely flinched.

I raised the sword above my head and brought it down hard. The sharp steel sliced through both his wrists. Kari dropped to the ground and Rasputin howled. Staggering back, he glared at me, eyes wide with surprise, before he turned and jumped through the same broken window his men had crashed through earlier. The severed hands clawed at the ground, as if searching for their lost body.

'Let me take that,' Sam said and gently retrieved his sword from my grasp.

Kari blinked up at me. Bile rose up in my throat at the realisation of what I had just done, and I barely had time to run from the room and lean over the side before I threw up.

I was vaguely aware of voices, and the light pad of feet on the deck.

'It's okay, Laura, dear. Your mother's here.' Judy drew my hair back from my face while I emptied my stomach contents into the water.

Alec's voice came from a few feet away. 'Laura! What's wrong?' He was at my side in an instant, water dripping from his hair and jeans. I grabbed his hand.

Luc's voice, a hand on my shoulder. 'Laura, ma petite.'

'What happened?' Alec asked.

'Rasputin was here. Tried to take Laura,' Judy said.

Luc swore.

'I cut off his hands.' I heaved again.

'I'll stay with her,' Alec said. His hand replaced Judy's and held back my hair.

'Everyone's okay,' she said, but before I could add anything, another wrenching wave of nausea hit me.

Fish are getting a free feed tonight, I perversely thought.

'Come, ma cherie,' Luc said. 'She's in good hands.'

Luc and Judy left. With nothing left to expel, my vomiting ceased. Alec wiped my brow with a wet handkerchief he'd retrieved from his jeans while I leant against him, exhausted, trembling.

He handed the handkerchief to me, wrapped his arms around me and swore under his breath, his voice grim. 'This won't happen again.'

I wiped my mouth and streaming eyes and tried to dislodge the disgusting image of Rasputin's severed hands from my mind. 'I think you like getting wet.'

My cheek vibrated from the light rumble of Alec's chest, before he sobered. 'The Rebels were beneath the boat. It was a setup to draw us away from you and allow Rasputin to board.' From the dangerous tone of his voice, I guessed he was angry with himself for allowing it to happen.

'He wanted me to come with him, and I nearly did. He was so persuasive – his voice, his eyes.' I shuddered at the memory. 'Now I know how Mrs. Henderson felt.'

Alec's arms tightened around me. 'Mesmerisation doesn't work on an Ingenii. Never has, and Brethren are immune to it. Yet, if Rasputin can....' His voice dipped almost to a whisper. I looked up. His worried frown didn't instill much confidence in me.

'You can't do that to each other?'

He shook his head. 'No. As far as I know, Rasputin's skill was limited to humans before Timur transformed him. How did you break his hold?'

'I didn't. It was the ring. It started to burn, as if trying to get my attention, forcing me to look into its eyes. And when I did—'

'You were free,' he finished.

'Uh huh.'

He gazed at me for a while, and my mind replayed the sickening moment when the steel I wielded sliced through flesh and bone, like a knife carving through a joint of meat. Another tremor racked me.

'You're in shock, darling. Let's get inside, and I'll figure this out later.'

'I cut off a man's hands, Alec. I cut off a man's hands.' I wondered if the horror of it would ever leave me.

'You saved your mother, Kari, Jenny and even Sam, from what I've heard. You did good, Laura. Keep telling yourself that. Your quick action saved their lives.'

He was right, yet the haunting image was difficult to forget. I'd never physically hurt anyone before in my life. There hadn't been any need. Was this yet another facet of my secure and sheltered old life slipping away? Who would've thought the old Laura could turn into Ingenii warrior princess? I'd surprised myself. But it was one experience I didn't want to repeat.

It had been such a brazen attack against the very heart of the Principate. I was their ticket to escape the endless nights that their existence decreed. Yet they had chosen this path; chosen to become Brethren, knowing the price of immortality meant sacrificing the daylight. What was the saying, having your cake and eating it, too?

The boat shuddered as the engines started. Cal appeared and unhitched the moorings. Tendrils of damp, sandy-coloured hair flopped down over his face as he bent to release the last thick coil of rope from one of the piers. 'Cruisin' around,' he said, as he straightened and faced us. 'Keep the mongrels guessing.'

'How's Sam?' I asked.

'Pissed off. He can't believe that juvenile got into his head. Embarrassed, too.' He grinned, and both his dimples showed. 'Saved by a couple of women.'

So much for feminism.

Cal's gaze moved to Alec. He jerked his head up, 'Top deck. When you're ready.' He disappeared in a burst of speed.

'Feeling better?'

'Yeah. Nothing left to feed the fishies.'

Alec looked at me and his eyes showing a mixture of pride and concern. 'You never cease to surprise me.' He kissed the top of my head, tucked me into his side. We made our way up another set of stairs.

'How come they're all up there?' I asked.

'Judy thought it best for your friend, Jenny, to be elsewhere while she and Luc cleaned up. It was a shock for her, too. Terens took her up.' Vampire hearing again. He must have been listening to the others in the stateroom while I was busy being sick.

I'd bolted out, leaving the severed hands behind, their blood staining the beige carpet. Poor Jenny saw it all. She'd been so excited to learn of the existence of vampires. After tonight's events though…. 'I wonder if she'll run away from me after this.'

'No way,' he said confidently.

'I assume Rasputin's hands will regenerate?'

'A couple of weeks from now, he'll have new ones. Pity you didn't remove his head.'

I looked at him in horror, and he grinned. His little joke worked. I was able to smile back, and my trembling eased. 'Terens's arm regenerated overnight.'

'The older a vampire, the faster they heal.'

'Thank goodness Rasputin's a juvenile, then. It gives us a two-week reprieve.'

'We can only hope.' He opened the door to the uppermost deck.

CHAPTER 24 – WOLF'S HEAD

LAURA

The top deck was the control centre of the yacht. Its three-metre-long, white-panelled console resembled a plane's cockpit with its array of computer screens and various other techno-gadgets at whose function I could only guess.

Sam was seated at the captain's white leather swivel chair, his back turned to the others as he maneuvered the boat from its mooring. The first-mate's chair beside him was empty.

Directly behind him stood a small cocktail bar against which Jake and Cal leant. Both were gazing intently at the ring Jake held between his fingers. It was the same wolf's head that had been on Rasputin's hand.

'Really cute,' Jake muttered facetiously. He pressed the side of it with his thumb and the deadly spike sprang out.

Terens was crouched on the floor in front of Jenny, who was seated with Kari on one of the L-shaped settees scattered around the deck. Both her hands were held in his. He must have said something to her, for she nodded, looked up, saw me and smiled. Terens turned and winked at me, then joined the others.

'Hey hon, you okay?' Jenny asked me, but before I could answer, Kari shot to my side and enveloped me in such a bear hug I thought my ribs would crack.

'Laura, you were incredible,' she said then sniffed and pulled back. 'That big ape would make anyone vomit.'

'Thanks Kari.' I was quickly learning that subtlety was not one of Kari's strong points.

'I'll get you some water,' Alec said.

Kari sat me on the settee between her and Jenny. 'You saved my life, and I'm the one who's supposed to be the bodyguard.' She looked crestfallen.

'You were great. How were you to know that man could mesmerise us all like that?' I patted her hand then turned to Jenny. 'I'm so sorry, Jen, I honestly thought you'd be safe with us.'

'I can cope, girlfriend.' She glanced in Terens's direction and smiled.

Thank you, Terens.

Alec returned and handed me a chilled bottle of Perrier then perched on the coffee table opposite me as I rinsed my mouth and drank. The water tasted cool and sweet. 'We didn't know what Rasputin was capable of, Kari. If Sam had trouble—'

'Then we're all in trouble.' Sam finished. 'Son-of-a-bitch can sniff out a weakness and twist it around in your head.' He briefly turned his head toward us. 'Laura, did he try that with you?'

'Sure did, but the ring brought me back.'

Alec repeated what I'd told him.

I looked at my hand. The eyes of the serpent glowed, as did its twin on Alec's hand. But then, they always did when either of us was close by, as if they relished each other's company. Luc told me the serpent rings were fashioned from the pendant the witch had worn around her neck; so perhaps it was true – they were two halves of a whole – the way Alec and I were, and whenever we came together, the rings blazed to life.

'Luc needs to know,' Sam said. 'As far as I remember, it's never done that.'

'Know what?' Luc's head emerged at the top of the stairs, Judy by his side. He must have been too preoccupied elsewhere to overhear our conversation.

'Rasputin tried to mesmerise me, and it would have worked, if not for the ring. It got my attention, burning my finger, as if willing me to look in its eyes. When I did, everything became clear.'

'Yep, we saw it, didn't we?' Kari said. She glanced at Jenny, who nodded.

'Interesting,' Luc said. While Judy pulled up a chair next to Alec, Luc strode over to the bar, poured himself a brandy and took something with care from his pocket. He laid it on the counter – another wolf's-head ring.

Jake did the same with the one he held.

'Here, add this,' Alec said, and removed another one from his own finger – one I hadn't noticed – and tossed it to Luc, who caught it and placed it with the others.

'So, now what?' Jake asked. 'Keep 'em or destroy 'em?'

For the length of a slow vampire-heartbeat nobody spoke, their gazes riveted on the three shiny objects with their deadly cargoes—death at the push of a hidden button.

Jenny nudged me and whispered. 'What's with the rings? Magic or something?'

'It's what's inside them. White-oak – that spikey thing that popped out. It's poisonous to vampires. That's why Rasputin made that pathetic joke, 'One scratch and you're ash!"

'Right.'

'It's outlawed among our kind. Anyone found in possession is usually executed on the spot,' Alec said.

Jenny stared at him, wide-eyed. I had the feeling whatever she knew about vampires, or thought she knew, was now overturned.

'I say we hang onto 'em.' Terens picked one up and held it to the light. 'I know it's against our laws, but this changes everything. If every damned Rebel has one of these, then our side doesn't stand a chance. And we're the good guys.' He dropped the ring back with the other two.

Cal nodded. 'Good point.' He pointed to the ring in Cal's hand. 'Those could even things up a bit.'

'I hate the whole idea.' Luc scowled, moved away from the bar and sat in the first-mate's chair next to Sam. 'Antonius and I made these laws only to break them now?'

'We've never been threatened like this before. New game, new rules,' Terens retorted.

'I agree.' Sam said without taking his eyes off the water

ahead. 'The enemy has a superior weapon and we'd be fools not to take advantage of it.'

'Jake, what do you think?' Alec asked.

He didn't answer straight away, but looked around until his gaze rested on Luc. 'I believe there comes a time when rules need to be amended. I can see no other way to get through this. Banning it no longer works, and not defending ourselves would also be wrong.'

'Alec, what about you?' Luc asked.

'Jake's right. There's no other choice. Enforcing the white-oak ban worked in the past, but not any more. Humans don't believe in us anymore and the last two centuries have seen an increase in our kind now that we're no longer hunted.'

'Not all humans,' Jenny pointed out.

Alec looked at her and smiled. 'No, not all.' He turned his attention back to Luc. 'It's difficult to police our laws. Even the Prefects struggle to maintain the ban in their Prefectures. I can't see any other solution but to allow the use of white-oak.'

Luc downed the rest of his brandy, rose to his feet and strode to the railing, letting his arms rest on it while he stared into the water. No one spoke, while he wrestled with the issue. 'I'll need to confer with Antonius and the other Elders,' he said at last without looking around.

'Of course,' Alec answered.

'There's a snag,' Cal said unexpectedly. 'Time. How long it would take to get the stuff and form it into something useable, like sword tips, bullets, or,' he pointed to the pile of wolf's-head rings, 'these things, could take weeks.'

'Agreed,' Terens remarked. 'Let's skip all that, find where the Rebels are hiding, rip the damned things off them –'

'And pulverise 'em before they do it to us,' Cal finished.

The two punched fists in a sign of solidarity.

'Use my blood.' The words left my mouth before I realised what I was saying. Something had prompted me, yet I had no idea who or what.

Luc swivelled around and glanced from me to Judy. 'No, Laura. That's not an option.'

'It makes sense,' I said. 'The Rebels are using an outlawed lethal weapon that would take time for us to obtain, while my blood is just as deadly and ready to use.'

'Luc's right. We're not going to use you as a weapon,' Alec said.

'Why not?'

'Yeah, why not?' Terens asked.

'Laura's blood is her protection – not for us to use as we'd like.' Alec's face was set in a resolute expression – which I ignored.

'Even if I let you?'

'Not even then.' His expression changed from stubborn determination to such tenderness that had my heart not already belonged to him, I would have dedicated it to him anew. 'Besides, I've just thought of something else which will solve this problem.' He turned around to face Luc. 'It might take a few days, but I want to find an antidote to white-oak.'

Jake shook his head. 'Tried several times.'

'Then we've got to try again. My lab's the best equipped in this country.'

'Think you can do it?' Luc moved from the railing to stand next to Judy. He placed a hand on her shoulder. She covered it with her own.

'I can only try,' Alec answered.

'*We* can only try,' Jake emphasised. 'Remember the old adage about two heads.'

Alec nodded his thanks.

'How long will you be away?' I asked, hating the idea of being separated from him, even for a few days.

'Not sure. As long as it takes – a few days perhaps. Between the two of us,' he glanced at Jake, 'working night and day, we should come up with something.' He took my hands in his and intertwined our fingers until the serpent rings touched. Their eyes lit up in an unearthly glow and bathed the faces of those around us in a ruby aura.

I heard Jenny's intake of breath. 'Wow. Don't think I'll ever get used to seeing those flarey eyes.'

'Couldn't buy that in K-Mart,' Kari quipped as she leaned forward to look past me to Jenny on my other side.

Alec rolled his eyes and I fought the urge to laugh. Kari had successfully killed the moment.

'I won't be far away,' he said squeezing my fingers. *Call and I'll come.* His voice sounded in my head.

I will, I sent back.

His mouth crinkled up into a smile.

'Ugh! Will you two quit making eyes at each other!' Kari said. This time I laughed.

Alec kissed me then rose and joined Jake and the others at the bar. They were all still bare-chested and barefoot. Alec's damp jeans hugged his body, which probably explained the sigh that came from Jenny.

Luc crouched down to speak to Judy, and while their conversation flowed around me, I was oblivious to it – too intent on the discussion Alec and the men were having. I saw him pocket the three wolf's-head rings, and Terens's protest, although I couldn't catch the words. They were speaking too fast and low.

'Jacuzzi, Laura.' Kari's face loomed in my vision and blocked Alec from my view.

'What? Sorry, I wasn't listening.' I angled my head to see around her, but Alec and Jake had gone. Blast!

Kari draped her arm around my shoulders. 'What I was saying was, I've got a great idea. Jacuzzi.' She beamed. 'It's exactly what you need right now.'

I could think of several reasons why that was a great idea, but one in particular stood out. 'Do I still smell of vomit?'

'Yep, and that ape's blood.' She paused then added, 'Handless and hairy. Hey, I like that. Think I'll call him that from now on – HH.' She laughed.

'The Jacuzzi will help relax you, Laura,' Judy said. 'Kari knows her way around and where the towels are kept.' She rose and stretched. 'I'm off to bed. Goodnight.' She kissed me on the cheek and walked down the stairs. Luc strode over to the men, whispered something before following her.

'Well, there goes any chance of skinny-dipping,' Kari said, and her pixie face contorted into a comical grimace. 'Seems you've got extra bodyguards tonight.'

The three of us looked in the men's direction. Terens smiled at Jenny and raised his glass.

She nudged my foot with hers and whispered, 'Chuck my bikini overboard.'

CHAPTER 25 – JENNY'S PROBLEM

LAURA

Two days had passed since Alec left to create the antidote in his hospital lab. I woke up to see him comfortably ensconced on my bed, looking down at me and twirling a strand of my hair around his fingers. He brought it to his lips and kissed it.

I sat up and threw my arms around his neck. 'How long have you been here?' My voice was still heavy from sleep.

'Couple of hours.'

'Why didn't you wake me? What time is it?"

'Still dark. You looked so peaceful. Besides, I enjoy watching you sleep.'

I pulled back to look at him. 'That's creepy you know.'

'Only if I make a habit of it. I've missed you.'

'Missed you, too. Got your antidote yet?'

He shook his head. 'We're close. I'm waiting on the results of a compound we synthesised last night. Jake's still at the lab, bunking down in my office.'

I ran my hands down the side of his face. There were dark circles under his eyes, and I remembered he hadn't fed from me in a few days. 'You need to eat.'

'You offering?' He gave me a lopsided grin.

'You want to go somewhere else?'

He chuckled, swept my hair to the side and claimed my mouth, before nuzzling my throat. No matter how many times he kissed me, I experienced a thrill in his arms and revelled in the anticipation of our joining. This morning was no exception. I melted into him. 'You know how to excite a girl.'

'I intend to satisfy her, too.' He licked the delicate skin on my throat and bit down. As always, his saliva numbed the pain of his bite. My body relaxed, and a sense of peace spread through me. I wondered how many chose to be donsangs if only to experience this. And how many didn't want the feeling to stop until too late?

Too soon his deep gulps slowed and it was over. He licked the wound closed, kissed it and lowered me back onto the bed.

We spent the next few hours making love.

I fell asleep afterwards. When I woke, I was alone in my queen-size bed. Yet the side of the bed he'd occupied still felt warm as I stretched my arm out over the sheet and caressed it. A knock on my bedroom door had me scrambling for my clothes. It was still dark outside.

'Won't be a moment,' I called as I picked up the dress I wore yesterday. It stunk of vomit and dried blood.

'It's me – Jen. I need to talk to you.'

I breathed a sigh of relief, dropped the dress on the floor, crawled back into bed and pulled the sheet over me. 'Door's unlocked.'

Jenny came in, closed the door and leant back against it. 'I've got a problem.'

'Let me guess. Terens?'

She bit down on her lip and nodded, but her laughter still managed to bubble up.

'But it's only been a couple of days.'

Her eyes widened and she gave me a reproachful look as she knelt in the middle of my bed. 'Who said that sometimes it only takes,' she made air quotes with her fingers, 'a few days to recognise a man's qualities?'

'Okay, I did, but—'

'But what, hon? It can happen to you and not me?' She sat

back on her heels, hands on her hips and glared at me.

'That's not what I'm saying.'

'Then what?'

What could I say, that I'd dreamt when I was in hospital that she'd become a vampire? Since when did I believe in dreams? Ever since vampires, magic serpent rings and witches curses had turned the pragmatic part of my brain into a believer. And now, her infatuation with Terens. The blood in my veins froze. I lunged forward, grabbed her wrists and turned them upward, looking for tell-tale bite marks. There were none.

She waved her arms in a shooing motion. 'Laura! What are you doing?'

I checked her neck. Nothing.

'Stop, you idiot.' She backed away to the end of the bed. 'He hasn't bitten me, if that's what you're looking for.'

'Yeah.' I sat back against the bedhead and hugged the sheet to me. How could I tell her I was afraid of losing my best friend to the dark – literally.

'So what if he had? You let Alec feed from you?'

'I'm different. I can't be transformed. The Ingenii mutation prevents it.' It took more than a few bites to change a human into a vampire, exchange of blood had to take place. But I knew Jenny well enough to know she was capable of going to extremes to please a man.

'So that's it. You're afraid I'll ask Terens to change me?' She rolled her eyes and threw her arms in the air. 'Oh, hon, no. I'm not ready for that. Still, I'd think about it.'

'Please don't, Jen.'

'Easy for you to say. Look at you.' She pointed. 'Fifty years old and you pass for a twenty-something, while I'm only thirty-four and I look older than you.'

'I didn't ask for this. And it comes with a price, remember?'

A cynical smile creased her face. 'Yeah and he so looks hot in wet jeans. Some price.'

Here it was, the growing difference between us. It had been simmering for some time and now was finally in the open – my youthful immortality, and her slowly-aging decay. It's what I'd feared for the past few months, and it made me both angry as well as scared that I could lose my best friend.

Yet she saw only the superficialities – youth, immortality, vitality. Who wouldn't be drawn to that? How could I blame her for wanting it? But it had a dark side too, and she'd already had a glimpse of that. It was time she knew more.

'All right, Jen, but let's put aside, "being young and immortal." ' I did my own air quotes. 'And consider the nastier side of what it is to be Brethren.'

She nodded. 'Terens told me. Also about the donsangs?'

'Donsangs. It means blood givers. They're human donors who like doing that sort of thing.'

She raised an eyebrow. I knew what that look meant. 'I have no choice in this, but the donsangs do. Anyway, the Brethren hunt and feed from *people*. Sometimes they kill them, and it isn't always an accident. You want to do that? Turn into a killer?'

Her face paled. 'Terens said they fed from blood bags.'

'True, but not always. They prefer to hunt. It's part of their instinct, I think. Now there's a whole bunch who want to do it all the time and leave no survivors. You met one.'

She looked up at the air-conditioning unit and pulled the lower end of the sheet over her legs. 'It's got really chilly in here.'

I doubted her sudden coldness stemmed from the air conditioning. She didn't want to hear this. Reality was clashing with her romantic illusions.

'They're not all like Terens and Alec, or even Kari. There are vicious ones, like those who kidnapped, tied me up, and tortured me.' Her eyes widened. 'And enjoyed it. They got a thrill from my pain.' I threw the sheet aside, stood up, naked as I was, and showed her the two red lines on my abdomen – the remains of the welts Maris had inflicted with her whip.

Jenny gasped, a look of horror crossing her face.

I slid back into bed and pulled the sheet over me again.

Her eyes welled up with tears. 'I could never be, never do....'

'Something like that?'

She nodded.

'They wanted to use me to breed another like myself so they could daywalk.'

She said nothing and wiped her eyes with the back of her hand. Her shocked expression was enough of a clue for me to know she may be rethinking her haste to become a vampire. I decided to press it further.

'Mind pulling back the curtains, Jen? I don't fancy appearing in the nude again.'

It was morning already and the sunlight was struggling to find its way in through the heavy, blockout curtains.

She gave me a lame grin. 'Hon, you don't have anything I don't have—'

'—unless you're a mutant.' We both finished together and laughed.

It was Jen's favourite line. She used it on her students whenever she marched into the locker room to hurry them up after Friday afternoon sport.

She climbed off the bed, swished aside the blue-striped drapes, and the sharp summer sunshine flooded the room. She looked out at the marine view. 'Wow. Isn't it glorious? Want me to open it?'

'Go ahead.'

I drew my knees up, wrapped my arms around them and took a deep breath of salty, sea air. 'Make the most of it, Jen,' I said. 'If you decide to become a vamp, no more glorious days, no more days at all, only night. Wouldn't you miss it? I don't think I could give it up.'

The window of my room was large enough that even from my vantage point, I could see the spectacular view. Sam must have moored the yacht while I slept. The scenery outside was different. *I should go up on deck and see exactly where we are.*

Her hand gripped the windowsill, and she stared out at the azure sky. I saw her swallow. 'I haven't made up my mind.'

'Jen? Don't do it because of Terens.'

She turned around and looked at me. That's when I properly noticed the T-shirt nightie she wore – dark grey with some kind of logo on it. 'Nice T-shirt.'

She looked down and ran her hands down its length. 'Mmmm. I like it, too. Pity it's not mine.'

'Who's then?'

She crossed her arms and looked at me. 'You sleep naked all the time?'

I knew Jenny's evasive tactics. 'Please don't tell. It's Terens's.'

She laughed. 'You know you can be such a prude sometimes?'

'I'm just … concerned. That's all.'

Jenny sat back down on the edge of the bed. 'I haven't slept with him. He lent me this when I mentioned I forgot to pack my PJs.' She paused. 'He's a nice guy.'

Who also happens to be nearly two-thousand years old and probably had just as many women in that time. *Does he remember any of their names?* I thought it best not to voice that thought. No woman likes to be considered one among many. At least I knew Alec's exes. Both were dead. 'Don't fall in love with him.'

She chewed the inside of her bottom lip and glanced out the window. 'I love daytime, too.'

We sat in silence for the next few minutes.

Jenny suddenly exclaimed. 'Hey, it's Christmas Eve.'

CHAPTER 26 - SERUM

LAURA

With the yacht moored at Darling Harbour we couldn't go back into the house, so Judy ordered Christmas decorations online. They arrived at the wharf within twenty-four hours, while the presents I ordered arrived soon after.

We'd spent the day stringing fairy lights above and around windows, and along the outside railings. Kari joined us at sunset, and she and Jenny hung mistletoe from just about every doorframe they could find. It wasn't hard to guess which two men they aimed to pin beneath those plastic green sprigs. We'd erected floor-to-ceiling Christmas tree in the main stateroom and draped its green boughs with crystal, and delicate, beaded glass ornaments; some shaped like snow flakes, others as glittery bows, balls or tassels. A pearl garland of lights created a jewel-like effect when Judy pressed the switch and the tiny lights blinked into life.

'My first Christmas with my family.' Judy took my hand as we stepped back and admired our handiwork, her face alight with joy.

I kissed her cheek.

We had just finished dinner – take away Thai – and cleared

away the empty containers from the coffee table around which we sat, when Alec appeared. He picked me up and spun me around. 'We've got it!' His eyes shone.

'The antidote?'

'Not so much an antidote, as a serum. It'll counteract the poisonous effect of white-oak; a kind of immunisation.' He lowered me to the floor. 'Plus an extra surprise, and something we weren't expecting. Jake's telling Luc and the others about it now. Our results revealed you and I, although not immune, have a high tolerance to white-oak.'

I was stunned. 'How?'

'As far as I can tell, it must be the Ingenii mutation. It's overriding your vampire blood. All previous Ingenii were immune.' He glanced at Judy.

'We don't need a serum, but,' I turned and looked at Kari, 'what about —'

'I didn't say we don't need it, darling. You and I may have a high tolerance, but it can still make us very sick. We need the serum, and what we've got looks promising.' He took a deep breath. 'We used samples of our blood – mine, Jake's, Luc's and the others – with the isolated compound added, then put in a tiny amount of crushed white-oak, enough to kill the most ancient of our kind and,' a broad smile lit his face, 'there was minimal reaction.'

'Minimal?' Kari asked.

'The sample didn't crystallise. In fact, the blood liquefied and then thickened again about fifty-five minutes later.'

'That's good?' I said.

'Yes.' He hesitated. 'I tested it on myself.'

I gasped. 'What if it hadn't worked? Alec, the risk you took!'

He placed his finger over my lips. 'I'm all right, as you can see. It was the only way to test the compound—see if there were side effects. We don't have the luxury of time to put it through all the necessary tests. That could take weeks, even months.'

I wasn't convinced and lightly nipped the tip of his finger. Alec only smiled, which infuriated me all the more. 'Laura, I was confident there was no danger. I would never risk leaving you alone. Never.' His face sobered and as his gaze bored into mine, his arms about me tightened.

I hugged his neck, and the sick feeling slowly receded.

'What does it do to you exactly?' Jenny said. She was sitting cross-legged on one of the sofas. 'Can someone fill me in on that?'

Jenny had learnt much about the Brethren in the last twelve hours, but not this. Perhaps she hadn't come across the fatal effects of white-oak on vampires in her research.

'You haven't heard of that?' I asked.

She thought a moment. 'Well, yes and no, hon. It's hard to know what you read on online is fact. But I worked out it must be bad by the way you reacted when Rasputin had Kari.'

'Most wood has little affect on us,' Alec said. 'Only there's something in the structure of white-oak that reacts with our blood. Kills us instantly.'

'So the wooden stake through the heart bit?'

'Still effective, but not as instantaneous as *that* particular wood,' Alec emphasised.

I explained its effects on a vampire's body, having seen it happen to Russell.

'Well, what do you know.' She looked at me and shook her head. 'This has been an education.'

She had no idea.

'We're still in the early stages. Jake injected himself first. Wouldn't let me try it on myself till he was sure.'

Kari gasped. 'He's—'

'He's all right, Kari. Only experienced a few side effects. Flu-like symptoms—high fever, aching muscles and weakness. Lasted just under an hour. For me, about half that.'

'And that's all?' she asked.

'That's all. But,' he emphasised, and he looked back to me. 'I'm not sure how long the serum lasts. There hasn't been enough time to check. It could be a day, a week, maybe a month. Plus I'm not sure if our blood's a representative sample because of the witch's curse. I need to test this on one of the Brethren transformed by a regular vampire, to know for sure.'

'So that counts me out?' Kari said.

Alec nodded. 'Anyone changed by any of us. Jake and I came up with someone who would be perfect. We're just not going to tell him beforehand.'

'Who?' Judy asked.

'Dawson.' Alec replied.

Kari laughed. She must know him, and why did she find it funny? They were considering risking a man's life.

'Who is this guy?' I asked.

'A temporarily-reprieved criminal; a former dealer in white-oak. We promised him his life in return for information, and … he's doing a little job for me.' A wide smile graced his face.

Jake and Cal came in. 'Ready?' Jake asked. They each had a sword strapped to their side. Jake also a small black bag tucked under his arm.

Looks like they were planning to go out again and test it on the poor guy. 'Criminal or not, is that fair, Alec? What if it doesn't work on him?'

He tucked a lock of hair behind my ear. 'We've got little choice and I don't want to ask for a volunteer. So far, we know it only works on us. Jake's injected the others.'

'What?' Judy asked, her face creased with concern. 'Luc too?'

'He's all right, Judy,' Jake called after her as she ran from the room. Presumably my father was somewhere on the upper deck.

'Kari.' Jake beckoned her over, placed the bag on the coffee table and opened it. 'Your turn.'

Kari skipped over to Jake and extended her arm in blind trust. Could I do any less with Alec?

A cold shudder swept through me as Jake lifted the syringe and plunged it gently into Kari's arm. I had an almost phobic fear of needles, which was ironic considering that I was the superfood, the Goji berry, of the vamp world, and sharp and pointy fangs were now part of my existence.

But, they were Alec's fangs, and that made all the difference.

I fought back my fear, disengaged myself from his embrace and bared my arm. 'Me too.'

'I know how much you hate these things.' He kissed me as a sudden burning sting tore through my upper arm.

'*Ouch!*'

He raised his head and smiled down at me. 'All over.'

'That was sneaky.' I rubbed the spot.

'But it worked.' He placed the syringe back into the black bag and sat me down on one of the sofas.

'Glad I don't need one,' Jenny said and grimaced.

'You're lucky.'

She turned her head in the direction of the stairs. Was she expecting to see Terens?

'How do you feel?' Alec crouched on the floor in front of me. 'Any weakness, aches and pains, soreness?'

'Fine.' I shrugged.

'Let's give it a few minutes.' He watched me, then after five, maybe ten minutes, he took my pulse and temperature. 'Humph! Normal. Still feeling okay?'

'Same as before. I feel great.'

Alec shook his head. 'You are an enigma.'

'Just as well you'll have eternity to figure me out then,' I said and smoothed the crease between his eyes with my finger.

Alec snatched it and brought it to his lips. 'Not long enough.'

'We need to go,' Jake said.

Alec rose and took my hand. 'We're going out.'

'To jab poor old Dawson? You don't need me along for that.'

'No, not for that. I have something else in mind.' He grinned.

'What?'

He wouldn't tell me and turned to Jenny instead. 'Jen, I believe Terens would appreciate some TLC right now. It's a long time since he's had the flu.'

Her eyes lit up. Uncurling herself from the settee, she said, 'Where is he?'

Alec indicated with a flick of his head. 'Wheelhouse. Upper deck. Splayed out on one of the deck chairs.'

She shot me a grin and waved. 'Have a nice night, you, two.'

I just had time to grab my bag off the settee as Alec led me from the stateroom, Cal and Jake following behind, carrying the little black bag.

My bodyguards.

A delicious array of aromas wafted from the string of restaurants and cafes along the pier as we got into the launch. Alec and I sat on one of the long benches at the back, his arm around me as Jake steered out of the busy hub of Darling Harbour.

The lights from the jetty danced on the waves as we cruised along the dark water towards Circular Quay. A train roared overhead as we passed beneath the dark shadow of the Harbour Bridge. I smiled inwardly – the people within had no idea the kind of beings passing below them.

While Jake moored the launch at a wharf near The Rocks, Cal lifted up the back seat, extracted two dark objects and shook them out – long, black leather coats. He tossed one to Jake, who threw it on as we climbed out. Presumably they were to hide the presence of the swords dangling from their hips. They stepped ashore, and like real minders, surveyed the scene before nodding to Alec.

I had to admit, in those coats, they looked quite intimidating. Several passers-by paused to look but quickly moved on.

The area around the Quay was milling with people, locals as well as tourists. Live bands entertained the crowd. Some listened while others danced, their sweaty gyrations becoming another source of entertainment.

Cal stopped and sniffed the air. 'There's a hunting party of four out.'

Alec looked around and murmured, 'Happy hunting.'

'Okay, let's go.' Jake led the way down Pitt Street, the crowd parting to let them through.

We walked about a block, the music and noise from the Quay receding behind us, until we entered an unlit side lane. I wrinkled my nose at the smell of stale urine and garbage from an open dumpster. A cockroach the size of a rat scurried past my foot, and I squealed.

'Appearances are deceptive,' Alec said. He smiled and squeezed my hand as we entered a darkened concrete building. Just inside the entrance, Jake stopped at the elevator. We rode up to the second floor, and the doors opened onto a wide corridor that led to a timbered double door with polished brass handles and an intercom. Apart from a room number, it had no other identification.

My curiosity went into hyperdrive. What on earth was he up to, apart from jabbing the guy who lived here?

Jake and Cal stood behind us as Alec pressed a button. A voice answered. 'Can I help you?'

'It's Dr Munro. I have an appointment.'

'Please come in.'

With a click, Alec pushed open the door. Hand in hand, we walked into one of the most luxurious jewellery shops I had ever seen. Gleaming glass counters ringed the room, and ceiling downlights shone upon tray after tray of glittering objects. In the centre of the room, perched on top of a polished jade column, stood a small fountain in the shape of a water lily rising from a crystal bowl. Water cascaded over the stem and leaves that appeared to be made entirely of crystal and gemstones, while the lily itself was encrusted with diamonds. More were scattered, like pebbles, in the centre of the bowl.

I was amazed, not just by the opulence, but by the fact that I'd lived in Sydney all my life and never knew about this place. Yet here it was, hidden away in a non-descript building, only reached by elevator and an appointment.

'How long has this place been here?'

'Nearly a century, I think,' Alec said.

With Jake in front and Cal behind us, we made our way through this Aladdin's cave toward one of the counters. Behind it stood a man of average height. Thick, wiry brown hair curled over the tips of his ears, and a scraggly, uneven moustache drooped over his upper lip.

This must be Dawson. I wondered if the moustache tickled the skin of his donsang when he fed, presuming he had one. On either side of him stood two others – also Brethren from the colour of their eyes – a man and a woman who looked so alike they could be twins. One stared at Jake, and the other's gaze never left Cal.

'Nice to see you again, Princeps,' Dawson said to Alec. His eyes darted nervously from Alec to Jake and Cal before resting on me. 'And, and is this the young lady in question? The Ingenii?'

'That's right. My fiancé, Lady Laura.'

Dawson's eyes widened just as he bowed his head to me before addressing Alec again. 'Shall I, uh, bring out the trays or the particular article you admired earlier?'

Alec glanced at me. 'Show Lady Laura both.'

By now, I was anticipating what he was up to, and it wasn't only to test his serum on Dawson.

Dawson dipped behind the counter and brought out a tray wrapped in green velvet. His hands shook as he laid it on the counter and unveiled half-a-dozen or so stunning diamond rings. The pleasant butterflies in my stomach went into free fall and my hand flew to my mouth.

'Here's the one you thought the lady might like.' He lifted the tray to reveal another beneath. He picked up a small, purple velvet bundle, slowly unwrapped it, and I found myself staring at a heart-shaped diamond tinged with a subtle pink glow set in a plain gold band.

It was so beautiful, for a second I stopped breathing.

'Let's see if it fits,' Alec suggested.

He took my left hand and gently slid the diamond in place. It fitted perfectly. 'It's about time I gave you an engagement ring.' He kissed my fingertips.

I gasped with pleasure, speechless. The diamond spanned the width of my finger and sparkled like raindrops in a sun shower. Alec had picked it especially for me. I could feel my eyes beginning to sting as my gaze shifted from my new diamond ring to Alec's smiling face.

That's why he'd been so mysterious.

'Would you like to see the others, my lady?' Dawson pushed the other tray toward me then stepped away, hands behind his back.

Perhaps he's afraid to touch me. Probably thinks even my skin is dangerous. Right then I didn't care. 'No. I love this one.' I threw my arms around Alec's neck and hugged him.

His arms encircled me. Over my head he said, 'We'll take it.'

'Would Lady Laura like it gift wrapped?'

'No. I'm never taking it off!'

Alec's whole body shook with laughter. 'Don't worry about the box.'

I lowered my left hand onto Alec's chest and admired my stunning engagement ring. The fire within seemed to grow and glow the more I gazed at it.

'You really like it?'

'How did you know?' I looked up at him.

'I didn't. It just looked the type of ring you'd wear – graceful and elegant.'

His words went straight to my heart and a tear trickled down my cheek. Alec brushed it away, raised my chin and kissed me.

'I'm happy to have been of service, and since the lady is satisfied—' Dawson began.

'Just one more thing.' Jake placed the black medical bag on the glass counter, and I swung around in Alec's arms in time to see

Cal leap over, and haul the look-alikes aside.

They struggled in his grip. 'Don't hurt him! Uncle's done nothing wrong.'

Uncle? I couldn't see any similarity, except for their eyes, which had nothing to do with shared DNA.

Dawson's face paled. He backed away, hitting the wall behind him. 'I've done everything you asked!' His gaze ranged the room like a cornered rabbit looking for escape.

I felt sorry for him.

'Calm down. We've come to ask if you'd like to be immunised against white-oak,' Jake said.

Dawson's eyes narrowed and slowly shifted from Jake to Alec. 'You're not here to ex—execute me?' He swallowed hard.

'No,' Alec replied. 'If we were, would I have brought Lady Laura?'

He looked at me, but remained braced against the wall, wary. 'Please, release my niece and nephew.'

So they were twins.

Alec said. 'Not till you answer Jake's question.'

Jake held up the syringe. 'This serum will protect you from white-oak.'

'How do I know it works?'

'We've all been injected, and as you can see, we're fine,' Jake replied.

He moved a fraction from the wall, closer to the counter. 'Why offer it to me?'

Good point. Like offering a cancer cure to a death row inmate.

'You do a valuable service for us,' Alec said. 'And you've made a lot of enemies in the process. Still, the choice is yours.'

Jake shrugged and made a show of packing the syringe back into its little black bag. Dawson's gaze followed. He licked his lips, and in a sudden movement, his hand circled Jake's wrist. 'Wait,' he said, then let go when Jake glared at him. 'There's a lot of it on the streets. You'll never be able to stop it. But if that really works, I want some.'

'Wise decision,' Jake said.

'Them too?' He jerked his head in the twins' direction.

Jake glanced at Alec as Dawson rolled up his white shirtsleeve and bared his arm.

'Them, too,' Alec said.

Jake took a blood sample first before administering the serum. It seemed to take longer than injections I'd seen with ordinary people. Perhaps it had to do with the fact that vampire blood flowed more slowly then a human's.

When it was over, Alec asked. 'Feeling okay?'

'S'pose. Is that it?'

'Give it a few minutes.'

Dawson's head jerked up. He'd been rolling his sleeve back down. 'You said you'd already tested it.'

'Best to be sure.' Jake dug his hand into the black bag and brought out a wolf's-head ring. 'Seen this before, kids?' he asked the twins.

They looked at it and shook their heads.

Dawson's brow creased. 'What the hell's that?'

'I'm glad you don't know,' Alec said. 'Confirms my faith in you.'

Before Dawson could reply, Jake scratched the back of his hand with the white-oak spike, enough to draw blood.

'Hey!' Dawson sucked at the wound.

I held my breath, afraid the white marbling and almost-immediate crystallisation of his body would occur. But it didn't.

'Congratulations Dawson. You're immune to white-oak,' Alec said.

Dawson's eyes widened. He stared at his hand, a horrified expression on his face before sliding behind the counter to land with a thud. The twins cried out. Cal must have let them go, for they ran to their uncle's side.

'He'll be fine, kids,' Jake said. 'Only shock. Haul him up.'

They lifted him up. Dawson raised his head, a smooth sheen of sweat on his brow. 'I feel like shit! What did you do to me?'

'Just the effect of the serum. It won't last long – about an hour,' Alec said before addressing the twins. 'Take him to the back room.'

'Um...' They glanced at each other, reluctant.

'We won't tell where the room is,' Alec said. 'Take him in there and lay him down. He'll be okay.'

'C'mon, Unc,' one of them said. 'The princeps said you'll be okay.' He pressed something beneath the counter and the wall behind him swung open. They picked their uncle off the floor and carried him inside the secret room.

'Laura, we'll have to watch him for the next hour, or so, just to be sure,' Alec said. 'You can browse the shelves and pick out something you like.'

His generosity stunned me, but I had all I wanted. I lifted my hand and wiggled my newly ringed finger. 'This is all I want.'

He flashed me a grin.

'I'll stay with you.'

'All right.' His lips grazed mine then he and Jake turned their attention to Dawson.

Cal moved to stand near the front entrance, hands crossed over his chest.

'Right, you two. You're next.' Jake told the twins and loaded a new syringe.

They glanced at each other, their uncle, then at Jake and shook their heads.

'Your choice.' Jake packed the syringe away, and over the next hour, he and Alec conferred while Dawson moaned.

I entertained myself by trying on the various pieces of jewellery, including a few tiaras. Not my thing, I concluded.

Eventually the fever abated, and in a little over an hour later, Dawson was on his feet.

'We done here?' Cal asked.

'All done.' Alec took my hand, kissed it, and the shiny pink rock on my finger winked up at him. 'Thanks for waiting.'

I smiled. 'Let's go home.'

Jake and Cal once again took up position in front and behind us as we exited the building and made our way to the launch.

As the boat skimmed over the waves I leaned back against Alec and looked up at the crescent moon. Clouds scurried across the sky and dimmed the stars, but nothing could dim the joy that filled my heart when I glanced at the beautiful pink diamond on my finger. It glowed with its own fire, almost complimenting the dull scarlet blaze from the eyes of the serpent ring on my other hand.

Alec whispered, 'I love you,' in my ear and pressed me closer.

I snuggled into the comfort of his arms and uttered a silent prayer that this night would indeed be the beginning of our happily-ever-after.

For that one glorious moment I forgot I was the centre of a war with creatures who would do anything to prevent the curse from ending.

CHAPTER 27 – A VERY VAMPIRE CHRISTMAS

LAURA

It was midnight when we sat down, to what Judy described as a vampire Christmas. Earlier in the day, she, Jenny and I had celebrated with my foster-parents, John and Eilene, and we were still recovering from that meal. My mum had created an amazing spread – a four-course gastronomic delight that could have come from the pages of *Delicious* magazine.

Jenny had gone to bed, no longer able to stay awake. In spite of my own drowsiness, I was determined not to miss my first official Christmas with my immortal family.

The dining room on the main deck was dark, except for the light created by two exquisite golden candelabras, shaped like twisting vines, in the centre of the glass dining table. Twelve silver candles – six in each – rose from their scrolled-leaf beds and threw flickering shadows across the room. On either side of each candelabrum, four crystal decanters filled with wine caught the glow of the candlelight, their burgundy contents appeared as if lit from within. A fifth crystal decanter filled with clear liquid, sat on the table in front of me. White wine or water?

Marcus sat at one end of the table, Luc on his right, Judy on his left. Alec and I sat together at the other end, Jake and Cal on my right, Kari, Sam and Terens opposite. Each of the men had an empty wine glass in front of him, as well as a small vial the size of a man's thumb, filled with red liquid.

It must be blood. But why such a miniscule amount?

There was a quiet solemnity about this gathering that I didn't understand. Most of my Christmas dinners with friends and family had been noisy, jovial affairs, with each person attempting to talk over the other. I glanced at Terens. His gaze was riveted on the glass vial in front of him. The other men seemed just as mesmerised by theirs, staring at the delicate-looking containers hungrily.

What was in them? Something similar to the ruby pendant-vial that Luc had given me? I leaned over to ask Alec, when Marcus stood.

'My family,' he began, looking around at each of us, 'this night is special, for we celebrate the homecoming of my granddaughter, Laura.' He looked at me. 'Our first Christmas together since you were a baby. My life is now complete.' He reached for the decanter and filled his, Luc's and Judy's goblet. His men did the same.

Alec reached for the clear decanter and poured its contents into my glass. 'A precaution,' he whispered.

I sniffed the glass. Water. In case I was already pregnant? 'You know something I don't?' I whispered back.

'Not for want of trying.' He smiled and tipped the rest of the water from the decanter into his own wine glass.

Marcus raised his, 'To the Child of Light and Darkness, daughter of Lucius Antonius Pulcher, my son, and Judith Dantonville. To Laura, last of the Ingenii.'

Beneath the table, Alec took my hand and gave it a gentle squeeze.

Everyone rose, turned to me and chanted in unison. 'To Laura, last of the Ingenii.' They downed their glasses.

Touched by Marcus's welcome, I could appreciate what it meant to him. He was there at the beginning of the curse, and now he was here, at what I hoped was its end. What would his choice be? Life as a vampire – a nightwalker – or a higher form of life throughout eternity? Maybe I was selfish, but I didn't want him to choose. Although I knew how old he was, my grandfather had the appearance of a young man; and young men should not die. He'd suffered enough and deserved his own happy ending.

'Thank you.' I sipped my water.

The men remained standing and refilled their glasses as Marcus spoke again. 'According to our tradition, we remember our fallen comrades.'

Kari rose from her seat, and I did the same.

'Fallen comrades,' they repeated, raised their glasses in another toast, and then refilled.

Terens suddenly uttered, 'Melander.' He leant forward and blew out one of the silver candles before throwing his head back and emptying his glass.

'Nepos.' Jake puffed out the next one and downed his toast.

'Appius,' Sam said, and another candle died.

'Pudens.' Cal followed suit.

Four silver candles had been snuffed out. The aroma of burnt wax filled the room.

'Martius,' Marcus said and blew out another one.

'Galen,' Luc said. Another candle spluttered out and the last toast was drunk.

Six extinguished candles to represent six dead soldiers. I guessed those on the candelabra that remained represented Marcus and the four living members of the original Roman patrol, as well as Luc, his son. Luc had told me the story of the deaths of two of them in particular. They'd been caught up in the terror when Marcus and his men were transformed by the witch's curse and were killed by their comrades. From the sad expression on Terens's face, he must have been responsible for one of those deaths. Perhaps Melander's, the name he called out.

We resumed our seats, but Luc remained standing. 'And now, to The Second Cohort of Frisians,' the others rose and stood to attention, 'my customary gift.' He indicated the crimson vials in front of each of his men. 'Tribune Sextus Terentius, Troopers Quintus Sempronius, Caius Justinius and Calixtus. May you enjoy the day and the light of the sun. May the strength of the gods be yours, and the swiftness of their steeds speed your feet. May your enemies cower and prostrate themselves before you.' When he finished, Luc gave them a nod.

The men bowed low to him and Marcus, picked up the vials and drained their precious contents. Yet another ritual, but without the biting. Its ancient formal language embodied romantic images of soldiers in red cloaks riding on white horses into battle.

'Oh man, I'd forgotten how damned good that is,' Terens remarked as he sat back down.

'Can we know whose blood we've been given this year?' Jake asked.

Luc looked at Judith, and she smiled. 'My gift to you. A way to say thank you for looking after our child.' She and Luc linked hands on the tabletop. 'It's First Blood.'

I was stunned at my parent's generosity. First Blood, I'd been told, is the most potent, filled with energy and power unmatched later in an Ingenii's lifetime. It slowly declines over time, hence the need for a changeover every fifty years.

Cal, who sat closest to them, took Judy's hand, brought it to his lips and kissed it. 'Thank you, lady. I speak for us all.'

The other three acknowledged with 'Aye's'.

'What are you going to do in your three days of sunshine?' Judy asked him.

He ran his finger around the rim of the wine glass. 'Botanical gardens. A lot of flowers only open in the day. I want to see and smell them.'

Everyone nodded. There were no chuckles or smirks. It was the last thing I expected to hear from an ancient warrior. Who would've guessed that Cal liked flowers? I found myself waiting to hear what the others would do with their fleeting time in the sunshine.

'Jake, what about you?' Alec asked.

'Been thinking about that since this time last year.' He paused. 'I'm gonna take off my shirt and stroll along the beach. Then sit and watch the sunset.' A beaming smile lit his face.

I looked at Terens. He was lounging back in his chair, rubbing the diamond stud in his ear and staring into space. 'Terens? What are you going to do?'

He glanced at me. 'I had considered skydiving, pet. I've always wanted to see the world in the daylight from that height, but I've had a change of plan.'

'You're not going to make a hole in the ground if the 'chute doesn't open?' Sam said.

'Nope. Going hunting.' Terens poured himself another glass of wine. 'Lost an arm to that bastard, Timur. He left his sidekick, Rasputin, behind who knows where that slime of a master of his is holed up.'

'Why didn't you tell me?' Sam turned in his chair and faced him.

'Just did.'

'I'm after that son-of-a-bitch myself. I'm going with you.'

'Count me in, as well. Luc, bring me one of the vials.' At Marcus's sudden pronouncement the room became deathly quiet.

'But, you never—' Luc began.

'This time it's different. I can't hide in a monastery and let you battle this alone.'

Terens grinned and slammed the table top with the flat of his hand. The candelabras bounced. 'Like old times!'

'Well, there goes the beach.' Jake rose and hammered on the table's surface as well.

Sam did the same and muttered, 'I'll smell the roses next year.'

The table vibrated with their rhythmic thumping, and the entire room reverberated to the accompanying cry, 'Mar-cus! Mar-cus! Mar-cus!'

In that moment I was drawn into another world, another era, like a bystander from another time witnessing a scene that had disappeared from the planet, centuries before. Here they were, Roman soldiers saluting their commander – my grandfather.

The passage of time had become irrelevant.

A broad smile lit Luc's face as he and Marcus clasped forearms and exchanged words, so low and fast I could only guess what passed between them. Whatever it was, the men thumped the table even harder, the din so loud my ears began to ring.

Next to me, Alec rose and joined in the salute. I wondered how much the glass table could take till it shattered under their prolonged assault. I glanced at Kari. She was staring open-mouthed at Jake, hero worship evident in her eyes. *How long will it take for him to see it?*

Luc spun on his heel and left the room.

Marcus raised his hand for silence and looked at Alec. 'With your permission, I'd like to resume permanent command of my men.'

'You have it. Welcome back, Lord Marcus.'

Marcus bowed his head then motioned for us to be seated. His gaze went straight to me. 'Laura, when Luc first told me about finding Alec, I knew we wouldn't have long to wait for your arrival. But, by Deus, neither he nor I guessed how all this would come about.' He smiled briefly at Judith. 'It all comes full circle, and where it began, it shall end.'

The curse began in a remote Pictish village in Scotland. That's where I would have to give birth to a child conceived with Alec in order to end it. I had no idea if I was even pregnant and inwardly laughed as my twenty-first century feminist ideas were jettisoned in the face of the ancient juggernaut that had taken over my life.

Luc returned and handed Marcus the little red vial. Marcus swallowed hard and straightened his shoulders. 'The time has come.' Everyone around the table watched as he removed the stopper, stared at its contents then gulped it down. 'Deus!' His eyes widened. 'I could lift a house off its foundations. My entire body's tingling.'

'Welcome to my world, Father,' Luc said.

Marcus placed a hand on Luc's shoulder and squeezed. His gaze went to his men. 'We leave at dawn.' His chin quivered.

'Been a long time since you've given that command, Marcus Antonius Pulcher,' Terens said, a note of reverence in his voice. 'It's good to hear.'

'Why did it take you so long?' Luc asked.

Marcus sat back down, and with a wave of his hand, indicated his men. 'I brought them into this, so I took the brunt of the punishment. I could have acted more nobly and showed clemency in the face of *her* cruelty that day. But I did not. I showed myself to be no better. She as much as said so, and I've carried that guilt for nearly two-thousand years.'

'No!' Luc cried. 'The bitch cursed us all; the innocent with the so-called guilty. I'll never accept it as punishment. It was vengeance, Father, and no less. To be condemned for all eternity to live without light, far outweighed the so-called crime.'

Marcus continued. 'I've had a long time to think about it. She and I were both wrong. But I believe she relented after her death. Hence the Ingenii.' He glanced at Judy, then at me before returning his attention to Luc. 'You have been privileged to enjoy the sun, Luc, and I am proud of you for sharing it with our men. Any more than once a year, though and who knows how the curse would have reacted.'

'You talk of it like a living thing,' I said.

'Laura, these things are like an entity, an extension of the one who uttered it – like a lost spirit who hovers on earth waiting for Judgment Day. It cannot leave till all things are properly fulfilled.'

The hairs on my arms stood on end.

Alec squeezed my hand. 'We'll end it, darling, and it'll haunt us no more.' His eyes looked into mine with such assurance, I wanted to believe everything was going to be all right.

'You could've shared in this once a year,' Jake said. 'It wouldn't've affected the curse. Why didn't you?'

'I had my reasons.' Marcus waved his hand. 'No longer relevant.' He looked at the wine glass in his hand and drank down whatever was left.

It occurred to me that they always spoke English. Did they ever use their own language when alone? Would it be Latin? I whispered the question to Alec.

'Only Marcus, Luc and Terens are from a Roman background,' he answered. 'Cal, Jake and Sam are Frisians – from the Netherlands. Latin isn't their native tongue. In fact, Frisian is the ancestor of modern English.'

Terens turned toward me, wearing a mischievous smile. 'You should hear Sam speak Latin, pet.' He shook his head in mock disgust. 'Worst thing I've ever heard. At least in French or English I can understand what he's saying.'

Sam slowly turned his head in Terens's direction as quiet chuckles filled the room.

'For example,' Terens went on, 'I remember a particular incident when he was stopped by that old, bandy-legged centurion, Nemius –'

'Not that old story,' Sam protested.

Kari sat forward in her chair and asked Jake, 'Have I heard this one?'

'Probably. Terens loves to repeat it.' Jake's eyes crinkled up at the corners as he sipped on his wine.

' "*Festinabimus Taberna!*" he said.' Terens mocked Sam's voice. Even Sam cracked a smile.

Of course, I didn't have a clue what they were on about. I looked at Alec for clarification. 'Sam said he and his companions were hurrying to the tavern, but he used the feminine form of the verb, as if they were women.'

I could see how that would've been embarrassing to his fellow soldiers.

'I got a week's latrine duties for getting it wrong,' Sam said.

'As I recall,' Terens remarked, 'he said you accomplished what no enemy of Rome had done – destroy the Roman language.'

Marcus and Luc roared with laughter.

'You'll never let me live that down, will you?'

'Not in a million years,' Terens answered, leaned forward and slapped Sam on the back.

'Don't you think it's ironic. Nobody speaks Latin anymore, yet Frisian's everywhere – in modern English? Maybe it's just as well I didn't waste my time learning to speak your language.'

Cal guffawed, reached for the decanter and poured himself another glass of wine. 'How you gonna counter that one, Terens?'

'Only one way I know.' Terens stood and flexed his right arm. 'Brand new model.'

'By all means, test it out.' Sam's chair scraped across the floor as he, too, rose and began flexing his right arm. 'Ready to lose some fingers?' The two faced each other, grinning.

Kari rolled her eyes. 'Oh no, not this stupid game.'

Alec leaned toward me and whispered, 'Maybe we should go for a stroll around the deck.'

'Why?' I asked. 'What are they going to do?'

'Their version of an arm wrestle.' Alec looked uncomfortable. 'They do it every Christmas.'

'It's gross, Laura.' Kari grimaced. 'The loser must chop off a finger and hand it over. The one with the biggest collection wins.'

'You're kidding. At Christmas?'

'It's the only time they can do it – good way to test the strength of the Ingenii blood. Any lost appendage regenerates in an instant,' Alec said.

'Sorry, boys, you know I can't stay to watch,' Judy said. 'If anyone wants me I'll be in my room.' She wished us goodnight and kissed Luc and Marcus on the cheek. The men rose and bowed as she left.

'Think I'll do the same,' I said when I saw Terens move one of the candelabra aside and pull a blade from beneath his trouser leg. 'No way am I going to watch them cut off fingers, even if it is some weird Christmas tradition.'

'Allez, ma petite, this is not for a lady's eyes.'

'I agree,' Kari said and skipped to my side of the table. 'Let's join Judy.'

I still had Alec's Christmas present. This was a good time to slip away and give it to him. 'Meet you there, Kari. There's something I need to do first.' I mouthed the words, 'Present for Alec.'

She nodded and gave me a knowing smile as she left.

I turned to Alec. 'I accept your offer of a stroll around the deck.'

With his arm around my waist, Alec led me from the dining room just as Sam and Terens took up their positions, elbows on the table, hands clasped, steely gazes locked. Two long, menacing-looking knives lay in the centre of the table.

I shuddered and turned away.

The night air was cool and sweet as we stepped through the doors. I took a deep gulp to rid myself of the warm scent of burnt candle wax, along with the image of disembodied fingers. It brought back the sickening memory of Rasputin's severed hands clawing at the ground.

Although it was cloudy, the air was still, and every sound was magnified – the hum of the crickets in the bush across the bay, gentle lapping of waves against the sides of the boat. Several smaller boats were anchored nearby, their lights reflecting off the dark, mirrored waters.

I reached into the pocket of my taffeta, black and white polka-dot dress, pulled out a tiny parcel and held it out to Alec. 'Merry Christmas.'

'Laura, I didn't expect—'

'Ssshh, open it.'

While he and Jake had been away at the lab searching for an antidote for white-oak, I'd done some searching of my own. After several hours trawling through the net, I'd found it – the perfect gift – on a Scottish Clans site.

Alec tore off the wrapping and sucked in a breath when he opened the little box.

'I hope it fits,' I said.

A dazzling smile lit his face. 'It will, darling.' He lifted the gold ring from its box and slipped it on. It fitted. A gold eagle perched on top of a strap and buckle – the ancient family crest of the Munro clan – sat comfortably on his left, index finger. He pocketed the box and wrapper, took me in his arms and kissed me with a passion that made my thighs tremble.

'So, you like it?' I asked after a while.

Alec chuckled. 'Very much. Where did you find it?'

'Online. You asked me not to leave the boat.'

He brought his hand up and gazed at the ring. 'It's perfect. Now it's my turn to ask – how did you know?'

'I didn't. Only knew you had a set of bagpipes, and since there's no other ring on your finger apart from wee serpent here,' I put on a mock Scottish accent and wriggled my finger, 'I thought to get you one.'

'Our clan crest.' He chuckled and kissed me again. 'Merry Christmas,' he murmured into my mouth. As we were locked in each other's embrace, faint growls and swearing drifted out from the stateroom. I didn't want to know who was losing a finger.

I pressed closer to Alec. The drumming of my heartbeat drowned out any other sound.

CHAPTER 28 – PORTRAIT

LAURA

I grabbed a pillow and covered my head to muffle the ringing of my mobile phone. Any message could wait. I was having such a wonderful dream about Alec making love to me. Last night, there was no part of my body he hadn't lavished with attention – he had raised me to heights I never thought possible.

I dumped the pillow when the phone beeped again, picked it up and checked the time. 1pm. My stomach grumbled. Another beep. 'For goodness sake.' I pressed the message button. 'Who's messaging me on Boxing Day?'

My sleepy brain spluttered into life when I saw who the messages were from.

Matt!

I sat bolt upright. *Why does he still have my number?* 'What do you want, Matt?' I said rhetorically to his name on the small screen. After our less-than-congenial-parting, I was reluctant to have any further contact with him. But he'd been my first lover; and I would always have affection for him.

I placed the phone down on the bedcover and stared at it.

It beeped again. I jumped. There was no avoiding it. I scrolled through the messages.

Have 2 c u urgently where r u moored? It's important; can I meet you today? Need 2 show u s/thing.

My curiosity was piqued – Matt never exaggerated. If he said something was important, then it was. I glanced at Alec's side of the bed. A pale, blue sheet of paper lay neatly folded on his pillow. I picked it up and brought it to my nose. His scent. Images of our lovemaking flooded my mind. Even his smell set me on fire.

Good morning, my sleeping beauty. Didn't want to wake you. Will be at the lab most of the day checking on the serum. Should you need me… you know what to do. Hope to be done by early this evening. Need to have you in my arms.

Yours for eternity, Alec

Even his written words made my heart melt. The phone beeped again. I sighed and checked the screen.

Pls answer, Laura!

Nope. No avoiding it. I messaged him back. *Come to the boat, Matt. We're moored at Balmoral Marina*

Thx. On way.

He could be here in less than thirty minutes if he was at his home in Glebe. I threw aside the bedcover and raced for the shower, before realising I hadn't asked either Judy or Luc if inviting him was okay. As soon as I was dressed, I'd do so.

I made my way up to the galley on the next deck. No one seemed to be about. Perhaps Judy still slept. Kari surely would be. Antonius and his men would be out hunting Rasputin – I would've loved to have seen my grandfather experience his first morning in nearly two-thousand years. I was sure Luc had been present to see it with him. The thought occurred to me, would he be still awake? *He needs to know about Matt.*

'Papa, are you awake?' His hearing was as acute as Alec's. 'Matt's coming over,' I said, as I grabbed a mince pie out of the well-stocked pantry, full of leftovers from Christmas luncheon.

'How do you feel about that, ma petite?'

I spun around. He stood by the door, arms crossed over his chest, blonde hair slightly tousled, as if he'd just gotten out of bed.

Maybe he had.

'Awkward.' I took a bite of the pastry. It was good. 'Did I, ah, wake you up?'

He dismissed the suggestion with a wave of his hand. 'Why does he want to see you?'

'Not sure. Something about needing to show me something. He sent me urgent texts.' I set the espresso coffee machine, and, while it bubbled away I showed him the messages.

His brow creased. 'Mmm.' He handed back the mobile. 'You think he might be trying…?'

'To get me back?' I thought it through. Although we were together for only four months, Matt never came across as that duplicitous. He was one of those what-you-see-is-what-you-get type of guys. I shook my head. 'No, that's not the way he operates.'

'How well do you know him?'

I took a deep breath. It was a question that had been put to me before, and at the time I had dismissed it. 'Not that well.'

'You don't have to see him.'

'I told him I would.'

'Ah!' Luc stepped further into the galley. The espresso machine hissed, and I placed my cup beneath the nozzle. 'Pour me one, too, ma petite.'

He pulled down the blinds and I wondered if he was becoming averse to sunlight. As far as I knew, he still fed from my mother, and being an outgoing Ingenii, the special qualities her blood once possessed would be waning.

I filled two cups and handed him one. We sat together at the breakfast bar, sipping in silence as the delicious aroma of freshly brewed coffee wafted around us.

'You still feel anything for this man?'

'Fondness. I can't wipe out the time I spent with him, even if it was only for a short time. I enjoyed those four months.' He said nothing, and I added, 'It's Alec I love, Papa. No man will ever compare to him.'

'Bien!' He smiled and patted my hand.

I finished my coffee and took my cup to the sink. 'By the way, you know if Jen's still asleep?'

'She's awake and in the Jacuzzi.' He indicated the next deck up with a jerk of his head. 'I like her. She's been a good friend to you all these years.'

'How do you…?' I shook my head. Naturally he knew. He'd been keeping watch over me since I was a baby. He probably had a list of all my friends, acquaintances and who knows who or what else. Yet – I could forgive him as he did it for my protection.

His grin confirmed it. He swivelled his head toward the door. 'Ah! He's here, ma petite. Coming down the jetty.'

My stomach fluttered. 'What could be so urgent that he has to see me in person?' Luc's brow furrowed. 'I'd better go.' I kissed his cheek then I went out onto the main deck.

It was a warm day, and I blamed that for my sweaty palms as Matt strode along the pier. He wore jeans and a plain, white T-shirt. His face was grim. There was a newspaper tucked beneath his arm.

I took a deep breath.

'Laura.' I'm sure his eyes softened, if only for a moment, until he looked down at my hand. My engagement ring glinted in the sunlight. His jaw tightened. 'Didn't waste any time, did he? One hell of a rock.'

I slid my hand from the railing and tucked it into the pocket of my shorts. 'Alec told me about your … memory.'

His face hardened. 'And you're okay with that?'

'He saved your life, Matt. My father would've killed you.'

Matt huffed. 'Yeah, don't know whether I owe him one, or should hate him more. I'm still deciding.' He looked past me. 'He around?'

'No, he's at the lab. What's this about, Matt?'

His gaze came back to me. 'Can't I see my *ex*-girlfriend?' A hint of a sardonic smile played around his lips as he emphasised the "ex."

In the bright sunlight it was impossible not to miss the stubble on his chin, and the dark circles under his eyes. A twinge of guilt shot through me.

'Lebrettan in there?' With a jerk of his head he indicated the boat.

'Yes.'

He looked away and swore under his breath.

'Whatever you need to say, or show me, you can do it here.'

He shook his head. 'Better inside.'

With two clenched fists in my pockets, I led the way into the main salon conscious of Matt's burning gaze on my back. Only two weeks ago ... I quashed the memory. 'You dating that ER doctor who treated you?' I shot back over my shoulder.

'Who?'

'The one whose hand you didn't want to let go when you told me to get lost.'

Silence behind me, except for heavy footsteps on the gangplank. I thought to make myself feel better by reminding him of his infatuation with the pretty brunette doctor. It made leaving him for Alec easier. That, and the fact he'd been planning to kill the fanged side of my family in a misguided attempt to protect me. Instead, it was no better than a petty remark. *No good, Laura,* my conscience chastised. 'Can I get you a drink?'

'No thanks.' He stood in the entrance and gazed at me.

'Please sit down.' I perched on the edge of the closest sofa, hands clasped tightly in my lap.

Matt didn't move. He lowered his head and shoved his hands into his jeans pockets. 'Look, Laura, that day at the hospital, what I said.' His head jerked up. 'I'm sorry. I was angry. I'd lost my memory and then you came in and said you were leaving me—'

'You couldn't remember me. Why did it matter?'

'Look, call it wounded pride, whatever you want, I, ah, had no right speaking to you like I did.'

So he wasn't dating her. He feigned it so I wouldn't pity him. Another rush of conscience assailed me, and I conjured Alec's face in my mind. Instantly, I knew I had made the right decision. 'Let's forget it, then. Can we be friends?' As it came out of my mouth I knew the stupidity of what I'd just said. Can ex-lovers ever be friends?

He stared at me for a while, before he finally said, 'No.'

Perhaps it was for the best. 'Okay.' I released a breath. 'What do you need to see me about?'

He removed the newspaper from beneath his arm and joined me on the sofa.

'Seen the papers recently?'

'No, not interested.'

He spread the paper open, placed it on the coffee table in front of me, and pointed to the bottom of the page. 'You ought to take a look at this.'

I glanced down. My picture stared back at me, or rather, a portrait of me. One I instantly recognised. I'd seen it before – in Jean-Philippe's makeshift studio. Some of the details had been altered, but it was essentially the one *he* had shown me, the night…

My stomach churned.

'Know him?' I didn't like the tone of Matt's voice, or the way it sliced through me. His finger moved to a smiling photo of Jean-Philippe – young, handsome, and according to the headline, missing.

A dreadful coldness crept over me as I skimmed through the article.

Portrait Artist Goes Missing
Recently nominated for the Sydney Emerging Artists Prize for his portrait of "Laura", John-Phillip Reynold has not responded to emails or calls. My eyes scanned to the last line.
If anyone knows of his whereabouts, please contact….

John-Phillip Reynold. He had anglicised his name – to avoid detection? I had hoped never to hear him mentioned again, or see the disturbing images he had painted of me. Yet here they were, for the whole world to see. How on earth could I explain it to Matt? Our relationship was over, and he was here, not as my protector, but as a detective. How could I tell him what happened? What Jean-Philippe had tried to do to me – how he had attempted to kill Alec? How could I tell him he was enquiring after a man who was dead?

The dreaded thought occurred to me – would he try to arrest Alec? Unfortunately, Matt knew me, knew I hiccupped if I attempted to lie. 'He's my half-brother,' I answered.

He frowned. 'I though you were an only child.'

'I only found out last week. He was Luc's son – *is* Luc's son.' I could have bitten my tongue at the slip up.

'Was?'

'Is. Anyway, aren't you off duty? Why come here with that?' I slid the newspaper back to him.

His eyes narrowed. 'Why so defensive?'

'We're not together. Why should it interest you?'

Matt shot to his feet. 'You always interest me. I'm sure you understand why.'

In a moment of silence, our gazes locked. His eyes were pale blue, like Antarctic ice, the shade they always turned when he was angry.

'It's none of your business, Matt. Let it go.'

'A half-brother who paints a semi-nude portrait of his sister who just happens to be my ex-half-vampire girlfriend; a man whose eyes are the same strange shade of lavender? Oh yeah, I looked him up online. Now he's suddenly disappeared after winning a major art prize. And you're asking me to let it go?'

'Yes.' My mouth was a hard line.

He shook his head. 'You have no idea.' His fists clenched as he spoke. 'There's a good chance it'll land on the desk of someone in Missing Persons, who just might recognise your picture. It'll get around the station. If this guy doesn't show up soon, it *could* go to Homicide.'

My mouth dried up, and I swallowed hard at that last word.

'Where is he?' Matt pursued.

I looked up to where he stood, hands crunching the top of the settee opposite me. Was he pursuing this for his own reputation, or was it out of genuine concern for me.

'Why are you doing this? For you, or me?'

His brow creased, and tense lines around his mouth – a mouth I had often kissed – tightened. 'If you have to ask me that question, then we don't know each other, do we?'

The silence stretched between us again.

'I guess we weren't together long enough.'

'That wasn't my choice.' He gave me an accusing glare, hurt burning in his eyes.

I stood and faced him. There was no way I was going to take the blame for our break up. 'No? You were planning to murder my family, Matt. I know about the white-oak bullets. You had them the night we were attacked. How could I stay with a man capable of that?'

He took a step back. 'I won't deny it, and won't apologise for it. But let's qualify the word, "murder." That relates to humans, not the *undead*.'

His words burned inside me. 'Half of me is *undead!* Where does that place me in your limited category of who is and is not human? Killing me wouldn't be murder?'

His face paled.

'It's you who has no idea.'

'I would never hurt you.'

'You already have, by what you planned to do.'

He took a deep breath. 'I see.' A heavy silence settled between us. He turned and strode to the door. 'If someone wants to pursue this missing person and Homicide gets hold of it, be prepared – it could land on my desk. From that point, address me as Detective Inspector. Our friendship is over.'

Matt was relentless. Unless I told him the truth, he'd keep digging. I dreaded the thought of having to face his icy stare on the other side of an interrogation table. Who would've believed that our relationship would come to this.

'Matt, wait.'

He stopped mid stride, hand on the door handle and looked at me over his shoulder.

'I'll tell you.' I blinked. 'But you have to promise something first.'

'I can't do that.'

'Then I can't tell you.'

He exhaled and turned to face me fully. 'All right, what do you want?'

CHAPTER 29 – MESMERISED

ALEC

I glanced at my watch – it was going on three. Six hours of daylight remained and I still had other experiments needing my attention. The vision of Laura in my arms last night filled my mind, and I had to force my thoughts to stay on task.

The serum was still active in the blood samples I took from Luc and each of the men, including Dawson. I was placing the tubes back into the centrifuge when I heard Jake's voice.

'Alec, where are you?'

He must be within a six-mile radius if he wanted an answer. The Ingenii blood had doubled the hearing range. 'At the lab. Why?'

'Four assassins are after you. Get back to the yacht.'

I looked down at the serpent ring – its eyes were black. How long had they been like that? Why didn't I notice sooner?

I extended my senses and tried to locate any unusual emotional scents. Professional assassins would exude blank signals; a deadly intent to complete a task, while most humans exuded a variety of scents that mirrored their thoughts and emotions. But no success – too many people about. If these assassins were close, then my staff were in danger as well. I had to get out, into the open.

I removed my lab coat and dropped it into the laundry chute on my way out. The long corridor that led to the hospital wing and reception was empty, so I sped down its length to the emergency exit. To my left was the Staff Only car park, to my right a small tree-covered copse; occasionally, staff members and visitors sat in the shade to eat their lunch. While deciding which way to go – my car or tree cover – something whizzed past my ear. I caught the whiff of white-oak.

'One's already here,' I said.

'We're close,' Marcus's voice sounded in my ear. 'Contain them till we come.'

'Will do.' I raced to the nearest tree and, hoping no human was around to witness, shimmied up to the highest branch that would support my weight. From my vantage point, I scanned for my attacker.

He was behind a van, his gaze darting about trying to find where I'd gone. To his human senses, I'd simply disappeared. The gun trembled in his hand. This was no professional killer. I inhaled his scent, and it surprised me. This human's partner was a friend of the Principate. When did she become turncoat? No, that didn't make sense. *There has to be something... Rasputin!* There could be no other explanation. If he could mesmerise Sam, then he could do the same to fellow Brethren, and use their donsangs. These so-called assassins were mesmerised *donsangs.*

Typical of Rasputin to choose innocent victims. If he can succeed in controlling the will of every Principate supporter in the city.... Suddenly I feared I might be witnessing the ending of the Principate in a manner unforeseen by either Marcus or Luc. The scenario I envisaged horrified me.

As I watched, I sensed another arrival. The newcomer gestured to the man behind the van, before crouching down behind the low hedge between the Staff Only car park and the public parking. He, too, had a gun aimed at the copse of trees where I hid.

How long before someone walks out, sees them and calls the police? I had to end this. There was no sign of the other two assassins. Jake had mentioned four.

The man behind the hedge was nearer to my hiding place. I moved fast – faster then their slow human senses could perceive – and grabbed him by the throat. The man's eyes bulged and he clawed at my hand, as I took his gun and shoved it in my pocket. No smell of white-oak. As I decided what to do with him, I recalled Laura saying how her ring had enabled her to overcome Rasputin's mesmerisation. It was worth a try.

I relaxed my grip on his throat, raised the serpent ring until the man's eyes focused on it. A faint light streamed through my fingers. The man blinked and his eyes flared. He looked about him in confusion.

After releasing his throat, I placed my finger on his lips and whispered in his ear, 'Stay here. Don't speak or move till I say so.'

He nodded vigorously.

Good. Now for the next one.

An extra heartbeat drummed in my ears, this one from the other end of the car park. The emotional blankness I sensed identified him as another assassin. *One down, two to go. How did they know I'd be here today?* Crouching low, I found a break in the hedge that brought me to the van. The man had his back to me. I dashed beneath the vehicle, grabbed his legs and dragged him under.

The gun dropped from his hand and clacked on the concrete, alerting the other assassin. Footsteps drew close. The man lay unconscious – he'd hit his head on the pavement. I pocketed his gun, and as I dragged his prone body from beneath the van, he stirred and opened his eyes. They widened as they focused on me crouching next to him.

I held my ringed finger in his line of vision. 'Look at its eyes.' As before, the eyes of the serpent flared then dimmed.

The man blinked, refocused on me, paled and swore.

Behind me, I sensed Jake, his Range Rover screeching to a halt only yards away. 'Get the others. Don't kill them, they're mesmerised,' I said as he, Cal and Marcus sprang out.

To the human I said, 'Who ordered you to kill me?'

'Snake eyes.' He sat up and dropped his head into his hands. 'My head.'

'My fault. Only way to stop you.' Marcus approached, dragging a man by the arm. Behind him, Jake held another who struggled in his grip. 'I left one sitting beneath the hedge.' I indicated his position with a flick of my head.

'I'll get him.' Cal jogged over.

'Can you stand?' I returned my attention to my would-be assassin. We couldn't stay out here, in the open, yet I didn't want to take them to my office either.

The staff would be shocked to see us striding through the hospital. Where to interrogate them? Snake eyes, he said. Had to have been Rasputin.

He looked up at me, panic in his eyes. 'Annalise! I need to know if she's okay.'

'We'll check later. Can you get up?'

He rose tentatively, palm pressed to his forehead. 'Brethren, they came to our house.'

'How many?' Marcus asked. He and Jake joined me, pushing their captives beside the one I held. The mesmerised donsangs stared at me blankly. 'Three, no, four. There were four.'

I glanced around after sensing several humans enter the car park. 'Get them into the car – question them there,' I said to Marcus.

Cal climbed in first and sat cross-legged in the space between the back door and the extra back seats, blocking any escape. The donsangs went in next, and I took the seat by the door. Jake got behind the driver's wheel and Marcus slammed the door shut before joining Jake in the front.

I turned and faced the remaining two. 'You and you. Eyes here.' I raised the ring. Though still mesmerised, it drew their gazes. The light flared and I saw understanding, then fear, replace their dull, expressionless stares.

'Deus! I've never seen it do that before.' Marcus removed the headrest and folded his arms along the top of the seat.

'Tell me what you remember?' I asked them.

They all babbled at once, and one thing became clear – Rasputin had visited each one in their own homes – he'd been the one who had mesmerised them.

'I don't know what happened after that snake-eyed devil did this to me,' one of them said. 'All I remember is an urge to kill you.'

The others nodded.

'I woke up on the floor, a gun beside me,' another said and shivered.

'What about our procters?' The first man asked me. 'I need to know if Annalise is safe. I need to check on her.' He tried to rise from the seat, but Jake pushed him back.

'If she's safe, then she's resting. If not, well, it's too late for you to do anything.'

The *Procters*, the corrupted form for the French term for protector, was what the donsangs called their Brethren lovers. Most unions formed strong, almost lifetime bonds, but rarely did it result in the transformation of the human partner, for it would signal the end of their blood sharing relationship. Brethren cannot feed from each other, as our blood's too thick.

The man looked back at him with panic in his eyes.

'What's your name?' I asked him.

'Grayson.'

'The more you tell us, Grayson, the sooner we'll be able to catch them and prevent this from happening again. Now take a deep breath and tell us anything else you can recall.'

'Annalise, they held her down – two women and one man. Never saw them before.' He shook his head, as if trying to clear it. 'Can't remember, damn it! Just snake eyes.' His desperate gaze slid to me. 'I need to know if she's okay; if they haven't....' He swallowed, and I could smell the sweat trickling down the inside of his shirt.

'Describe them,' I said.

'Ah, the man was bald; had some kind of tattoo on his neck. The women, both dark haired, wore black leather.'

I had no doubt who they were – Stockton and his two females accomplices.

'The guy's tattoo said, "Bite Me",' the other man added. 'I saw it.'

Double confirmation.

I looked at Marcus. He nodded and said to the donsangs, 'You're free to go. See if your procters are alive, and if they are, leave them word to go to the nearest safe house when they rise. You do the same, and stay there till this situation is resolved.'

'If they're dead?' Grayson looked ashen.

'We'll avenge them.' Cal replied.

I turned to Jake. 'Where are Terens and Sam?'

'Searching the waterways in case Rasputin is holed up in an underwater wreck.'

'Anything yet?'

He shook his head. I saw the worry in his eyes. They didn't have much time – three days only, and today was nearly over. After that, the Ingenii blood would start to wane together with their daylight tolerance, and their advantage.

I slid open the door and the men clambered out, still dazed and shocked.

Cal unfurled himself from his cramped position and stood beside the car, watching as the donsangs sprinted down the driveway. 'Their procters are probably dead,' he said.

'We don't know for sure,' Jake replied. 'Rasputin may have mesmerised them, too.'

'Into following him? No, I don't think so. I reckon what he's got in mind is the less competition the better,' he said, his tone grim.

'Are those Timur's orders, or is he acting on his own? That's what I'd like to know.' Marcus's gaze roamed between the four of us. 'Could he mesmerise his own sire?' He stepped out of the car and paced a few steps, before turning to face us. 'We're going about this the wrong way.'

Cal's brow creased in a frown. 'What do you mean?'

'Remember what we did with the barbarian tribes? Pay one to attack the other, or start a rumour; spread a seed of distrust; turn them against each other. Deus! We should approach this the old Roman way – divide and conquer – and set those two worms against each other.'

'Worth a try,' I said. It was about time we went on the offensive.

Jake stroked his beard. 'From my dealings with him, Timur's a paranoid enough bastard to believe someone's plotting against him. And after the way Karl fooled him, he'll be even more suspicious.'

'It has to come from someone Timur trusts, to give it more credibility,' I said, as an idea began to form.

Marcus braced one arm against the side of the car and regarded me. 'Who've you got in mind?'

'Stockton.'

A moment of silence ensued. 'I hate to point out the obvious, but how will you persuade him to do that, when we haven't caught him?' Cal asked.

'No need. Sam can hack into Stockton's computer and send Timur a message, saying,' I thought a moment, ' "Rasputin's got his own army and is planning to overthrow you." And for good measure, let's send Rasputin an anonymous tip-off saying something like; "Don't trust Stockton. He'll turn you in." '

Cal looked doubtful. 'Think they'll fall for it?'

'They've been proscribed. Hell yeah, they'll fall for it,' Jake said.

'It's worth a try.' Marcus's gaze slid from me to Cal.

'Okay, I'll run with it. But if they end up killing each other, Terens and Sam aren't going to be happy. They got plans.' Cal raised his eyebrows.

'I'm sure we'll find a way for those two to be satisfied,' Marcus replied with a grim smile.

Another thought occurred to me. 'Contact all donsangs and tell them to go to the nearest safe house while it's still daylight and wait for their procters there. Messages also need to be left with all Brethren to make their way there as soon as they rise, without delay. I have a feeling Rasputin and his mob will be doing the rounds tonight.'

'And we'll be able to track 'em,' Cal said.

'If I were him,' Marcus began slowly, his eyes a study in concentration, 'I'd head to the houses of the most loyal Principate supporters and either mesmerise or kill them.'

'Makes sense. Which is why we need to be there to prevent it happening. And since they won't sense me, I can pick up their scent and catch them before they get close.' The serpent ring would block my presence to their senses, giving me that much-needed edge, while the men had the advantage of the Ingenii blood. I doubted Luc and I could have contained the rebellion on our own. In some way, it could not have come at a better time.

'That's assuming you're at one of the houses they decide to visit,' Marcus pointed out.

'Whoever senses them first, can get word to me and I'll be there is seconds.' I mentally ran through a list of the most loyal friends of the Principate and narrowed it down to nine clans. We couldn't protect all of them. *Which ones would Rasputin choose?*

Then it came to me – Rasputin wouldn't know, but Stockton was local. 'There are four clans, I reckon he'd try for, the McMillans in Edgecliffe, Chus in Rose Bay, Norssons in Potts Point and the Beckmanns in Bondi. Each of us will stake one out.'

'What if he attempts to mesmerise us, as he did with Sam?' Jake had a point.

I glanced at the serpent ring. *It's worth a try. If it can restore a mind, could it prevent it from being captured in the first place?* I glanced at Jake. Should I try? No. Better test it on myself first.

'Let me try something.' I raised my hand in front of my eyes and gazed at the serpent's eyes.

Jake lunged forward and grabbed my wrist. 'What are you doing?'

'Experiment. I need to see if the ring can protect my mind from Rasputin's power. If it works, I'll do the same for all of us.'

'How will you know?' He looked at me with concern. 'What if it does something to your mind instead?'

'I doubt it will harm the one it's meant to protect,' Marcus said. 'We saw what it did to the donsangs. '

The slight shake of his head indicated Jake wasn't convinced, but he released my wrist and sat angled on his seat as if ready to intervene.

I turned my gaze back to the ring and stared intently at the serpent's eyes. Nothing happened – only Jake's rapid breathing filled the confined space in the vehicle – until I brought up an image of Rasputin in my mind. The serpent's eyes blazed to life and emitted a blinding beam that filled my vision with a burst of vivid scarlet.

The men gasped and Jake called out.

'No! Don't do anything,' I said. 'Wait.'

Cleansing. That was the only way to describe the light that filled my mind and blasted away Rasputin's image. Seconds later, the beam died down and retreated into the serpent's eyes. Golden daylight replaced scarlet.

'Alec?' I looked up to see Marcus staring at me, brow creased, lips a tight line.

I nodded. 'I'm okay.'

'What did you feel?' he asked.

'Nothing; only light.'

'So how do we know it's worked?' Cal asked. 'It's not like that injection against white-oak you gave us. We saw the proof of that in Dawson.'

I described what had happened when I thought of Rasputin.

'Do me next.' Jake leaned forward in his seat.

'No. Me,' Marcus said. 'I should take the risk before any of my men.' He climbed back into the passenger seat and turned to face me. 'Best done in here, just in case.'

So far we'd been lucky, and the car park had remained empty. But any moment, someone might walk out and see something they shouldn't.

'Conjure an image of Rasputin in your mind.' I raised the ring. Marcus focused on it. The serpent's eyes flared briefly, and the same beam of light erupted before dying down again.

'Deus!' Marcus blinked and rubbed his eyes.

'Okay, Alec. My turn.' Jake focused his eyes on the ring.

'You know what to do.' I raised my hand to his eye level. 'Think of that—'

'I know, that son-of-a—Whoa!' There was a flash and a bright, red glint.

'Jake?' I snapped my fingers in front if his eyes. He blinked.

'Yeah, I'm fine,' he answered. 'It was like a laser beam – Rasputin's image disintegrated.'

'Okay, that's good. I like that.' Cal smiled. 'S'pose it's my turn now.' He grasped the top of the vehicle and leaned in. 'I'm ready. Go.'

The scarlet light flared to life again.

'Am I immune now?' he asked when his eyes regained focus.

'Let's hope you don't need to find out,' I replied.

Marcus pulled out his mobile phone. 'Terentius and Sempronius need to be here.' He whipped around to face the front as he made the call. Only Marcus still referred to his men using their Roman names. Everyone else had stopped doing so long before.

'I want to extend our odds and take six houses instead of four,' Jake suggested. 'It'll give us a better chance of catching them.'

'Agreed, although they'll sense our presence,' Cal said.

'Yours yes, mine no, because of the ring. We can use that to our advantage to herd them toward The Residence and execute them there.'

A grim smile lit Cal's face. 'Or hand them over to Terens and Sam.'

I had no doubt those two would derive pleasure from exacting as much pain on their enemies as the night hours would allow before ending their lives, but I couldn't condone it. Although the Rebels deserved to die, torture was repugnant to me.

'They're on their way.' Marcus turned back to face us. 'Sam's particularly interested.'

I could understand why he would be. Jake lifted the back seat and pulled out several dark coats and swords. Marcus raised an eyebrow. 'One for me in there?'

'I always carry spares.'

Marcus smiled and took the one Jake held out.

We discussed the logistics of lying in wait for the Rebels when I sensed Sam and Terens arrive in Terens's Porsche.

'What's this about the ring blocking Timur's pet snake,' Sam asked as he leapt from the vehicle.

CHAPTER 30 – HOW TO EXPLAIN A DEATH

LAURA

Matt closed the door and took a step back into the room, his eyes glacial. I'm sure the temperature around him dropped.

I swallowed, unsure where to begin, or even how to begin telling him about Jean-Philippe and what he tried to do to me.

Matt waited.

'The man you're looking for is dead.'

His eyes narrowed. 'How do you know?'

'I saw it happen.' Every muscle in my body tensed.

For the longest second I'd ever experienced, Matt watched me, face utterly blank before he said, 'I want to know everything you saw, and be careful how you tell me. I may be off duty but I'm still obliged to report anything suspicious. You understand me, Laura?'

I nodded and buried my shaking hands inside my pockets. This side of Matt frightened me. Would he be "obliged" to arrest me if I didn't report it?

He sat back down on the sofa, leaned forward and clasped his hands in front of him; his mouth a tight line as he stared at me.

I perched on the edge of my seat and rehearsed the words I

had to say to convince him that Alec had had no other choice but to kill him – Jean-Philippe had been deranged.

'His real name is Jean-Philippe Reynard. He tried to rape and kill me.' My hands began to shake.

Matt's eyes widened and his fists clenched. 'When was this?'

'Several days ago; at Alec's place. He climbed up the outside of the building, crashed through the window and grabbed me after stabbing Alec. He said killing me was the only way he could be free, but first he wanted to rape me; said I'd enjoy it if I didn't struggle.'

Matt swore and appeared to be about to say something.

'No, let me finish, Matt.'

He nodded, breathing hard.

'He nearly succeeded – I hadn't the strength to fight him. Alec somehow managed to pull the stake from his chest, drag him off me, and stab Jean-Philippe with it. Luc and the other men arrived at the same time, but he was dead. They took his body away. I don't know what they did with it.'

That was the truth and Matt knew it – I didn't hiccup once.

Matt's gaze never left my face, and for a fraction of a second his eyes softened as he looked at me. 'You okay?'

I shrugged. 'I suppose. Alec made me talk about it, to let it out. He was there for me, even though he was hurt and nearly killed, too.'

Matt dropped his head into hands, ran them through his hair then rose and paced the floor. 'Why did the stake—' he looked at me. 'I assume it was wooden?' I nodded. 'Why did it kill Jean-Philippe and not Munro?'

'My blood. It saved him.'

Matt frowned and his gaze slid from my face to somewhere behind me, out the window. I knew that look – he was working something out. 'Why did this Jean-Philippe want to kill you?'

'We knew each other a long time ago.' I related the story of our first meeting in Italy. 'He thought we could rekindle it, and when I refused….'

'You were only a kid then.' His eyes blazed as he focused on me again.

'He didn't see it that way.'

'And you never saw him after that?'

I shook my head. 'Only at the Ritual. From a distance, I didn't realise it was him. Italy happened so long ago.'

'He didn't approach you?'

This is Matt, the Detective, and I'm on the other side of the metaphorical interrogation table. It was what I feared. 'Wasn't allowed to, he told me. Luc forbade him.'

'Because he was your half-brother?'

'Maybe, but we didn't know that then. Neither did Luc. Alec did the DNA test.'

'How convenient.'

I stood up. 'What do you mean by that? The test results arrived on Luc's fax and Alec passed it to him. It wasn't rigged, if that's what you think.'

His eyes narrowed. 'He could've told the lab to skew the result.'

'Why? So I wouldn't go with Jean-Philippe? That's ridiculous. Even if the results were otherwise, I would've still chosen Alec.'

Matt reared back like I'd slapped him in the face.

'I'm sorry I didn't mean it to sound—'

'Leave it.' His expression hardened again.

I sat back down and decided to fill him in a bit more about Jean-Philippe. 'He had a studio in Luc's house, walls covered in photos he'd taken of me. He'd been stalking me all these years.' I recalled the unease, even fear, I'd experienced as he proudly showed them off. I'd been his obsession.

Matt stood behind the sofa, his fists white where they clutched the top of the soft leather. 'Lebrettan?' His voice was strained.

'He didn't know. No one knew.'

Matt was silent a while, then he said, 'You've put me in a difficult position.'

I stood and came over to him. 'I told you only because you promised not to tell anyone.'

'I made no such promise.'

'You did. It was implied. You know that.'

Matt lowered his head and tucked his hands into his pockets. I could only guess what he was thinking and hoped it had nothing to do with an arrest.

'I want to protect you, Laura but....'

'Protect me? I've done nothing wrong. Except not allow

myself to get raped and murdered.'

'You should have gone to the police.'

I waved my arms in the air. 'And say what? That a vampire tried to kill me, and another vampire killed him instead, and the body's probably turned to ash? Is that what I should do?'

He swore and pointed to the newspaper. 'That can't be explained away. If it hadn't found its way into the papers, no one would be any the wiser, and I couldn't have cared less. Actually, I'm kind of glad there's one less vampire in the world. But people know his name, Laura, and it's associated with yours. There'll be questions.'

'Which you can deflect because you know the truth.'

Matt spun away from me and faced the windows on the other side of the room. 'I don't think I can.'

'Why not? It's not like I'm asking you to cover up a murder.' I moved to stand in front of him as a horrid thought occurred to me. 'Look at me, Matt,' I said when he continued to stare at the view behind me, his expression stone hard. Slowly his gaze drifted to me. 'What if I had told you it'd been Judy who'd killed Jean-Philippe rather than Alec?'

He frowned. 'It'd make no difference. I'd still want to take her in for questioning.'

'But you're not dealing with humans, here. Your rules don't apply; they simply don't work. Matt, please.' I placed my hand on his chest, almost imploringly.

He looked at my hand resting on his chest, and for a moment, his eyes softened. I felt his heartbeat beneath my palm before removing my hand. He still loved me but I could never use that to my advantage. Ever.

'Sorry, I....' My heart stopped as I realised the serpent's eyes were black. How long had they been that way? I was about to cry out to Luc when they slowly returned to their normal blood red. *Alec! It has to be Alec. It can't mean I'm in danger, otherwise Luc'd be here in a shot. But whatever danger it was must be gone because the eyes are red now. No danger. Breathe Laura.*

'What's wrong, Laura? You've gone white as death.'

'Nothing. Sorry.' I walked to the window and looked out, trying to rid myself of the nauseating wave that had swept over me. It was late afternoon, and the yacht's dark silhouette floated out over the water. *Alec, be safe.* My heart leapt at the thought of him. 'You should go,' I said to Matt.

Silence behind me. Then, 'You're going through with it – having his kid?'

I spun around to face him. 'Our child. You know the stipulations of the curse. It's the only way to end it and free my family.'

'What then? Stay with him?'

'I love him.'

Matt's jaw twitched. 'Relay a message for me. I said I'd come after him if we found another drained body. In the last few days there've been so many.' His expression darkened.

My stomach hollowed out. 'You can't do that! Alec's the only one who can stop them. His men are out there right now tracking them down.' I pointed out the window. *It's Rasputin,* my inner voice screamed. *Doesn't he know?*

'He's lost control. More and more bodies are turning up.' He angled his head and looked at me through narrowed eyes. 'What do you mean right now? In the daylight?'

Crap. I bit my lip and nodded. 'Ingenii blood. From Judith,' I quickly added when Matt's nostrils flared. 'A present from Luc; once a year.'

'Now they're out during the day.' He swore again, raised his arms and let them drop to his side.

'It's the only way they can find and get rid of them. Don't worry; it only lasts a couple of days.'

'How many more are going to die before they do? Dave's already mentioned the media's sniffing around, sensing we're covering something up. The victims' families have been asked not to go on social media, but it's all over it.'

'You're supposed to be on sick leave.'

He glared. 'Didn't you hear what I said, Laura? People are dying!' He paused, then said, 'I'm bringing Munro in.'

'How do you propose to do that?' The low, chill tone of Luc's voice signalled danger. He must have been listening from the galley.

Matt's neck muscles tensed as he turned to face Luc. 'Not even you can stop the police, Lebrettan.'

My father strode to the bar. 'No, but I have powerful friends.

I'm sure you don't need me to explain,' he said meaningfully as he poured himself a brandy.

I wondered if some of them were donsangs. Anything was possible.

Matt stood there for a moment, lips a tight line, eyes cold as a glacier. 'I understand, all right. You get Munro off on a technicality and I'm the one reprimanded, maybe even demoted and shunted off to some outback town where I can't do any damage. Is that how it works?'

'I'm glad you understand,' Luc answered.

I glared at Matt and clasped my hands behind my back to stop myself from slapping him. 'Alec is no criminal, how dare you.'

'Alive but compromised. Is that it?' His gaze was glued on Luc. Had he even heard me?

'I believe you have it,' Luc answered and calmly downed his brandy.

'You manipulate everything and everyone around you,' he glanced at me, 'even your own daughter.'

'Matt!'

Luc stepped out from behind the bar, eyes narrowed. 'Be careful what you say, Detective Inspector. Everything I do is to safeguard my family. Be thankful you've never been in a position where you've had to compromise and make hard decisions to protect the ones you love.'

Matt swallowed as Luc bared his fangs, but just as quickly, he retracted them.

'Show me this newspaper,' he growled.

Matt stepped back as Luc picked the newspaper from the table. A sad expression flitted across his face as – I guessed – he gazed at the picture of Jean-Philippe. 'My daughter spoke the truth. Alec saved her life, and I will not allow you to arrest him.' Luc raised his head from the paper and gazed dangerously at Matt.

'I don't doubt her, nor you—'

'Yet you come here and threaten?' Luc's eyes lightened.

Oh crap.

Matt paled.

'You think I would let you jeopardise everything I've worked for all these centuries?'

In the fraction of a second it took to blink, Matt ended up

unconscious on the floor, Luc standing over him.

My heart jumped sickeningly. 'Is he…?'

'No, ma petite, he's not dead. I only pressed a nerve to knock him out until I decide what to do with him.' He picked Matt up, tossed him over his shoulder and headed for the stairs leading down to the cabins.

'Please don't kill him.'

'I have no intention of doing so. I know it would hurt you.'

'Couldn't you have mesmerised him?' I traipsed after him, visions of police raids, arrests and years of imprisonment parading through my mind.

'It's not healthy to use that too often on a human, especially by different Brethren, so I dare not. On the weaker minded, it could lead to brain damage. And this one,' he swatted Matt's rear end, 'has experienced it twice. Only Alec can do it to him again safely.'

Luc opened one of the cabin doors nearest the corridor and dumped Matt's body on the queen-sized bed, located his mobile phone and pocketed it.

'Is he okay?' I asked.

He stared at Matt intently for a few seconds. 'Heartbeat's fine, but he'll have a headache and nausea when he wakes. It'll keep him in bed for the next hour or so.'

I smoothed the hair from Matt's forehead. 'I'm so sorry, Matt.' I doubt he heard me.

Luc secured the porthole. 'Now he won't get out.'

'How long before he wakes up?'

'Few minutes. Come.' Luc took my hand, led me from the room and locked the door. 'You're not to worry, ma petit. He's in a comfortable room and in no danger. I'll sort this out.'

He sounded so confident, yet a tiny niggle at the back of my mind told me things are never that straight forward. Matt was stubborn; I'd been with him long enough to know. Although I hated the idea, perhaps mesmerisation was the only answer. At least he would be alive. But now, we had the missing persons article to worry about.

'What if Jean's disappearance comes to the police?'

Luc rubbed his chin. 'It may not. So let's not think on it.' He smiled and placed his hand on my shoulder. 'Your friend, Jenny, is in the Jacuzzi. Why not join her?'

Jen! What would she say if she found out my father was holding my police detective ex-boyfriend prisoner in one of the guest cabins? I closed my eyes and groaned. 'What am I going to tell her? She'll freak!'

'Then don't.' He said it so calmly, as if it was no great matter.

I gazed at him open mouthed. 'And when Matt starts yelling and banging on the door?' I could so picture it.

Luc grinned. 'Don't worry, he won't wake the dead. Kari's not due to rise for another few hours.'

'If that's meant to be a joke, it's not funny.' Kari. I'd forgotten she was asleep in one of the cabins. What if she woke up hungry? 'She wont, you know...?'

He pursed his lips. 'We might get lucky.'

'Papa!'

He laughed and placed his arm around my shoulder. 'Only kidding. Kari prefers the more expensive types—billionaires.'

I wondered if he knew how she acquired extra "pocket-money."

We made our way back up the stairs to the top deck, and my gut churned all the way. At this rate, I risked getting an ulcer.

Luc took me gently by the shoulders to face him. 'Ma petite, you are not to be concerned. I forbid it.' His face softened. 'I want you to be happy. Alec and I will speak with Sommers and get him to see reason. If not, Alec will mesmerise him again and there it will end.'

'And no brain damage?'

He was silent a moment, his eyes serious. 'It's always a risk, but it's my belief Alec could do it without causing him harm. Sommers is quite strong-minded.'

Understatement. I nodded. What else could I do? Why couldn't Matt just leave things alone?

'Now, take a deep breath,' Luc said. 'Let it out. And again.'

I did so and felt better.

'Good. Go and relax in the spa.' He kissed me on the brow and left.

With my father's assurances echoing in my head, I went to the towel room on the upper deck, retrieved my swimming costume and joined Jen. She was reclining against the edge, her dark hair piled on top of her head, her gaze focused on the harbour views as she sipped a cocktail. She appeared the picture of relaxation – just how I wanted to be.

'Hey Laura.' She spied me and raised her glass. 'I could so get used to this.'

'Move over; I'm joining you.'

'Grab a drink. But, ah, ignore the cocktail recipes on the inside door of the bar.' She pointed. 'They're not meant for us.'

That comment took my mind off Matt. 'Got blood in them?'

'Uh huh. Check out the Bloody Cally. Think it refers to Cal?'

'Maybe.'

½ glass O+, ½ glass Smirnov was hand written on a sheet of paper stuck to the inside of the door. It was one of a list of other similar 'cocktails.'

'Saw Matt come up the jetty. Everything okay, hon?' She gazed at me with concern.

There was no way I could hide this latest development from her. 'How open-minded are you?' I poured myself a cold glass of chardonnay and slid into the water beside her.

CHAPTER 31 – CHASE

ALEC

I glanced at my watch – 8.15pm. The summer sun had set. I hid in the shadows of the McMillan house in Edgecliffe, one of those closest to the centre of the city, and the one I hoped Rasputin would visit first. I could feel the executioner's sword strapped to my side, through the thin leather of my coat.

Sam and Jake lay in wait at the Chu's in Rose Bay; Terens and Cal were at the Beckmann's, and Marcus had taken the Norssons in Potts Point. Should either Rasputin or Stockton and his gang show, they'd sense their presence and stay away and hopefully head here.

Sam had sped back to the yacht to hack into Timur and Rasputin's accounts and leave those incriminating messages before joining Terens. We'd know soon enough if the ruse worked.

McMillan and his clan had just awoken.

'Stay in the house, Eric,' I told him. 'Rasputin might be on his way here.'

'I can help.' McMillan's clear voice rang in my ears.

'Not this time. Rasputin can mesmerize you. Stay safe. The

men and I've got this.'

He swore. 'Lord Marcus?'

'Covering the Norssons.'

He informed the other two with him. I sensed ripples of fear and anger course through them.

'They're coming out of the water now,' Jake's voice broke through the babble of voices around me. Rose Bay was roughly three miles from where I was, meaning not only could they sense him, but they'd hear our conversation. 'It's Stockton, and he's got two females with him.'

'Got four here. Came straight out of the waves. Rasputin's not among them,' Terens said from his position at Bondi Beach, his voice low with disappointment. There was a pause, then; 'They know we're here. They're running.'

'Don't let them slip back into the water.' Where was Rasputin? I extended my senses to my six-mile limit. Nothing. Had Timur already read Sam's fake message and recalled him? I hoped so. Shutting my mind to the incessant flow of human conversations around me, I concentrated on detecting the Rebels' conversation, Stockton in particular.

I sensed surprise. Stockton wasn't expecting Luc's men to be there, and now he was desperate to shake them. And there was something else – he was afraid of Rasputin.

'Did one of you tell him I was disloyal?' I heard anger in his voice.

The two women with him denied it vehemently.

They ran and argued, Jake and Cal hot on their heels. Meanwhile, in the house behind me, I sensed the need for the McMillans to feed. I glanced at the ring. The serpent's eyes were red – all clear.

'Eric, I'll escort your household to Amanda's. I know you need to feed.'

'What about Rasputin?'

'Can't sense him anywhere near.'

The front door opened and all three came to my side – Eric, his wife, Alexandra, and their daughter, Catherine. From what I knew they'd all been transformed at the same time, saved from a cholera epidemic in London in the early 1830s. Eric and Alexandra had been in their late thirties; Catherine had only just turned eighteen. Rumour had it, she'd persuaded her parents to immigrate to Australia, due to her supposed crush on Sam. He'd never mentioned it.

'Let's run,' I said.

With the two women between us, we sped through the dark streets of Edgecliffe, past the string of embassies and consulates that dominated the suburb and to Amanda's, three miles away. It was faster than using a car, and traffic lights wouldn't stop us.

No one spoke for fear of being overheard by the Rebels, and the serpent ring effectively provided a sensory shield none of our kind could penetrate. I doubted even Rasputin could break through it.

Past the spreading branches of the horse-chestnut trees that lined the street, we slowed as we neared the Bondi house – a street back from the main corso, it was an imposing 1930s, two level brick house on one-acre. The air was scented with sea salt, coconut oil and frangipani; and white-oak. I could see where the bullets left an imprint in the brick from the drive-by shooting a few days earlier. Coloured-glass splinters from what was left of the windows lay scattered on the ground. The shutters had been lowered, concealing the extent of the damage.

The door opened. 'Princeps, please come in.' Amanda stepped aside, and I ushered the McMillans in.

'Can't stay. Spread the word – no one is to approach Rasputin in case he mesmerizes us.'

'I'll get the word out.'

I nodded my thanks, turned and left. It was then that I sensed him, somewhere in the city. He was being careful, as a wanted man should be.

'We need to talk, Princeps,' he said. The Brethren inside the house would hear, as Rasputin surely intended. 'My master has recalled me.' There was a raw, angry edge to his voice.

Seems Timur got Sam's fake message. I chuckled and sped away from the safe house, in the direction of his voice. *Keep talking. I'll find you.*

'Why should he do that? He's always trusted me. You're responsible.'

Oh yes, he was enraged. Even at this distance, I could sense that. Good. It might cause him to make a mistake. He was just out of reach, and since he couldn't sense my presence, he was guessing where I was. So far, he was lucky. *Not for long.*

'The only way I can prove my loyalty to my master is to bring him a remarkable gift. What do you suggest?' He sniggered.

Gift? The hair on the back of my neck prickled. I inhaled, yet couldn't pick up his scent. He had to be either in, or on, the water. But where? If two groups came out of the water at Rose Bay and Bondi, then somewhere between?

I heard Jake's grunt of satisfaction. 'Got three. One's still on the loose. Cal's after him.'

'The bodies?' I asked.

'We'll dispose of them.'

Our collection was growing.

Terens swore. 'The women have been terminated, but Stockton got away.'

'Which way is he headed?' My guess was he'd go for the nearest heavily populated area – slow us down. Stockton's cunning enough to know we'd avoid endangering humans.

'Westfield, Bondi Junction,' Terens answered.

Damn! I was right. It was one of the biggest shopping centres in the southern hemisphere. Even at this time of night, it would be teeming with tourists and locals at the Boxing Day sales. I could hear Terens cursing as he trailed Stockton through the streets. 'Bastard's just gone in, and he's got two mates.'

'On my way.' I sped there as fast as I could. 'Sam?'

'Getting rid of the bodies,' he said.

The Junction wasn't far. I sensed Marcus close by. 'Terens, stay on Stockton. Alec and I will take the other two,' he said.

That suited me.

Careful to keep my sword concealed, I strode into the crowded mall and was at once hit by a battery of senses – sharp lights, cacophony of sounds pumping from every store, and the enticing smell of blood drumming through human veins. The last mingled with the aromas from the food court, cosmetics and perfume counters and human emotions – all masking the ones I was trying to locate.

If my senses were strained, then the Rebels' would be even worse; they'd be almost blind, but they'd be safe. They knew we wouldn't try anything here and expose our world to humans. But they couldn't remain here for long; eventually the mall would close for the night. Perhaps they planned to hide till then, or hoped to lose us in the sensory overload. That made more sense.

Several people gave me a passing look – my long, leather coat wasn't exactly summer wear.

'Security,' I said as I pushed through the crowds. It seemed to work.

It was difficult to concentrate on Marcus and Terens's voices amidst the human babble. Then I spotted him, weaving his way through a group of people standing around a juice bar. Terens wasn't far behind. Stockton momentarily stopped and looked behind. His eyes narrowed as he spied him, but he didn't seem to notice me. His companions left him, scattering in separate directions.

I signalled Terens to trail one. Stockton was mine. If the situation had allowed, I would've smiled at the gaggle of teenage girls who stared after him as he passed.

Stockton edged closer to one of the exits that led to the underground car parking. Glancing behind again, he went through the sliding glass doors and into the dark.

I touched the sword at my side and followed.

CHAPTER 32 – COMPLICATIONS

LAURA

Jenny let out a high-pitched giggle, a trait of hers when she was nervous or didn't know what to say. Hmmm, not a good sign. Nothing much shocked Jen, but my story about Luc knocking Matt out and locking him in one of the guest rooms did.

'He's a cop, Laura.'

'I know. I dated him four months, remember?'

She stared at me a moment longer before climbing out of the water and going to the bar. 'Maybe if I get drunk enough the police'll see me as incompetent and they won't arrest me.'

'You're safe; you had nothing to do with it. Besides, he doesn't know you're on board. It's me they'll haul away.' I gulped down the rest of my cocktail and wondered how many years I'd get for being complicit in knocking out and holding a detective captive.

'Why did Luc do that?'

'Matt wants to arrest Alec.'

'Whaaat? Why?'

I took a deep breath – it was time for Jenny to know about

Jean-Philippe. She sat quietly when I explained our meeting in Italy, and then no contact till the Ritual, last week. Her face paled when I described what he later tried to do to me. When I finished, she shook her head, her breath rapid. Next minute she was in the water, arms around me in a fierce hug. 'Oh, hon!'

'I didn't know how to tell you sooner. And there was so much going on, you know?'

'It's okay, it's okay,' she repeated, rubbing my back. 'That son-of-a-bitch! Alec was right to kill him; he was crazy.'

'Yeah, but look at the mess it's created. My picture's in the paper, he's missing, and all because he sent a portrait of me to some contest. And now Matt's onto it like some bloody hound on a scent—'

'He's jealous, hon.'

I pulled back, looked at her and nodded. 'I know that. But what can I do about it?'

She thought a moment, a slight frown crossing her face. 'Luc wouldn't, you know, kill him?'

I shook my head. 'I'd never forgive him. He promised.'

'Well, hon, looks like mesmerisation's the way to go. I read vampires, um, I mean Brethren, are good at that. If Matt's memory can be wiped and nobody comes looking for that Philippe guy … I mean, some people go missing because they want to, and the police don't bother to follow it up.'

'That we should be so lucky.' There was a note of despair in my voice, and just as I said it, I heard banging and Matt bellowing, 'Laura! Open this door!'

I closed my eyes and groaned.

'What is it?' Jenny asked.

'You didn't hear that?'

'Hear what?'

'Matt's banging on the door and yelling to be let out.'

'Didn't hear a thing.' She looked at me closely. 'If I can't hear that and you can….'

We gazed at each other as the scary implication dawned on me. Vampire hearing? Was this the start of my coming-of-age? I swallowed. What else could I expect? I ran my tongue along my top teeth and sighed in relief. No fangs – yet.

'Let's try something?' Jenny suggested.

I nodded. My throat had developed a tight knot.

'Listen for anything else, apart from you-know-who down in you-know-where.' I frowned. 'What else can you hear? Just on the boat for starters.'

I concentrated. Judy talking to someone, but not Luc. Was she on the phone? Then Luc's voice – he was talking to someone too; about it being time to use the stores in the bloodvault. I sucked in a breath when Antonius replied. My father and grandfather were having a conversation that I could hear, and Antonius was not on the yacht.

A jolt of fear mixed with exhilaration shot through me. Hadn't I wished for vampire hearing? What if it was really happening? A faint, regular thumping came from somewhere close – Jenny's heartbeat. 'I can hear everyone on the boat, Jen, even your heartbeat, I think.'

'Shoooot!' She folded her arms over her stomach. 'You sure?' The thumping increased.

'Uh huh.' Luc needed to know. My legs were shaky as I climbed out of the hot tub, grabbed a towel and raced to Luc's office, Jenny right behind me. I wasn't exactly sure where it was, but it was the room from where he'd entered the smaller dining room on the main deck.

'Luc, I need to see you now. Something's happening to me.'

I'd barely reached the bottom of the stairs when Luc appeared, brow creased. 'Ma petite, are you hurt?'

'No, nothing like that. I can hear … I mean, I could hear you talking to Antonius and him answering you. I know he's not on the yacht – is he?' He shook his head. 'I think I'm developing vampire hearing.'

His eyebrows shot up. 'First time?'

'Just now. I can hear Jen's heartbeat and,' I listened carefully, 'Judy's. She's in there.' I pointed to a door off the dining room. 'On the phone to someone.'

'She's on Skype to friends in Britain.' Luc looked at me and stroked his chin. 'I wonder.' He turned me to face the window and pointed. 'Other side of the bay. Tell me what you see.'

Everything seemed clearer and closer. 'A few large houses; a road leading up from the wharf, and a few shops.'

'Can you read the shop signs?'

'There's one outside a café, and a chalkboard that reads, "Devonshire Teas $8.99, Smoothies $5.99—'

'Good,' Luc said.

Next to me Jenny gasped. 'You can see that?'

Luc turned to her. 'How about you?'

'Nothing like that. Houses mostly, between the bush, but I can't even see the shops, let alone the signs. It's too far away.' She gazed at me in awe. 'That's freaky, Laura.'

That raised another issue – what if vampire hearing wasn't the only new thing I could expect? What if my appetite began to change as well? Could I develop into a blood drinker?

I must have had a panicky look on my face for Luc placed his hand on my shoulder and said, 'It's only natural that you're beginning to manifest these signs, ma petite. Your coming-of-age is your vampire-puberty, but that does not mean you're transforming into one – the Ingenii gene prevents that.'

'Positive?'

He smiled. 'You'll have the best of both worlds without any of the drawbacks.'

I had a feeling he was referring to the blood drinking bit. 'You miss it? Food, the aromas?' Imagine not being able to eat chocolate or mangoes, custard, apple strudel or potato pancakes. My mouth watered as all my favourite foods skipped through my mind. I could almost smell them.

He took a deep breath and released it. 'I can smell the ham and cheese croissants over in that café,' he tilted his chin in the direction of the window, 'and it's enough to turn my stomach. No, ma petite, I don't miss it. Only the scent of blood entices me.'

Jenny nodded. 'Makes sense. Imagine craving food and not being able to eat it because it makes you sick. Awful.'

'Exactly. It's a small mercy in compensation,' Luc replied.

In those seconds, I became aware of other sounds, like an insect buzzing nearby. When I looked around to locate the source, I was shocked to see it came from the bar-b-que table in the park, at least five-hundred metres from the jetty where we were moored. Then more sounds – the clanging of metal rings against boats, people speaking although they were nowhere in sight, the lapping of water against the boat, even the sudden swish as if a large fish had swum beneath us – a jumble of noises swamped me all at once; every sound magnified a thousand times. I didn't know where to look first.

I closed my eyes and clapped my hands over my ears. 'Too much! How can you stand this?'

'Laura.' Luc gripped my upper arms. 'Open your eyes. Look at me, ma petite.'

His voice was calm, comforting. Slowly, I did as he asked.

'Lower your hands and tune out all other sounds except the ones you want to hear; concentrate on those. Ignore everything else. Try.'

'Is this how it was for Alec at first?'

He nodded. 'All juveniles have to be trained to deal with sensory overload.'

Now it was my turn. I followed Luc's instructions and tried to ignore all sounds except those in my immediate vicinity. It seemed to work.

'Well done,' he said.

Of course, he could hear my heartbeat as clearly as I could hear Jenny's, and even Judy's in the other room. And mine had calmed.

'Now hum a favourite tune in your mind; carry it with you when you want to relax – it'll help drown out everything else.'

I brought to mind a movie theme I'd always loved and hummed often to myself; a beautiful haunting melody – Adventures in Paradise. With the romantic theme running through my head, other sounds faded into a distant buzz until I forgot they were there. Yet I still retained an awareness of what was around me. This was what Alec must have meant when he'd spoken of vampire etiquette; the ability to tune out, especially when living in close proximity to others.

'It's working.' I turned to Luc.

A beaming smile lit his face. 'You're a fast learner. Let's try some more exercises.'

Jenny coughed. 'Look, I'm going to get changed.'

I'd forgotten I was still in my swimmers with a towel wrapped around me. A small puddle of water had formed at my feet. 'Oops, sorry Papa. I—'

He raised his hand, palm outwards and shook his head. 'Don't worry, ma petite, it was important you see me. Go get changed. I'll wait.'

Jenny and I dashed down the stairs to the lower deck, and as we entered the corridor leading to our cabins, I grabbed her arm. 'Don't let Matt hear you, Jen. I don't want him to know you're here.'

She nodded, and we tiptoed past the room Luc had locked him in. Jenny continued to her cabin, but I paused outside his door – it was quiet. I used my newly developed skill to listen for his heartbeat. It was strong and steady. Perhaps he was lying on the bed plotting how to get out of there. I debating whether to knock. But then what? Ask if he wants a cup of coffee? *Don't be an idiot, Laura. What Matt wants, you can't give him.*

The bed creaked and footsteps padded toward the door. 'Laura, is that you?' he yelled.

Crap. He must have better hearing than me.

'If you don't let me out of here you'll face serious charges.'

'Sorry, Matt, I can't.'

'He's planning to kill me. Are you complicit with that?'

'No one's going to hurt you, I promise.'

'Then why am I locked in here?'

'You threatened to arrest Alec.' I ran to my cabin as he yelled and banged on the door. I tried to block him out, the way Luc taught me, yet his words hammered in my ears.

'Laura, listen to me.' Another bang on the door. 'You can't keep me here.'

As I dressed, I thought through the implications if I let him out. Would Luc keep his promise and not hurt him? And what could Matt do anyway? No one would believe him, and if Luc went through with his threat to use his influence, Matt could be demoted and shunted off somewhere remote. It would crush him. How could I let that happen?

I stepped into the corridor. Jenny stood there, grimacing. 'We can't hold him like this,' she whispered. 'What if he breaks the door down?'

'Let's hope he won't,' I whispered back.

'Can't Luc mesmerize him and send him home? Cause this isn't good, hon.'

'I know, Jen, I know. Only Alec can safely do that, and I've got no idea what time he'll be back from the lab.'

'I'm uncomfortable about this,' she began slowly. 'When you invited me here, I didn't expect it would involve the police.'

I was suddenly afraid she'd want to leave, and I couldn't blame her. But the danger wasn't over yet; not until Rasputin and the other Rebels were caught.

We couldn't stand out here and whisper. I clutched her arm, led her to my room and closed the door. 'Neither did I. But it's not the police, really – it's only Matt.'

Incredulous, she folded her arms and looked at me. 'Who are you kidding? He's a cop!'

I bit my lip to stop the hysterical laugh that threatened.

'Laura, this isn't funny.'

'I know, but I can't help it. This whole situation, everything's that happened to me since my birthday and now this.' I waved my arm at the door.

Jenny's eyes softened and she sighed. 'I guess that's as good a reason as any to lose it. I was so enjoying this holiday.'

We gazed at one another before Jenny laughed. I wished Alec would arrive and fix this mess. I toyed with the idea of contacting him, either telepathically or using my new-found hearing, but I didn't want to disturb him. I knew he was perfecting the anti-white-oak serum. I glanced at the serpent ring. Its eyes pulsed a comforting scarlet. I wouldn't disturb him.

'C'mon, Jen, let's get back. Luc's waiting.'

In the corridor, I glanced at the other closed doors. Which room was Kari sleeping in? I tiptoed past Matt's room. Once again I listened – no heartbeat. I turned and looked at Jenny. I could hear hers, why not Matt's? *Oh crap.*

'What's up?' she whispered.

'Can't hear his heartbeat.'

She paled, and her eyes widened. 'Open it.'

'How? Luc locked it. I don't have vampire strength.' I tried anyway, and the door opened. It shouldn't have done that. 'Matt?' The room was empty. My stomach sank. Had Luc taken him? My head spun at the possibility. How could he do such a thing? He promised. My foot kicked something as I took a step into the room – a metal coat hanger, its hook unbent. I picked it up. Matt once mentioned he'd been shown how to pick a lock using a coat hanger.

A strange mix of relief and fear flooded through me. Relief that Luc hadn't secretly taken him – and fear for Matt's safety.

'Jen, he's picked the lock.' I showed her the evidence.

'Holy hell. If Luc finds out—'

'I know.' He'd go after him and…. I didn't want to imagine the rest. I had to find him. Apart from Jenny's heartbeat, the only other one I heard was Judy's. Matt was no longer on board.

I dropped the coat hanger, dashed up the stairs to the next level and leaned over the railing facing the jetty. No sign of Matt. I listened for his car, but there were too many other sounds, and one car sounded much the same as another to me.

Jenny joined me, her heart beating fast from the exertion. 'Don't even think of going after him, Laura.'

'Then what do you suggest?'

She shrugged. 'Ring him. Talk to him.'

'Luc's got his phone. Took it from him when he locked him up.'

'Shit!' She paused. 'You've got to tell Luc.'

'No need; I heard.' Luc leaned his arms on the railing beside me. Jenny squeaked in surprise. 'I hoped to mesmerize him rather than use my contacts to keep him contained. Foolish young man.' He sighed.

Young man? Matt was thirty-eight, but, to Luc, anyone under a thousand would be young. And foolish? Perhaps, as only an angry and hurt man who can't let go could be.

The afternoon shadows had lengthened, casting dark silhouettes of the trees onto the house. Most of the scaffolding had already been removed, but what remained clung to the walls like the skeletal remains of a giant creature. It gave the place a forbidding air—'Here there be vampires'. Yet I knew the ones that lived within its walls posed less threat to humanity than the ones that lurked outside it. They were the real monsters; who chose to indulge their baser urges and who regarded humans as nothing more than fodder.

I shivered and automatically glanced at the serpent ring, Alec never far from my thoughts. It's scarlet eyes blinked up at me. *Stay safe, my love.*

Jenny linked her arm through mine. 'Forget about Matt for now, and let's grab something to eat then maybe watch a movie.

It'll keep your mind off things for a while.'

Doubt it.

We sauntered back into the stateroom. Jenny picked through the extensive range of DVDs, while I couldn't help wondering what Matt was up to. If he hated Luc and Alec before, what must he be feeling now? A sense of dread clutched at my heart, and despite Luc's assurances I couldn't dislodge the feeling.

CHAPTER 33 - ROUND THREE TO THE REBELS

ALEC

People were about – strolling to cars, or loading shopping bags into the back of them. I couldn't unsheathe my sword here. As if he sensed me following, Stockton stopped, turned and looked back. I ducked behind one of the concrete pillars. I heard him sniff. Had he caught my scent?

In a sudden burst of speed, he took off. I gave chase, but he kept to the populated streets, heading for the centre of the city – Hyde Park. Although lit by tree lights, there were many dark spots where Brethren could feed uninterrupted. If that was his intention, I was about to spoil it for him.

As I unsheathed my sword, I became aware of another, darker, presence – Rasputin.

In the shadows of the giant Morton Bay fig trees I stood, until I spied him on the stone seating that ringed the Archibald Fountain. A laughing group of humans passed, and his eyes narrowed into slits.

My hand tingled as I ran my thumb along the hilt of my sword.

He was choosing his prey. His hands, mere stumps covered by the black gloves he wore, rested on his lap. He would have difficulty grabbing his prey, unless Stockton helped. I smiled when I thought of the way he'd lost his hands and my chest swelled with pride – *my Laura.*

Stockton strode up to him.

They would be unaware of me; unaware of being observed until I strode into their midst. The serpent ring blocked their senses.

Now, I thought. *I can take them both out.*

My scalp prickled as Stockton said, 'Is he here?'

Rasputin grinned and his gaze seemed to pinpoint exactly where I stood. 'Yes. I can feel him. The others?'

'Sacrificing themselves for you.'

'As they should.' He laughed.

Leading Marcus and Terens on a chase, I'll be damned. I gripped the sword tightly, took stock of my surroundings – no humans around, and the moon behind clouds.

'Come out, Princeps. Let's face one another,' Rasputin said.

How the hell did he know? The serpent ring on my hand flared for an instant, and I didn't need to look to know its eyes had turned black. My senses tingled as I picked up the presence of at least a dozen Brethren – not Principate supporters.

A trap, and I had walked right into it.

How many could I take out before they overpowered me? Even the strength of the Ingenii blood had its limitations. My hand tightened around my sword hilt, and I stepped out from the cover of the trees.

'Princeps!' Rasputin's grin widened. 'What a pleasure to see you again.'

'Is it? Last time we met, you didn't appear that thrilled.' He'd been marched into a cage at sword point by Terens.

'That was then.' He spread his arms out then dropped them back onto his lap. A snide grin curled his lips. 'Here we are now.'

Two Brethren joined him and Stockton. Behind me, I sensed four more, while six jumped down from the branches and stood, three by three, on either side of me. I smelled white-oak and caught the glint of the wolf's-head ring on Stockton's hand.

Time for backup, and there was only one way to do that

without alerting present company. *Laura, tell Luc to send backup. Now! Archibald Fountain, Hyde Park.*

I sensed her fear; heard her calling Luc.

The circle around me closed.

CHAPTER 34 – DUCK, SWIPE AND SLICE

LAURA

'Where is everyone?' Kari flopped onto the sofa next to me. She smelled of jasmine and rose geranium, and her short, blonde spikey hair was wet – probably just stepped out of a shower.

'Apart from Alec, everyone else is out chasing the bad guys,' I said. Yes, I sounded petulant. I missed him.

As the sun had set, Luc had maneuvered the yacht out into the harbour. Surrounded by water, we were virtually invisible to Brethren senses. Safe. Jenny and I were onto our second DVD. Earlier, we'd ordered Mexican for dinner. The empty containers were scattered on the coffee table. Neither of us felt like cleaning up. Kari's nose wrinkled.

Jenny was leafing through a fashion magazine and only half watching the movie.

For the umpteenth time, I glanced at the serpent ring and wondered how Alec was, and if his experiments were working. Earlier this afternoon, its eyes had gone black, but then returned to red. I had no idea whether the danger sign had been for me – and Luc had averted it by knocking out Matt – or for Alec. Not for a minute did I believe Matt would hurt me, but then I'd thought the same of Jean-Philippe.

As I watched, the serpent's eyes darkened until a pair of black orbs stared back at me. I sat bolt upright. My breath caught in my throat.

'What's up?' Kari asked.

'Danger! Look.' I practically shoved the ring beneath her nose.

Kari shot to her feet, her pixie face tight with concentration, and looked around. 'Can't sense anyone on the boat apart from us, but with the water....'

Alec's voice boomed in my head, *Laura, tell Luc to send backup. Now! Archibald Fountain, Hyde Park.*

'It's Alec!' I raced for Luc's room, calling out as I went.

Luc met me halfway. 'What did he say, ma petite?'

'Hyde Park, the Archibald Fountain. He needs backup. Now!' I couldn't get the words out fast enough. 'What's he doing there? I thought he was in his lab, at the hospital?'

'An incident.' He held his palm up, stared straight ahead and said, 'Marcus, Alec's in trouble. Hyde Park, Archibald Fountain. Meet you there.'

An incident. So the warning had been for Alec, not me.

'Deus. I knew it. On my way.' I heard Antonius's voice as clearly as if he stood beside me.

'What's happening?'

'No time to explain, ma petite. Stay here.' He glanced behind me. 'Kari, you're on guard.'

'I'm coming with you,' I said.

'No, stay here.' He turned on his heel, sped down the stairs. By the time I followed, he was returning in a long, black coat strapping a sword to his side.

'I'm coming.' I blocked his way.

'Laura, the danger.'

'Please, Papa. I'll go insane here waiting. If you refuse, I'll grab Kari, and we'll go regardless.' I held my ground.

'To put you both in harm's way? Think Laura!'

'But—'

He took me by the shoulders. 'I said, no. Consider your mother. Would you leave her and your friend unguarded without

Kari?' Luc's lips tightened.

'No.'

'That's right, you haven't thought of that. What if they were to come here and take your mother to use as leverage to hand you over? Do you think I could make such a choice?' His voice had risen, and I couldn't miss the flash of fear in his eyes.

I swallowed.

'Don't put me in that position, ma petite,' he whispered. 'I've only just gotten you back.'

I nodded. He was right. 'Bring him safely home to me.'

'I'll bring him home.' He kissed my cheek and sped past me up the stairs.

'You okay, hon?' Jenny asked as I trudged back up. There was concern in her warm, chocolate-brown eyes.

She and Kari stood there looking at me.

I shook my head, fighting back tears of fear and frustration. Had Luc allowed me to go with him, I would've been a liability – a magnet to the Rebels and a hindrance to him and the men.

'I can't stand this!' I closed my eyes and tried contacting him. A series of images flashed through my mind, but nothing coherent – trees, a statue spurting water, Rasputin. My heart rate doubled. 'Alec, talk to me. What's happening?' I waited. Nothing. 'Alec!' I strained my hearing as far as it could take me and only received a jumble of sounds in return, but not the voice I longed to hear.

The sound of bare feet padding on the carpet and the scent of Chanel No.9 – Judy. 'Luc told me.' She grasped my ringed hand and stared intently at the serpent's eyes before her gaze lifted to me. 'As long as they stay glossy black, he's alive.'

'What colour do they turn when…?' No way could I say the word "die." My mind, let alone my tongue, wouldn't let me.

'Milky opaque.' She clasped my hand between hers. 'He's alive. Hold onto that.'

'Why can't I get through to him, even telepathically?'

'Remember the last time he didn't answer? He didn't want you worrying and everything turned out fine.'

I let out a pent-up breath. 'I *hate* when this happens. And if he thinks this'll stop me worrying, then he's wrong.' *Please, let it turn out fine this time, too.*

Judy nodded. For the first time, I noticed fine lines around her eyes and deepening ones ringing her mouth. Tendrils of grey snaked through her thick copper locks. The past couple of weeks had taken its toll. How much more in the weeks, or even months, that lay ahead?

A steely resolve took hold of me, and easing my hands from Judy's, I faced Kari. 'Teach me to fight.'

She cocked her head and regarded me. 'Against Brethren?'

'Laura, dear, you can't be serious. Your human strength can't begin to match theirs.' Judy looked at Kari as if for confirmation.

Kari nodded and added, 'Plus, you're slower and less agile.'

'They have a point.' Jenny shrugged.

'I have to do something practical, otherwise I'll go nuts.'

'Why not carry a syringe with your blood in it? I reckon that'd be a pretty good deterrent. Worked on that creep, Rasputin. He backed off,' Jenny said.

'It's too dangerous. What if I accidently stab one of our guys?' I shook my head. Even though it sickened me to suggest the next thing – especially from recent memory – there was no other option. 'A sword. I need to learn how to handle a sword, and how to cut off a vampire's head.'

The three of them gazed at me like I'd lost my mind.

'Think about it. If I jab one of our guys at least it won't kill them. Everything they have regenerates.' Kari snorted. 'But one drop of my blood is worse than white-oak.'

'You're determined about this, aren't you?' Judy's curt tone was matched by her disapproving expression.

'When Rasputin had Kari, I felt so helpless. She was fighting to protect me, as was Sam, yet here I was, totally powerless. And then, when I grabbed Sam's sword, it felt good to be able to do *something*. If I'm going to live for the next thousand years, or whatever, do I always rely on others? Forever the "damsel in distress" whenever bad guys show up?' I paused as I framed my next words. 'When Alec and I have a baby, do you expect me to stand by and do nothing to defend my own child – or the man I love?'

Silence.

What I thought was admiration appeared in Judy's eyes. She smiled and enveloped me in a hug. 'You've come a long way, my dear Laura. I always knew you were stubborn, but in the last couple of weeks I've seen that develop into steadfast courage and strength. And I want you to know I'm proud of you. I may not express it as readily, nor as easily, as your father, but don't doubt it.'

I hugged her back, fighting back the tears her words evoked.

'Know something, Laura? I reckon you'd be good with a sword after what you did to hairy and handless.' She grinned, her lavender eyes sparkling. Clearly she enjoyed her nickname for Rasputin.

I glanced at Jenny who shrugged. 'You've convinced me.'

'Let's do it.' Kari disappeared up stairs, and within a heartbeat re-entered with two menacing-looking swords. 'From the gym. The guys keep a weapons stash in there.' She waved them in the air, and the glint of cold steel caught the light. 'They're practice ones – blunt.'

They may not be sharp and nasty, but they were still pointy and heavy. But there was no going back after my speech. *You've opened your mouth, now bite the bullet, Laura.*

'Here.' She handed one to me then proceeded to swing hers around, balancing the tip on her finger before flicking it back upright, catching the hilt.

'Still sure you want to do this?' Jenny asked.

'Absolutely.' I thought of Alec, and his handsome face appeared in my mind. My body ached for him.

Jenny and Judy moved the coffee table and pushed the sofas back to give Kari and me room to move.

'This is a thrusting and cutting blade,' she pointed to the tip and edges, 'and perfect for slicing.' Kari accompanied each word with the appropriate action. The sword whistled through the air, forward and back, like a professional tennis player with a racket. 'All you need do is strike your opponent to get them off guard, then go straight for the neck.' The edge of the sword stopped millimetres from my throat. I heard Judy gasp. 'A good sharp blade can take a head off in one stroke.'

The horrible image of me cutting off Rasputin's hands surfaced in my mind, and I had to force down the bile. 'Did Jake teach you this, Kari?'

She shook her head. 'My papa mostly. I didn't have any brothers to protect me and he wanted to make sure I could defend myself. He taught Ma, too. But we weren't allowed to use swords. Only the nobility were permitted to.'

It was easy to forget Kari came from the eighteenth century, in a society where most men carried weapons and preyed upon women. *Hummphh. Nothing much has changed.*

'Hold the grip firmly – no, not like that, Laura. Like me. See? It's a sword, not a tennis racket. One hand only.' Kari sidled up next to me and demonstrated the correct hold.

Jenny laughed. I shot her a filthy look, which only made her laugh harder. 'Ouch!' Something hard swiped the back of my knees and brought me down.

'That's what you need to do to your opponent. See where I am now, and where my sword is?'

I was on my knees looking up at her. Kari and I were the same height – five foot five. But right now she had the advantage. The edge of the blade lay against my neck.

'You let yourself get distracted. That's a no, no. See how I brought you down?'

I nodded. This was good. 'Okay, let's try again.'

Kari thrust out her hand and helped me up. 'You need to bring your opponent down to your size – literally. Most Brethren guys are tall, so use that against them. Do what they won't expect; diss 'em—D-S-S—Duck, Swipe and Slice.'

We could've been discussing a cooking recipe, but at least it was easy to remember. *DSS – duck, swipe, slice; duck, swipe, slice…*

For the next hour or so, Kari drilled me till my perspiration made the sword slip in my grip, and I accidentally nicked the back of her leg.

'Sorry, sorry, I didn't mean to do that.' Just as well the sword was blunt – no blood escaped.

She smiled. 'Finally!'

Although I never succeeded in bringing her down, I managed to duck and swipe, an achievement in such a short time. Judy and Jenny clapped.

'Okay, again,' Kari said.

That tiny triumph gave me confidence, yet sparring with Kari was a far cry from facing one of the Brethren. Could I ever slice off an enemy's head? The very thought made me sick, but so did

the possibility of losing Alec.
    'Again,' I said.

CHAPTER 35 – REBELS STRIKE BACK

ALEC

Each man displayed his wolf's-head ring. Unlike Stockton, they weren't grinning. I smelled their fear, yet it didn't hold them back. These Brethren weren't mesmerized – they wanted to be free to kill. *And there lies the irony*, I mused. *They fear death, yet don't hesitate to kill their victims.*

'A reward to the one who brings me the serpent ring, as a gift for my master,' Rasputin said.

I glanced at the men surrounding me. They were eager – I could smell excitement. 'Who wants to be first?' I said, raising my sword.

Eager or not, they hesitated, giving me time to spin around and decapitate the two directly behind me. I leapt over their bodies and into the high branches above.

Stockton growled. 'After him.'

They scaled the branches and darted around me, scattering fruit bats nesting in the giant fig trees. Their powerful scent, as well as my black coat and serpent ring, hid my presence.

'Where the fuck did he go?'

'Shutup! He can hear.'

That's right, I can. I dropped behind one and quietly struck. Rather than leave his remains in the tree, I took his wolf's-head ring and pierced his skin. In seconds, both head and body turned to dust.

Three down, seven to go, not including Stockton and Rasputin. Where was Marcus?

Humans strolled nearby, their scent strong and sweet. I needed to lead the Rebels away from them, even if it meant leaving the location I'd told Laura. Marcus and Luc would have to follow my scent. Bligh Street, the business district would be dark and quiet. Offices were closed for the holidays.

The humans were getting closer. No time for a debate. I landed back on the pavement. 'Looking for me?' And I took off at full speed, my senses alert to them close behind.

The park and the streetlights faded to a blur as I ran, and the tall office buildings crowded in on one another, leaving little space between. Turning into a side alley, I scaled the walls to the roof and hid behind the large, concrete air-conditioning unit.

I didn't have to wait long. Three figures alighted, stopped and sniffed, then spread out. With their hands curled into fists, they aimed the wolf's-head rings like weapons.

I hoped the serum still worked. White-oak may not kill me, but the weakness it would cause would render me powerless.

'We know you're here, Princeps. Let's end this.'

'Good idea. Who's first?' I strode out to meet them, waving the wolf's-head ring I had taken from the last dead Rebel, as well as my sword. 'Headless or shiny ash? Your choice.'

They snarled and came at me. I did the same then ducked, bowled one over and dug the spike of the wolf's head ring into his leg, at the same time swinging out with my blade. I twisted around and faced the third attacker. He looked at his two companions – one a headless corpse, it's hands searching – I kicked the head over the side of the building – the other, tearing at his pants' leg, screaming as the venom spread.

'Which way do you prefer?' I asked.

His shook his head, snarled, turned and ran.

Five down, seven to go. This time I included Rasputin and his sidekick, Stockton.

I walked to the edge of the building and looked out over the city expanse. 'Marcus, where the hell are you?' There was a tear down the side of my coat where the spike of a wolf's-head ring connected. Too close.

'Ambushed. Where are you?'

I was about to give away my position, but there was nothing for it. 'Top of 1 Bligh St.' I inhaled. 'Rasputin's heading my way.' Couldn't miss his particular stench.

'Get back to the boat. Leave him to us.'

'All yours.' I looked back at the remains littering the roof of this impressive new building. One was already a pile of ash. The other would be, come sunrise.

I didn't have much time. I sensed a group of Rebels closing in on me. Leading them to the yacht was the last thing I had in mind. I'd left my car at the McMillans in Edgecliffe. That's where I'd go. I jumped back down into the street, and the Rebels surrounded me.

'Thanks for the address.' Rasputin gave a low whistle and they came at me at once.

I lunged at Stockton first, when a burning pain shot through the back of my head and another through my sword hand. Sudden weakness paralysed me. White-oak. Not good. I struggled to stay upright, but my body ached in every joint. My grip loosened. The sword dropped, and so did I.

'Why isn't he crystallizing?' One raspy voice asked.

They stared curiously down at me.

'Try again,' Rasputin said. 'I want that ring.'

'My pleasure,' Stockton said as he leaned over me and stabbed the point of the spike into my neck.

My body convulsed as the venom – and weakness – spread. My vision blurred. How much could the serum handle?

'They're coming!'

'Shit.'

'Just cut his finger off,' Stockton said.

'No. Pick him up. Bring him with us. I want to know why the poison hasn't killed him.'

Stockton hoisted me onto his shoulder and ran.

I gritted my teeth at the pain that wracked my body as I dangled helplessly over the bastard's back, each bump a fiery, electric jolt. They took the route through the Botanical Gardens –

the gates were already shut – and leapt into the water. I heard Luc yell out just as we went under.

CHAPTER 36 – BAD NEWS

LAURA

'Merde!'

Kari and I stopped and stared at each other. 'Did you hear that?' I asked. 'It was Luc's voice, and it was loud. I'm sure every Brethren in the city must have heard.'

She nodded, eyes wide. 'But how could you?'

'I can see and hear like you now.' My gaze automatically swept to the ring. The serpent's eyes were still black. What was going on?

'What is it, dear? What did you hear?' Judy rose from one of the sofas where she and Jenny had been watching the training session.

'Luc swore. Something's wrong.' The old cliché about the hairs on the back of my neck standing up was never more apt. I closed my eyes and called out to Alec. 'Where are you? What's going on?' Nothing. I tried again. 'Alec!'

My heart raced. All I could think was that he was in trouble. In desperation, I called out to Luc, past caring who heard. 'Luc, is he okay? Are you with him?'

'What colour are the serpent's eyes?'

If he had to ask that question, then Alec wasn't with them. 'Black.'

'Then he's alive.'

'Where is he?' I held my breath waiting for his answer while the seconds ticked by. 'Rasputin has him.'

My body went cold, and the sword dropped from my grasp. The blood roared in my ears. Somewhere in the haze, Kari told Judy and Jenny the news. My mother gasped.

'I've got to go to him.' Before they could stop me, I ran down the steps to the lowest deck where Judy had mentioned they stored the jet skis – a garage of sorts. Regardless of my pathetic sword skills, I couldn't stay here, doing nothing.

Footsteps behind me, something whizzed over my head, and Kari stood before me.

'Don't even think of stopping me.' I told her.

'I'm not.' She held out what appeared to be either a short sword or a long dagger. Either way, it looked lethal. 'You'll need this. Luc never mentioned anything about me knocking you out to keep you here.' She made a face.' 'Don't reckon he'd like me doing that. So, as your bodyguard, I have to go with you.'

I took the weapon as footsteps sounded on the stairs behind me.

Judy stood on the bottom step, Jenny at her back. 'Laura, you can't. They're out there, and it's you they want.'

'They've got Alec. You really expect me to stay here?'

'I expect you to use your sense and not put yourself in danger.' Her pleading tone made me pause.

'What should I do, then?'

'Contact Alec again. Find out where he is, so we can let Luc know.'

I took a deep breath, closed my eyes and called out to him. Alec, please answer me.

Laura. Snapper Island. His voice sounded distant and weak. Rather than words, images floated into my mind – grey walls, peeling paint, a single pale light bulb hanging from the ceiling and a dark shadow I couldn't make out. The images faded too soon.

'Snapper Island. That's where they took him.' My gaze instantly shot to the serpent's eyes. They hadn't changed – their glossy black hue stared back at me.

'Where's that?' Jenny asked.

'Not sure. Somewhere at the other end of the harbour, maybe.' Judy looked past me to Kari. 'Check the location on the GPS, and I'll steer.'

'Yes!' Kari pumped a fist and zipped back up stairs.

'Steer? You know how to drive this boat?' The few times I'd been in the wheelhouse, Sam had been in the skipper's seat.

'Laura, dear, your father bought this yacht for me; it has my name. And yes, I jolly well know how to steer it. You think I'd let you and Kari go on your own?' She shook her head. 'Not going to happen. We'll go to the island, moor as close to the jetty as we can and wait for Luc and the men to get him out. I'm not letting you off this boat. Do you understand?' Her determined expression effectively ended any further protest on my part. I resisted the urge to pout. 'Now, tell your father what we're doing so it won't come as a nasty surprise to him.'

'Yes, Mum.' I rolled my eyes.

Judy laughed. 'If that was meant to be a facetious jibe, it didn't work. I quite like you calling me mum.' With that, she turned and walked up the stairs. 'Wheelhouse, girls,' she called back over her shoulder before disappearing from sight.

Jenny grinned and raised an eyebrow at me. She didn't need to say anything, it was all there in the look – no matter how old a girl is, her mum is still boss.

I sighed, picked up the blade Kari had handed me, and tucked it into the belt of my shirtdress. As we made our way to the uppermost deck, I told Luc where Alec was, and that we'd meet him there.

He wasn't happy.

I ignored his protests, drowning it out the way he taught me. Instead, I concentrated on what I would do once we got there. Although the Rebel Brethren couldn't sense us while we were out on the water, it would be a different matter once we docked. They'd sense us and might even attempt to board. What could two humans, one vampire and one half-human/half-vampire do against a group of nasty rogue vampires?

'Jen, wait.' We'd reached the main stateroom when I remembered something. I dashed across to the bar, pulled open the cutlery drawer and rummaged around till I found the corkscrew I'd threatened Rasputin with earlier. Why not? I thought and tucked it into my belt as well.

'A corkscrew?' Jenny looked at me incredulously.

'It worked last time.' I tapped it. 'Insurance policy.'

She shuddered. 'Let's hope not.'

We joined Judy and Kari on the uppermost deck. While Kari navigated, Judy deftly maneuvered the boat, avoiding the many smaller craft that swarmed the harbour at this time of the year. Many were here, not only to escape the harsh northern hemisphere winter, but to enjoy the spectacle of one of the most famous nautical events in the world – the Sydney to Hobart Yacht Race. Everyone who owned anything that could float seemed to be out enjoying the balmy summer night.

'Next stop Snapper Island,' Judy declared.

'We're coming, my love. Hang on,' I whispered into the night, and for the thousandth time checked the serpent's eyes. Black was becoming my next pet hate.

CHAPTER 37 - SNAPPER ISLAND

ALEC

Stockton pulled my head back and I tried not to grimace as pain shot through my body. The chair to which I was bound, creaked with every movement.

'Why aren't you dead?' His face was inches from mine, brow furrowed.

Another thin, red line burned across my chest where he'd dragged the white-oak spike across my skin.

My weakness grew with every passing second. A haze fell across my eyes, and my body ached as if I'd been stretched out along the wrack – every joint pulled out of place, muscles screaming in agony. Even my breathing was laboured. Would the serum last? How much more could it take? My only hope was that Marcus would somehow pick up my scent.

'Interesting.' Rasputin's face loomed next to Stockton's. 'Your body's fighting the poison instead of being destroyed by it. Why is that?'

'Guess.' I said, although the effort drained me. It was imperative he believe it was the Ingenii blood that created my immunity. Otherwise I, too, could become their puppet – kept alive to create the serum for Timur, and maybe Rasputin's exclusive use.

He angled his head, gaze boring into mine. 'Ingenii blood. Why did we not know about this before?'

'Not my problem,' I said.

'No, Princeps. I think there's something more here; more secrets, and unless you share them with me, it will be your problem.'

'You really think so?'

'A man can endure only so much pain.' He inhaled. 'And I can smell yours. The pain's increasing, isn't it? Look at you – you're shivering, sweating. It doesn't have to be this way. If only you would join me.' His voice dipped to a lulling, soothing tone. 'I could make it all go away. We're Brethren. We shouldn't fight.'

He was trying to mesmerize me again. I gave him my best sneer. 'It didn't work last time. Why do you think it'll work now?'

He sighed. 'I had to try. Perhaps in your weakened state, you'd be more amenable.'

'Sorry to disappoint you.'

'Oh no Princeps, I don't believe you're sorry at all.'

'You're right. I'm not.'

He laughed. 'I'm enjoying this!'

'Let's just kill him.' Stockton wrenched my head back. I groaned. 'He won't tell you anything and I've had enough.'

'Why so impatient? I don't have all my answers yet. Patience, patience.'

Stockton growled. 'We don't have much time. They're probably out looking for him.'

'You told me they'll never find us here.' His voice dripped with menace.

Stockton had a fistful of my hair, and I felt his hand tremble. 'With all this water around? No way. But why take a chance?' He exuded fear – of his new pal, Rasputin, or being caught by Marcus and the men?

Rasputin returned his attention to me. 'Why don't you succumb to my will like all the others? Is that another of the gifts of the Ingenii?'

'Seems you have all the answers.'

His gaze slid to the chain around my neck. I tried not to tense.

He jerked his head at Stockton and indicated for him to remove it. My breathing became more laboured, and I strained at the chains binding my wrists behind my back.

Stockton gave me a fanged smile and released my head. He grabbed the chain with the crucifix and bloodvault key and ripped it from my neck.

My head dropped onto my chest, barely able to lift my gaze.

Stockton dangled it and its precious contents before Rasputin, whose handless arms remained in his coat pockets.

'It was my mother's,' I said. 'No value to you.'

'You surprise me. I never took you for the sentimental type.' He gazed at the crucifix, his eyes taking on a distant look. Unexpectedly he said, 'I once had one, too. Gift from the Czarina – *Matushka*. Most prized thing I ever owned. Wore it always. Used to exorcise demons with it.' He paused and laughed. 'Now I am a demon.'

He had once been friend and confidant to the Romanovs, the last Russian ruling dynasty. Many blamed him for their demise and thought him a devil. 'Only if you want to be,' I said.

He blinked and spread his arms, the sleeves of his coat covering the gap where his hands once were. 'This,' he slammed his chest, 'is what I am!'

I didn't have the strength to argue.

Rasputin's eyes narrowed as he gazed at the key. 'What's this for?'

'Unlocks her vault,' I lied. I pictured my mother's grave in my mind, imagined inserting the key, turning the lock, trying to convince my body to give off the required scent.

His eyebrows shot up and he stared at me. 'The crucifix I understand, but that,' his head jerked toward the key, 'I do not.' He leaned toward me and sniffed. 'The scent of truth, yet…. I always know when someone lies. The Czar depended on me; so many lied to him, and I exposed them.'

No wonder the Russian nobility tried to kill him.

'I suspect you're lying, Princeps.'

'Suspect all you want. I told you—' I coughed for the first time in nearly a century. Damn! My lungs were filling with fluid. So much poison must be flowing through my system, both serum and the Ingenii immunity were struggling under the onslaught.

Stockton smirked and dropped the chain on the table in front of me, next to my sword. 'I'd say your immunity is going for a dive, Princeps.'

Bastard. I had to stay alive; had to, for Laura's sake. I called her name as my body grew numb and I drifted into unconsciousness.

Suddenly my head was wrenched back again. 'Not yet, Munro.' Stockton's voice hissed in my ear.

'Our donsangs saw your men out in the daylight.'

'Yeah, they're allowed to daywalk, even if only once a year. But no, not the rest of us. We don't fit in to your exclusive little club.' Stockton sneered, his fist twisting my hair more tightly. The muscles on my neck strained to breaking point.

'You know why,' I struggled to say. 'Principate would have fallen long ago if all Brethren had shared in the *Gift.*'

'Yeah, that would've been a real tragedy.'

Rasputin's eyes narrowed in concentration. 'Who's blood were they given, I wonder. Not Lady Judith's, surely. Hasn't hers begun to wane? And that little bitch who did this to me.' His eyes paled as he thrust his handless stumps at my face. 'Show him,' he said.

Stockton released me and removed Rasputin's gloves. The skin had healed and where his hands once were, small, pale protrusions had begun to grow – the beginnings of fingers. Juveniles healed more slowly than mature Brethren, and it would be weeks before Rasputin would have a new pair of hands.

'She did a good job,' I said, my blood boiling at his reference to Laura.

Rasputin's fangs slid from his upper lip. He glanced at Stockton and jerked his head in my direction. Stockton backhanded me and I tasted blood on my lip.

'Her blood is poison, which leads me to ask, who's blood were they given?' He stared at me while Stockton replaced the gloves.

Rasputin was cunning. Nearly an hour had past since Stockton had infected me with white-oak. I had faith in the serum, but with the amount of poison circulating through my system, recovery would take longer. Did I have the time? 'What answer do you get?'

He grinned, and his gaze flashed from me, to my chain, and back again. 'Come, Princeps, let's not play games. You and I know that key is not for any burial vault. It has the smell of blood on it, not earth. In particular, Ingenii blood.'

'Ha, brilliant. I feed from an Ingenii, the key's on my chest and a drop of blood spills on it. What reasoning!' I attempted a feeble laugh.

He leaned over the table, a snarl pulling his upper lip back. 'Whose blood did your men receive? The only answer that comes to me is stored blood – stored *First Blood*. Lord Luc has a cache somewhere, hasn't he? Somewhere he can easily access it.' His eyes flared. 'Like The Residence.'

My heart hammered in my throat. Could I convince him otherwise? 'Wrong—'

'Yes, yes, that's it!' His grin was triumphant. 'I remember the scent of blood somehow mixed with all those wine bottles in the cellar where you held me.' He laughed aloud. 'And to think I almost burnt it down.'

I strained against my bonds – too damn weak.

He and Stockton exchanged glances. 'The place is empty. They're all on his yacht,' Stockton said. 'Want me to find where Lebrettan has it stored?'

Rasputin looked at Stockton. 'No, we'll go together. The temptation might be too great for you.'

'What the fuck is that supposed to mean?' Stockton glared, fists clenched at his sides. 'You questioning my loyalty?'

That gave me hope – Rasputin didn't trust him. I silently thanked Sam.

Rasputin levelled his gaze at him, but Stockton shielded his eyes. 'Don't you try that on me, you son-of-a-bitch.'

The door burst open, and a Rebel, whose face I recognized, strode in. 'Two boats speeding in this direction. The Principate's found us.'

'You sure?' Stockton asked.

'I'm sure. The big one's called "Judy" and the smaller one's "Judy II." It's Lord Luc all right.'

'Fuck! How?' Stockton spun around and glared at me.

For a split second I saw fear in the Rebels' eyes. 'Dunno. Reckon we've got five minutes. I'm off.'

'No, wait,' Rasputin said. 'This is perfect. You,' he addressed the Rebel. 'Take one other, go to The Residence, and wait for me at the entrance to the cellar. Do not go in. Understand?'

The man nodded and departed, leaving the door ajar.

Rasputin turned back to me, a wide grin on his face. 'I could not have planned this better – the Prime Elders running around here while I help myself to Lord Luc's little secret.' If he could, I'm sure he would've rubbed his hands together.

I called to Laura. *Warn Luc. They're headed for the house. The Rebels know about the bloodvault.* To Rasputin I said, 'The Residence is guarded. Your men won't get through.' A necessary lie.

'Really? I thought they were all hiding in their safe houses?'

'You thought wrong.'

He rubbed his forearm along his chin. 'No, I don't believe I am. My men won't have any trouble. Which brings me to my next question. How much does he have?'

'You expect me to answer that?'

'No, in fact I don't. My friend here's getting restless and needs an excuse to play with his ring.'

Stockton leered at me and dug the spike of the white-oak deep into the side of my neck, creating a long gash as he dragged it along my skin.

I felt blood trickle down. My body convulsed as the deadly poison snaked through my system. Another wave of pain engulfed me and leached into every muscle, nerve and sinew. I became so weak I could barely raise my head.

'Amazing. The strength of Ingenii blood.' Rasputin gazed at me with the impassioned stare of a sadist. 'No wonder he hoards it and refuses to share. How much does he have?'

Fluid filled my lungs, and I coughed.

He ran his fingers through his beard. 'Perhaps Lord Luc only keeps a small amount of Ingenii blood here. There's got to be more. But where?'

'Maybe not here – where they lived before,' Stockton said.

Rasputin's eyes gleamed. 'Of course. The Dantonville Chateau in France; the original Residence. Together with the serpent ring, what better gift to present to my master.' He turned to Stockton. 'Send a message to Lord Timur. Tell him what we discovered, with my compliments, and place the chain in my pocket. I mean to discover what it unlocks.'

Helpless, I could only watch as Stockton relayed the message on his mobile then dropped my chain with the crucifix and bloodvault key into Rasputin's coat pocket.

Rasputin strode to the door. 'Nothing compares with the satisfaction of a job well done. Don't forget the ring, Stockton.' He kicked the door open and walked out.

Stockton grabbed the sword from the table and stalked toward me.

CHAPTER 38 – NOT HELPLESS

LAURA

The western end of the harbour, along the Parramatta River, was less densely populated. Being further from the touristy sections of the city, few ventured this way. This was where the locals moored their boats; where the old industrial wharves and factories had been transformed into trendy suburbs; of high-rise apartment blocks with million dollar views.

We passed the former naval dockyard of Cockatoo Island, when Kari cried out, 'That's it, over there.' She pointed to a large outcrop jutting from the water. It looked tiny – our boat was bigger. Lights on either end blinked as a warning to passing ships. 'The jetty's next to those two palm trees,' she said.

A smaller boat appeared, its engines roaring louder the closer it came.

'It's Luc,' Judy said.

I leaned out of the window for a better view. It was speeding to catch up with us. With my enhanced vision, I could clearly see his face. 'He's not happy,' I said.

'Laura, tell your mother to stop that boat.' His voice carried clearly over the water.

'He wants you to stop.'

'Leave your father to me.'

'I hate domestics,' Kari said, screwing up her nose as she gazed towards the black expanse.

Next to her, Jenny looked tense and pensive, unlike her usual bubbly self. 'Is Terens on the boat following us?'

'Uh huh.'

'That's good.' She gave me a wan smile, but I could tell she was anxious.

She's really fallen for him. 'I'm sorry all this happened while you're here, Jen.'

'Not your fault, hon. I wanted to know about vamps, uh, Brethren, and, well, now I know.'

Warn Luc! They're headed for the house. They know about the bloodvault. I jumped at Alec's voice in my head. The serpent ring erupted in a blaze of light and just as suddenly dimmed.

For a split second I debated what to do first – contact Alec or tell Luc, but his message sounded urgent. 'They know about the bloodvault,' I threw over my shoulder to Judy as I raced out of the wheelhouse. I leaned over the railing and called to Luc in the motor launch, its lights gaining on us.

'Papa, the Rebels know about the bloodvault. They're on their way to the house now.'

Luc swore. 'Alec told you?'

'Yes. He's okay, but I have a bad feeling.'

'We're coming alongside.'

The launch sped up, and within minutes, had maneuvered close enough for Sam to leap onto the main deck and secure it with a line of rope. A noise caught my attention. Although it was dark I saw the outline of a small vessel speed away from the island.

'It's them,' I called down to Luc and pointed at the departing vessel.

He spun around and issued orders to the men, and then he and Marcus joined Sam on the main deck. Jake threw the rope down, took the launch wheel and with Terens and Cal, sped after the Rebels, leaving nothing but the smell of diesel, and churned waves, in their wake.

Rather then take the stairs, Sam, Marcus and Luc bounded up, landing on the deck in front of me. In their long, black leather coats, swords at their sides, they looked intimidating, until Marcus smiled, leaned down and kissed me on the cheek. 'We'll get him back,' he said.

Sam gave me a brief nod as he strode past, on the way to the helm I presumed.

'I should be angry with you,' Luc said, lips a thin line.

'With both of us.' Judy came to stand beside me.

Luc shook his head then enveloped us in a fierce hug. 'Thank God, you're both safe.'

'Do you know how many are left on the island,' Marcus asked.

'No, Alec didn't say.'

Luc released us and we joined Sam at the console. 'Dock at the jetty, next to the two palm trees,' Luc told Sam, who had replaced Judy at the wheel. 'Laura,' there was an edge to Luc's voice, 'what is that matchstick tucked into your belt?'

Kari and I exchanged a glance, and she gave me an encouraging grin.

'I wanted to know how to use a sword. Kari taught me.'

'Good for you.' Sam said.

Luc rolled his eyes, but there was a smile on Marcus's lips.

'I'm not going to be helpless, Papa, with you, Alec or the men coming to my rescue. Not any more.' I stood facing him.

'We're here,' Sam announced. He'd sidled the boat alongside a crumbling, wooden jetty. *Probably riddled with termites.* He cut the engine.

Two lone palms stood at the other end, behind which were huddled a group of dilapidated, derelict, corrugated-iron buildings. The weathered sign read, 'Snapper Island,' and featured a picture of a naval ship. A smaller sign nearby showed it had once, long ago, been a boys' naval training facility.

'The moment we step on land, they'll know we're here,' Marcus said.

Luc looked directly at me. 'I know you're brave, ma petite, and I'm proud of you for that, but you're no match for the two Rebels we're going after. And we move too fast for you keep up.' He glanced at my sword. 'Keep that on and pray you won't have to use it.'

'Ready?' Sam asked.

Luc kissed Judy then he, Marcus and Sam leapt over the side and disappeared. The four of us stood silent at the railing looking out. I drowned out all other sounds and concentrated on locating Alec's voice somewhere within those shabby buildings.

Jenny touched my arm. 'Can you hear?' she whispered.

'I'm trying. Mostly shouting and swearing. I think someone's dead!' My heart jolted. It couldn't be one of ours. Automatically I glanced at the serpent ring – eyes still black. My heartbeat returned to normal. It wasn't Alec.

A ferry loaded with partygoers chugged past, the loud music amplified as it boomed across the water. I clapped my hands over my ears. Talk about bad timing. Some of the revellers called, 'Merry Christmas' and waved. Obviously they'd been celebrating for a while – Christmas was yesterday.

Kari waved back.

'If only they knew what's really going on in the world,' Jenny said and shook her head.

I turned to look at her. 'I don't blame you that you regret coming.'

She linked her arm through mine. "No way, hon, wouldn't have missed it for anything. Well,' she shrugged, 'except for a few bits.'

We leant our heads together and stood like that for a while as I peered through the dim lighting to the row of buildings ahead. *Please come out Alec.* I prayed Luc and Marcus would reach him in time.

Jenny patted my hand. 'They'll get him out, hon.'

We stood and waited.

CHAPTER 39 - CLOSE CALL

ALEC

Stockton raised my sword above his head. With every ounce of strength I had left, I overturned the chair as the sword swished through the air. I crashed to the ground. My shoulder and head connected with the concrete. Blood trickled into my eye. I lay there panting, drained, knowing he'd strike again immediately.

Stockton swore.

There was nothing else I could do as the chains held me to the chair. I sensed Marcus, Luc and Sam somewhere nearby. Did I have the strength to groan for help? Stockton loomed over me, sword raised. Helpless, I waited for the blade to descend. Suddenly, his head swivelled toward the door. He must have sensed them also, for he snarled and turned back to me, indecision creasing his face.

The door flew open. Marcus entered, growled, and in a blink Stockton's head flew from his shoulders. The sword clattered to the floor.

Marcus sprinted to my side, nostrils flaring as he assessed my wounds. 'Deus!'

I tried to speak. 'Be, all, right. Serum's working.'

He ripped the chains that bound me, righted the chair and sat me back in it. I sagged into it, my head dropping onto the back of the backrest.

'I'll finish this business and we'll get you out of here.' He picked up Stockton's head and placed it on the table, out of reach of the grasping hands, afterward removing the wolf's-head ring from his finger. He plunged the spike into the Rebel leader's thrashing body. In seconds, all that remained was crystalline dust. Stockton's clothes collapsed into the space left by his now-disintegrating body. Marcus stabbed Stockton's head with the ring, and then spat on the remains. The wolf's-head ring he slid onto his little finger.

'Take the phone,' I managed to say, my voice barely above a whisper. 'Don't... destroy it. Bloodvault ... Rasputin knows.'

His eyes flared as he gazed at me, and I knew what sped through his mind.

My speech was frustratingly slow. 'No, I didn't tell them. Donsangs saw the men. He worked it out ... knew the blood couldn't come from Judith or Laura. Got Stockton to ring Timur. Took my key.'

'I don't doubt *you*. Rasputin is a dangerous snake.' Marcus searched Stockton's clothes, found the mobile and pocketed it. 'Come, my boy.' He draped my arm around his shoulders as he levered me up, supporting my weight. My legs dragged on the ground as we exited into a narrow corridor.

'Where's Luc?'

'With Sempronius, making sure no Rebels are left alive.'

Marcus half-carried me down a corridor, which turned right into another and ended at a set of closed double doors. He kicked them open. The smell of cordite permeated the empty space – the room may once have been used to store ammunition. To our left, a set of half-rusted stairs led upwards, hanging precariously from equally rusted brackets.

Luc's head peered down at us. 'You look like shit.'

I croaked a laugh, 'Least ... not dead.'

He jumped down, took my other arm and draped it around his shoulders. 'Heard what you told Marcus. Merde. My fault. I took a risk sharing the Ingenii blood this year. I hoped nobody would ask questions.'

'Get Sempronius to hack into Timur's mobile – stop that message getting through,' Marcus suggested.

'Soon as we get back to the boat.'

Supporting me between them, they vaulted up the stairs. We emerged inside a low-roofed, corrugated-iron building I didn't recognize. Hanging upside down, semi-conscious from Stockton's back hadn't helped my orientation, either.

We stepped through the door at the other end of the room. Fresh sea air stung my face, and I took a deep gulp. Slowly, strength began seeping back into my legs and I was able to shuffle along.

Sam appeared, wet, his coat hung over one shoulder. His eyes flared on seeing me, then his gaze shifted to Marcus.

'Stockton paid.'

Sam swore. 'Wish I could say the same about Rasputin. He got away. Nearly had him before he slipped through a hole. Went after him and lost his scent.'

Marcus handed him Stockton's mobile. 'Can you stop a message reaching Timur?'

'What's on it?'

'Bloodvault,' Marcus answered.

Sam inhaled sharply. 'How the hell?'

'Someone saw you.'

Sam frowned, 'But all the Brethren know every year....' He stopped and gritted his teeth. 'Shit. I didn't think of that. Laura's off limits, so where else would Ingenii blood come from unless Luc bottled the stuff.'

'Get back to the boat and see what you can do.'

With a nod, Sam sped off.

'How long before you're fit?' Luc asked me.

'Not sure. Give me an hour.'

We followed the path toward the jetty, the lights from the yacht illuminating our way. I spied Laura at the railing, scanning the distance before her, her beautiful eyes wide with concern. She alone gave me the strength to move my weakened body. I couldn't wait to wrap her in my arms.

CHAPTER 40 – ALL BETTER

LAURA

'Here they come,' Kari said.

Soon, forms appeared – three of them. As they neared, I recognized Alec's bowed figure supported by the other two.

My heart lurched. Someone sprinted ahead and rushed past me – Sam.

Ignoring Judy's protest, I ran down the stairs to the main deck and onto the rickety jetty. It swayed as I dashed to his side. Luc and Marcus half carried him onto the wharf.

'Alec!'

He raised his head, and I gasped. He was pale. There was blood on his face and neck, and his lower lip was swollen as if he'd been struck there. A light sheen of perspiration glistened on his skin, and his shirt had been ripped open, revealing dark red scratch lines across his chest and neck.

I touched them tenderly, and raised my eyes in question.

'Wolf's-head ring.' His voice was barely above a whisper.

Tears of anger stung my eyes. 'They tried to kill you!'

'They failed.' He gave me a weak smile. 'Serum worked.'

I took his face between my hands and kissed him. 'Let me,' I took his arm from Marcus and placed it around my shoulders. 'Rasputin?'

'Got away,' Luc replied.

'Sam chased him through a maze of corridors and lost his scent. Must be a passage that leads straight to the water,' Marcus said. 'Deus. We were so close.'

'Why do the bad guys always get away?'

'Not all,' Luc answered as we shuffled back to the boat. 'Stockton and the other Rebels are dead.'

After we lay Alec down on one of the sofas in the stateroom, the others left us alone. I bit back tears of anger as I examined his injuries. *Bastards!* I rarely swore, but to see the way they had made him suffer was enough for me to want to utter every obscenity I knew.

He didn't speak, only winced, as, with a wet cloth, I gently dabbed at the dried blood that stained his lip, forehead and neck. I followed it with a kiss. His gaze remained on me as I cleaned the rest of his face then kissed each pale cheek, his eyes and brow, his chin, his throat and lastly his mouth again, as if by doing so I could erase the pain he'd undergone. 'I love you,' I murmured against his lips.

Alec's hand slid into my hair, and he twirled the strands around his finger. 'Thoughts of you gave me the strength I needed.' His other hand cupped the side of my face. I turned my head and kissed the inside of his palm.

The boat shuddered as the engines started and we moved away from the wharf. I could hear everyone talking in the wheelhouse and silently prayed Terens, Cal and Jake had caught up with the other Rebels. I didn't want to imagine the consequences if they found the bloodvault. Yet how would they get in without the keys?

I lowered his hands from my face and laved his chest with the wet cloth next, kissing each angry gash. Alec sighed, but my mouth went dry. His gold chain was missing.

'Your chain with the bloodvault key.'

'Rasputin's got it – for now.'

I gasped, and a cold wave ran through me.

'I will get it back.' Steely resolve appeared in his eyes.

'But doesn't it—'

'No, it takes two keys to unlock the vault. The third was an extra in case one was lost. He can't use it to get in even if he were to find it – which I doubt.' He coughed. I'd never heard him cough before, and it scared me.

'Shhhh, don't talk. Rest and get your strength back.'

He closed his eyes and I sat watching his breathing. Although I trusted Alec's serum, I clutched his hand and brought it to my cheek as if that would prevent the dreaded crystallisation.

Five or ten minutes later, his chest rose as he took a deep breath, opened his eyes and looked at me. 'My strength's coming back.' Even his voice sounded stronger, and the ugly, red marks on his chest and neck had faded.

He tried to rise, but I placed a hand on his shoulder and urged him to stay down. 'No, lie still. Give it time.'

'We don't have time. When Timur sees that message....' He closed his eyes. 'He's holed up in his castle outside Budapest, and it's still day there, but sunset's not far off. We've got to intercept that message before he rises.'

'What message?'

He explained and my hand flew to my mouth. 'Does Luc know?'

He nodded and lay still for another few minutes. Suddenly he opened his eyes and turned his head to gaze at me, squeezing my hand. 'I never tire of looking at you.' He unlocked our hands, clasped the back of my head and kissed me – long, hungry and with passion that left me quivering.

'Feeling better?' I smiled at him.

Alec smiled, nipped me lightly on the lips and said, 'Yes. Help me up.'

I held his arm, which trembled slightly. He sat up and flexed them both. 'Much better.' Another deep breath. He stood and caught me up in his arms. 'I feel good.'

Was it his kiss or the adrenaline of nearly having lost him that had me wanting him? Well, now wasn't the time. 'Perfect. Now tell me everything that happened, and don't leave out one detail. I was going crazy and even got Kari to teach me how to use this.' I tapped the sword at my side.

He raised an eyebrow. 'I noticed.'

'Don't even think of objecting.'

I was ready to launch into my speech, when he said, 'It's a good idea. Should have thought of it sooner. I'll give you some extra lessons later.' I was speechless, and he took advantage of it by kissing me again.

'Talk now, kiss later,' I said.

He chuckled and sat on the sofa with me on his lap. 'Okay, I was led into a trap. Rasputin was waiting with too many for me to fight off. They'd been hiding out at that old navy training base and took me back there to interrogate.'

That explained the scratches on his chest. 'But using white-oak....'

'That's why. They couldn't understand why I wasn't dust, so they kept trying.' He tucked a lock of my hair behind my ear. 'Rasputin realized we must have another source of blood when our guys were out in the daytime. He knew we couldn't use your blood or Judith's.'

Just then I heard what sounded like cheering from Kari, up in the wheelhouse. 'I knew the guys'd get 'em. Does that mean the rebellion's over?' she said.

'Is Kari right about the rebellion being over?' I asked.

Alec looked at me dumbfounded. 'How did you hear that?'

'I haven't told you about that development.'

His brow furrowed as I explained my increased vision and hearing, and for a while he said nothing. 'Mmmm. Let me know if there are any other changes.'

'Like a craving for blood perhaps?' *Oh lord, I hope not.*

'Exactly.' He gazed at me as if expecting a set of fangs to erupt from my mouth at any moment.

I suddenly remembered. 'There's something else you need to know.' I leapt off his lap and went over to the coffee table. It was still there, open at the page Matt had shown me. 'Look at this.' I handed him the newspaper with Jean-Philippe's portrait of me.

A muscle in Alec's jaw ticked as he perused the article. 'Holy mother of....'

'Matt came here to show it to me, and warn me that there might be an investigation. He also said more bodies were turning up; that you'd lost control and ... he was going to bring you in.'

This time both his eyebrows shot upwards. When I told him the rest, he rose and paced. All sign of weakness was gone. 'That portrait poses more of a problem than Sommers does.' He dug his hands into his pockets and gazed out the window.

'What are you thinking?'

'How to get hold of that portrait and hide it.'

'That'd be one solution. But what's the point of stressing over something that mightn't eventuate?'

He took my fingers and brought them to his lips. 'True, but we still need to be prepared.'

'And the rebellion?'

'It may be finished here, with Stockton dead, but with Timur we could be facing something worse.'

'What could be worse?'

He let out a breath. 'It was one thing for Luc to share Ingenii blood once a year with his men, but to have a store of it spanning centuries for all to share.' He paused, 'Timur could use it to turn our allies against us.'

I thought of Karl and Milena, O'Toole and the other Prefects. Would they turn against the Principate for this? The thought frightened me. 'Is there anything we can do?'

'Not sure.'

'If we could tell them the blood was only for emergencies?'

'There've been two rebellions prior to this, Laura. Each would've been considered an emergency at the time. Yet the stored blood was not used. How to explain that?'

'It all depends on what you call an emergency. I'd say the ending of the Ingenii and the threat it brings to the Principate qualifies.'

'I agree. But would others?'

'If their homes and lives were threatened, and the Principate was the only thing that stood between them and destruction? I think they would. And if the stored Ingenii blood gave their protectors the edge, do you think they'd object?'

'You should've been a diplomat, Miss Dantonville.'

'I'm a primary school teacher – same thing.'

Alec chuckled and drew me into his arms again. 'I believe you'd persuade them, too.'

'What about Rasputin?'

'He's finished, here at least. The Rebels are dead and he's temporarily disabled, thanks to you.' He kissed me on the nose.

'And he's alone and hunted – there's a price on his head. My guess is, he'll try to get out of the country. But it'll take him days before he sets foot in Europe, in the meantime we might be able to intercept that message and stop it reaching Timur.'

His gaze bored into mine, and in his eyes I saw strength, confidence and determination, and whatever doubts I had harbored, dissipated like mist on an autumn morning. My heart soared and I hugged his neck.

'We've won, darling. The Principate has survived the first hurdle, and we're sure to win.'

For now, that was all that mattered. Whatever was happening among the Brethren in the rest of the world seemed far away. Here, at least, the rebellion had been defeated. Hurdle number two would come soon enough, but not today. Today was good, my family was safe, and the man I loved was secure in my arms. As for tomorrow? What did Scarlet O'Hara say about leaving things for another day?

Sensible idea.

EPILOGUE

Rasputin's head broke the surface of the water, his piercing gaze levelled at the departing Principate yacht. Stockton had failed him. The princeps was still alive and, no doubt, wearing the serpent ring – the priceless gift he'd promised to deliver to his master, Timur. And here he was, handless and helpless – thanks to that little bitch— and hunted.

Rage seethed through him. She would pay. Oh yes, she would suffer. He would see to it. He smiled and licked the salt from his lips. But that pleasure would have to wait. His sire, Timur, had ordered his return. At least he could offer the knowledge of Lebrettan's secret blood stash to deflect some of his master's wrath.

Rasputin scanned the horizon. A water taxi seemed to be headed his way. No passengers, one skipper – perfect. He submerged and waited till it came within range, launching himself from the water and onto the deck.

'What the hell?'

The man stilled as Rasputin's gaze bored into his mind and fastened on a weakness. 'My boat sank, and I need to get to the airport. I'll pay you triple to take me there.'

The man grinned, steered the boat around and made straight for the coast, expertly negotiating the waves as he exited the harbour and motored down the coast to the next bay.

Rasputin sat in the stern, watching the pulse throb in the man's neck, smelt the blood beneath his skin, and his hunger grew. He swallowed saliva and covered his mouth with a sleeve as the tips of his incisors protruded from his upper lip.

'What's your name?' Some people collected coins or stamps; Rasputin collected the names of those he killed.

'Stavros.'

Greek. On the dashboard sat an icon of the virgin and photo of a woman with four children. A rosary dangled from a hook next to them. Rasputin remembered a similar icon. *Matuschka* used to pray before it.

'You a good son of Holy Mother Church?'

'Of course.' The man angled his head toward his passenger. 'Are you Orthodox?'

Images paraded through Rasputin's head – ones he'd rather forget. 'I was a priest once.' He watched with interest as the man's head swivelled around to get a better look. Should he drop his sleeve and reveal what lay beneath?

The smell of jet fuel alerted his senses. They were close. 'Drop me at the next wharf.' He needed to feed.

The skipper slowed his taxi to a halt, threw a line and secured it to a pole.

'Come sit next to me.' Rasputin beckoned him with jerk of his head. Voice and eyes persuasive, the man obeyed. 'Bare me your throat.'

He saw the man's eyes flare, smelled his body tense and knew that, somewhere in the dulled corner of his mind, horror silently crept. Yet that would not delay the inevitable. Without the use of his hands, Rasputin still managed to wrap his arms around the Greek's shoulders and hold him in place as he drank.

Long, sweet draughts slid down his throat. As his strength grew so the man's heartbeat slowed and stuttered to a halt. He let the body drop, wiped his mouth with his sleeve and alighted from the boat.

'Spasiba.' He thanked the man in his native tongue, then

turned and sped off into the darkness.

END OF BOOK 2

Turn the page to read Chapter 1 from book 3 – BloodVault.

BLOODVAULT

"So many out-of-the-way things had happened lately, that Alice had begun to think that very few things indeed were really impossible." Alice in Wonderland by Lewis Carroll

CHAPTER 1 – DESTINY

LAURA

Whoever said we are captains of our own destiny had no idea. Not a clue. Mistakenly, I once believed my life was mine to control, but that illusion has been shattered. Once, I was ordinary Laura Dantonville, primary school teacher, and soon-to-be engaged to Matt Sommers, Detective Inspector and all round nice guy – or so I thought. That was only a few weeks ago. Now....

My pink-diamond engagement ring flashed up at me as I examined the result of my home pregnancy kit. And I had to concede that fate and destiny had control; the strip showed two coloured bands.

I was pregnant.

Nothing unusual in that, except that Alec, my fiancé, is a vampire.

My ex-boyfriend, Matt, hated vampires and wouldn't hesitate to kill them, even if it meant wiping out half my family – the vampire half. I'd had to end our relationship.

Placing the strip of paper on the edge of the sink, I looked down at my flat belly. *Not for much longer.* I rubbed my hands over the spot where, deep within, a little life had been conceived. Soon my warm and fuzzy feeling evaporated, and fear took hold – the birth of our child would mean the end of the curse. For centuries, the firstborn in each generation carried the Ingenii gene, which provided longevity and youthfulness, and gave the chosen Brethren who fed from us the greatest gift of all – the ability to daywalk. That was all about to end, and for many among the Brethren, it meant losing any chance to share in that privilege. Would they be desperate enough to kill my baby? To hinder its birth?

I hugged my arms about me, stepped out of the ensuite into my bedroom and called Alec. 'I need to see you.'

We were still on the *Judy* – Luc's yacht – moored in Double Bay, not far from his Vaucluse mansion. Repairs on the house were only weeks away from completion after the fire that had caused extensive damage to the lower floors but had, thankfully, destroyed nothing major. So for now, *Judy,* was our temporary home.

'Anything wrong, darling?' Alec stood in the doorway, his six-feet-one frame dominating the narrow space. The injuries he'd sustained after being captured by the Rebels had healed, and his lavender eyes sparkled as they surveyed me. Only he could make my body tingle with the slightest glance.

I took a deep breath. 'I'm pregnant.'

His smile faded as his gaze darted from my face to my belly. 'You sure?'

'My period's late, so I did the test – three times with three different kits. Each with the same result.' I gave a nod toward the bathroom. 'It's on the basin.'

Alec stared at me, eyes wide, fists clenched.

Okay, not the reaction I expected. 'What's wrong? I thought….'

He shook his head, closed his eyes and the crease between them deepened. 'No, nothing....' In a blink, he was at my side, holding me close.

I sucked in a breath as I remembered what Alec told me weeks ago – his first wife and baby died in childbirth. Did he fear the same would happen to me? Or, was it something else?

I took his face between my hands. 'Tell me.'

He licked his lips, and his breath came rapidly. 'I can't lose you.'

'I won't die, Alec. Women don't die in childbirth anymore. There are modern—'

'I know, Laura, but you won't be in a hospital. To end the curse, you have to give birth at that damn witch's grave, somewhere,' —he waved his arm— 'in the wilds of Scotland. Do you know what that means?' His pupils dilated.

The curse. I had thought it through; I knew what it meant. Luc had told me the stipulations of the curse the day after the Ritual. At the time I didn't think it applied to me. By the time it did, I had no choice – I was the Child of Light and Darkness who was supposed to mate with the witch's descendant and bear the Child of Promise. Then, and only then, would my father, Luc, and grandfather, Marcus, their men, and all whom they transformed, be given a choice: to return to their human state – and die immediately as age caught up with them – or remain vampire.

Alec had decided on the latter. I wasn't going to die on any witch's grave, nor be transformed into one of the Brethren as a last resort, either. Just as well, as the Ingenii gene I carried prevented it anyway. But, I trusted in my father's – and Alec's – ability to keep me and the baby safe when the time came.

'You'll be there - you're a doctor, and so is Jake.'

'But I'm not an obstetrician, Laura, and neither is he.'

'Well, if other women can give birth in' —I thought of recent incidents on the news— 'parking lots and service stations with no qualified medical people around, and be all right, then so can I.' *I hope.*

It took him a while to answer, the skin around his eyes and mouth tight with anxiety. 'If it came to a choice' —he began slowly— 'between you and the baby, I choose you. I don't give a damn about the curse - that's Luc's obsession. I care about you. Do you understand? I can't lose you…. I can't allow it!'

The passion in his voice, the fear in his eyes, caught at my heart. I placed my finger over his lips. 'Shhh … Don't say that. I love you, and I can't imagine anything more beautiful than having a child with you. I want you both.'

Alec took my hand and kissed the inside of my palm. 'Darling, if there are any complications, even the hint of one, I'll whisk you to the nearest hospital. Luc and the curse be damned!'

I hoped my father didn't hear. He was Alec's sire, and he'd been waiting and planning for the day when the curse would end and our family would no longer be vampire food. In the past, the Brethren had fought battles over us. The most recent rebellion had been defeated here, but a threat still loomed in Europe. My father and his men were in the wheelhouse, on the uppermost deck, trying to intercept a text message and stop an attack on our chateau in France. Alec and I had been with them until I'd been hit by a wave of nausea and excused myself. The sea was particularly choppy tonight, and my sea legs had never been good.

I pulled out of his embrace and stared at him. 'We have no choice. You know that. Unless the curse ends with us, our baby will be the next Ingenii. You want to see our child undergo the Ritual? Will you be princeps … to your own child?'

Alec ran a hand through his hair, and his expression darkened. 'Holy mother of … No! I will not feed from my own child.' The thought of it sickened me, too. 'Now I understand how Luc feels.'

I nodded. My parents faced the same problem when my mother fell pregnant with me. No wonder my father had appointed Alec as princeps instead. He couldn't bear feeding from his own child, just as Alec couldn't face the idea now.

He came towards me and leaned down so our foreheads touched.

'It didn't bother you before,' I said.

'It didn't hit home till now.'

We stood like that as the enormity of it sank in. I silently prayed that when the time came, there would be no unforeseen complications – nothing that would force either of us into making a heart-wrenching choice.

He took a deep breath. 'It's very subtle, but I can smell the hormonal changes on you.'

'Who needs a pregnancy test when you're around?'

He chuckled before sobering and tilting my chin up so I would meet his gaze. 'We won't be able to hide this for long. Others will soon detect your scent.'

'But hasn't the rebellion been defeated here? Who'd attack now? Isn't Rasputin gone?' Rasputin – his name alone made me shiver – a vampire who could mesmerise his own kind into doing his will and who led a rebellion against the Principate. I'd injured him severely to save Kari's life – chopped off his hands. Last I heard, he was on the run.

'As far as we know, he's no longer in the country, but that doesn't mean other Rebels won't swarm here.' His voice dropped. 'They could try to harm the baby … prevent its birth.'

I shuddered. My fears were justified.

'We can't stay here indefinitely, and the residence here is not designed for defence. I'm taking you to France – to the chateau. It's the safest place.' He paused. 'For you both. The security system's one of the best. The sooner we get there the better.'

My heart stuttered. I knew we would have to leave Sydney when the time came, but it had seemed so far away. Now, I wasn't prepared. A million questions rushed through my mind – work, my flat, car … and my passport – who knew where that was? I hadn't used it in years, and I wasn't sure if it was still valid. What if we didn't make it back by the end of January, when the new term began? I hadn't farewelled the kids, parents, other staff at the school. Things were moving too quickly.

'Alec, I'm not ready for this.'

His arm tightened around my waist. 'Laura….' Lines around his eyes creased with concern. 'I know it's sudden, taking you away from all you know—'

'Do I have time to say goodbye?' I thought of John and Eilene. Up until a few weeks ago, I had believed them to be my parents.

He shook his head. 'No time for a personal visit. Call them.'

What a terrible way to say goodbye after everything they had done for me. I could be away for a year, perhaps more. A lump rose in my throat.

He rubbed his thumb gently across my lower lip. 'I know it's hard, but they'll understand. I'm sorry about your teaching job, too.'

So was I. But that didn't compare with having to leave the two beloved people who had raised me, like this. It broke my heart. Yet did I have a choice? 'What about you, the hospital?'

'I have processes in place for such an emergency. I'll let the Board know.'

I sighed and lowered my head onto his chest, fearful of what lay ahead, yet fiercely resolved to see it through.

GLOSSARY OF CHARACTERS AND NAMES

Alec Munro – Vampire, princeps and together with Lucien Lebrettan, leader of the 'Brethren', a community of vampires living in Sydney. Originally a doctor, he had enlisted in the AIF soon after the death of his wife and child. He was later transformed by Lucien while serving in an army medical field hospital in northern France in 1918. He owns and manages a private hospital in Sydney dedicated to blood disease research.

Antonia Pulchra – Daughter of Marcus Antonius Pulcher, twin sister to Lucius. Antonia was the first to carry the Ingenii mutation. She lived for 218 years and was the mother of Paulus, the next Ingenii.

Appius – Vampire, former Roman soldier, and part of the First Cohort of Frisians cavalry unit, stationed at Vindobala (Rudchester). Unable to bear life any longer as a blood drinker, he took his own life by walking out into the sun, soon after his transformation into vampire form by the Pictish witch, Eithne.

Bloodgifted – Term given to certain members of the Dantonville family who carry the cursed gene, giving them unnatural long life and youthfulness. Their blood alone provides vampires with superior strength and senses and the ability to daywalk. The Bloodgifted – Ingenii – are much coveted by the Brethren community and were the epicentre of two previous rebellions; the first taking place in the tenth century, resulting in the deaths of tow of Luc's men – Galen and Martius – and the other in the seventeenth century.

Cal (Calixtus) – Vampire, former Roman soldier, First Frisian Cavalry Regiment, stationed at Vindobala (Rudchester), on Hadrian's Wall, northern Britain. Part of Marcus Antonius Pulcher's cohort, he was cursed (along with his comrades) by a Pictish witch into vampire form. Cal is also a widower, having lost his wife in childbirth. Currently he is bodyguard to the Ingenii, friend to Alec Munro and he owns an Armagnac distillery in France.

Dave Delaney – Human, Detective Senior Constable, friend and mentor of Matthew Sommers, in charge of the investigation into his assault.

Elders – Group of the world's oldest vampires, who set the rules by which all blood drinkers must abide, in order to keep their presence hidden from the human world. They have power over life and death in the Brethren community. They also officiate at every Coming-of-Age ceremony and induct the princeps. They are among the oldest living creatures on Earth.

Eilene Dantonville – Human, wife of John Dantonville. Her first child, a baby named Katie, died of SIDS at aged three months. She and John accepted the infant Laura in place of their deceased daughter, in order to help out Lucien and Judith. She loved Laura as her own child.

Eithne – Pictish witch and high priestess of the Caledonian goddess, Melusine. She cursed Marcus Antonius Pulcher and his men for killing her people in the mid 3rd century, effectively turning him and his men into vampires. She used kidnapped Roman captives as human sacrifices in bloody religious rites.

Galen – Former Roman soldier in the First Frisian Cohort Cavalry Regiment stationed at Vindobala (Rudchester). Along with his comrades, he was cursed into vampire form by the Pictish witch, Eithne. Until his death – at the hands of vampire hunters in the First Rebellion – he was one of the bodyguards to the Ingenii.

Ingenii – Latin term meaning 'Bloodgifted'.

Jake (Caius Justinius) – Vampire, former Roman soldier and physician attached to the First Frisian Cavalry Regiment, stationed at Vindobala (Rudchester) on Hadrian's Wall, northern Britain. Along with his comrades, he was cursed by a Pictish witch into becoming a vampire. He is close friend of Alec Munro, and loves sports cars and racing horses. Currently he is bodyguard to the Ingenii.

Jean-Philippe Louis Auguste de Reynard – Vampire, and 18th century French nobleman who once fought for Napoleon. He was Lucien's illegitimate son and Laura's half-brother. His mother was the Duchess D'Orleans. He was also a well-known portrait artist who first met Laura in Italy where he fell in love with her unaware he was her half-brother. Jean introduced himself to her by his second name, Philippe. Lucien broke up the relationship. Their romance is the subject of the short story, **Laura's Locket**.

Jenny Callen – Human, Laura's best friend and work colleague in a primary school in Balmain. She's had several failed relationships and is currently single.

John Dantonville – Human, Laura's foster-father and maternal uncle. He is Judith's youngest brother and Eilene Dantonville's husband. He and Eilene adopted Laura as a favour to Lucien and Judith, but came to love her as their own. His pet name for her is, 'Baby'.

Judith Dantonville Lebrettan – Human, thirty-third Ingenii. Pressured into marrying her first husband, William Allerdyce, by her father, Owen Dantonville to clear gambling debts. Only meant to be a business arrangement, he raped her on their wedding night. Judith met Lucien some time after and they became lovers. Later she divorced William and secretly married Luc after giving birth to their child, Laura.

Kari (Karelia Anakeinen) – Born in Finland in the late eighteenth-century, Kari's family moved to France when her father was offered the position of chief stonemason on the D'Antonville estate in the Rhone Valley. She had been transformed by Jake, when the rest of her family died in an epidemic which swept the region. Kari is Judith Dantonville's best friend, and unofficial bodyguard to the current Ingenii, Laura Dantonville. She is also secretly in love with Jake.

Karl – Czech Prefect, Count Karel von Czernin; vampire and Principate spy who befriended Count Timur Széchenyi, the Hungarian Prefect, and infiltrated the Rebels ranks to learn of their plans and report back to Luc. His easy-going nature hides a sharp mind and decisive nature. He's friends with Alec Munro, and secretly in love with Baroness Milena Flaks.

Kwome – One of the Elders, and originally king of the ancient kingdom of Benin. He was transformed by his teacher and mentor.

Laura Dantonville – Part human/part vampire, thirty-fourth and current serving Ingenii, and Lucien and Judith's biological daughter. She is a primary school teacher and former girlfriend of Detective Inspector Matthew Sommers, before meeting Alec Munro. Laura was raised by John and Eilene Dantonville, who she believed to be her parents. She was also Jean-Philippe's half-sister.

Lucien Lebrettan – Vampire who underwent transformation at puberty. Known as 'Luc' to his friends, Lucius Antonius Pulcher was born in the mid 3rd century AD to, the son of Marcus Antonius and Gallia. He was the first princeps, and Alec Munro's sire and friend, and Laura Dantonville's father. He secretly married her mother, Judith, a week after Laura was born. Lucien Lebrettan is the Gallic version of his Roman name, and means 'Lucius the Briton.'

Marcus Antonius Pulcher – Vampire, former Roman legionary cavalry commander – Praefectus Equituum – stationed in Vindobala (Rudchester) in Britain in the mid 3rd century AD. It was his actions, which led to him, and his men, to be cursed by the witch Eithne. Marcus Antonius is the father of the twins, Lucius and Antonia, and husband to Gallia. He departed from Britain after his transformation into a vampire, and went into hiding in his villa in Gaul (France).

Martius – Vampire, former Roman soldier in the First Frisian Cohort cavalry unit stationed at Vindobala (Rudchester). Along with his comrades, he was cursed into vampire form by the Pictish witch, Eithne. Before his death, Martius was one of the bodyguards to the Ingenii. He was killed by vampire hunters during the First Rebellion.

Matthew Sommers – Human, Police Detective Inspector. He was Laura's boyfriend and rival with Alec Munro for Laura's affections. He was attacked and nearly killed by rogue vampires while trying to protect her. Laura broke off their relationship at the end of Book 1 when she learnt he was planning to kill the vampire side of her family in a misguided attempt to protect her.

Melander – Human, former Roman soldier of the First Frisian Cohort Cavalry Regiment stationed at Vindobala (Rudchester). Sent back as guard to Nepos who had been wounded in a surprise Pict attack. Killed by Calixtus during the early stages of his transformation.

Milena – Baroness Milena Flaks, vampire, the Slovakian Prefect and supporter of the Principate. Her concerns over Count Timur's ambitions – and threat to her territory – has led her to approach Jake into becoming her consort, and thus her protector. Like other aristocrats of her generation (eighteenth-century) she believes in the superiority of her noble blood, although Brethren law discourages class discrimination. Her old-world attitude leads to clashes with more-recently transformed Brethren.

Nepos – Human, Roman soldier of the First Frisian Cohort Cavalry Regiment stationed at Vindobala (Rudchester). He was seriously wounded in a surprise attack by Pictish raiders and sent back to the fort by his commander, Marcus Antonius Pulcher. While recovering from his wounds, he was killed by Terens during the early stages of his transformation.

Princeps – Latin term for First Citizen and the origin of the English word for Prince.

Principate – The Brethren political system established by Marcus Antonius Pulcher and his son, Lucius (Lucien) to control the Brethren and protect humans. It's composed of the Elders – Kwome and Zhao – as well as Marcus, Luc and Alec. As a result of the death of Maris Quesnel, there is a vacancy in the Eldership for a female representative.

Pudens – Vampire, former Roman soldier in the First Frisian Cohort Cavalry Regiment stationed at Vindobala (Rudchester). Along with his comrades, he was cursed into vampire form by the Pictish witch, Eithne. Unable to endure life as a blood drinker, he took his own life by walking out into the sun.

Rasputin – Vampire and former confidant of the last Russian royal family, the Romanovs. He was transformed in 1917 by Hungarian noble, Count Timur Széchenyi, the Brethren Hungarian Prefect. Many blame him for the demise of the monarchy in Russia, and his sinister influence over the Russian royal family. He has the ability to mesmerise humans as well as vampires, and uses that to further his master's ambitions to overthrow the Principate.

Sam (Sempronius) – Vampire, former Roman soldier in the First Frisian Cavalry Regiment, stationed at Vindobala (Rudchester) in northern Britain. Along with his comrades, he was cursed by the Pictish witch, Eithne, into vampire form. He is also the former lover and sire of Maris Quesnel. Sam is a Techno wiz and responsible for security in the Lebrettan household. Currently, when not hacking into Rebel phones and computers, he is one of the bodyguards to the Ingenii.

Serpent Ring – Ancient artefact created by Marcus Antonius Pulcher on the instructions of the Pictish witch, Eithne. It's in the form of a golden serpent with blazing red eyes—symbol of Melusine, Caledonian goddess of vengeance. It renders the wearer invisible to vampire senses as well as burning the fingers of imposters, and shooting fire from the serpents' eyes, destroying those who physically threaten either princeps or Ingenii. In times of danger, the eyes turn black. Every fifty years the ring is passed down to the next Ingenii.

Terens (Sextus Terentius) – Vampire, former Tribune attached to the First Frisian Cavalry Regiment, stationed at Vindobala (Rudchester), northern Britain. Along with the rest of the cohort, he was cursed by the Pictish witch, Eithne, into vampire form. Although he has a reputation as a ladies man, Terens is also a deadly swordsman and is known to have fought off eight armed Rebels in the last Rebellion. He's always wanted to try skydiving. Currently, he is one of the bodyguards to the Ingenii.

Timur – Count Timur Széchenyi, Hungarian Prefect, and leader of the rebellion to overthrow the Principate and kidnap the Ingenii to breed her with a human and produce the next generation of Ingenii. He used his family crest – a snarling wolf's-head – to create the outlawed wolf's-head ring, which contains a deadly white-oak spike. It's believed he is the centre of the illegal blood-slave racket, which traffics in selling under-age humans to the Brethren. Timur is also Rasputin's sire.
His castle is located outside Budapest.

Zhao – One of the Elders. Ancient Chinese warlord turned philosopher. His sire is unknown.

A Note From The Author

Hi, I'm Tima Maria, and I write vampire books, but not just any vamp books—mine are Roman soldiers cursed by a Pictish witch in the 3rd century. So, how did I start this series? In a previous life (before I started writing) I was a practicing archaeologist and historian, specializing in Roman Britain. Later, I took up high school teaching, as It gave me the opportunity to take my students on overseas excursions to visit the amazing archaeological sites they'd only seen in books. Then one day, I surrendered to the itch of writing. After many years reading and correcting my students' creative writing tasks and essays, I decided it was time to write my own. I couldn't hold it in any longer. Bloodgifted is the result. In 2011, it was shortlisted in the Atlas Award—sponsored by a boutique Brisbane publisher—and eventually came fourth. In 2012, it was listed among the top ten in the Choclit, Search for an Aussie Star Competition. In 2013, I was offered a publishing contract, but declined in favour of going indie. I liked the idea of being in charge of my own creation. Bloodgifted is just the start of a three part series I've entitled, The Dantonville Legacy. Later, I intend writing individual books on the other characters in the series, for they all have their own story. Currently, I live on the Central Coast, an hour's drive north of Sydney, surrounded by wooded hills, possums and seed-dropping rosellas. Between bouts of writing, I teach English and History, enjoy long walks while dodging the nesting magpies and plot the next series of books I'd like to write.

CONTACT

Tima Maria Lacoba
Visit me at my website:
http://www.timamarialacoba.com

If you enjoyed reading this book, I'd love you to share it with others, RECOMMEND it to friends, family, and reading groups or clubs, or online forums. You can also REVIEW this book at the site where you purchased it. That is the best gift, you as a reader, can give an author. And if you happen to do that, email me at, timamarialacoba@bigpond.com and I'll send you a personal message of thanks.

You can also connect with me at:
Facebook – http://www.facebook.com/TimaMariaLacoba
Twitter – http://www.twitter.com/timamarialacoba

Tima Maria Lacoba

http://www.timamarialacoba.blogspot.com.au/p/home.html
https://www.facebook.com/timamarialacoba

Paradox Book
Cover Designs

PARADOX BOOKS FORMATTING

www.ingramcontent.com/pod-product-compliance
Lightning Source LLC
Chambersburg PA
CBHW030626110726
47901CB00002B/331